THE

999 PORTAL

Starseed Academy
Book 1

N. L. MYSTIC

Cover design by N.L. Mystic
Stock art by Canva

Paperback ISBN 979-8-9990094-0-1
EBook ISBN 979-8-9990094-1-8

To all the homesick aliens who incarnated on Earth.

You are not alone.

CHAPTER ONE

There is a world inside this one. A secret realm hidden beneath the surface of Earth, where reincarnated souls study the healing arts. At least that's what it says in this strange little book I found in a free library box: *A Starseed's Guide to Agartha.*

Its once-vibrant cover is now dulled with age, the image of ancient pyramids dissolving into a backdrop of symbols that seem to shift when you stare at them too long.

According to the text, portals open every year in special locations around the world to transport students to a school unlike anything found on the surface.

This year's portal? September 9th.

That's why I'm in Shasta.

One of the few perks of living in your car is being able to chase a portal to the center of the Earth on a whim.

"Are you a first-year too?" A girl with beach-blonde dreads and a septum ring grins at me. She looks about my age. Early twenties, tan, freckled, and beaming like she's already been chosen.

"I guess. I've never walked through a portal before, if that's what you mean."

"Same. My name's Mae." She adjusts the ukulele strapped across her back like it's a purse.

"Hi. I'm Synchronicity."

"Oh my God. I love your name."

"My parents were amateur Jungians. You'd think with all that shadow work, they'd be a little more self-aware."

Mae laughs. "Hey, that's why we're here, right? To heal the generational trauma."

We're gathered around a natural spring on the western slope of Mount Shasta, maybe fifteen of us total, dressed like festival castoffs and cult recruits. The crisp mountain air nips at my skin despite the bright morning sun.

"Most of these people won't even see it," Mae says, tossing her dreads over one shoulder. "The portal only appears to those who are chosen to attend the Academy."

"How do you know all this?" I ask.

"My dad. He told me stories growing up. Never went himself, but he met people who had. He used to read me that same book." She nods toward the copy in my hand. "It's rare. I'm surprised you found one."

I glance down at the timetable in my book. It claims the portal will open at 9:09 a.m. Strangely specific for a prophecy, but that's what it says. I run my thumb over the dog-eared page, wondering for the hundredth time if any of this is real.

"Why 9:09?" I ask, not quite skeptical, but not convinced either.

"I don't know," Mae says. "Something about numerology. Portals love symmetry."

As the scheduled time approaches, a hush descends over the crowd. The only sounds are the babble of the spring, a lone raven's croak overhead, and the crunch of gravel under nervous feet.

Then, a man with shoulder-length black hair and a full sleeve of alien tattoos shouts, "I see it! The portal!"

For a moment, I think he's crazy, until he steps forward and vanishes.

"Me too!" someone yells, and they disappear at the same spot on the edge of the creek.

One by one, people vanish before my eyes. I blink hard, heart hammering in my chest.

"Can you see anything?" I whisper to Mae.

She narrows her eyes, scanning the rocks. "Wait... yes! Right there. In front of the spring!"

I stare. Nothing.

"Oh my God," she breathes. "I can't believe I've been chosen. My dad's gonna freak."

"Yeah. Wow. Congrats." My voice sounds far away.

"You don't see it?"

"Nope."

"Don't give up. Sometimes it takes a second. And even if you don't get accepted this year, you can always come back. Some people try for decades."

"Well, don't wait on my account," I say, watching a few more people disappear.

"Are you sure?" Mae shifts her weight from foot to foot.

"Go. This is your dream."

"Thanks," she says, but before she goes, she turns toward me and places a warm hand on my arm. "Just wait. I know you'll get accepted. You have such good energy."

I let out a sigh. "I'm not so sure about that, but thanks."

Her eyes linger on mine for a beat longer, then she turns around and approaches the edge of the creek. It looks like she's going to step right into the water, but at the last second, she vanishes.

After a few more minutes of this, there are only seven of us left. We wait and wait, but no portal appears.

A guy with a man bun picks up his pack and trudges back down the trail, shoulders slumped. The others file slowly after him.

An older couple passes me last, the woman smiling faintly. "Beautiful day, isn't it?" she says, as if the weather might make up for the magic that never came. They amble down the mountain, arm in arm, leaving me finally and utterly alone on the banks of the creek.

What the hell am I doing here? Did I seriously think that someone like me would be accepted into some cosmic boarding school for energy healers?

I don't leave. Not because I have hope, but because I have nowhere else to go. My friend group back home won't talk to me, my family disowned me, and my credit cards are just about maxed out.

Instead, I strip off my clothes and step into the water.

The cold hits like a slap. I walk deeper until the current reaches my waist, then sink backward into the stream, letting it swallow me.

This is what got me into this mess in the first place.

Maybe I'll just stay here.

Maybe I'll die, and nature can take me back.

I close my eyes and tilt my head into the current, letting it leech the heat from my skull.

My skin numbs.

My thoughts don't.

The ache inside me, the one I've carried since that day six months ago, doesn't fade. It never does.

I submerge completely and start counting heartbeats, waiting for the darkness to win.

But something inside me resists.

At the last second, a wild, animal instinct claws to the surface. I break through the stream, gasping, coughing, water streaming from my hair and eyes.

And there it is.

Glowing in front of me.

A six-foot rift in time and space, shimmering violet and humming with impossible energy.

The portal.

I scramble to my feet, but the smooth river stones betray me. I slip hard, gashing my ankle on a rock.

"Shit."

I crawl out of the water, pull a sock over the wound, and stare. The portal pulses like it's alive.

My clothes go on in a flurry. I think about running back to the car, grabbing a bag, something, but the portal starts to flicker.

No time.

I shove my copy of *A Starseed's Guide to Agartha* into my hoodie pocket, and with three steps, I leave my old life behind forever.

CHAPTER TWO

The portal to the Starseed Academy opens into a mystical courtyard teeming with students and celestial beings of every shape and hue. Honest-to-God *aliens* mingle with wide-eyed humans like it's no big deal.

My shock is interrupted by a familiar voice.

"Synchronicity! You made it!" Mae barrels toward me and wraps me in a hug like we've known each other for years. "Isn't it amazing?"

My breath catches."I can't believe my eyes."

The courtyard is dominated by a central obelisk, and beyond it, a massive pyramid rises in the distance, layers of stone interspersed with sections made of glass and capped by a shimmering triangular gem.

"Did your portal open up underwater or something?" A woman with perfectly straight, long brown hair and loose linen clothes approaches us, flanked by two similarly dressed women who snicker at her remark.

My hair is still soaked from the dip I took in the creek, and my ankle throbs where I bashed it against that rock. "It was in Shasta, actually," I say, trying to keep my voice calm, but my eyes shoot daggers.

"I'm only teasing, darling." She extends a hand and pats me condescendingly on the forearm. "My name's Vaylen. This is Kara and June. We just arrived from Boulder."

"We've been practicing to come here for *years*," the one named June says. She has two small braids framing the sides of her face and a messy blonde bun held up with chopsticks. "Vaylen's mom is a Starseed. She taught us everything."

"June, that's enough." Vaylen's tone sharpens. "Anyway, it was a pleasure meeting you... Shasta, was it?"

"Synchronicity," I grit.

She lets out a performative little laugh behind tattooed fingers.

"Don't I know you from somewhere?" she asks, leaning in

a little closer.

"I don't think so," I say, trying to avoid her gaze.

She searches my face a little longer, then steps back.

"Well, *Synchronicity*, I wish you nothing but love and light."

They vanish into the crowd like they were summoned somewhere more important.

"What a bitch," Mae mutters. "She didn't even ask *my* name."

"Don't listen to them," says a new voice behind us.

A young man with a mop of black hair and an eccentric outfit of multi-colored clothes approaches us. On his shoulder perches what looks like a fuzzy red raccoon.

"There are girls like that every year. All surface-level spiritual signaling on the outside, nothing but ego on the inside. Hi, I'm Jasper. And this," he gestures, "is my spirit animal, Mochi."

"He's adorable." Mae rushes forward and tries to nuzzle Mochi, who squeaks and darts to Jasper's opposite shoulder.

"He's just a little skittish," Jasper says. "Don't worry, he'll warm up to you."

"What is he?" Mae asks.

"A red panda. They're native to the eastern Himalayas, but I found him down here in Agartha."

"Hi Mochi. My name's Mae, and this is Synchronicity." Mae extends her hand palm up, and the creature gives it a tentative sniff. "Do we get spirit animals too?"

"That depends on what type of Starseed you are. I'm an Arcturian Starseed, which means I have a closer connection to animals and nature."

"How do we find out what kind of Starseed we are?" I ask, curious about my own cosmic origins.

"C'mon, I'll show you." Jasper leads us through the maze of students appearing from portals around the courtyard. My ankle throbs with every step as we weave our way through the crowd to a line forming in front of the obelisk. "The Entrance Obelisk," he explains. "This is where you find out what kind of Starseed you are and how many times you've incarnated."

"You seem to know a lot," Mae says. "Are you a second-year or something?"

"You could say that. You could also say I'm re-taking my first year." Jasper tousles his hair and smiles sheepishly.

"But why…" I begin, but Jasper cuts me off.

"It was entirely political. One of my professors didn't see eye-to-eye with me about my interpretation of a certain scholar's work. They just weren't ready for my level of genius."

"So you cheated," Mae deadpans.

"Let's not get into details on such a glorious day. Don't you want to know what star system your soul originated from?"

"I've been dying to know my whole life," Mae says. "I hope I'm a Pleiadian. They're the rarest."

"I'm sorry," I interject, "But are these *actually* aliens walking around?"

"Naturally," Jasper shrugs. "Who else would teach a bunch of half-awake humans how to ascend?" He nods toward a long-necked being with pale yellow skin. "That's Alien Olbos. He teaches Sound Healing to the first-years. And those glowing orbs of light over there? That's Alien Lumari. He teaches Galactic History. His species has attained such high levels of consciousness that they basically just exist as condensed balls of light now."

We take our place at the back of the line, and I consciously try to keep myself from gawking at the incredible beings walking around the courtyard. "I still can't believe all of this is real," I murmur.

"Oh, it's real." Jasper produces a treat from his pocket and holds it up to Mochi, who snatches it into his mouth. "Sometimes it feels *more* real than the surface world. I'd choose to live down here any day, but I have to remind myself that I incarnated here to help the people of Earth."

I glance upward. "If we're in the Hollow Earth… then how can I see the sun?"

"It's an artificial sun. They made it using ancient technology. Held in place by a magnetic field or something. They'll go over all that in orientation."

"What are the dorms like?" Mae asks, moving forward in line.

"They're quite nice, actually. It's group living. Twenty or so people to a dorm with a communal kitchen where everyone cooks meals together and catches up on each other's lives."

As Jasper rambles on about the living situation at school, I am overcome with the uncomfortable sensation of being watched.

I scan the courtyard, and my heart skips.

Leaning against the far wall is a tall, brooding, human-like being. His massive arms are crossed against his chest, skin a deep crimson with intricate black markings that may or may not be tattoos. He has a strong jaw, firmly set into a brutal face. His features are decidedly alien, but alien in a way like some god took all the facets of human masculinity and pushed them to their logical extreme.

And his eyes, his larger-than-life, almond eyes with irises of glowing amber, are boring into mine like he can see straight through to my soul.

My heart jumps and lodges in my throat.

"Synchronicity, come on!" Mae shouts. "What are you doing?" She and Jasper have moved up several places in line, and there is now a large gap between us.

"I was just..." But when I look back, the figure is gone, lost among the bustling crowd of students and teachers.

"You're holding up the line," another first-year behind me says.

I quickly step forward and regain my spot.

Jasper glances at me. "First time in Agartha hits hard, huh?"

"Yeah." I swallow. "Like a punch to the soul."

The line moves. A voice calls out: "Arcturian Starseed, third incarnation!"

A lithe blue-skinned alien with big black eyes and petite antennas protruding from her forehead stands at the base of the obelisk. She's all elegance and severity in a flowing white robe.

"Alien Sylestra," Jasper whispers.

At her announcement, the student at the front of the line jumps up in joy. I recognize her as the woman named June I had met earlier. She embraces her friends before a human instructor hands her some kind of crystal tablet.

Vaylen steps up next. I watch as she approaches the towering stone monolith and places her hand on an angled indentation carved into the rock. She closes her eyes, and a moment later, two hieroglyphs on different parts of the obelisk glow a striking blue. Alien Sylestra reads them off. "Sirian Starseed, twelfth incarnation."

Her friends swarm her, but she bats them off and fixes her hair. She takes her tablet and joins June with the group of newly recognized Starseeds.

"Makes sense she's Sirian," Jasper huffs. "They're the most stuck up."

"Do they have any spiritual, you know, powers?" Mae asks.

"Well, the Sirians are the most powerful group in the Galactic Federation. They can heal people with their minds. It's pretty cool, but the downside is that they have to do a lot of meditation to access their powers. That, and it hurts like hell to get a treatment from them."

"Okay, this might be a dumb question," I say, "but why does everyone speak English?"

"Not dumb at all," Jasper says as we move forward. "See that gleaming stone at the top of the main pyramid? It's a Logos Stone. It projects an energy field that works on the level of the subconscious to translate any language into your native tongue."

Vaylen's other friend, Kara, steps up to the obelisk.

"Lyran Starseed, eleventh incarnation," Alien Sylestra calls out. Kara takes her tablet from the man standing next to Alien Sylestra and joins her friends in the growing semi-circle of admitted students.

Only a few people are left between me and the obelisk.

My stomach twists.

What if I'm not supposed to be here? Will that obelisk know everything about my past?

Jasper continues his commentary. "Lyran Starseeds are the musical ones. They're known for being easygoing, and their spiritual power is healing with sound. There's a band of Lyran Starseeds at school called Supermoon. I'll have to take you guys to one of their shows."

Two Sirians. One Arcturian. Then it's our turn.

"Jasper Collins," Alien Sylestra drones out in an elegant voice. "If I'm not mistaken, you already know your star system of origin."

"Yes, Alien Sylestra. Arcturian Starseed, sixteenth incarnation. I was just helping these new students with the particulars of their first day at Agartha."

"I'm quite certain they would be better off *without* your help, Mr. Collins." Alien Sylestra's long, blue fingers grasp one of the crystal tablets. "Unless, of course, they would also like to be held back a year."

"About that," Jasper says, taking a tablet of his own from the man standing next to her. "I was hoping I could talk to you in private about perhaps taking some second-year courses, seeing as I already..."

"Mr. Collins, you are lucky the portal even let you return after the stunt you pulled last year. If I were you, I would be grateful I got a second chance to attend this prestigious academy."

"But Alien Sylestra, I've already taken all these courses." Jasper gestures to a few lines of script glowing on the tablet.

"Then you should have no problem passing them *without* cheating. May I remind you that your attendance here is a privilege, Mr. Collins. Do I make myself clear?"

"Yes, of course, Alien Sylestra." Jasper bows profusely while Mochi wobbles on his shoulders. "I'll just join the rest of the first-years over here then." He slinks over to the other students while Sylestra follows him with a cold stare before turning her gaze to Mae.

"Name?"

"Mae Rivers."

"Step up to the obelisk, Miss Rivers."

Mae approaches the towering stone structure. It is etched from top to bottom with alien symbols. She places her hand on the angled slab inset into the rock. A moment later, two symbols flare to life.

"Lyran Starseed, second incarnation." Alien Sylestra's voice resounds over the clamor of the crowd. Mae squeals and spins, her ukulele banging against her back, before running up to me and embracing me with another one of her deep hugs.

"I can't believe it! Looks like I'm going to be healing people with this old thing." She swings the ukulele around to her front and plays a few chords. "Second incarnation, too. I knew I had a young soul."

"I would agree with that," I say.

"Miss Rivers," the man with the tablets calls, holding out one of the sleek translucent slates.

My heart stumbles.

It's the first time I've gotten a good look at him. It's hard not to notice how handsome he is. A head full of mahogany hair, soft brown eyes, and a beautiful, warm smile.

Mae steps forward and accepts her crystal tablet before joining Jasper and the rest of the first-years.

Now there is no one between me, Alien Sylestra, and the obelisk. "Name?" she says, her gaze sharp as obsidian.

"Synchronicity Jones."

She taps something on her tablet and gestures with her four-fingered hand toward the Entrance Obelisk. I take a tentative step forward, trying not to limp on my wounded ankle. The man with the tablets offers me an encouraging smile, but I'm too nervous to smile back.

I step into the shadow of the monolith, trying to make sense of the mysterious engravings that mark its surface. I take a deep breath and place my hand on the flat depression carved into the stone. The granite is worn smooth here from generations of students inquiring about their cosmic origins.

I close my eyes and wonder what this stone knows. If it

knows where my soul came from, does it also know the things I've done in my life?

Could someone like me really be allowed in a school like this?

It feels like I've been standing here for a long time, much longer than the other students, when I hear Alien Sylestra say, "It can't be..."

I open my eyes and look up at the obelisk. Two symbols are illuminated that I haven't seen on anyone else's results.

"Something must be wrong," Alien Sylestra says in an accusatory tone.

"What is it?" The man puts down his tablets and walks over to Sylestra's side. They both stare up at the pair of glowing hieroglyphs, astonished.

"What does it say?" I ask, heart thudding in my chest.

Alien Sylestra looks at me like I'm a glitch in the matrix.

"Earthseed. First incarnation."

CHAPTER
THREE

All hell has broken loose in the courtyard.

A congregation of teachers, alien and human alike, has gathered near the Entrance Obelisk, arguing fiercely about me, seemingly unaware that I am standing just a few feet away.

"Earthseeds don't belong in this school!"

"A first incarnation? That's unheard of!"

Mae and Jasper rush to my side.

"Are you okay?" Mae asks, her hand fluttering to my shoulder, eyes wide with concern.

"I'm fine... I think." My voice comes out smaller than I want it to. "But what the hell is an Earthseed?"

"Someone whose soul originated on Earth," Jasper explains, swiping his floppy black hair off his forehead. "It means you've never incarnated in another star system. No lifetimes in Lyra or Sirius or the Pleiades. You're... brand new."

"Is that a bad thing?" I ask.

Jasper winces. "Not *bad*, just rare. Most humans are Earthseeds, but as far as I know, an Earthseed has never been allowed into Agartha before."

"Why not?"

Before he can answer, a voice cuts through the noise like a serrated blade. "Because human souls haven't attained a sufficient level of consciousness to perform the kind of spiritual work that *real* Starseeds can do." Vaylen strides toward us with her two minions flanking her. Her tone drips superiority like perfume. "It's nothing personal, darling. The portal must have let you in by mistake."

Mae steps forward like she's ready to throw hands. "The only mistake the portal made was letting *you* in. You think you're spiritual because you memorized your mom's affirmations? Please."

"Careful, second-incarnation," Kara hisses. Her

Cleopatra bob swings like a blade as she steps forward, framing her harshly exotic face. "You wouldn't want to make enemies on your first day."

Vaylen fakes a warm smile. "C'mon, girls. Let's find our dorms." She pauses to look back at me. "Oh, and Synchronicity? I really do wish you the best. Maybe I'll see you back on the surface someday." She tacks on a saccharine, "Ciao," with a vocal fry so sharp it could cut quartz. Then the trio disappears into the crowd, giggling amongst themselves.

"Harpies," Jasper mutters, feeding a piece of dried fruit to Mochi, who snatches it like he, too, is done with the drama.

"I'm really sorry about them, Synchronicity. Don't listen to what they say." Mae offers a consoling hand on my shoulder.

"I'm more worried about what the faculty thinks," I say, nodding toward the shouting match still raging by the obelisk. "What do you think they're going to decide?"

Jasper's tone shifts. "It's an interesting case. This is a Starseed Academy, so as an Earthseed, the curriculum isn't really designed for you, but..." He tilts his head, watching me. "You came through the portal. And the portal only appears to souls chosen for this path."

The debate among the teachers grows more intense.

"Where is Xion?" Alien Sylestra barks. "Someone needs to escort this girl back to the surface immediately."

"That is completely uncalled for." The handsome man who had been giving out the crystal tablets is right in her face. "She has a right to be here just like everyone else."

"Who is that?" I ask quietly.

"Kai Moongate," Jasper replies. "Interim healer. Basically the most eligible bachelor in the school. Spiritual, gifted, emotionally available... and tragically straight."

My gaze stays locked on Kai as he steps closer to Sylestra.

"Earthseeds have no place in Agartha," Sylestra insists. "Her presence lowers the collective frequency. She should be returned to the surface at once."

"You do not have the authority to make that decision," Kai says, every word measured but molten underneath. "Only the Spiritual Director can expel a student."

"Then maybe we should take this to Alien Isis herself," Sylestra snaps, trying to retake the ground she just lost.

Kai doesn't flinch. "Gladly."

There's a tense pause.

Sylestra recovers her poise, just barely. "You really want to waste the Spiritual Director's time on a portal fluke?"

"I don't consider attempted expulsion a *waste* of anyone's time," Kai says. "Especially not hers."

Alien Sylestra considers the proposition for a moment. "As you wish," she says, finally turning her penetrating gaze on me. "Miss Jones, would you accompany Mr. Moongate and me to the Spiritual Director's office?"

The Great Pyramid of Agartha rises up against the blue sky, its translucent capstone shimmering like a diamond in the sunlight. Alien Sylestra leads the way, every step clicking with purpose as she guides us up the causeway.

Beside me walks the man who defended me in front of everyone. He's calm and composed, like even this moment can't shake him.

"I'm truly sorry for all this," he says, his voice gentle but earnest. "I'm Kai, by the way. Interim healer."

He's a few inches taller than me, and the way he looks down at me with those gorgeous eyes makes my heart flutter. There are plenty of reasons I don't want to get sent back to the surface, but the chance of getting to see this man again is quickly moving up on the list.

"I'm Synchronicity," I say, trying not to sound like I'm unraveling. "And don't worry. Getting kicked out of an alien healing school wouldn't be the worst thing that's happened to me this year."

He is dressed in brown pants with a blazer over a loose linen shirt that shows off his tanned chest. "Let's hope it doesn't come to that."

The pyramid looms larger as we reach its base and begin ascending wide stone steps toward an arched entryway. I pull in a sharp breath. Words cannot describe how overwhelmingly beautiful, how intricate and vast the inside of this pyramid is. The interior of the massive temple is not dark like I assumed, but bathed in luminous beams filtering through crystalline panes high above, illuminating elaborate gardens thriving along the vast central chamber.

We walk past a series of towering geometric columns etched with alien glyphs, and behind translucent walls, administrators work quietly on glowing crystal tablets. Alien Sylestra's shoes click rhythmically against the polished marble floor. On either side, amphitheater-like classrooms carved seamlessly from stone await eager students, while at the hall's end, a monumental staircase of immense granite blocks rises sharply, spiraling upward toward an unseen apex drenched in celestial light.

"It's magnificent, isn't it?" Kai looks around the interior of the pyramid with genuine wonder.

"It's amazing," I say, trying not to limp as Alien Sylestra leads us up the staircase at a swift pace. "Did humans build it?"

"It was a joint effort between the Sirians and the Pleiadians when Earth was added as a candidate for the Galactic Federation. As far as I know, you are the first Earthseed to ever step foot inside of it."

"If I'm being honest, it's still a little hard to believe that I'm at a spiritual arts school in the center of the Earth."

"You'll get used to it. Before long, this place will start to feel like home." His smile sends heat pumping through my veins.

"That's enough chit chat," Alien Sylestra says. "We're here."

The stairway terminates at a set of intricate wooden doors inlaid with gems. Alien Sylestra pushes them open, and we step into a large chamber with soaring ceilings and one wall made entirely of angled glass that looks out over the campus below.

Behind a carved desk sits a being so radiant I forget how to speak.

Alien Isis.

She has a human silhouette, tall, elegant, but her skin is a lattice of shifting geometric patterns, refracting the light in a kaleidoscope of color. Her hair flows like liquid silver, and a shimmering halo of energy floats just above her head. But it's her eyes that stop me. Piercing, glacial blue, completely and terrifyingly aware.

"Alien Isis," Sylestra says with a deep bow. "Forgive the interruption, but we have an urgent issue regarding admissions."

"And what is the matter?" Alien Isis says. Her voice is pure, like a vibration ringing across the cosmos.

"It's rather unprecedented," Sylestra says, adjusting her robe. "But somehow an Earthseed managed to infiltrate the entrance proceedings today."

"I didn't infiltrate anything!" I pipe up. "I came through the portal just like everyone else."

"Can you confirm this, Mr. Moongate?" Isis turns her head in Kai's direction.

"Yes, Spiritual Director Isis. I noted her when she entered the courtyard. I saw her pass through the portal myself."

Alien Isis raises an incredulous crystalline eyebrow. "Among the hundreds of students arriving today, you noted her in particular?"

My pulse quickens at the thought that I caught this man's attention. Maybe I'm his type just as much as he is mine.

Kai hesitates for a moment. "Her hair was dripping wet. She was hard to miss."

Welp... so much for being his type.

Sylestra cuts in. "Regardless of whether or not she came through the portal, Earthseeds simply do not have the spiritual capacity to perform the kind of powers we teach at Agartha." Her tiny nostrils dilate on the part of her smooth blue face where a nose should be. "That's the entire reason the school exists. Because human souls are not spiritually evolved enough to join the Galactic Federation."

"I know why the school exists, Sylestra." Alien Isis's face

betrays a level of compassion, but her tone is firm. "I was here when it was founded."

"Yes, of course, Alien Isis. I meant no offense." Sylestra gives a slight bow.

"Mr. Moongate, what is your position on this?" Isis turns her crystal gaze on Kai.

"The Agartha bylaws are very clear. The portal system was constructed to allow only those souls who are chosen and ready to receive the Academy's teachings. Any student who passes through the portal must be accepted into the school." Kai's features bristle with determination as he pleads my case.

"As for her condition as an Earthseed, I can only say that if we did not believe that humans were capable of raising their level of consciousness, why else would we be educating Starseeds and sending them to the surface? Surely humans must be capable of some spiritual advancement, otherwise everything we teach here would be for naught."

He's not just beautiful. He *believes* what he says. That might be worse.

"Alien Isis," Sylestra interjects, "obviously human souls have the potential for expansion, otherwise we wouldn't be out here in this Source forsaken part of the galaxy, but we have never taught an Earthseed at Agartha. We simply do not know what sort of ramifications or dangers her presence here could precipitate."

Alien Isis leans back in her chair, the halo above her head shifting from gold to violet. The room stills.

"May I say something?" I take a step forward on my unwounded ankle, swallowing down the panic.

"You may," she says.

"My name is Synchronicity Jones. I don't know why the portal chose me—I honestly don't. But the way things unfolded this past year, maybe even my whole life, it feels like something was guiding me here. Like, on some cosmic level, I was *meant* to go to this school. I don't know how to explain it other than that there is some element of fate to my being here today. Maybe I'm not as spiritually advanced as the other students, but I'll study harder, train longer. Even if it seems strange now, I feel like I'm here for a reason."

Alien Isis ponders for a moment.

"When you've lived as long as I have," she says at last, "fate stops feeling like such a strange idea." She taps her finger on the desk. "I find myself tempted to side with you and Mr. Moongate."

Waves of relief wash over me.

"But," she adds, gaze sharpening, "do not make me regret my decision to let you stay. Is that understood?"

"Of course, Alien Isis. I won't let you down." A well of joy springs up inside me, a joy I haven't felt in a long time.

"Unbelievable," Alien Sylestra mutters. "She's a *first* incarnation. That means she hasn't even paid her tuition! Where will she stay?"

"Didn't you submit a request for an aide, Sylestra? Put her up in one of the extra rooms in the Energy Work School. She can work off her tuition as your assistant."

"But Alien Isis..."

"I have made my decision." The halo above her head flashes crimson. "I suggest you honor it. We have greater challenges to face this year."

Alien Sylestra scoffs. "Fine. But don't expect me to go easy on her just because she's an Earthseed. She will be expected to do everything that is required of all the other students."

"I would expect nothing less, Sylestra. Now, Mr. Moongate, will you please take Miss Jones and fix that ankle of hers?"

I look down. My sock is soaked scarlet with blood.

CHAPTER FOUR

Kai's house is tucked just outside the main pyramid, nestled among flowering hedges and ancient stone monoliths. The path to his door winds through a garden of sunflowers, rose bushes, and something that smells like vanilla and honeysuckle.

His front door glides open at a touch. Inside, the space is calm and curated, sunlight bouncing off rows of hanging plants and shelves lined with herbs, minerals, and softly glowing crystals. A small fountain gurgles gently in the corner.

"You can sit wherever," Kai says, brushing a strand of hair behind his ear as he leads me in.

I limp toward the couch and sink into it.

"Thanks again," I say. "For sticking up for me back there. And not letting them beam me back to my car and my overdue credit card bills."

He smiles and shrugs off his jacket, revealing a loose linen shirt that only highlights how golden his skin is. "It was the right thing to do. I know what it's like not to be seen as enough."

"Hard to imagine you ever being the underdog," I say.

"For a while, second incarnations weren't allowed at Agartha either," he says. "But luckily, I paid my tuition in my first incarnation, and I petitioned Alien Isis to change the rules."

"What's the deal with tuition anyway? I didn't know I was supposed to pay something before I came here."

"Tuition is paid in Galactic Credits, which you can't acquire on Earth. That's why everyone pays their tuition before they incarnate here."

"So before you die, you make a donation to the school just hoping that you'll reincarnate on Earth?"

"The soul can choose where it incarnates in the in-between place." He settles down on the couch next to me.

"Do you remember your last incarnation?"

"In the later years, there is a class for past life regression. I always had fleeting memories of my life in the Pleiades when I was growing up on Earth, but I got the full picture when I took the past life regression class."

"So you're a Pleiadian?" I remember Mae saying something about them being the rarest type of Starseed.

"Yes. Just like Alien Isis."

"But she's not a Starseed..."

"No, she's a native Pleiadian."

"And Sylestra?"

"Alien Sylestra is Sirian. You always want to use the title 'Alien' before your professors' names. It's a term of respect within the Galactic Federation."

"She didn't seem to like me very much." I adjust myself on his couch, taking the pressure off my injured foot.

"Sirians are one of the most spiritually advanced races in the Galactic Federation, and they hold a lot of political power. They have a tendency to look down on some of the other alien races."

"What did Isis, I mean Alien Isis, mean about having bigger challenges to face this year?"

"I'm not sure. Alien Isis has a lot on her plate as the Spiritual Director. I'm just glad she was able to see our side today. Now let's have a look at that ankle." Kai kneels down next to me and pulls up my legging. "How does it feel?" he asks, slowly rotating my foot back and forth and looking up at me with those beautiful brown eyes.

I wince as he moves it a bit too far in one direction. "Not the best," I say.

"Hold still. I'm going to take off your shoe." He sits cross-legged on the floor and rests my foot between his legs. He unties the laces and eases the sneaker off my swollen foot. My sock is soaked through with blood. "What happened here?"

"I slipped in a stream right before I came through the portal."

"That would explain the wet hair."

I blush. Disheveled and bleeding certainly isn't the way I want to look meeting a man like him.

"This might hurt a little." He peels the blood-soaked sock off my foot, ripping it away from the spot where the wound had already started to congeal to the fabric. I breathe in sharply between my teeth.

"Sorry," he murmurs.

I grit my teeth as he eases the sock fully off my foot. "So this is the part where I ask if bringing injured girls back here is a habit of yours."

A corner of his mouth turns up into a smirk. "Only the really special ones."

"Oh shut up," I say, rolling my eyes and trying to conceal a smile.

"I'm just teasing," he says, adjusting my leg across his lap. "Now let's get you healed up."

He closes his eyes. His hands hover an inch above my skin. His lips move in a whisper I don't understand, and then...

The light comes.

It pours from his palms in threads of translucent opal, the same color as Alien Isis's skin. The strands wrap around my ankle like ribbons of warmth, tightening, pulsing, seeping into my bones.

For a moment, the light becomes too bright to look at. I close my eyes and lean back on his couch as hot waves of energy shoot up my leg. It doesn't sting. It feels... good. Almost *too* good.

My back arches slightly. I consciously will myself not to moan as the intense pleasure radiates up my spine. My whole body feels alive, every part flushed, heated, *glowing*, and then just as quickly, the sensation fades. I open my eyes.

The wound is gone. Just a smear of dried blood remains.

"Holy shit," I whisper.

"Pleiadian healing," Kai says softly. "We work through light and frequency. It's usually... pleasant."

"Yeah," I say, breathless. "I noticed."

"Agartha's magnetic field makes spiritual powers appear as visual light," Kai says, getting up. "A lot like the Aurora Borealis on Earth."

He hands me a cloth to wipe the blood away, then disappears for a second and returns with a crystal tablet just like the ones the other students received at the Entrance Obelisk. "Here. You'll need this."

I take the translucent slate and hold it between my hands. The edges are straight but the top and bottom are rough and natural, like it was hewn from a living crystal. It's only a few millimeters thick. "It's beautiful."

He sits beside me on the couch now, close enough that our shoulders nearly touch. "It's called a selenite tablet. Has your schedule, communications, assignments. Just place your palm on the surface."

I do. The surface glows beneath my touch, etched with blue alien symbols that shimmer like water.

"Most of it's written in Light Language," he says. "It's meant to be read intuitively, not literally. You'll pick it up."

He takes the tablet and starts scrolling through the course listings. His fingers move with confidence, but there's something tender in the way he handles the slate, like he's adjusting my future, one class at a time.

"All first-years have to take Energy Work, Galactic History, and Craft. Most take something based on their Starseed origin as their fourth class, but... since you're an Earthseed, you have some flexibility." Kai taps on the screen and scrolls through a list. "There's Musical Healing Theory, Intro to Meditation, Herbalism..."

"Ooh, do Herbalism. I've always wanted to learn that."

"Herbalism it is." He makes some final adjustments by swiping things around the glowing crystal face. "Okay. Herbalism and Galactic History, Tuesdays and Thursdays. Energy Work and Craft, Monday, Wednesday, Friday. You're officially enrolled."

I take the tablet and hold it to my chest like a passport.

"Wait, what's Craft?" I ask. "Please tell me it's not alien macaroni art."

He laughs. "Close. It's actually UFO flight training."

"You're joking."

"Not even a little. Eldercraft are ancient vehicles left behind by advanced civilizations. The Academy trains Starseeds to fly the reverse-engineered models. Personally, I think it's more of a distraction than anything, but some students claim to get a spiritual boost from connecting with a craft."

"And you just casually teach people to pilot UFOs?"

"Well, I don't," he says. "That's Xion's class."

Something about the way he says the name puts me on edge.

"Xion?"

"He's... complicated." Kai leans back against the couch, his expression darkening just slightly. "A Maldekian. One of the last. Their planet was destroyed centuries ago in what the Federation calls a self-inflicted collapse. Most Maldekians didn't survive."

I blink. "And he's a teacher here?"

"He's one of the best pilots in the galaxy. But..." Kai hesitates. "Maldekians aren't exactly trusted. Not after what happened to their world. The Federation considers them a cautionary tale, what happens when a species fails to evolve spiritually."

"That seems harsh."

"Maybe. But it's the reality. He's never been officially accepted into the Galactic Federation. Neither have his people. He keeps to himself, doesn't get along well with students. Alien Isis defends him, but it's controversial. I'd give him a wide berth if I were you. He's not too fond of Earthseeds."

I nod slowly, something cold curling in my chest.

"They still let him teach?"

"He's valuable," Kai says carefully. "And divisive. Just... be cautious, okay?"

I nod, but my thoughts are already spinning.

Xion. The name echoes in the back of my mind like a

warning.

Kai sighs, rubbing the back of his neck. "I don't get it. Why Isis lets someone like that teach here. The Maldekians *destroyed* their own world, and he's a living reminder of it."

My stomach drops. I wonder if Kai would feel the same way about me if he knew the truth.

That I've destroyed something too.

CHAPTER
FIVE

Kai walks me back to the Entrance Obelisk where Alien Sylestra has resumed reading off the Starseed origins of excited first-years. A new teacher is handing out the tablets.

"I have to prepare for the class I'm teaching this year." Kai's gaze is warm, and he puts a comforting hand on my shoulder. "Just hang out here until Alien Sylestra finishes. She'll get you set up in your room and tell you what she expects of you as her aide."

"Can't wait," I mutter.

He laughs. "You'll be fine. Plus, you'll get experience working for the Academy. In that regard, you'll be way ahead of the other first-years."

"Lucky me."

"Hey, you're gonna do great." Kai walks backward away from me. "See you around campus. And if you slip in another creek, you know where to find me."

I watch him get smaller as he walks down the causeway toward the Great Pyramid, eventually losing him among the crowds of teachers and students.

"Altairian Starseed, ninth incarnation." Alien Sylestra's voice is harsh against the cool afternoon breeze wafting through the courtyard. She hasn't so much as acknowledged me since I showed up.

"Alien Sylestra, I just wanted to let you know I'm here whenever you want to show me where I'll be staying."

"Not now, Synchronicity. I'm working." She doesn't even look at me.

"Well, do you know how much longer you'll be here?"

"I said, not now," she hisses before calling the next student forward.

I take the hint and retreat to a bench on the side of the courtyard. The portals are opening much less frequently now, and the line for the Entrance Obelisk is dwindling.

I think about Mae and Jasper and wonder where they're

staying. They're probably enjoying dinner with a bunch of other new students. Meanwhile, I'm waiting for Alien Sinister over there to finish her work so she can come up with ways to torment me.

The shadows grow longer, and at last, the final first-year approaches the obelisk.

"Name?" I hear my new boss call out.

"Bo Kingscott." He's short with a shock of red hair.

"Go ahead and place your hand on the obelisk, Bo." I don't remember Alien Sylestra being so accommodating with me.

The young man walks up to the towering piece of granite and lays his palm on the singular recess in the rock. After a few moments, two symbols light up on the stone face, and Alien Sylestra reads them off. "Sirian Starseed, fifth incarnation."

Bo pumps his fist in the air and yells out, "Yes!"

"Congratulations, Mr. Kingscott. If you need any help channeling your spiritual powers, my doors are always open," Alien Sylestra says loud enough for me to hear. "Although, as a fellow Sirian, I suspect you should have no trouble at all."

Apparently, these spiritually evolved teachers aren't above showing favoritism.

"Thank you," Bo says and moves on to receive his selenite tablet.

Finally. I'm exhausted and can't wait to decompress in a room of my own. But when Alien Sylestra finishes conferring with another teacher, she simply walks off toward an arched exit in the courtyard.

Without even looking back at me.

I get up and run after her.

"Alien Sylestra, I was told you would show me to my room."

"Oh yes, dear. I completely forgot you were waiting for me."

Sure she did.

"Follow me. I'm excited to have an aide this year. There's simply *so* much work that needs to be done in the Energy Work School."

"I'm happy to help," I say, glad that she's taken a friendlier attitude towards me.

"The Energy Work School houses the College of Massage, the Reiki Center, the day spa, and the yoga classrooms. You'll be responsible for wiping down and rolling all the mats and washing all the linens from the massage tables, among other things."

When I heard teacher's aide, I had imagined myself grading papers and making worksheets, not cleaning and doing laundry. But if this is my ticket into Agartha, then so be it.

"I think I can handle that," I say.

An elaborate domed complex rises ahead of us, framed by the orange and pink sky. Each building is a curved stone circle with round windows, intersecting with others to form a temple of interlocking rotundas. It looks like someone carved giant soap bubbles out of stone.

"I certainly hope you can," Alien Sylestra continues. "Your enrollment here depends on it."

Her voice is amiable, but I hear the threat.

We step into the nearest building, and the air shifts. It feels like a cross between a monastery and a wellness spa—gleaming white floors, copper inlays catching the light, and shelves brimming with tinctures, salt lamps, and herbal tonics. Crystals pulse softly from recessed alcoves, casting warm amber refractions across cushions and meditation benches. The scent of eucalyptus and tea tree hangs in the air, grounding and bracing.

Sylestra leads me into a yoga studio stacked with multicolored mats. "I'm afraid we're a little backed up after the break. I'll need all of these wiped down and restocked in each of the classrooms before class starts tomorrow."

"Wait, you want me to do all of this... tonight?"

"Oh yes," she says with a sadistic gleam in her big alien eyes. "And I'll need all of the linens washed for the massage tables as well."

I follow her down the hall to a storage room that is absolutely packed with dirty blankets.

"You can't be serious."

"Of course. You didn't actually expect to attend this school for free, did you? You're going to have to earn your keep."

"Okay... where are the washing machines?"

Alien Sylestra lets out a condescending laugh. "Oh, we don't use *washing machines*, darling. You Earthseeds and your simple ideas."

We continue down the hall and turn a corner into another passage. Sylestra opens a door and we enter a large recessed room filled with steam and lit by large glowing crystals on the wall.

"The Energy Work School was built over very unique geothermal springs and vents. The hot spring water is piped into the spa for soaking and mineral baths, but here you'll use it to wash laundry." She leads me to a stream of steaming water bubbling forth from rocks set right into the floor of the room. The water spirals over smooth river stones into a whirlpool that disappears into a hole below.

"Like this." Alien Sylestra extracts a wrinkled towel from a pile of laundry and sets it loose in the stream. The whirlpool of hot water carries it over the rocks, jostling it as it goes until the towel disappears into the dark hole.

"But how do I..."

"Just wait."

A moment later, the towel emerges from another hole in the floor, this one larger and lined with rough boulders, propelled upward by a gust of hot air.

"That's actually amazing," I say.

"Let it dry a moment longer, then you can grab it."

The towel tumbles in midair, suspended by the rush of hot wind pouring from the geothermal vent. I reach out to grab it, and it feels like I'm putting my hand in front of a giant hair dryer. The towel is completely dry. The whole process couldn't have taken more than a couple minutes.

"Like I said, I need all of the linens washed and restocked in the classrooms and massage studios before classes start tomorrow. Do you have any questions?"

"Not about the laundry, but where exactly am I staying?"

"Oh yes. Come."

Back in the hall, I follow Alien Sylestra to the next door.

"I'm afraid it's not much." She opens the door to a small storage room lit by a single glowing crystal and lined on one side by wooden shelves filled with cleaning supplies. "I don't know what Isis was thinking, allowing you to stay with no tuition and no student housing. You should really consider yourself lucky you have a place to stay at all."

A massage table sits folded up in the corner.

"You want me to sleep on that?"

"Why yes, dear. They're quite comfortable. I myself have fallen asleep on them on more than one occasion while receiving energy work."

Even though the room is small, I'm grateful for it. Anything is better than sleeping in my car. At least I'll get to fully extend my legs.

"Is there anywhere I could get some food?" I ask. I haven't eaten all day.

"Well, let's see. Your work-study credits won't get applied to your tablet for two weeks, so you won't be able to buy anything from the student market until then, but in the meantime, there's a little cafe further down the hall. They haven't been open all summer, but I suppose you could help yourself to whatever you find there."

"Thank you." My stomach grumbles as if on cue.

"Now, do you need anything else from me? I really must be getting back."

I set my selenite tablet down on the cluttered shelf and try to imagine spending a whole year in this room. "I think I'm all set."

"Good. I'll see you first thing tomorrow. You're in my 8:00 class, right?"

I hadn't realized my Energy Work class was with Sylestra.

"I guess so."

"And remember, the mats and linens. All of them." With that, she vanishes into the corridor. I hear the double doors shut at the front of the building and find myself eerily alone in this huge complex.

I decide to deal with my room later and walk off down the hall in search of something to eat. The Agarthan sun is falling behind the horizon, sending rays of golden light through the round windows. I pass more yoga studios and classrooms before finding a vacant little cafe at the end of the passage.

The display cases are empty, but inside one of the cabinets, I find some granola and dried fruit, and make myself a light meal.

I tell myself it's dinner, but really it's trail mix.

I find a bar of dark chocolate hidden behind some coffee filters and eat a few squares as the light fades from the sky. I'm not full, but it's enough to keep me going for now.

The halls are lit by crystal light now, and I make my way back to the room filled with yoga mats. In the closet, I find a washcloth and a glass bottle filled with clear liquid that smells like lavender. Dabbing the cloth in the cleaning fluid, I set to work wiping down the mats.

One by one, I clean them and stack them into neat piles and take the piles down the hall to the various classrooms and stack them in the corner. After the first trip, it barely looks like I've made a dent in the mountain of dirty mats. The longer I go, the further I have to venture out in the school to find unstocked classrooms. It's like a giant circular maze that seems to stretch on for miles.

The glowing clocks etched into stone on some of the walls use alien symbols, but they are divided into twelve segments just like on the surface, and when I finally finish with the mats, I deduce that it is close to 11:00 at night.

Shit.

I'm bone tired, but I still have all the linens to do.

I know it's not wise to drink coffee this late at night, but I need something to keep me awake, so I fix myself a shot of espresso at the cafe. Even though I'm away from all my peers, it's kind of nice having this whole place to myself at night.

The espresso is bitter and smooth and buttery and I savor every sip before going back to work. I'll be lucky if I get done by 2:00.

There is no cart, so I have to take the piles of dirty linens by the armload from the closet to the laundry room. Every time I open the door, the hot, humid air blasts me in the face.

It's oddly meditative, sitting next to the hot spring and dropping blankets into the stream, watching them swirl and jostle among the rocks as the whirlpool pulls them down into the dark abyss below. Moments later, they shoot back up the geothermal vent, and when there's enough of them dancing in the jet of hot air, I get up and fold them into tidy stacks.

It was one thing finding all the rooms in need of yoga mats, but the massage tables are spread out between classrooms and smaller individual studios. I line the headrests and make the tables up as neatly as possible, given the time constraints.

When I finish drying the final load, I have to venture farther into the Energy Work School than I have before to find the last remaining studios. Somewhere on the third floor, I stumble upon a long hall with a single door at the end lit by a green crystal overhead. Thinking that this is where the last few studios must be, I walk down the hall and try the handle. It's locked, which is strange, considering every other door in this building has been open. I peer through the small rectangular window into the hall beyond.

Whereas the rest of the school has been lit with soft, warm light, the corridor on the other side of the locked door glares with a harsh fluorescence like something you would see in a modern hospital. I try the handle again out of curiosity, but it remains steadfast.

After one last glance down the mysterious passageway, I find the remaining studios and stock them with freshly cleaned linens. When I'm finally done, the clock reads 4:00 a.m.

I stumble back to my room and unfold the massage table,

lining it with an extra set of blankets. After I adjust the legs to the lowest setting, I collapse back onto it and stare up at the ceiling.

Old pipes jitter and groan, carrying the hot spring water to other parts of the school, and the single crystal affixed to my wall with a copper wire wrap emits a soothing otherworldly glow.

I reach into the pocket of my hoodie and pull out my copy of *A Starseed's Guide to Agartha*. If it weren't for this little book, I wouldn't be here right now.

I flip it open to a random page. "*All the spiritual technology that Agartha is built upon, from the artificial sun to the quadrupole magnetic field that holds it in place, was given to us by the Elders, an advanced race of ancient beings whose ruins can be found throughout the galaxy. Although we owe much of our progress to the Elders, very little is known about who they were or why they disappeared.*"

As interesting as this section is, I can barely keep my eyes open. I prop the book between two bottles of cleaning solution in a feeble attempt at a bookshelf. It's not much, but it makes my glorified supply closet feel a little more like home.

I reach up and instinctively tap the crystal. The light clicks off, shrouding me in utter darkness, and I am asleep before my head hits the pillow.

CHAPTER
SIX

The sound of voices jolts me awake. Laughter and footsteps echo just outside my door.

Shit.

I scramble for my tablet, tapping wildly at the glowing interface. No obvious clock. No idea how long I've been out. My heart starts pounding.

First class. Sylestra's class. I'm already late.

There's no time to change. Not that I could. All my other outfits are still in my car... on the surface.

I throw open the door and slip into the current of students streaming through the halls of the Energy Work School. I feel like a paperclip caught in a magnetic storm of flowing robes, crystal necklaces, and perfectly serene expressions.

I spot a tall alien teacher with a long neck and luminescent eyes and flag them down. "Excuse me. Do you know where Alien Sylestra's class is?"

"Second floor. Room 217," they say, blinking slowly. "But you're late. Nearly fifteen minutes."

"Thank you very much." I sprint up the staircase, darting past wide-eyed first-years and teachers gliding by in silence. I rush down the hall, glancing in each classroom until I spot Alien Sylestra, poised in front of a packed classroom like a queen before her court. I push the door open as quietly as I can, but it's no use. Sylestra pins me with her gaze as soon as I step foot inside.

"Synchronicity Jones," her voice lances across the room like a blade wrapped in velvet. "So glad you could join us."

A wave of snickers ripples through the class.

"Oh my God, is she wearing the same clothes as yesterday?" It's June, blonde baby braids perfectly framing her face, sitting right in the front row with Vaylen and Kara.

"How embarrassing," Kara says.

Vaylen just looks at me with a patronizing smile, and

somehow that's worse than the comments from her friends. All three look like they stepped off the cover of a galactic wellness catalog, flowing linen, effortless grace. Meanwhile, I'm standing there in my thrifted hoodie and knockoff leggings.

"Class," Sylestra purrs, "Synchronicity has just volunteered to be our demonstration subject today. How generous."

I freeze, but she gestures to a massage table set up in the front of the classroom with an expectant smile.

This feels like a bad idea, but I don't have much of a choice. I walk up to the table and lie down. Sylestra leans her head in close to mine, pretending to adjust the headrest. "If you're ever late to my class again, I'll fail you," she whispers in my ear.

She straightens and addresses the class. "The physical body is merely the echo of the etheric body. Shift the current of energy, and the body will follow."

Sylestra waves her hand over me, and all of a sudden, my throat is overcome with an intense, dry itching sensation. I try to control it, but it's useless. I let out a barrage of hoarse coughs that do nothing to ease the itch.

"By sensing the subtle currents of the etheric body, one can manipulate them into, or out of, alignment," Sylestra continues. "In this case, I have given Synchronicity a mild cough by reversing the direction of one of her many etheric currents. Would anyone care to attempt a correction?"

"I'd like to volunteer, Alien Sylestra." It's Vaylen. She flips her long brown hair over her shoulder and steps to the front of the class.

"Vaylen Blair, you're a Sirian Starseed, isn't that right?"

"Yes, Professor."

"Then you're like me. Our kind heal with thoughts alone."

"Actually, Professor, I've found that my abilities are enhanced when I use a particular element. May I?"

Vaylen takes a candlestick from the side of the room and places it on the counter next to me. From her pocket, she produces a box of matches and lights the candle. The sulfur smell of the match immediately fills my nostrils, triggering another coughing fit that wracks my whole body.

"So you're an elemental healer. Those are quite rare." The hint of praise in Sylestra's voice is apparent.

"Yes, Professor. I've been drawn to the element of fire from a young age."

Of course she was. Psychopath.

"Good. Now, using what I taught you this morning, try to feel into the energy imbalance in Synchronicity's body and channel your healing powers there."

Vaylen puts one hand near the candle and the other over my throat. I let loose a particularly wet cough, hoping to get some spittle on her.

"Gross," she says, jerking her hand back and wiping it on her pant leg. This time, she keeps her hand safely over my forehead, out of coughing range.

I watch her close her eyes in concentration, and the flame on the candle begins to glow blue. Soon, a burning sensation overtakes my throat. I feel the muscles in my windpipe constrict, and I can only get air into my lungs in small gasps.

Liquid wax runs freely down the side of the candle as the flame burns brighter. It feels like my esophagus is literally on fire. I sit up on the table, gesturing wildly to my throat. I try to heave in another lungful of air, but my windpipe is now completely closed off.

"Hey, stop that! You're hurting her," a woman from the back of the room calls out.

"Let her finish," Sylestra says calmly.

I clutch at my throat as the pain sears my windpipe. I turn to Vaylen, pleading with my eyes, but her gaze is fixed on the blue flame, which is now towering almost a foot into the air and giving off a column of thick black smoke like something summoned.

The pain in my throat is unlike anything I've ever felt before. I look at Alien Sylestra in a last attempt to be saved from this torture, but she simply regards me with cool indifference.

That's it. I'm going to die here. On my first day of class.

I collapse onto the floor, but just as my vision starts to go dark, the pain fades, my throat opens back up, and I pull in lungful after lungful of deep, rich, life-giving oxygen.

The class applauds.

"Excellent work, Vaylen," Sylestra says. "Synchronicity, how does your throat feel?"

"Pretty terrible," I manage to get out.

"Synchronicity raises an excellent point. Healing can often be painful, especially when administered by a Sirian Starseed, but with practice, the painful side effects can be reduced. Thank you, ladies. You can return to your seats."

Vaylen rejoins her friends in the front row, and I find a seat somewhere on the edge of the classroom, my throat still aching from Vaylen's "healing."

"By midterms, you will all be expected to locate an ailment in the body and heal it, just like Vaylen did today."

"Except if you're an Earthseed," someone says loud enough for the whole class to hear. It's the red-haired boy who was last in line at the obelisk yesterday. Muffled laughter arises from the class, and I shrink into myself, feeling the eyes of my fellow students on me.

"Miss Jones will be expected to produce healing powers just like everyone else," Alien Sylestra says. "And I do not appreciate being interrupted in the middle of a lecture, Mr. Kingscott."

"I'm sorry, Professor. I just fear that her lower vibration is going to affect my own healing powers." He shoots a smirk back at me before continuing on. "Don't you think it would be better if she had her own private energy work class for spiritually challenged healers such as herself?"

Ass.

The classroom erupts in laughter while Vaylen, Kara, and June snicker amongst themselves in the front row.

"Your cleverness will only get you so far, Mr. Kingscott." Alien Sylestra narrows her gaze on Bo. "If I were you, I'd focus on manifesting my own healing powers and less on the vibratory state of your classmates."

"Yes, Professor," he says, the smirk is still plastered across his face.

"Now, for your homework, each of you will check out *Energy Flow in the Etheric Body* from the library and read chapters one through three. If you have any questions, don't hesitate to visit me during my office hours. Thank you, and I'll see you on Wednesday."

Alien Sylestra sits down behind her desk, and the students begin to gather their things and stand up. I hurry toward the back door, hoping to avoid Bo, Vaylen, and her clique of spiritually perfect followers, but before I reach the back of the room, someone stops me.

"Hey, I just wanted to say I was worried for you up there. That looked really painful." She's a thin, pale young woman with waist-length platinum-blonde hair and mousy features.

"Thanks," I say. "I think you were probably the only one rooting for me."

"I noticed you on Entrance Day. I actually think it's cool that you're an Earthseed." She pushes a strand of hair behind her ear. "My name's Cassandra, by the way."

"I'm Synchronicity, but I guess you probably know that. I like your necklace," I say, trying to be nice.

"Thanks!" Cassandra's muted grey eyes light up. "It's a meteorite. I saw it fall from the sky about a year ago and followed it to where it landed. All I could find was this little piece." Her voice is so soft I can barely hear her.

"That's really cool," I say. "Hey, do you know where they hold the Craft classes? I've got one in like fifteen minutes."

"Yes, the craft site. It's near the hangars. Go past the Entrance Obelisk, then veer left toward the pyramid. I can show you, if—"

"No, that's okay. I think I can find it."

She nods. "See you Wednesday?"

"Yeah. See you."

I slip into the hall, sore, shaking, but somehow still here.

CHAPTER
SEVEN

"Synchronicity! We were sure you got sent back to the surface." Jasper's voice cuts through the buzz of students gathered across a vast field lined with gleaming silver saucers.

Real-life flying saucers.

Dozens of them, glinting in the Agarthan sunlight like ancient gods waiting to be awakened.

"No, we weren't," Mae corrects him, barreling toward me with arms wide. "I knew you'd make it."

The warmth of her hug dissolves the edge I didn't know I was carrying. I feel my shoulders drop for the first time all morning.

"What dorm did you get?" Jasper asks, his red panda spirit animal, Mochi, perched lazily on his shoulder. "You missed the party last night."

"I didn't even know there *was* a party. I was working for Sylestra."

"On your first night? That's downright cruel." Jasper's floppy mass of curly black hair nearly blocks his vision.

"She had me doing laundry till 4 in the morning."

Jasper eyes my crumpled hoodie. "That explains the look. No judgment, but you're giving interdimensional gym rat."

"Asshole," I laugh, swatting his arm. He's dressed like a velvet prince from a space opera: maroon coat with faux fur lapels, silk shirt unbuttoned just shy of scandalous. "I wasn't exactly planning on walking through a portal to the center of the Earth yesterday."

"Don't worry, we'll take you to Deechin's vintage shop later today. He's got an awesome selection."

"Which dorm are you in?" Mae asks. "I want to come and visit you." Her blonde dreads are interwoven with green ribbons and feathers.

"I... uh... didn't get a dorm. Sylestra put me up in the Energy Work School. I'm her aide now."

"More like indentured servant," Jasper quips.

"She didn't seem too happy after Kai showed her up in front of Alien Isis," I explain.

"Oh, that's right. You went off with hot tablet guy," Mae grins. "Did he ask you out on a date after all that?"

"Actually, he brought me back to his place."

"Get out!" She pushes me backward with both hands in disbelief. "Did you hook up with him?"

My cheeks flush. "It wasn't like that."

"Uh-huh. And I suppose he healed your ankle out of the kindness of his chiseled heart?"

"I'm pretty sure he glows when he concentrates," I admit.

Mae gasps. "Synchronicity's got a celestial crush!"

Before I can defend myself, an impossibly low voice ripples across the field.

"Good morning, first-years,"

The crowd hushes. The crimson-skinned alien I locked eyes with on Entrance Day strides into view, his very presence pulling the air taut.

He's massive, shoulders like stone, tattoos curling over muscle and bone like sentient ink. A leather vest leaves his chest bare, revealing a heavily built physique. He's probably a foot taller than the tallest student, and his mouth is so perfect I feel like I could stare at it for hours. When his gaze sweeps the class and catches on me, my heart squeezes like a vice.

"My name is Xion Da'ath. I'll be your craft instructor for the year."

The silence is reverent.

"Craftwork is not only essential for intergalactic travel, but it can also help you channel your spiritual abilities and gain a clearer mind." His voice commands the attention of the entire class without him having to raise it. "Eldercraft are composed of both metallic and biologic material. That means that when you connect to one, it increases your own neurological capacity. It's like hooking your brain up to an even bigger brain. This allows you to access your spiritual powers more easily, export your tedious thoughts to its neural network, and ultimately live more in the moment."

He paces in front of us, boots thudding like war drums.

"In this class, you will not only learn how to connect to a craft, but also how to repair it and, ultimately, the basics of flying it. Some of you will be more naturally inclined to this than others." He stops in front of me, and a shiver shoots down my spine. I try to maintain my composure, but when he looks down at me with those uncompromising amber eyes, glowing like twin embers, my heart skitters.

"There are two types of craft," he continues. "Eldercraft, which have been recovered around the galaxy from the remains of the Elder civilization, and reverse-engineered craft, which are built by our own scientists using the technology we have gleaned from the ancient ships. Connections with true Eldercraft are powerful but extremely rare. In fact, the only two people in Agartha connected to true Eldercraft are myself and Alien Isis."

A quiet murmur spreads through the students.

"In this class, we will only be using the reverse-engineered models, otherwise known as RE craft." He gestures towards the rows of UFOs behind him. "It will be your responsibility not only to repair and maintain these vehicles but to cultivate a meaningful connection with them throughout the year, because a craft will only fly reliably if it can trust its pilot."

"I want that one," Bo says, pointing to a sleek black ship with three long, pointed tails, set apart from the rest of the ships on the far edge of the field.

Silence reigns over the group. Xion slowly approaches Bo until he's towering over him.

"What's your name, Starseed?" His tone is inscrutable.

"Bo. Bo Kingscott."

Every student stiffens.

"Starseed Kingscott here says he wants to connect with an Eldercraft after I specifically said you would only be assigned *RE* craft. And not just any Eldercraft, but *my* Eldercraft. If Starseed Kingscott even attempted to connect with my ship, his small brain would be so overwhelmed with spiritual downloads that he would most likely end up with permanent psychosis. So tell me again, Starseed." Xion leans in so close to Bo that their faces are practically touching. "Which craft do you want?"

"Not that one," he mumbles.

"What's that?" Xion cups his hand over his ear. "I couldn't hear you."

"I said, not that one."

"That's right, Starseed Kingscott. Your arrogance has earned you the privilege of repairing this relic." Xion slaps the metal hull of the UFO directly behind him. "Sirian Class G Y-80. Learn it. Love it. Try not to crash it."

"Yes sir."

"What is it called?"

"A Sirian..." I can see beads of sweat on Bo's forehead.

"A Sirian Class G Y-80."

"A Sirian Class G Y-80," Bo repeats.

"That's right. By the end of the year you will know the name and part number of every piece of this craft, down to the smallest screw." Xion opens a hatch and pulls out a heavily used book. "That's the user's manual," he says, throwing it in the dirt at Bo's feet. "I suggest you become intimately familiar with it."

Bo bends to pick it up with shaking hands.

Xion moves on.

"Now, who wants to go next?"

The class is silent.

"How about you," Xion says, walking in front of June. "What kind of Starseed are you?"

"I'm Arcturian, sir."

"No spirit animal?"

"I, uh, haven't had that class yet." June adjusts one of her braids. "Sir."

"Well, for now, you can consider your craft as your spirit animal. You'll be taking care of that one back there. A Denebian UH-44."

"Thank you, sir," she says before walking over and

standing next to her craft.

One by one, Xion walks down the line, assigning a craft to each student until he reaches me. He crosses his arms, sending the muscles in his chest rippling. My pulse spikes.

"And you. What's your name?" His eyes dart back and forth between mine, like he's looking for something. I have to tilt my head up just to meet his gaze.

"Synchronicity Jones."

"What kind of Starseed are you, Synchronicity?"

"I'm not a Starseed, sir. I'm an Earthseed."

A few students snicker behind me.

His lip quivers almost imperceptibly. What was it Kai said about him? That he hated Earthseeds for some reason?

"Well then, Earthseed Jones, I have a special craft for you." A hint of malice flashes across his eyes.

Great. Another teacher with a vendetta against me.

He walks me down to the very end of the row to a flying saucer that looks more like something you'd find in a junkyard than a spaceship capable of interstellar travel. "This is a Castor 5. Originally one of the most successful reverse-engineered craft, however, it's become somewhat... obsolete." He slaps the hull, and a rusty piece of metal comes clattering to the ground.

I can't believe it, but my instructor is actually smirking at me.

"Wow. Thanks," I say.

We're separated from the rest of the students, and the thought that I am suddenly alone with this alien brute sends a wave of thrill and fear through my body.

He leans in, close enough that I catch a whiff of something electric and sharp. "This older craft should be more than enough work for an Earthseed like you." His voice is like gravel.

I tilt my chin up and lock my muscles to keep from trembling. "I've had to replace the alternator *and* the radiator on my Subaru, so I think I'm more than qualified."

He laughs a deep booming laugh and leans his massive,

muscled arm on the craft he's assigned to me. "There's a little more to craftwork than alternators and radiators, I'm afraid."

I lift my head up another inch to hold his gaze, challenge flaring in my eyes. "I taught myself to drive stick in the middle of winter in Colorado. I think I can handle this bucket of bolts."

Just then, a horrendous screeching erupts somewhere across the craft site. We both look up and see Bo's craft lurching into Xion's pristine black ship.

Xion sprints back to the front of the field with me following close behind. Everyone is looking on confused, except for Bo, whose face is as white as a sheet of paper.

"What the fuck did you do?" Xion screams.

"I just wanted to see if I could connect with it..." Bo stammers.

Xion runs up to the colliding ships and somehow gains control of Bo's clunky saucer and wills it with his mind back onto the ground before turning to face Bo.

"Did I tell you that you could connect with your craft?" he bites out.

"I'm sorry. You said we needed to form a bond with our craft if we wanted to fly them."

"You call that forming a bond? Taking shoddy control and crashing it into *my* Eldercraft?" Xion is shaking with fury. "If you ever pull a stunt like that again, I will not only fail you but I'll make sure you'll be cleaning out oil condensers until your last day at Agartha."

No one laughs.

I should be horrified. But instead, somewhere deep, deep inside, I'm lit up like a fuse.

This man is dangerous. Commanding. Utterly unapproachable.

But God help me, I want him.

CHAPTER
EIGHT

"I thought Xion was *literally* going to kill Bo," Mae says, laughing as she loops her arm through mine. We walk beneath the pearlescent sky, back toward the Great Pyramid. Jasper appears at my other side, his coat flaring like he timed his entrance.

"He could have," he says. "Wouldn't even have blinked. Maldekians aren't known for their mercy."

"But he looks so human," I murmur.

"It's the sun," Jasper replies. "Planets in the same solar system develop life along similar patterns. Same magnetic field, same frequencies."

"Wait, you're saying Maldek was in our solar system?" I ask.

"It was," he says. "You know the asteroid belt? That's what's left of it."

"They destroyed themselves," I say, Kai's words still echoing in my head.

Jasper nods. "And the survivors, those who didn't get consumed in the collapse, have been wandering the galaxy ever since."

"No wonder he's grumpy. He's got no home to go back to," I say, perhaps speaking more about my own situation than his.

"Did anyone else think he was hot?" Mae flicks her dreads off her shoulder, feathers catching the breeze.

"Alien Da'ath may be a prime specimen of masculinity, but interspecies relationships are strictly forbidden. The offspring of such unions can get... how shall I say it?" Jasper ponders for a moment. "Messy."

"So we're allowed to drool but not touch," Mae says. "Got it."

"I still can't believe we're learning to fly *UFOs*," I say. "This is all so crazy to me." And it's true. Yesterday I woke up in the back of my car, crammed in among piles of clothes and bags of groceries. Now I'm attending a spiritual healing arts school inside the Hollow Earth.

Mae beams. "It's magic. All of it."

"Craft are impressive, sure, but remember, ladies, the real goal here is to cultivate an equanimous mind and manifest your spiritual powers." Jasper reaches into his coat pocket and pulls out a morsel for Mochi, who devours it with gusto. "It's kind of hard to do that when you're speeding around the galaxy at multiple times the speed of light."

"Craft *help* you manifest your spiritual powers," Mae retorts. "You're just mad your craft looks like a toaster."

"What are you talking about?" Jasper drawls sarcastically. "The dull exterior and harsh angles of the Arcturan B Class Flying Cube are the perfect complement to a man of style such as myself." He tugs on the lapels of his coat with exaggerated pride, and I grin despite myself.

"And speaking of style, we need to get you a wardrobe upgrade," he says, eyeing my hoodie like it's a personal insult. "Something planetary yet poetic."

"Do you mind if we stop by your dorm first?" I ask. "I haven't eaten anything except some granola and a bar of chocolate since I got here."

There's part of me that feels ashamed asking my new friends for food. I have never been one to ask for help, but my stomach feels like it's going to eat itself alive.

"Of course, Sync! You must be starving. Plus, I want to show you my room," Mae says. "I picked up these amazing crystal string lights at the entrance swap last night."

"It sounds like I missed a lot last night."

"Don't worry. There will be more fun stuff. Did I tell you I'm auditioning for Supermoon?"

"No. That's amazing!"

"I met some guy last night who's a friend of the guitar player. He said they always like to have seven members in the band, one for each of the classical planets, and their mandolin player graduated last year."

"Yes, our little Mae certainly made some... exciting connections last night," Jasper interjects.

Mae's face turns beet red.

"What happened?" I ask.

"It was nothing," she says.

"This morning, while I was making maté, who do I see stumbling out of Mae's room? None other than the black-haired harpy Kara."

"We had a moment during the ecstatic dance!" Mae protests.

"Hey, I'm not judging." Jasper puts his hands up. "I'm just glad one of us is getting some action."

"It was a temporary soul contract. Our souls decided to bond for one night and one night alone," she says, but I can tell by the glow in her cheeks that she hopes it might be something more.

"Good for you," I say. "Wish I'd gotten one of those with Kai."

We round a curve in the path and stop before an enchanting house nestled in a grove of lilac and wisteria. A carved wooden sign sways gently overhead: *Larimar House*.

It's like something out of a coastal fairytale—weathered shingles, rounded alcoves, blue-glass windows that catch the light just right.

"Oh my God, guys, this place is beautiful. This is really where you live?"

"Where we live, laugh, and desperately wait for our turn in the bathroom," Jasper quips.

Inside, the air is warm and alive. We enter a common area with a bookshelf, hanging plants, and coffee tables of various sizes and designs. Two students are sitting on a couch, deep in conversation, and a gloomy man with straight black hair sits sketching symbols on a pad of paper.

We continue down a hall to a communal kitchen. "You guys, this place is amazing. You should see where I'm staying."

"It's so messed up they won't let you stay in a dorm with other students," Mae says. "Human connection is one of the best parts of this place."

"What would you like to eat?" Jasper asks. "I could whip

up some pasta, there's a ton of fresh fruit, or there's leftover rice and beans from last night." Mochi jumps off his shoulder and scurries along the counter to a bowl full of pears.

"Rice and beans are fine." I'm so jealous of their kitchen. It's like they're living in a hostel.

Mae hoists herself onto the counter and strums a few chords on her ukulele. "I got a job at the student market. You should come see me sometime. It's like a big farmer's market, and they grow all the food right here at Agartha."

"I was starting to think I was the only one with a job," I say. "Sylestra's got me scrubbing linens and wiping down yoga mats like it's my soul's penance."

"It depends on how much you donated to the school in your previous incarnation," Jasper explains. "Apparently I used to be Arcturian royalty. My student account could buy a moon."

"Mine's the opposite of that," I mutter between grateful bites of jasmine rice and spicy black beans.

"Don't worry, Sync," Mae says. "We've got you. We already decided we're your Hollow Earth parents."

I laugh. "You mean that?"

"We were so worried when they dragged you off to Alien Isis yesterday," she says.

"She was otherworldly," I say. "Like a living crystal carved into the most beautiful woman you've ever seen."

"I need to meet her," Mae says dreamily.

"You will," Jasper says. "Alien Isis is very hands-on. This school is her grand experiment. She wants it to succeed."

The sullen man who was drawing in his notepad walks into the kitchen, grabs some bread, and nods to us before heading up the stairs.

"Strange fellow," Jasper says. "I haven't heard a single word come out of his mouth since school started."

"We're all a little strange here," Mae replies, and the truth of it strikes me deep in the chest. For a moment, I believe that maybe there is a place for me here among these strange, wonderful souls.

Even if they don't know what I'm running from.

* * *

Later that night, I hang my new clothes on a freshly cleared shelf in my not-quite-a-bedroom. Jasper's generosity still hums around me like incense. He refused to let me leave Deechin's without at least one bag of essentials. But "essentials" at Deechin's meant a gold-threaded bomber jacket, embroidered tank tops, and yoga pants with constellations stitched into the hems. Everything in that little pop-up shop felt enchanted, like it had been waiting just for me.

With everything hung, my little supply closet is beginning to feel more like home.

Then I hear footsteps.

They echo down the stone corridor, steady and slow, and my body stills before I even realize I've stopped breathing.

I hadn't fully let myself register how alone I've been here in the Energy Work School. But now, as those footsteps approach, the solitude feels fragile, like something is trespassing through it.

The steps pause.

Right outside my door.

I hold perfectly still, heart thudding in my ears, until they continue on. Only once they fade do I crack open the door and peer down the hall, catching a glimpse of Alien Sylestra just before she turns down an adjoining passage.

There's nothing odd about her being here. She is the director of the Energy Work School after all. But something about the way she moves, the timing, the silence... it doesn't feel like casual administrative business.

It feels like secrecy.

And I can't help myself.

I slip into the hallway and follow, bare feet ghosting over the cold tile. When I reach the junction, I glance around the corner just as my toe clips the baseboard. Sylestra stops in her tracks.

I flatten myself against the wall, pulse hammering in my throat.

The pause stretches on. Then the footsteps resume,

unhurried, unaffected.

More carefully this time, I peek my head out and watch as she ascends a stairway. I creep after her, breath tight, until I reach the foot of the stairs and hear the soft sound of a door opening. But it's not the second floor. She's gone to the third.

My heart pounds with the thrill of doing something I probably shouldn't be doing. If Alien Sylestra caught me following her, she'd probably have me scrubbing the floor with a toothbrush, if not expelled.

I creep up the stairs, careful not to make a sound, and ease the door open to the third floor, where I see Sylestra disappear down the mysterious, green-lit hall. I race over to that corner, and when I peek around it, Sylestra has passed through the locked door, which shuts with a metallic clang behind her.

I risk a look through the small rectangular window into the sterile corridor beyond, but Sylestra is nowhere to be seen. Just the flicker of fluorescent light on linoleum, so out of place in this otherwise earth-toned school.

CHAPTER
NINE

I wake up early and make my way across the campus toward my first Herbalism class. The pyramid glints in the morning sun, and dewdrops hang on the grass like miniature jewels. Jasper's directions take me past the craft site where our assigned UFOs are lined up in rows, each with its own distinct design and character. I spot mine at the end of a row, rusty and nearly falling apart, with big circular windows looking into a messy cockpit. I was hoping I'd catch a glimpse of my flight instructor, but the massive tattooed alien is nowhere to be seen.

The path turns, slipping through a grove of trees, where I pass the remnants of a fire pit. A perfect pentagram made from white and black stones encircles the still-smoldering embers. Whoever made it is long gone.

At the far end of the grove, the land falls away, and I am greeted by a spectacular sight.

Before me lies a giant crater lined with lush terraces that overflow with hanging gardens. There are ponds with lily pads and beds of succulents and flower gardens and draping vines. The far edge of the crater has been eroded away into a narrow canyon through which the rising sun sends its golden rays and at the very bottom of this verdant hemispherical basin lies a pool of blue so vibrant it looks unreal, rimmed with yellow and orange mineral deposits like fire against water.

The wind carries the scent of herbs and damp soil as other students begin to arrive behind me. We descend the long, wending stairway together, past flowerbeds, mossy stones, and delicate trellises of medicinal herbs. Puffs of respiration rise from our breaths like clouds of spirit, condensing for a brief moment before dissolving once again into the ether.

I try to count the steps, but lose track somewhere after 400. At the bottom, on the crystalline shore of the blue pool, waits a squat figure in dirt-stained overalls, sandals, and a woven sun hat.

"Glorious morning," the alien says, her voice loamy and rich. "I'm Alien Thumgren. Native Arcturian. Keeper of roots, weeds, blooms, and wisdom. I'll be your Herbalism professor."

She's unlike any teacher I've had. Her skin is a soft, earthen green, ears long and pointed, hair a chaotic nest of brown frizz. Her toes, hairy and sharp-nailed, peek out from leather sandals like old roots.

"This," she says, gesturing expansively toward the natural amphitheater that surrounds us, "is Atum Crater. Born of fire. A meteor struck through the crust of your Earth and into Agartha. The wound became a gift."

She points to the pool.

"The force of the impact revealed the living waters which you see behind me. Rising up from the depths of Agartha, these waters remain at near-freezing temperatures year-round, and they have fed the gardens you see around you for millennia."

She waves a hand around the gardens. "Over time, we shaped this scar into a sanctuary. We built the terraces that wrap around the crater like rings to slow the erosion of this natural wonder. Today, it is one of the most diverse living gardens in all of Inner Earth, supporting all types of plants and animals."

At the mention of animals, a squirrel-like creature with mossy fur and the nose of a mole scurries out from a bush and climbs onto Alien Thumgren's shoulder. "This is Myco, my spirit animal. He comes from the Arcturian star system, but everything else here was collected from the surface of Earth. Do I have any Arcturian Starseeds in this class?"

A few of the students raise their hands. One of them, I notice, is the gloomy man from Larimar House.

"You may very well encounter your spirit animal in Atum Crater, but I assume all of you are taking Spirit Animal Calling as well." The students who raised their hands all nod their heads.

"Just to give you a breakdown of how the crater is

organized, the south-facing wall is where you'll find all the desert plants and plants that like a lot of sun." Alien Thumgren points to her right, where the crater wall is lined with cacti and palo verdes and big flowering vegetable gardens.

"The north-facing wall," she says, pointing to her left, "is where the plants from colder climates reside, as well as those that don't like direct sun. Up near the rim, you'll find sub-alpine herbs and even wildflowers from the tundra, whereas closer to the bottom of the crater, there are plants more typical of rainforest environments.

"The east-facing and west-facing walls are for everything in between. The unique geology of Atum Crater provides a distinct habitat for almost every type of plant, making it a perfect natural herbarium."

She smiles with the kind of pride only a gardener can have.

"This is a living library. Your task is to learn its language."

I can already tell this is going to be my favorite class.

"Throughout the year, we will learn how to propagate clippings, how to make tinctures and salves, and of course learn the medicinal properties of as many plants as we can. For instance, this plant right here is a hawthorn." She walks over to a dense, many-trunked tree with small, intricate leaves. "The red berries this tree produces in the fall are an excellent heart tonic which can open up the heart to process past traumas and even relieve heart palpitations."

Cassandra, the pale blonde girl from my Energy Work class, raises her hand timidly. "Alien Thumgren, is it true that the shape of a plant can correspond to the part of the body that it heals?" She says it so quietly I'm not sure anyone else heard her.

"What's that, dear? Speak up," Alien Thumgren says.

"She asked if the shape of a plant corresponds to the part of the body it heals," I offer, glancing at Cassandra with a smile. She blushes and looks away.

"Ah! Yes. That's called the Doctrine of Signatures.

Ancient knowing. A walnut resembles the brain, good for memory. Eyebright for the eyes. But here in Agartha, we go a step further. We practice florachanneling."

"Flora-what-now?" someone whispers.

"Florachanneling," she repeats. "You learn to listen. The plants will tell you what they heal. You don't memorize flashcards. You cultivate a relationship."

"That's so cool," I blurt out.

"Yes, it is cool." She says the last word like it's a novelty. "What's your name, young lady?"

"Synchronicity, Professor."

"And what kind of Starseed are you, Synchronicity?"

I was hoping she didn't ask that.

"I'm... I'm not. I'm an Earthseed."

A ripple of snickering murmurs through the students.

"Ah, yes, I heard about you," Alien Thumgren says, while two girls in front of me whisper to each other and shoot surreptitious glances back at me. "You may actually have an advantage in this class, Synchronicity. With a native human soul, I suspect your connection to the plants will be stronger than those of your classmates."

The snickering stops, and a small feeling of pride rises in my chest.

"Are you in my lab, Synchronicity?"

"Yes, I believe so."

"Good. For those of you taking the lab, you will be assigned a plot of land somewhere in the crater. In this plot, you will tend to the plants there until harvest later this fall and then cultivate new varieties of your choosing next spring. The soil will teach you more than I can. Fail to care for it, and it will let you know. The plants here are not just alive, they're awake."

A thrill runs through me.

Of all the classes I've had so far, this is the first where I feel like I belong.

CHAPTER
TEN

I have fifteen minutes to make it from Herbalism to Galactic History, and I'm hopelessly lost.

Jasper's directions were cryptic at best. Something about "the sixth stairwell" and "a mural of twelve suns..." and now I've ended up deep in the bowels of the Great Pyramid. The halls down here are colder, damp with condensation, and lit only by sporadic citrine crystals embedded in the stone.

I haven't seen another student in at least five minutes.

I'm about to double back when I hear voices. Low. Urgent.

I peer past a massive block of carved sandstone and see two figures engaged in a heated conversation.

Xion.

And Alien Isis.

The violet glow of her energy halo illuminates the hall, and her iridescent skin shimmers in the darkness. "I appreciate your secrecy regarding your involvement in the recovery mission, Alien Da'ath, but I'm afraid you must continue to keep it hidden until I figure out our next move." Her voice is low and tense.

"We should report it to the Galactic Federation," Xion hisses. "Keeping something like this a secret is a capital offense. Maybe not for someone like you. But me? I'd be vaporized before I could offer a defense."

There's a pause, thick with the weight of unspoken history.

"I understand the risk you are taking for me, Xion, and you will be duly compensated. There is more going on here than you realize, and getting the Galactic Federation involved is in neither of our best interests."

"But housing that thing so close to the craft site... It's dangerous. We don't know what it could do."

"For now, that is the only place we can hide it. I'll let you know if anything changes." Alien Isis turns to walk away. "And next time, if you want to meet with me, please do it through the usual channels."

Her light fades into the corridor. For a moment, Xion remains still, fists clenched, his silhouette flickering in and out of the low light. Then, with a guttural growl, he punches the wall, and little bits of stone come raining onto me from the ceiling. He turns in my direction, and I dart back into the shadows, hiding behind a statue in a recessed part of the wall.

For a moment, I think he'll storm past me, but as he comes level with the statue, he stops in his tracks and sniffs the air.

He turns.

His glowing amber eyes lock on mine.

"Jones. What the fuck are you doing down here?" His voice rumbles like an approaching freight train.

"I was looking for my Galactic History class." I step out, heart pounding.

"Behind a statue of Hermes Trismegistus?" The intricate black patterns on his face accentuate his mouth as it curls into a smirk.

"I got lost."

He lets out an exasperated sigh. "Fucking Earthseed."

"Are your anger issues the dangerous thing you're hiding at the craft site?" I ask, before immediately regretting it.

"Eavesdropping on sensitive school secrets, were we?" Rage flashes through his eyes. "Give me one reason I shouldn't kill you right here."

I swallow the knot in my throat and take a step closer to him. "A teacher threatening a student? That could get you in a lot of trouble. Especially for someone with a reputation like yours."

"If you knew anything about my reputation, you'd know you shouldn't get caught alone with me in the dark," he growls.

"I'm not afraid of you," I lie.

He shoves me against the wall like I weigh nothing, pinning me with his forearm against my throat.

"Listen to me, Earthseed. Don't give me a reason to find you in an even darker and more secluded part of the school."

"Who says I don't want that?" I shoot back, a spark of flirtation slipping through before I can stop it.

A smile spreads across his lips. "Believe me. You don't."

"Fine then," I say, struggling against his arm. "Just tell me where Galactic History is and I'll be on my way."

He doesn't budge.

"Do you plan on telling anyone what you heard down here today?" His eyes search mine with a cruel, calculating curiosity.

"No." I glare back at him, defiant.

He looks at me like he did that first day I saw him in the courtyard, like he's trying to see straight through to my soul. I hold his gaze, but a shiver runs down my spine. He could snap my neck right here and hide my body somewhere in the depths of this damned pyramid and nobody would ever know what happened to me. My life is entirely in his hands.

"We'll see if you keep your word," he says, loosening his hold on me.

I heave a deep breath of air into my lungs.

"I'll see you in class tomorrow, Jones. Try not to be late." He steps away from me and turns down the hall, walking off toward a stairway at the end of the passage.

"Wait," I call after him. "What about my class?"

"Two floors up, second door on the right," he tosses over his shoulder.

"Thanks," I say, but he's already gone, swallowed by the shadows of a pyramid that suddenly feels a lot darker than it did before.

"Galactic History is the story of consciousness," says a voice like starlight through water. "It is the chronicle of our ascent. The record of those who came before."

The voice belongs to Alien Lumari, if he can be said to possess anything at all. He doesn't have a body in the traditional sense, only a cluster of luminous orbs floating near the front of the amphitheater-style classroom. They pulse in slow spirals, casting shimmering bands of light across the stone walls of the pyramid's lower level. A few crystalline sconces provide ambient illumination, but the room is otherwise dim, almost sacred.

I slip in through the back, trying not to draw attention. The subterranean chill clings to me like fog, the air steeped with the stillness of ancient things.

"Long before the Federation, before names like Pleiadian or Arcturian were spoken," Lumari continues, "there were the Elders. An ancient, enlightened civilization. Their ships seeded the stars."

I spot Mae halfway down the aisle, waving at me with a smile. She's managed to save me a seat. I begin making my way toward her when a foot juts out from one of the rows.

I catch the toe of my shoe on it and go flying, sprawled across stone, scattering tablets and notebooks in a loud, humiliating clatter.

A ripple of gasps stirs the silence.

Bo Kingscott leans back in his seat, smirking. "Oops," he mouths, palms raised in mock innocence.

I glare at him as I scramble to my feet, my cheeks burning. Students gather their scattered notes with cold politeness. I mutter apologies and reach for my selenite tablet, only to find it already being handed to me.

"Here." It's Cassandra. She's holding my tablet out like a peace offering, her pale fingers ghost-like against the glowing crystal.

"Thanks," I say, brushing the hair from my face. Her silver eyes flicker in the low light.

"Anytime," she says quietly, and returns to her seat.

I finally reach Mae, who's sitting with concern etched across her face. "I'm fine," I whisper, settling in beside her. "Honestly. Just bruised pride."

"I thought you were about to throw him through a wall," she whispers, impressed.

"I considered it."

Alien Lumari's voice continues, calm as ever, as though

my public faceplant was part of the curriculum.

"The Elder Civilization achieved heights of spiritual and technological advancement we still do not fully comprehend. It is from them that we have the Eldercraft, the vessels recovered across the galaxy, older than any known race. These relics helped birth the age of interstellar travel."

Mae stifles a yawn. "Please tell me this isn't the whole hour."

"Just wait until we get to the galactic tax codes," I whisper.

She snorts. A few students glance back.

Vaylen turns with a glare and raises a manicured finger to her lips. "Shhhh."

I slouch down in my seat, embarrassed, and Mae makes a sarcastic face at her.

Lumari pulses gently. "The Elders vanished long ago. No record of their downfall remains. No transmissions. No debris fields. Only their ships remain—silent, waiting. Their disappearance is one of the great mysteries of galactic history."

Even with the dreamy cadence of his voice, I catch myself leaning in.

"After their departure, it was the Lyrans, the Arcturians, the Sirians, and the Pleiadians who formed the foundation of what would become the Galactic Federation. These civilizations reached the necessary vibrational thresholds of peace, cooperation, and self-awareness."

Mae raises an eyebrow. "Vibrational threshold?" she whispers.

I shrug. "Cosmic GPA?"

"In time," Lumari goes on, "other worlds were considered for membership. Some were granted entry. Others... failed to meet the criteria."

And now he says it.

"Maldek," he intones. "A planet of extraordinary ambition and technological prowess. A candidate for the Federation. But they did not ascend. Instead, they fell to internal conflict and self-destruction. Their planet is now no more than a ring of asteroids between Mars and Jupiter."

A somber hush drapes the room.

"Maldek serves as a reminder," Lumari says. "That power without wisdom leads only to ruin."

A hand rises near the front. "Professor, did the Federation intervene when Maldek collapsed?"

A long pause.

"No. The Non-Interference Doctrine had already been established. The Federation does not meddle in the spiritual evolution of other worlds, no matter how dire. We observe. We support. But we do not steer. That said, Maldek's collapse did lead to loosened restrictions, which ultimately made possible the founding of this school."

"Professor," a voice pipes up from the far end of the room. "How does one know when they've gone too far down the path of power?" It's the boy with greasy black hair from Mae's dorm again.

"A profound question," Lumari says. "What's your name?"

"Peter Quinn, Professor."

Alien Lumari's orbs spiral briefly in thoughtful synchrony. "That is a question that echoes through every civilization we've studied. The answer often arrives too late, when the consequences of the choice have already begun to manifest."

Peter nods, his eyes catching the dim light, eager, unblinking. "Is there anywhere I could read more about civilizations that chose power over love?"

Lumari pauses a beat longer than necessary.

"Most students explore that material in their third or fourth year. But if you're interested, I can recommend a few texts after class. Use discernment. Some of those stories are more allegory than history."

"Thank you, Professor." Peter slides back into his seat, already scribbling.

"Creep," Bo mutters loud enough for the students around him to hear. A ripple of stifled laughter moves through his corner of the room.

I turn in my seat and fix Bo with a death glare. He just raises his eyebrows and stretches back like he owns the place.

"After Maldek's fall, the Federation recognized the unique complexity of Earth. A rare convergence of soul types. A world on the brink. Thus, the Agarthan Starseed Academy was approved. A school, not to interfere, but to teach. To raise the frequency of Earth's timeline through reincarnated Starseeds, acting from within."

Mae leans over, whispering, "So... basically intergalactic Montessori?"

"Shh," I say. "I'm actually kind of into this."

"Students," Lumari concludes, "we do not study history to memorize it. We study it to remember who we are, and to glimpse what we might become."

As the lights dim further and Lumari begins reciting the dates of Federation milestones, my mind drifts—not away from the lesson, but deeper into it.

What if history isn't just memory?

What if it's prophecy in disguise?

CHAPTER
ELEVEN

"That was so *boring*," Mae groans as we file toward the back of the classroom.

"I don't know," I murmur. "I thought it was kind of... interesting."

She narrows her eyes at me. "You're going to be a lifesaver in this class. Seriously." We jostle with the other students up the stairs. "Why were you late, by the way?"

"I got lost." It's mostly true. But I don't know how to explain the other part, the hushed conversation, the look in Xion's eyes. Would he really do something if I told?

"This whole place is like a rabbit warren," Mae sighs. "A glowing, psychic rabbit warren with way too many stairs."

"Isn't Jasper supposed to be in this class?" I ask.

"He bailed. Said Lumari's voice makes him feel like he's floating out of his body, which apparently is *not* ideal before lunch."

We push open the door to the corridor—

and immediately stop in our tracks.

The hallway buzzes with students, but a wide circle has formed around something, or someone, lying crumpled on the ground.

It's Bo.

His body is unnaturally stiff, arms locked against his sides, face ashen and frozen. Wisps of black energy curl off his limbs like smoke, forming thin, spiraling tendrils that vanish just inches from his skin.

Mae gasps.

I lurch forward.

"Help!" I yell, my voice raw. "Somebody help!"

Heads turn. Someone backs away. For a moment, no one moves, just the flicker of shadows dancing across Bo's rigid frame.

Then I spot him, Kai, moving fast through the crowd, a look of practiced calm on his face overlaid with real urgency.

"What happened?" he demands, kneeling beside Bo and placing two fingers against the boy's temple.

"We... we just found him," I stammer. "We came out of class and he was already... like that."

Kai's brow furrows. "You two, help me," he says, pointing to me and Mae. "We have to get him to the Energy Work School. Now."

Crystals and books crash to the floor as Kai clears a space on the table for Bo's rigid body. His face is locked in a grimace, his limbs unmoving as black tendrils of energy curl and recoil off his skin.

"What's going on here?" Alien Sylestra says, sweeping into the room with her robe trailing behind her.

"I don't know. I've never seen anything like this." A look of deep concern darkens Kai's face, his hands hovering just above Bo's chest. "The girls found him outside the history hall like this."

Alien Sylestra's gaze darts to me like a heat-seeking missile. I brace myself, but after a tense pause, she turns to Kai instead. "Help me feel into his etheric body. Let's see what we're dealing with."

Kai nods. He moves to Bo's feet while Alien Sylestra positions herself at the head of the table. Together, they extend their hands, moving slowly through the air above his body like they're reading the braille of another dimension.

The dark energy shivers and withdraws slightly under their presence, but it doesn't dissipate.

Mae and I hover near the wall, silent, watching.

The room feels colder. The only sound is the soft whoosh of Kai's breathing as he concentrates.

They work like that for several minutes. The black tendrils twist and flutter, almost sentient.

Alien Sylestra draws back her hands and inhales sharply.

"His auric field is fully collapsed," she says, voice clipped and serious. "Whatever did this... it bypassed all his energetic defenses."

"Do you know what it is?" I ask.

Sylestra's eyes cut to me, flat and cold. "Not yet." She turns back to Kai. "Gather the other Energy Work instructors. I'll try to figure out what's going on here."

Without a word, Kai gives a nod and steps away from the table.

Sylestra glances at Mae and me. "You two. Out. There's nothing more you can do."

We're barely out the door when she shuts it firmly behind us.

"Thanks for your help," Kai says as he turns to face us in the hall. His gaze lingers on me for a second longer than necessary. "We'll handle it from here."

"Do you think he'll be okay?" Mae asks, her voice small.

"We have some of the best healers in the galaxy working at this school. I'm sure he'll be fine." His expression betrays a flicker of doubt. "I'll keep you posted."

"Thanks," I say quietly.

He nods, then disappears down the corridor.

"Well," Mae exhales. "That was mildly terrifying."

"Do things like that happen here normally?"

"I don't think so," she says. "It seemed really odd. Especially that neither of them could figure out what it was."

"Maybe it's just karmic justice," I mutter. "He was kind of an ass."

Mae nudges me. "Synchronicity, be nice. He might really be hurt."

"I am being nice. I'm just saying... cosmic rebalancing."

She snorts despite herself. "Alright, Miss Karma. Since we're already in this part of the school, you have to show me your room."

"I don't think you're ready for the emotional devastation," I say.

"Try me."

I lead her past the laundry chamber and down the narrow hall until we reach my door. When I open it, she gasps and clutches her heart dramatically.

"Oh no, no, no... Sync, this is criminal. Are you seriously

sleeping on a massage table?"

"Would you believe me if I told you it's better than sleeping in my car?"

"Barely." Mae walks in, her sandals echoing softly on the floor. She idly strums a few soft chords on her ukulele and glances around. "You know, with a few string lights and a tapestry or two, this place could actually pass for a decent bedroom."

"Yeah, I haven't exactly got around to decorating it yet," I say, leaning against the doorway.

"Come on, let's go back to my dorm," she says, springing up. "We'll debrief with Jasper, and I'll let you raid my decor stash from the entrance fair."

"Deal," I say, a smile creeping across my face.

But as we walk off down the hallway, I can't shake the feeling that whatever happened to Bo... wasn't just an accident.

Later that night, I return to the Energy Work School and notice a glowing light spilling out from beneath the door of the healing chamber where we left Bo.

I creep closer, pulse quickening, and risk a glance through the narrow window.

Inside, seven beings are gathered. Alien Isis, Sylestra, and five other instructors I don't recognize. Each one stands like a pillar, palms extended over Bo's motionless form. Streams of multicolored energy arc from their hands, twisting into a vortex of violet, gold, and deep indigo above his chest. The light refracts across the walls, pulsing to the rhythm of an unearthly chant that reverberates straight through the glass.

And yet, despite all their power, Bo looks worse. His skin has taken on a sickly grey hue, and his features are drawn and hollowed, like something's gnawing at his soul. Those clouds of black energy haven't faded. They've grown thicker, darker, circling him like vultures waiting for the last breath.

I back away from the door before someone sees me, my mind spinning.

I creep back to my room and dig for answers in the only place I can: *A Starseed's Guide to Agartha.*

I flip to a random page, hoping the universe wants me to know something.

The healing arts have greatly advanced through the ages, with many new discoveries coming from the Sirian star system in the fields of quantum mechanics and consciousness shifting. But as advanced as our healing powers are, there is still no cure for death. Dying, it seems, is a necessary part of existence.

I close the book. The quote lands in the pit of my stomach like a stone.

Just as sleep begins to pull at me, I hear voices on the other side of the wall, faint but unmistakable.

"This is bad, isn't it?" Sylestra's voice, clipped and tense.

"Yes," says Alien Isis. Her voice, usually calm as still water, is now strained. "It appears he's suffered some kind of psychic attack."

"Do you think it has to do with... the object we recovered?"

A longer pause. Then Isis, quiet: "I don't know. It would be strange. But we can't rule out the possibility."

"I don't like this, Isis. First the Earthseed... then the recovery mission... now this? These are troubling signs."

There's a rustle, a soft hum of footsteps fading.

"Get some sleep, Sylestra. I'll watch over Bo. I'll see you when you return in the morning."

CHAPTER
TWELVE

A note taped to the door of my first class reads:

"All students report to Atum Crater. Mandatory assembly."

When I arrive, the terraces are packed. Students have claimed shady spots under eucalyptus and cedar trees, perched on boulders, or stretched out in the herb-scented grass. The crater's blue pool gleams under the morning sun, and the air feels too still.

I spot Mae and Jasper sitting under a low-sweeping cypress near the front.

"What do you think this is about?" I ask, sliding in beside them.

"I'd bet my last stick of incense it's Bo," Jasper says. He looks incomplete without Mochi on his shoulders, but I catch a glimpse of the red panda scurrying through the branches.

The sight of Xion in the line of faculty gathered by the pool sends heat rushing through me. His expression is unreadable, but the tension in his shoulders tells me he doesn't want to be here. I'm not sure I want to be either.

"That whole thing yesterday was freaky," Mae says. Her blonde locs are freshly beaded, and her septum ring now sports a tiny golden ankh. "Did you hear anything when you went back to the Energy Work School?"

"Yeah," I say. "I overheard Isis and Sylestra in the hall."

"What did they say?" Jasper leans in, but before I can answer, a commotion erupts on the terrace behind us.

"Excuse me! Spirit animal coming through!" June calls cheerily, leading a wide-eyed white stallion through a crowd of students.

"Wow, nice spirit animal," I say, making an effort to be nice. Kara and Vaylen follow behind, looking flawless and annoyed.

"Isn't he beautiful?" June says dreamily, stroking the stallion's flowing white mane. "His name is Edmund. I connected with him in my spirit animal class yesterday. Would you believe he was just standing there by himself in the middle of a green pasture?"

Mae gets up and approaches Kara, tucking a stray strand of hair behind her ear. "How are you doing?" she asks, her expression hopeful.

"Fine," Kara says coolly. Her dark, winged eyes don't even make contact with Mae's. I see the downcast look on Mae's face and feel for her. I know she felt a connection to Kara after they hooked up that night, but it seems the feeling is not reciprocated.

"My professor says he hasn't seen someone bond with a white stallion in at least ten years," June continues, visibly excited.

Vaylen steps forward. "You might want to be careful who you let near him, June," she says, her eyes narrowing on me.

"What's that supposed to mean?" I ask.

"Nothing. Just... things tend to go dark around you. That's all." She folds her arms, her gaze cool and appraising, like she's daring me to deny it.

"I found Bo just like everyone else," I say. "It wasn't me."

"Didn't say it was," Vaylen adds, faux-innocent. "But let's not pretend it isn't weird. Earthseed shows up. Starseed comes down with a mysterious illness. Funny coincidence, huh?"

"Whatever," I say. "You know, we might actually get along if you weren't so determined to hate me."

"Oh sweetie," she says with a smile like broken glass, "this isn't hate. It's discernment."

The three women make a calamitous exit as June struggles to lead the reluctant horse through a crowd of seated students.

"God. Sirian women," Jasper says. "Walking moral superiority complexes."

"I'm sorry about Kara," I say, extending a comforting hand to Mae.

"It's whatever," Mae shrugs, but I can see the disappointment in her face. "She said our soul contract was only for one night. But I felt something."

"I know," I say. "Maybe she'll come around."

Jasper slings an arm around her shoulder. "Not to worry. There are plenty of Starseeds in the sea." He winks at a handsome man a few terraces down, who waves back at us, smiling.

I wish it was another student I was interested in, but the only man who holds my attention in this whole crater is a seven-foot alien with deep red skin etched with tattoos and arms that could quite possibly crush me. I try to catch his eye for some recognition of our encounter yesterday, but his gaze is directed at Alien Isis. She raises her hands and the crowd hushes like the breath has been sucked from the crater.

"Thank you all for joining us this morning on such late notice." Her voice rings, amplified by some unseen force. "If you haven't met me yet, my name is Alien Isis. I am the Spiritual Director at Agartha."

She pauses, and for the first time since I arrived at this school, she looks almost... human. Burdened.

"It is with deep sadness that I inform you, one of your classmates, Bo Kingscott, passed away early this morning."

Gasps ripple through the terraces.

"What the fuck?" Jasper whispers.

Mae's hand flies to her mouth. "Oh no..."

"Apparently Mr. Kingscott," Isis continues, "smuggled in some human drugs to Agartha, notably Adderall and Xanax. Human pharmaceuticals react unpredictably in the magnetic field and unique microbiome of Agartha. We believe this is what took Mr. Kingscott's life."

"She's covering it up," I whisper.

"What?" Jasper says, leaning in.

"Last night, I heard her tell Sylestra it was a psychic attack."

"This is an unfortunate way to start a school year, but do not be saddened. Bo's soul has simply moved on to its next incarnation, and we expect him back at the Academy when he is once again of age."

Now Alien Sylestra steps forward. "Bo's death is

unfortunate indeed, but this should be a warning to anyone considering using synthetic human drugs in Agartha. Like the Spiritual Director said, they can have unpredictable effects in Agartha's unique magnetic field. If you have any ailments that require a prescription, you can visit the campus apothecary for safe, spiritually aligned alternatives."

She scans the crowd of gathered students.

"Bo will be sorely missed. It's rare that we receive a Starseed of such caliber. May his soul reunite with Source before returning to this plane." Sylestra bows her head in a solemn prayer.

Tears run down Mae's face but Jasper whispers, "Caliber my ass. That guy was an asshole."

"Hey! Not nice!" Mae punches him in the arm.

"Asshole or not, he didn't deserve to die." I scoot over on the rock ledge a little closer to Mae.

Alien Isis retakes the center stage. "Your classes for the rest of the day are canceled. Please keep Bo in your thoughts and consider what the ending of his incarnation means to you. Classes will resume as usual tomorrow. Thank you."

She bows her head, and the teachers gather in a murmured huddle.

Students begin rising, grabbing bags, drifting out through the terraces. I look at Mae and Jasper.

"That was no overdose," I say. "Bo didn't look drugged. He looked... drained."

"Could've been Xion," Jasper says. "You saw how furious he was when Bo scratched his ship."

"That's true," Mae says. "He *is* connected to that Eldercraft. You heard him, a connection to an Eldercraft enhances your spiritual powers. Maybe that includes... dark ones."

"I need to tell you something," I start, but then—

Xion looks up from the teacher huddle.

And locks eyes with me.

The weight of his stare lands like a thunderclap.

I freeze.

"Don't look," I hiss. "He's watching us."

Jasper follows my gaze. "Shit. Yep. That is not a friendly look."

Mae shudders. "Let's go. I'm not trying to get hexed today."

We gather our things and slip out of the crater, hearts pounding.

CHAPTER
THIRTEEN

"That's it. He did it. He killed Bo." Jasper's eyes gleam with conspiratorial certainty as he paces along the edge of the library's mezzanine. "If what you're saying is true, that he was in the pyramid that morning, then it's obvious."

I haven't told them about Xion's conversation with Isis, just that I saw him in the corridor. I don't know why I'm protecting him. Maybe because I'm scared. Or maybe because some sick, broken part of me wants him to trust me.

"He probably bumped into Bo outside your class," Jasper continues, "and that was enough to reignite the rage. Boom. Uncontrolled surge of dark Maldekian energy. The guy practically glows with pent-up wrath."

We sit beneath the towering shelves of the Agartha Library, where beams of sunlight pierce the pyramid's slanted glass walls, catching on motes of dust like suspended galaxies. The place smells like sandalwood and old paper, a hushed temple of alien thought.

Mae's perched beside me, flipping through a heavy leather-bound tome written in neat bilingual columns. "It says here that Maldek was once a thriving world. High technology, crystalline cities, all of it. But toward the end... something else crept in."

"Something else?" I ask, inching closer.

"It doesn't say what. Just that... something infiltrated the population. And that whatever it was, it wasn't entirely physical."

Jasper snatches the book, skimming the paragraph. "Fifth-dimensional energy vampires," he mutters, index finger skimming the page.

"Energy vampires?" I glance around, suddenly paranoid. Even surrounded by books and sunlight, the idea sends a shiver down my spine.

"Yeah, but it doesn't explain anything. Just calls them 'the corruption.' No origin, no taxonomy. Just... warnings."

"I'm sure there's something about them somewhere in this library," Mae says, standing and eyeing the spiral staircase that winds to the upper level. "This place goes on forever."

It's nothing like the public libraries I used to haunt back on the surface. When you're broke, it becomes prohibitively expensive to hang out in cafés, so whenever there was bad weather, I would find the nearest public library. They were usually noisy with glaring lights and lots of homeless people. Like myself.

But this library was unlike anything I had seen before. Ornate wood shelves with beautifully bound first edition books, some covered with strange alien symbols in glowing blue ink. The angled ceiling, which is really the glass outer wall of the pyramid, must be at least fifty feet tall at its highest point.

"While we're here, I still need my history book," Mae says.

"Me too," I say. "I still need *all* my books."

We make our way to the circulation desk, where an ancient-looking blue alien with feathers and a beak scrolls through a selenite screen.

"Excuse me, we'd like to check out a few books," I say.

The blue avian looks over his full moon spectacles and regards us indifferently. "And which books would you like to check out?" he asks, choosing each word with slow precision.

"Well, we're first-years, so we need the books for Galactic History, Energy Work, and Craft. I have Herbalism and Mae, what do you have?"

"Sound Healing," she says, "with Alien Olbos."

"And also anything you have on fifth-dimensional energy vampires," Jasper chimes in. "Preferably the soul-sucking kind."

The librarian arches a feathered eyebrow. "Excuse me?"

"You know. The kind that may or may not have brought down an entire planet."

"Such tales are apocryphal," he says carefully. "Maldekian authors have a flair for the dramatic. One must learn to discern between allegory and archive."

"But the book said—"

"The books say many things," the librarian interrupts, eyes sharpening like daggers. "Not all of them are true."

There's a beat of silence.

"Right," Jasper says, backing down. "No energy vampires. Got it."

The librarian continues without missing a beat. "History texts can be found in Section 112-C. Energy work in 204-A. Craft manuals are on the upper tier. That's also where you'll find your electives. Of course, you'll also need a book on basic Galactic Script so that you can make sense of these. You'll find that in the Light Language section."

"Thanks, Alien..." Jasper gestures vaguely.

"Tiryx."

"Thank you, Alien Tiryx," Jasper says, flashing a mock-formal bow.

We walk away in a hush. The further we go into the stacks, the quieter it gets, like the books themselves are listening.

"Well," Mae says finally, "I guess there's no such thing as fifth-dimensional energy vampires."

"I guess not," I murmur, but inside, my stomach twists. Something about the librarian's explanation was not entirely convincing.

CHAPTER
FOURTEEN

"Connecting to a craft is an intimate art, like sharing secrets with a lover." Xion paces in front of our class like a drill sergeant, and I can't help but quiver each time he passes me. Hearing him talk about lovers is so discordant with his harsh personality that, for a second, I think he might be capable of some tenderness. "This is something that your deceased classmate didn't understand."

The reference to Bo sets off alarm bells in my body, and I exchange a glance with Jasper and Mae.

Xion continues. "He rushed into his connection with his craft like a drunk frat boy getting his first taste of pussy."

I flush. The vulgarity is shocking, even coming from him.

"Today I will teach you the basics of the delicate art of craft connection. The process is like two minds becoming one, so if you've been in a deep relationship in the past, you will most likely be better at this part of the course. Remember, craft are made from both metallic and biologic material, so each of them has its own distinct personality."

I notice that the gleaming rows of RE craft have been rearranged, and now my rusty, jerry-built saucer sits right in the front. Xion's own UFO, the jet-black Eldercraft with the long pointed tails, has, notably, been moved beyond the reach of any reckless student pilots.

"I need a volunteer. Synchronicity, would you join me in front of your craft, please?"

I hesitate. My instincts scream trap. This is probably his way of punishing me for eavesdropping the other day. But I force my body to move. I won't give him the satisfaction of thinking I'm afraid.

Xion walks up to me and, dear God, I barely reach his collarbone. His eyes glint with something between malice and jest, like I'm something he's toying with before he devours me whole. "Tell me, Synchronicity, have you ever been in an intimate relationship?"

I blink.

Did he seriously just ask me that?

"One," I say.

"What was it like?" He cocks his head to the side and looks at me with genuine curiosity.

"I'm not sure what you mean..."

"To be in an intimate relationship with someone, to feel that your souls were bound for each other throughout all time. Surely you felt something."

"I'd rather not."

"Come on, Synchronicity. If you can't be honest with us, how can you be honest with your craft?"

I scan the row of my classmates, all looking on with anticipation. Mae gives me an encouraging look. Vaylen just rolls her eyes.

"It was like..." My throat tightens. "It was like finding an echo of myself in the world. An echo so deep and faithful that I could fall into it forever because it was like I was getting lost in myself." I'm surprised to feel tears wet my cheek as my memories drift back to Aidan.

"Good." Xion's gruff voice brings me back to the present. "That's exactly the kind of feeling you want to cultivate with your craft. The more you put into it, the more you'll get out of it. A healthy relationship with a craft can be an extremely rewarding experience, even outside of the obvious benefits of enhanced spiritual abilities and faster-than-light travel."

I reach up and pull a fleck of rust off my Castor 5, doubting whether this thing is capable of any flight at all, let alone faster-than-light travel.

"Your initial connection attempts will take place remotely, from outside the craft. The goal today is simple: get your ship to hover a few feet above the ground. Synchronicity, please face your craft and find a comfortable seat in the grass."

I do as he instructs.

"Now close your eyes. This is going to be a little like a meditation."

I feel him crouch behind me, close enough that I catch a

whiff of his scent, like leather and smoke.

Why does he have to smell so damn good?

He leans into my right ear and whispers, "When I say 'focus,' repeat the word 'Geminorum' in your mind."

The low rumble of his voice sends my heart into a gallop, stirring an unmistakable warmth in my lower stomach. "What?" I say, trying to compose myself.

"Just trust me," he whispers, then stands back up to address the class. "I'm about to put Synchronicity into a Theta brainwave state."

What the hell was that? Is he really trying to help me? This has to be some kind of trick.

"A Theta brainwave state is the most effective way to connect to a craft. Now, Synchronicity, I want you to relax. Drop your shoulders... Good. Now take three deep breaths."

The man who literally threatened to kill me yesterday is now leading me in a guided meditation. What the hell kind of school is this?

"Relax the muscles on your cheeks, the muscles around your eyes. Now let that feeling of relaxation seep deep into your brain. Deep, deep into your brain and imagine yourself walking down a flight of stairs into the deepest parts of your mind."

His voice starts to feel further away, like I'm underwater.

"Once you've reached the bottom of the stairs, create a mental image of your craft exactly as you remember seeing it. Every window, fin, and rivet."

I imagine myself in a large underground chamber with a vaulted stone ceiling. My mental projection of the Castor 5 sits in the center of the space, but there's something else down here, too. A door that I don't want to open...

Xion's voice cuts through. "When the mental image is complete, I want you to focus. *Focus*, Synchronicity."

I bring my focus back to the ship. What word did he tell me to say again? Geminorum? It's probably the command to self-destruct or to make the ship spray oil on me or something. I definitely don't trust Xion, but UFOs seem to be the one thing he cares about, so I give it a try.

Geminorum... Geminorum... Geminorum.

Nothing. Why did he tell me to repeat this anyway? Just so he could get close to me? I toss the thought from my mind. It's surprisingly easy in this meditative state.

Geminorum... Geminorum... Geminorum.

Then, suddenly, another voice pops into my head, cheery and mechanical.

HeLlo. I aM zX240G, a FiFtH gEnErAtIoN rEvErSe EnGiNeErEd CrAfT fRoM tHe CaStOr StAr SyStEm, BuT yOu CaN cAlL mE CaStOr. HoW cAn I bE oF sErViCe ToDaY?

Holy shit, am I actually talking to a UFO?

YeS. I aM zX240G, BuT yOu CaN cAlL mE CaStOr. HoW cAn I bE oF sErViCe ToDaY?

You can hear my thoughts??

YeS. wHeN wE aRe CoNnEcTeD lIkE tHiS i CaN hEaR yOuR tHoUgHtS.

This is so wild. Can you hover for me, I guess?

In OrDeR tO cOnTrOl My FlIgHt YoU mUsT fIrSt PoRt YoUr CoNsCiOuSnEsS iNtO mInE.

And how exactly do I do that?

MoVe ThE mEnTaL pRoJeCtIoN oF yOuRsElF iNsIdE tHe CrAfT. iNsIdE yOuR mEnTaL pRoJeCtIoN oF mE.

In my mind, I walk toward the image of my rusty saucer, open an imaginary hatch, and picture myself in the cockpit.

Suddenly my entire perspective changes.

I can see the craft site, all the other UFOs lined up around me, and my classmates all looking on expectantly. It's like I have a 360° view of everything around me. I can even see my own *self* sitting cross-legged in the grass.

What the hell just happened?

YoU hAvE sUcCeSsFuLlY pOrTeD yOuR cOnScIoUsNeSs InTo MiNe. ThIs Is HoW i SeE tHe WoRlD.

This feels so *weird*. It feels like I'm made up of wires and bolts.

RiGhT nOw, YoU aRe.

And if I want to fly?

ThAt's Up To YoU. yOu'rE iN cOnTrOl NoW.

I focus on the idea of levitating, not as a task, but as a feeling. Not something to do, but something to become. I reach for the sensation like it's a thread in the dark, like trying to remember a dream I never fully woke from.

What would it feel like to rise? To drift? I picture the press of the earth against my body easing, loosening its grip. I imagine the air around me becoming thick and full of lift, like water holding me aloft.

It's awkward at first, like flexing a part of myself I didn't know existed. A strange, subtle muscle beneath layers of thought. But then something clicks. I don't push. I release. And the ground is no longer beneath me. There is no weight. Only stillness. Only air.

Then, through the quiet, I hear Xion's voice, low, reverent, proud. "Excellent work. Class, you would all do well to follow Synchronicity's example."

It jolts me out of my concentration and back into my body. I open my eyes and, for a split second, see my Castor 5 hovering nearly ten feet off the ground, before it comes crashing back to earth. Several poorly attached scraps of metal break loose with the force of the impact.

"Good job," Xion says as he walks over to me. "We'll just have to work on the landing." A hint of a smirk curls the edges of his perfect lips.

"I would have had it if you hadn't interrupted me." I stand up and meet his gaze, having to tilt my head up several inches to do so.

"Am I a distraction to you, Synchronicity?" There's a definite smirk on those lips.

"When you're talking while I'm in the middle of connecting to my craft, yeah, you kind of are."

"Craft connection is all about concentration. If you lose focus while you're hurtling through the cosmos at the speed of light, you die."

"I guess I'll just have to get better at ignoring you," I say.

"We'll see about that, Earthseed." Xion turns and addresses the rest of the class. "Find your assigned craft and practice what I just taught Synchronicity. I'll be around to help each of you individually. And if you do connect, don't even think of trying to do anything but hover. I put restrictors on all of the craft that limit their movement to twenty feet in any direction."

Jasper is a natural, having already taken the course. He moves his metallic cube up and down and in little circles. After several attempts, Mae manages to get her craft that looks something like a big copper handpan into a decent hover. Kara and June's crafts are bumping into one another, and to my guilty pleasure, Vaylen can't even get hers off the ground.

"Something's wrong with this one. Can I get another craft?" She stomps her knee-high leather boot into the grass, and I can't help but feel a surge of satisfaction that I am actually better than her at something for once.

"There's nothing wrong with that craft. I tested them all this morning." Xion talks to her like he would a child throwing a fit.

"Please, just let me try that white one over there. Or maybe an actual Eldercraft. That's probably why I can't connect. I'm meant to have an Eldercraft like you and Alien Isis."

Xion lets loose a big booming laugh. "Craft connection isn't like healing. It takes a raw primal energy that, frankly, I don't see coming from you. If you can't connect to this RE craft—which, as a newer model, is one of the easiest to connect to—then believe me, there's no way you're connecting to an Eldercraft."

Vaylen scoffs, speechless.

"Take my advice. Stop trying to do everything perfectly. That might work in your Energy Work class, but here you need to tap into your intuition."

"This is ridiculous," she spits before storming off the field. "I'm going to talk to Alien Sylestra about this. You can't just treat people this way!"

Xion rubs his hand over his head. "She'll be fine," he says to no one in particular. "She just needs to blow off some steam."

Kara and June's crafts screech horribly as they push into each other, and the two women flail their arms wildly trying to move the craft apart. Xion rushes to their side and expertly separates the ships and lowers them gently onto the ground.

"Sorry, Professor." June gazes up at Xion with beaming eyes. It looks like I'm not the only one with a crush on our instructor.

"It's okay. Just be a little more careful next time. I want both of you to assess the damage done to your craft and try to find the name of every part that was broken in your user's manuals, then report to me at the end of the class."

"Yes sir. Of course, sir." June nods obediently.

"How are you coming along, Synchronicity?" Xion walks over to where I'm trying to secure one of the pieces that fell off Castor.

"Did you really have to give me the jankiest ship in the fleet?"

"Oh, come on, the Castor 5 is a classic ship. There's still not a craft that's been made that can match it in canyon terrain. It would be my craft of choice if I wasn't tethered to that beautiful girl over there." He gestures toward the silhouette of his deadly-looking Eldercraft.

"Does she have a name?" I am surprised to find myself leaning in toward him as I admire his ship.

"Nyx Arcana."

"That's a beautiful name. How did you two, you know, meet?"

"I was following a distress beacon, years ago, when I was a salvager, just living from one job to the next. It led me to an uninhabited planet in the Sagittarius arm of the Milky Way, way out past the Lagoon Nebula. Anyway, I'm rummaging around this crash site when I feel an inexplicable pull into the dunes beyond. Like an idiot, I leave my craft behind and just wander out into the desert. I walk for what seems like hours, and the whole time this pull is just getting stronger. Then I see her. Just a tip of her, black as night against the sand."

"Wow." I wish I had something better to say, but seeing him open up like this leaves me dumbfounded.

"Then I just sat with her. It was like connecting with a goddess. Like finding a piece of myself scattered out there in the universe."

"That's beautiful," I say.

"Anything that happens to her, I feel it." His jaw ticks. "It's hard to understand for someone who hasn't connected to an Eldercraft, but I would do anything to protect her."

I believe him.

And somehow, that terrifies me more than anything else.

CHAPTER
FIFTEEN

"Come spy on Xion with us, Sync. It won't be the same without you." Jasper's eyes are wide, and even Mochi, perched dramatically on his shoulder, tilts his head like a begging puppy.

"It's been weeks," I say, leaning against the kitchen island. "You really think he's going to slip up in front of a couple of students armed with snacks and binoculars?"

"Someone *died*, Synchronicity," Mae says, dead serious for once. "And no one's giving us real answers."

We're huddled in the Larimar House kitchen, the warm heart of the dorm, imbued with amber light and the scent of tea steeping in mismatched mugs. It's become our gathering spot. Our haven.

A pang of guilt knots in my stomach. As close as I've gotten to these two, I still haven't told them about my past.

"I can't tonight. I've got my first big Energy Work exam tomorrow, and I can't even feel the damn energy half the time, let alone move it."

"It's messed up that Sylestra's making you take the same test as everyone else," Mae says, flipping her wrist to show off a fresh flower of life tattoo still glinting with healing balm. "She knows you're not a Starseed. What does she think's going to happen?"

"I don't know," I say, picking at the chipped counter. "But I'm going to see the one person who might actually be able to help me."

"Ohhh, you mean *Kai Moongate*," Mae sing-songs. "It's okay to admit it if this is really a late-night healing session." Her wink is almost weaponized.

"It's not like that," I say too quickly. My face burns. "Not that I would mind if it *were* like that. But it's more of a... mentorship thing."

"Yeah," Jasper says, rolling his eyes. "A *mentorship thing.* That's what they're calling it these days."

I groan. "Obviously he's hot, okay? But the moment just hasn't... happened."

"Well," Mae says, sipping her tea and raising an eyebrow, "maybe tonight's the moment. He is good with his hands."

"Stop," I laugh. "This is serious. If I can't figure out how to channel even a spark of healing energy, I'm toast tomorrow."

"Well then," Jasper says, reaching into the fruit bowl and handing me a pear like a talisman, "may the hot professor bless you with enlightenment... or at the very least, some chakra realignment."

I grin despite myself. "Thanks. I'll let you know if we do any... realigning."

The Agartha campus is beautiful at night. Light from a thousand fluorescing minerals on the underside of the Earth's surface illuminates the buildings in an otherworldly glow. The main pyramid looks like a gleaming monument to some cosmic god, channeling its energy into the very ground beneath my feet.

I follow the manicured paths through the grounds until I arrive at the gate to Kai's home. A breeze rustles the lavender stalks that line the walkway. Everything smells faintly of mint and moonflower. I slip through the gate and up the carved stone steps.

I take a breath, then knock.

The door opens.

"Well, if it isn't Miss Synchronicity Jones," Kai says with that warm, low voice. His hair is freshly trimmed, framing his face like a Renaissance painting. "To what do I owe the pleasure of a late-night visit?"

"You told me if I ever needed anything, I could come to you, right?" I shift my weight back and forth between my feet.

"Yes, of course. What's going on?" His compassionate brown eyes gaze into mine with a gentle kindness.

"It's about my Energy Work class. I need help healing."

Kai lets out a long sigh, shaking his head and looking at

me like I'm hopeless. "Okay. Come in. Let's talk about it."

His home is elegant and lived-in, the kind of space built by someone who's put thought into their healing. Bookshelves curve along the walls. Dim lighting glows from orbs embedded in mineral sconces. A painting above his couch shows a goddess floating on lily pads, her eyes closed in serenity.

I settle under the painting while Kai takes a seat across from me, legs folded like a monk. "Tell me what's going on."

"Basically, I have my first Energy Work exam with Alien Sylestra tomorrow, and I have no idea what I'm doing. Everyone else has manifested some sort of healing powers, meanwhile, I've got nothing."

"Whoa, slow down. You must have mastered the basics of changing energy flow direction. You don't need healing powers to do that."

I shake my head. "Sylestra kind of glazed over that part."

"Well, she's definitely not setting you up for success."

"Ever since that first day in Alien Isis's office, she's had a target on my back."

"Oh, I see. You wish I hadn't stood up for you." The tiniest smirk appears on his lips.

"No, no. Of course not. I'm so grateful for what you did for me. I just wish Alien Sylestra saw things the same as you."

"It just takes time. She'll come around to you."

"Not if I fail her exam tomorrow."

"I think I can help you with that. If it's your first exam, you'll probably be healing something simple like a headache or a sore throat. You don't need spiritual powers to fix those. Simple energy field manipulation will do the trick." Kai turns fully to me. "Here. Lay your head back in my lap and I'll show you."

I swivel sideways and lean back until I feel my neck cradled against his calves.

"This might feel a little... intense." He looks down at me from the top of my vision.

"I think I can handle it," I say, but worry what might

happen if it feels as good as last time.

"Your etheric body is composed of hundreds of little magnetic fields that add up to create your toroidal field. The easiest one to feel and manipulate sits at the crown of the head." Kai adjusts himself so that one of his palms is placed directly over the top of my head. "The normal direction that this energy center should be spinning is clockwise, just like yours is right now."

I close my eyes and settle into his lap.

"But if I spin it the other way, you should feel some pretty immediate discomfort."

Suddenly, it's like my mind is being wound too tight. My thoughts start to race, crazy thoughts about me and Kai... me and Xion... Xion killing Bo... me killing... and then a searing pain that appears visually like a spreading splotch of glaring white light.

"Oh fuck, stop. That feels terrible..." I try to suppress the urge to writhe in his lap.

"Okay, and now..." There's a brief moment where the pain feels unbearable before the winding sensation reverses and all that pressure begins to drain from my brain. "... You're spinning clockwise again."

"Kai, that felt horrible," I say, sitting up and punching him in the arm. "What did you do to me?"

"I gave you a migraine. They can be pretty awful if you've never experienced one before. Hell, they're pretty awful even if you *have* experienced them before."

"But you fixed it, just like that."

"Like I said. It all comes down to the spin of the energy centers."

"Okay, but how do I do that?"

"Let's switch positions. You can try it on me."

"You're not afraid I'm going to give you an aneurysm or something?"

He lets out a slight chuckle. "Synchronicity, at your level, I'd be surprised if you could give me an itch."

"Wow, thanks for the vote of confidence." I roll my eyes.

"But with just a little instruction," he says, laying his head down in my lap, "I'm sure you'll be a master headache healer."

"Okay, so what do I do?" I'm looking down on him, at those heart-melting eyes, those full lips, and I get the random urge to kiss him upside down like Spiderman.

No. Not tonight. Tonight is about learning.

"Just place your palm over the crown of my head. Tell me if you feel anything."

I arrange myself so that I can get my hand over the top of his head and hold it there for a moment, closing my eyes and trying to feel into the subtle lines of energy. "What exactly am I looking for?"

"It will feel like a vortex. Like water draining from a bowl."

"Okay... wait... yes! Yes, I feel it!" It's faint but unmistakable. A definite clockwise swirling motion.

"Good. Now I'm going to spin it the other way, and you tell me if you feel anything."

"You mean you can change the direction of your own energy field?"

"If you're me you can," he says with a cocky grin.

"Prove it." I look down at him, teasing him with my eyes.

"You asked for it," he says, and streams of his iridescent Pleiadian energy begin to emerge from the crown of his head, almost like an aurora swirling around his scalp.

"Oh my God... that's beautiful."

The swirling energy slows to a halt and then starts spinning in the opposite direction. The clouds of glowing radiance pass through my thighs, sending waves of pleasure shooting to my lower belly.

"Hey! You're doing that on purpose," I say, breath catching.

His smirk is criminal. "What, this?"

His energy swirls faster, stirring a deep ache between my thighs. I bite my lip to keep myself from moaning.

"Stop it. You're gonna make me..." but I'm cut off by

another surge of pleasure crashing through me.

"If you want it to stop, you're just going to have to figure out how to spin it the other way." The self-satisfaction on his face is infuriating.

"It's kind of hard when you're..."

"When I'm what?"

"When you're doing *that*." Sensations swirl inside me at the same rate as his rotating vortex of energy, pushing me to the edge.

"It's in your hands now," he says. "To stop it, you'll have to reverse the spin."

Challenge accepted.

I take a deep breath and try to calm the fire in my veins. Another deep breath, and I place both my hands over the crown of his head. His energy currents tug at my palms like luminescent seaweed.

I try to distance myself from the sensation in my loins and focus on the energy in my hands. I take one more breath, and on the exhale, I push with all the mental might I can muster, trying to spin the vortex in the other direction.

The currents slow down, and the stimulus they produce in my body wanes. As excited as I am that I'm figuring out this healing thing, part of me wants Kai's spiral to keep going.

"Good. You're getting it," he says. "One more just like that and you should have me spinning clockwise again."

With one final exhale, I send all the energy I have to my hands and visualize his toroidal field spinning in a clockwise direction. Slowly, the feeling he's stirring inside of me fades to little more than a tingle, and when I open my eyes, the glowing white lines of energy are once again spinning in the proper direction.

"Nice work." Kai rises to a seated position, and the visual clouds of energy above his head dissipate into the surrounding air. "I honestly didn't think you'd pick it up so fast."

"I would have picked it up a lot faster if you weren't distracting me."

"It's honestly just a side effect. One of the many challenges of being a Pleiadian Starseed."

"Sounds like a real challenge, inducing uncontrollable pleasure in women anytime you use your healing powers."

Kai shrugs. "Not just women. Anyone. Obviously it's better than getting healed by a Sirian, but try telling that to a guy who gets an erection after I fix his broken leg. It can get awkward."

"Yeah. Awkward," I say, heat flushing my cheeks.

"Look, the point is, you did great. I know I made my energy field easier for you to sense, but it works the same way with everyone. Even if you can't see it, you'll be able to feel into their vortex and get it spinning in the right direction.

"Well, thanks," I say. "You don't happen to have any wine... or maybe a cigarette?"

Kai laughs. "I don't really drink. And you should get some rest anyway if you want to be present for that exam tomorrow."

He leads me to the door and his hand lingers on the knob.

"Goodnight, Synchronicity."

I walk down the garden path, heart thudding in my chest. My thoughts swirl around Kai's smile, his warmth, his healing aura, but they crash like a wave against the image of someone else...

My mental ponderings are interrupted by the sound of a stone door sliding open at the base of the main pyramid. A cloaked figure emerges before the door once again slides shut. Although her features are hidden beneath the hood of the cloak, I immediately recognize Alien Isis's lilac energy halo. I scan the campus, but no one else is around.

That's odd.

Curiosity gets the better of me, and I follow her at a safe distance as she makes her way toward the craft site.

She steps purposefully through the rows of RE craft, the gravity of her character evident even under the concealment of a cloak.

I crouch behind one of the hulking UFOs and peer

through the shadows. Alien Isis crosses the gravel path. She stops in front of a low, bunker-like structure set apart from the rest of the buildings on the craft site. Its exterior is dark metal and scorched stone, patched together with plates that look salvaged from long-forgotten wreckage. Sparse lighting glows dimly from beneath the eaves, casting jagged shadows that stretch across the gravel like claw marks.

She knocks once.

Xion appears, bare-chested beneath his open vest, eyes sharp despite the late hour, as though he hadn't been sleeping at all. They exchange terse words I can't hear, the air between them thick with tension. Then, without another glance, Xion grabs a keyring from the hook beside the door and leads her across the gravel toward the edge of the craft site.

They stop at a massive hangar, unmarked, sealed, and shadowed in gloom. Xion fits one of the keys into a panel. There's a faint click, and the door swings open.

The two disappear into the darkness, sealing the door shut behind them.

Whatever they're hiding... It's in there.

CHAPTER SIXTEEN

'Name the three primary nadis that flow through the subtle body and their location relative to the spine.'

The final question on the exam stares back at me like a dare.

Easy.

I've studied this diagram until it felt like a tattoo on the inside of my eyelids. I scrawl the answer in tidy script: *The three primary nadis, or energy currents, in the subtle body are the ida, the pingala, and the sushumna. The ida flows to the left of the spine, the pingala to the right. The sushumna rises through the center, aligning with the chakras.*

Done.

I'm about to get up and turn in my paper when I notice Cassandra is stuck on the last question. She's the only person I get along with in this class, so we usually end up sitting next to each other. Her insanely long platinum blonde hair drapes around the desk, hiding her face, but I can see her slim, bony knuckles where she grips her pen in frustration.

I check to make sure Alien Sylestra isn't watching, then nudge her under the desk, pointing to the question on my own exam. She looks at me with an expression of gratitude on her wan face and surreptitiously copies down the answer.

I let her turn in her exam first, pretending to go back and double-check my answers, even though I'm confident I got them all right. I've worked so hard for this, studying every night between loads of laundry and scrubbing out the sauna. It's my first real attempt to prove I belong here.

After Cassandra returns to her seat, I hand in my own paper. Sylestra doesn't even look up from her desk to acknowledge me. After the last few stragglers turn in their tests, she stands up and addresses the class.

"Now that you've all finished the written portion of the exam, I will be bringing in third-years who have volunteered to be healed today." Alien Sylestra's big black eyes scan the crowd, and her blue skin glistens in the soft light of the classroom. "I have induced each one with a mild headache. It will be your job to feel into the ailment and correct the rotation of the affected energy center."

Sylestra goes out into the hall and returns with an older student who lies down on the massage table at the front of the classroom. "Who would like to start?"

From the front row, Kara raises her hand.

"Yes, Miss Volkova. Come on up."

Kara's lipstick is dark and severe against her pale skin, and her winged eyeliner extends almost to the edges of her Cleopatra-style haircut. It wouldn't surprise me if she actually was a Pharaoh in a past life.

She approaches the massage table. Each Lyran Starseed has chosen an instrument in their Sound Healing class to channel their unique healing powers. Kara's is the shamanic hand drum.

She momentarily sets the instrument down on Sylestra's desk and places her hands on either side of the third-year's head. I watch as she closes her eyes to feel into the patient's auric field.

Despite Mae's best efforts, Kara has remained as cool and impenetrable as ever. I know it shouldn't bother me, but it does. Mae is bright and kind, hilarious and brave, and one of the most luminous souls I've ever met. How could someone share a night like that with her and then pretend it meant nothing? How could you just throw someone like her away?

Kara picks up her drum and starts a gentle rhythm that gets stronger as she hums a mantra. Slowly, the glowing yellow energy streams that are characteristic of Lyran Starseeds start to emerge from the steady pounding of her drum. As many times as I've seen these healing powers, they still never cease to amaze me.

The golden currents of energy radiate from Kara's drum and swirl around the crown of the patient's head. After about five minutes, Kara completes her treatment and the energy fades. The patient sits up on the table and Sylestra checks the rotation of their crown chakra with her slender blue hand.

"How do you feel?"

"I feel fine," the third-year says. "She did great."

"Thank you, Kara. You can go back to your seat." Alien Sylestra follows the student out of the room and returns with another. "Who would like to go next?"

"Ooh, me!" June jabs her hand in the air with excitement.

Sylestra beckons her to the front of the class, and June whispers something in her ear. Alien Sylestra nods. "Yes... yes. That will be fine."

June walks over to the side door of the classroom that leads outside. She leaves for a moment, letting the cool morning air waft in before returning with her white stallion, leading it by the bridle to the front of the class.

"You've got to be kidding me," I mutter under my breath.

Cassandra mumbles something in reply, but I can't make it out. She talks so quietly it's hard to understand her sometimes.

"If you guys haven't met my spirit animal yet, this is Edmund." June's signature baby braids frame her smiling face as she pats Edmund's luxurious mane. "He'll be assisting me in my healing today."

"There's no need for a presentation, Miss Molyneux," Sylestra drawls from her desk. "Just the healing will suffice."

"Yes, of course, Professor." June stands a little straighter. "Right away." She leads the horse to the head of the massage table where the new third-year lies expectantly. Edmond rolls his big head back and forth nervously, looking around the room, but June grabs hold of him, trying to calm him down by murmuring softly and pressing her forehead to his.

Soon, the animal relaxes while June continues to mutter indecipherable nothings in his ear. June places both hands on the patient's head, and Edmund follows suit by nuzzling the afflicted student with his soft nose. June closes her eyes, facilitating the flow of a vibrant green energy from the horse's muzzle to the patient's skull. I've only seen this kind of Arcturian healing power once before, when Jasper and Mochi cured a fellow student's bloody nose.

Waves of radiant green light stream from Edmund

through June's hands to the patient, and in no time, she's sitting up on the massage table, cured.

"Great work, Miss Molyneux," Sylestra says while June leads her spirit animal back outside, giving it many congratulatory pats on the back. "Now, who's next?"

Vaylen performs her fire healing technique, sending out waves of cerulean healing energy while the flame on her candle flares blue. The volunteer lies still, brow furrowed in mild discomfort, nothing like the searing agony I remember.

Next up is Cassandra. I know she's a Lyran Starseed, but I've never seen her with any instrument. She stands over her patient, her long hair obscuring most of her face from view. Several minutes go by, and nothing happens.

"Is everything alright, Cassandra?" Alien Sylestra raises an arched eyebrow.

C'mon Cassy. You got this.

Just when I think she's going to walk back to her seat, or worse, break down and cry, Cassandra opens her mouth and the most hauntingly beautiful voice pierces the room.

It sounds like the purest tones of the universe are being channeled into this waifish girl's vocal cords. Yellow light streams forth from Cassandra's throat, which is glowing with the intensity of a golden sun. Her healing rays caress the scalp of her patient while her song reverberates in the classroom like a chorus of angels.

Just as quickly as it started, Cassandra stops singing and walks back to her seat, head bowed, not even waiting to hear Sylestra's assessment. The patient sits up on the massage table, tears streaming from her eyes. "Thank you," the third-year says, looking directly at Cassandra. "That was beautiful."

"Very impressive, Miss Holloway." Alien Sylestra has her palm outstretched over the third-year's head. "You have completely corrected the spin of her crown chakra."

Cassandra just looks down at her desk, scribbling an incoherent dark shape.

"That was amazing." I reach over and squeeze her unhealthily skinny thigh. "Really. I've never heard anyone sing like that."

Cassandra looks over at me with her pale grey eyes. "Thanks," she says, and a shy smile lights up her face.

"Synchronicity," Alien Sylestra's harsh tone rings out over the class. "Would you like to go next?"

It's the question I've been dreading.

I let out a long exhale. "I guess I don't have much of a choice."

My patient is an older man with a receding hairline and a calm, detached expression, like nothing that happens here could possibly rattle him. He gives me a small, reassuring nod and closes his eyes.

"This should be good," Kara mutters, reclining smugly in her chair, arms folded like she's already watching the train wreck. Vaylen just glares.

"That's enough, Miss Volkova." Sylestra's voice is stern. "Let's see if Synchronicity has learned anything in my course. Just remember, the practical application of your healing powers is fifty percent of the exam. If you fail this, you fail the whole test."

I force a smile I don't feel and give her a nod. "I've got it."

I move to the head of the table and place my hand gently above the man's crown. His subtle field hums faintly beneath my palm, or maybe I'm imagining it. There's something there, but the sensation is slippery, uncertain, like trying to track a breeze in a thunderstorm.

Okay, think. A headache means counterclockwise spin. I just have to reverse it. Clockwise. Like Kai showed me.

But Kai's vortex was strong. Obvious. I can't feel anything definite here. No whirlpool. No direction. It's like trying to tune into a signal through layers of static, and all I can hear is the erratic thud of my heartbeat, louder now that I know every eye is on me.

I put both hands over the crown of his head and imagine a whirlpool of light. In my mind's eye, I slow the spinning currents until they come to a standstill. So far, so good.

I take a deep breath and imagine my head filling up with bright, healing energy, and when I exhale, I send all that energy down to my hands, focusing it into a clockwise direction.

But something cracks open.

A memory, jagged and unwelcome, surges up from the depths of my mind.

The freezing creek. The gush of wind on my skin.

Aidan. Blue lips. Slack limbs.

I thought I could heal him.

I was so sure.

My throat tightens. The vision of light I was holding collapses.

"Synchronicity, what are you doing!" Alien Sylestra's voice pulls me back into the present, and my eyes shoot open.

My patient's face has gone green.

Panic flares in his expression as he bolts upright. "I..." He puts his hand to his mouth and puffs out his cheeks. "I think I'm gonna be sick."

I step out of the way just in time for the man to stumble past me to the trash can near the door. He clutches his stomach and vomits violently into the bin.

The class erupts into groans of disgust. Someone in the front row dry-heaves.

I stand frozen.

Sylestra rushes past me. "What did you do?" Her voice is sharp enough to draw blood. "His toroidal field is tangled into knots!"

"I... I didn't mean to..." I stammer, but it's useless. Everyone's looking at me like I'm a contagious disease.

Vaylen shakes her head with a smug look of satisfaction. "I knew Earthseeds couldn't heal."

The man heaves again and June runs out of the classroom, hand clapped over her mouth.

I take a hesitant step forward. "Is there anything I can do to help?"

Sylestra doesn't even look at me. "You've done quite enough. Take your seat."

Sylestra hums and her blue Sirian energy comes pouring

forth from her fingers, surrounding the sick man in a ball of healing light. The energy strands work like tentacles, pulling the man's toroidal field back into alignment. When she's done, the poor soul is left panting on the floor.

"I'm so sorry," I mouth to him, but he simply stands up and brushes himself off, jaw clenched with quiet humiliation. He doesn't say a word.

He just leaves.

"In all my years of teaching," Sylestra says, her voice barely concealing her rage, "I have never witnessed a student fumble the practical portion of this exam so completely."

Her gaze lands on me like a gavel.

"I suppose this is what I get for allowing an Earthseed into my class."

I sink into my chair like I could dissolve into it, feeling the judgment radiating from every corner of the room.

"We have two more exams left, Synchronicity. If you fail another one, you're done."

CHAPTER
SEVENTEEN

The grass is still damp with dew beneath me. I'm curled over with my head in my hands as if I can fold into myself, disappear into the soil.

"It'll be alright, Sync. We'll help you prep for the next exam. Don't worry." Mae rubs slow, gentle circles on my back as we wait for craft class to start. Her warmth is a balm, but it doesn't reach the hollow place inside me.

"It won't matter," I mutter. "I'm an Earthseed. I can't heal anyone."

My voice comes out flat, like it's already accepted the truth.

"Don't say that." Mae sits in the grass beside me, her knees tucked to her chest, shoulder to shoulder with mine. "It just takes practice."

"That's true," Jasper adds, flopping onto the ground with theatrical flair. "Mochi couldn't channel his healing powers for the first six months last year. I had to do all my practicals solo while my so-called sidekick just sat on my shoulder eating figs."

"You guys don't get it." I glance up at them. "You're *Starseeds*. Healing comes naturally to you."

"Sync, look at me." Mae tilts my chin up until her sea green eyes meet mine. "You were meant to be here. I knew it the second I met you, back at Shasta. Whatever's going on, it's not the end. We're going to figure this out. Together."

Her faith in me cuts and comforts all at once. I nod, swallowing the ache in my throat. I don't deserve her kindness.

Not after what I've done.

"Did I tell you what we saw Xion do last night?" Mae says.

The guilt hits me square in the gut. I haven't told them what I saw. Alien Isis and Xion's late-night rendezvous, entering the hangar like conspirators in a dream. I should tell them. But some part of me is still protecting him. Still keeping his secrets like they're mine.

"No," I say.

"Well, we were out here last night while you were with Mr. Magic Hands—remind me to ask you about that later. I'm *so* curious—and Xion was cleaning his ship, right? You know that big black Eldercraft."

"I'm familiar with it."

"Anyway, he's trying to scrub out the scratches that Bo left on his ship when he gets so angry he kicks over his bucket and lets out this gut-wrenching scream. I've never heard anything so scary in my life, Sync."

"I don't know..." I say, wary. "Getting angry over a damaged ship doesn't exactly make someone a murderer."

"That's not all," Jasper adds. "I dug up some more references to those fifth-dimensional energy vampires, otherwise known as Draconids."

He sits up, cross-legged, his face lit with conspiratorial energy.

"Beta Draconids are mostly harmless. They float through the galaxy completely inert, like spores. I say mostly harmless because in the presence of an Alpha, they activate. Go full predator mode. And Alpha Draconids, they're sentient. But they don't attack directly. They manipulate. They latch onto a host and use the Betas like leeches, draining the life force of their victims from a distance."

I glance toward the hangar. My pulse ticks up.

"Some theorists think the Alphas and Betas are just two aspects of one massive interdimensional being," Jasper continues. "Like a giant mushroom whose fruits are scattered across the universe."

I try to piece together everything Jasper just said. "So you think Xion is the host, and the thing that attacked Bo is one of the Betas?"

"I think it fits. The attack on Bo. The rage. Alphas feed on negative emotion. And Xion's got plenty of that." Jasper pauses. "He may not even know he's a host."

"But how would Xion even have come into contact with

something like this?"

"They hibernate for millennia," Jasper says, eyes gleaming. "As long as they're attached to something from their homeworld. That Eldercraft of his? If it crashed on a contaminated planet, or carried something back in the hull..."

I think back to the story of how Xion found his Eldercraft. Then my gaze drifts over to the hangar I saw him enter with Isis last night. Could the object he recovered for her have contained one of these evil fifth-dimensional energy vampires?

CHAPTER
EIGHTEEN

The Herbalism plot I inherited in Atum Crater is a strange patchwork of plants, like a dream someone else once had but forgot to finish. Slender stalks of sage-green mugwort sway beside broad, heavy comfrey leaves. Blades of iris push up through the soil like silent exclamations, mingling with unruly stands of mint and lemon balm. Near the center, a lone chaste tree rises with its delicate, fingered leaves spread wide, like it's waiting for something.

It's odd, stepping into a garden this late in the season, tending life you didn't plant. I wonder who chose these herbs, who arranged them in this quiet little jumble. A second-year, no doubt, probably off in their dormitory somewhere with new classes on their mind. I wonder if they still think about their plot from first-year Herbalism. I know I would.

My lab goes late into the evening, and the sun is low by the time I make my final trip down to the pool. Most of the other students have gone, their laughter echoing off the terraces as they ascend the crater walls and disappear into the trees. I crouch by the edge and splash the deep blue water onto my face. The cold snaps through me like a power line, lighting up my spine, jolting away the evening fog that's settled in my bones.

With a full bucket in hand, I climb the winding steps to my terrace on one of the middle rings. My plot is marked off from the others by a miniature picket fence and a sign I painted that reads *Synchronicity* in swirling, uneven letters.

I tip the bucket on each of my plants, taking note of their individual habits and personalities. The mugwort is dreamy, half in this world, half in the realm of sleep. The comfrey pulses with a heavy, matronly energy, and the lemon balm hums like sunlight. Nothing here has grown much since I took over, but the leaves are yellowing gracefully, pulling energy down into their roots. Alien Thumgren says this is the season of descent, of drawing inward, conserving magic for the long dark.

Soon we'll learn to transform these plants into tinctures, honey infusions, and healing salves. But tonight, my job is simpler: to be their witness. To steward their life force back into the earth.

I rest a hand on the damp soil and say a quiet thank you to the plants, to whoever planted them, maybe even to the version of myself who is finally starting to feel rooted here.

Then I rise and begin the long climb, step after step, toward the lip of the crater, where the final light of the Agarthan sun slips behind the rim and leaves only dusk in its wake.

I make my way through the stand of trees, and when I reach the craft site, I startle at the sound of someone shouting. Even though it's dark, I crouch behind the nearest UFO and turn my gaze to the source of the commotion.

"Stupid fucking thing..." Xion's gruff voice is unmistakable. The door to the mysterious hangar flies open, and my pulse detonates as the massive, muscled red alien storms out. Every nerve ending in my body comes alive with an electric heat.

The reaction I have to the sight of him is so fucking inconvenient.

"Snapped all my tools. Of course you did," he grumbles as he slams the hangar door shut with so much force that it rebounds back open a few inches, as if even the building's resisting him tonight.

He doesn't notice the breach in security, or doesn't care, and stomps off to his Eldercraft, which sits black and motionless on the craft field. A seamless hatch opens on its sleek exterior, and Xion steps up inside. Moments later, some unknowable engines hum to life and Nyx Arcana shoots off into the inky night.

I should turn around. I should go back to my room. Even if Xion isn't infested with some fifth-dimensional energy vampire, he'd probably still kill me if he found me snooping around his things. Especially a thing so secret that even Alien Isis wants to keep it hidden. And if she found out? She's one of the only—no, scratch that—*the only* reason I'm still at this school. Let's just say I'd be back to living in my car before I could say Galactic Federation.

Every logical nerve in my body is telling me to turn around and pretend I didn't see any of this, but something else takes over. Not logic. Not fear. Something quiet and enormous that pulls me toward the hangar.

I race, half crouched, across the craft field to the open door and slip inside, shutting it with a quiet click behind me. I fumble in the darkness for a switch. My fingers catch on one, and I flick it on, activating rows of overhead lights that click on, one after another.

Sitting in the middle of the hangar, supported by four pneumatic arms, is a large egg-shaped object. Its surface is a pure, creamy white broken only by a large crack that extends from the bottom and up the side. As I approach, I can see it's etched with strange symbols unlike anything I've seen at the school so far. Scattered at the base of this giant stone egg are various tools, all twisted and bent like someone was trying to pry open an impossibly tight door.

I take a cautious step forward.

My fingers hover over one of the symbols. I should stop. But the symbol seems to beckon to me.

I touch it.

The reaction is instant: a pulse of electric blue light shoots through the glyph, illuminating the next, and the next, until the entire surface is glowing like a living constellation. A deep, resonant hum shakes the floor as the egg lifts from its restraints, hovering in midair like it's waking up from a long dream.

I fall back on my ass.

"Oh shit. Oh shit."

I scramble backward, keeping my eyes locked on the floating, illuminated egg.

Xion is *literally* going to kill me.

"Go back down," I whisper, palms raised. "Turn off. You know, deactivate."

It just sits there, hovering.

"I'm sorry I disturbed you. I promise I won't touch you again if you go back to sleep."

The egg tilts slightly, as if considering me. The blue glow flickers. It emits a low, curious hum.

"You know, sleep." I put my hands together and lay my head on them like a pillow, making fake snoring sounds. "Honk shoo. Honk shoo."

"HROONK SHOOOOM. HROOONK SHOOOOM."

The egg mimics me with a seismic imitation, loud enough to rattle the walls. I wince.

"No, no. Shhh. Not like that." I wave frantically. "You have to power down."

But it just hovers there, watching me like a giant egg-shaped puppy that doesn't understand what it's done wrong.

And then I hear it. The low thrumming of Nyx Arcana returning.

Shit.

I sprint to the light switch and plunge the hangar back into darkness, but the egg still glows with that eerie, celestial light.

Desperate, I press both palms against it and try to remember what Xion taught me about connecting with crafts.

I close my eyes.

Down the staircase I go, floor by floor, into the stillness of my psyche. I picture the craft perfectly, every detail of the glyphs, the crack in its shell, the way it seemed to tilt its head. I whisper to it not with my voice, but with my mind:

Power down. Go still. Hide.

Outside, heavy footfalls echo.

Mercifully, the egg winds down with a decreasing hum. The glowing symbols fade, and it descends gently back onto its supports just as the door swings open.

"Who's in here?" Xion's voice cuts through the dark.

I creep quietly around the egg until it's positioned between me and him.

He switches on the lights, and they come flooding back to

life. I hear his footsteps as he approaches the egg, and I crouch down behind it, trying to muffle the thundering in my chest.

"Hmm, what's this?" Xion's steps come around the side of the egg, and out of the corner of my eye, I see him reach down and pick up a socket wrench. "I was looking for you."

He retreats back the way he came, and I hear him deposit the wrench in a toolbox with a clatter of metal. I let out a sigh of relief, but as I do, my back grazes the surface of the egg.

The hieroglyphs on its surface once again spring to life, turning blue in successive upward patterns as the egg rises four feet in the air, revealing me cowering on the ground behind it.

I freeze.

Xion stares, eyes wide, not with anger, but something stranger. Something deeper.

"You..." he breathes, looking up at the floating egg. "You connected to it."

"I swear I didn't mean to." I scramble to my feet, hands up. "I just brushed up against it. I wasn't trying to do anything. I promise."

His glowing amber eyes drop down to mine. "We have to talk."

CHAPTER
NINETEEN

"Coffee?" Xion pours himself a cup from a blackened, ancient-looking percolator shaped more like an alchemical device than a kitchen appliance.

"It's nine o'clock at night," I say.

Steam curls around the hard lines of his jaw as he lifts the cup to his mouth. "It's from Aldebaran. Twice as strong, but it metabolizes in half the time. You'll be asleep by midnight."

I shrug. "Fuck it."

He hands me a mug carved from some dark obsidian-like material. It radiates warmth as the comforting smell of the roast hits my nostrils. I sink into a low-slung chair, the only one not covered in star charts or scattered engine components. The rest of his living space is cavernous and cold, the walls forged from dark stone laced with glowing alien glyphs. Metalwork lines the ceiling in intricate patterns, humming softly with some forgotten frequency. A fire crackles low in a sunken pit at the center of the room, more ceremonial than comforting.

Xion takes a seat across from me at a stone table littered with fractured tech and what looks like a partially disassembled drone. His gaze pins me before I can even sip.

"So. What exactly happened back there?"

"I told you. I touched it. It came to life."

He doesn't blink. His eyes, coal-ringed and bottomless, don't just look at me, they press. I shift in my seat.

"Impossible," he says. "You're an Earthseed."

"I don't know how. You probably know more than I do. What *is* that thing, anyway?"

He leans back, shadows cutting across his sharp features as the firelight flickers. "An Eldercraft. But not like the others. Alien Isis picked up its energy signature when term began and sent me to retrieve it. We've been trying to access its memory banks for weeks. Nothing. Then you walk in and it responds like it's been waiting for you."

I freeze. "So I connected to an..."

"An Eldercraft, yes."

"Just like..."

"Like me. Like Isis."

"But what does that *mean*?"

He doesn't answer right away. Just studies me, like he's calculating how much truth I can handle. Then, softly:

"It means, from now until the day you die, you will feel the exquisite pain of having your soul exist outside of yourself."

The words cut deep. "It can't be me. It made a mistake. I'm not even supposed to be here. I'm a bad person, Xion."

He laughs, but there's no joy in it. "There are no good or bad people in the eyes of Source."

"I'm serious. I look at my classmates, Mae, Jasper, and they're so *good*. Their hearts are open, pure. They'd do anything for me. And I... I just think about myself. Like I'm some secret sociopath hiding in their sunshine."

Xion's expression doesn't change, but something in his posture tightens. "You can question your self-worth all you want, but that craft didn't. And not just any craft. Eldercraft are already rare, but this one? It's like nothing I've seen before. Nothing anyone's seen. Even Isis doesn't recognize it."

I swallow. "There are more things in heaven and earth..." I mutter under my breath.

He arches a brow. "Shakespeare?"

I'm shocked. "You got that reference?"

"If you want real poetry, look up Braghzor Zhurn'ekk. He was a classical Maldekian playwright. The pain and beauty in his work make Shakespeare look like pop fiction."

"Can I ask you something?"

He nods.

"Why do you hate Earthseeds so much?"

His jaw clenches. "It's nothing." He averts his gaze like he's suddenly more interested in the machine parts on the end table.

"It's not nothing. You make a comment about it every time we talk."

There's a long pause. He drags his gaze back over to mine. "Look at this place. The Academy. The resources. The teachers. Earth's getting a royal ascension package from the Galactic Federation."

"You're mad Maldek didn't get the same."

His voice drops into a growl. "We got *nothing*." The words ignite something in him, an ember turned inferno. "They watched us *burn*. Let us destroy ourselves. Like rats in a cage. And now the survivors, what's left of us, are scattered through the stars. You have no idea what it's like to live your life in exile from a home you can never go back to."

"I might have some idea what that feels like..." I mutter.

"What?"

"Nothing."

He searches me again, like he's peeling back layers with his eyes. "If the Federation had lifted a finger, just one, we wouldn't be ghosts. But now Maldek is a pile of asteroids, and our name is nothing more than a warning."

"If you hate being Maldekian so much, why not just incarnate as something else?"

He flinches, like I struck him. I regret it instantly.

"Maldekians never incarnate as other species," he says softly. "It's a vow. A pact we made with our ancestors. Our souls will fade with our people."

A solemn hush settles over the room. I watch the grief smolder in his eyes, and in that moment, God help me, I want to kiss him.

"But this is my burden. Better to die as a Maldekian than live as a Sirian."

"Is that like your family motto?"

He lets out a low breath. "Just an old saying my people have."

I collect myself. "So... what happens next?"

"We wander the cosmos until the last light of Maldek dies out."

"I meant with my Eldercraft."

He stands, crosses to a wall panel, and studies a map of the galaxy pinned there. "We talk to Isis."

"Does this mean I won't have to work with the Castor 5 anymore?"

"Absolutely not. There is a reason Isis wants this thing kept secret. You are not to speak of your connection to this craft to anybody."

"Hey. You can trust me. I've kept your secret so far."

He turns, fixing me with that same penetrating stare. "What's its name?"

"I don't know. It kind of acted... like a baby. Curious. Clumsy. Not exactly wise."

Xion's brow furrows. "That makes no sense. Eldercraft are ancient. Older than most of the known civilizations. Their minds are like vast libraries. When you connect, you commune with something immeasurably old."

"Well, this one felt... new. Like it was learning how to be alive."

He steps closer. "Show me."

As soon as we step into the hangar, it stirs.

The egg-shaped Eldercraft lifts slightly on its supports, a low harmonic hum vibrating through the air as luminous glyphs ignite across its surface like falling stars, each one trailing a stream of electric blue down the curve of its cracked shell.

"I want you to try to interface with it," Xion says, voice low. "Just like we did in class."

"Okay." Part of me relishes how easily I follow his commands.

I settle cross-legged in front of the egg and let my eyes drift shut. With each breath, I descend inward, down the spiraling staircase of my mind, deeper and deeper, until the light of thought thins into shadow and I find myself in the lowest chamber.

The one with the door.

It stands at the far end of the room, simple and wooden, but looking at it sends fear racing through my heart. I know I can't face what's on the other side. Not yet.

Instead, I turn my focus to what I came for.

I conjure the image of the Eldercraft hovering in the center of the space, as real and radiant as in waking life. Its creamy shell floats a few feet off the floor, inscribed with glowing glyphs that ripple with soft blue light. The crack that runs like a scar up his side gleams faintly in the stillness, like a wound that refuses to heal.

Here, in the heart of myself, we meet.

"Good. The display on its surface is changing. You're doing something," Xion says, but his voice sounds far away.

Hello? I echo out into the void.

The egg responds with its machine-like hums in a rough approximation of the word 'hello.' I can't tell if it's doing it in real life or only in my mind.

My name is Synchronicity. What's your name?

...Synchronicity.

The energy of its voice is surreal, masculine, almost childlike.

Yes, good! You said a word. That's my name, Synchronicity. What's *your* name?

Name?

The egg tilts itself at an angle, trying to understand.

Yes. What do you call yourself?

Ra.

Ra? Your name is Ra?

Ra.

Good! Yes, excellent! It's nice to meet you, Ra.

Synchronicity.

Yes, I'm Synchronicity, you're Ra.

The egg just sits there, blue symbols cascading down its surface.

Can you tell me where you came from?

No response.

How about who made you? Do you have a creator?

Nothing.

Maybe it's that crack. On your shell. Is that what made you forget?

I run my finger up my torso to mimic the crack. The egg tilts, then, after a beat...

Ra.

The single syllable is all he manages to intone.

I find the spiral staircase in my underground cathedral and ascend back to the surface of my conscious mind. When I open my eyes, the egg hovers in front of me just like before.

"Well, I think I figured out his name."

Xion is sitting across the hangar, leaning back against the corrugated metal wall in a chair. "You were out for a long time."

"How long?"

"It's 12:30." His tone is calm.

"You mean I was down there for two and a half hours?"

"Yes."

"It only felt like a few minutes."

"Connection can be like that sometimes."

"His name is Ra," I say. "I don't think he remembers anything else. It's like he's just waking up, or was just born."

Xion stands, slowly approaching Ra. "When I first connected with Nyx Arcana, she gave me a download. Stars, secrets, wars, histories. The whole map of galactic consciousness. But this?" He runs his hand gently along Ra's glowing surface. "This one's different."

"I don't know what to tell you. Ra is a baby. He's... innocent."

"Or empty," Xion replies, voice taut. "And an empty vessel is dangerous." He pauses for a beat. "It's getting late. You should probably get going back to your room."

"And leave Ra alone?" I blurt out. The prospect of being separated from my craft yanks at my heartstrings. How have I become so attached to him so quickly?

"Don't worry. He'll be fine here."

"No." I put my foot down with force.

"Excuse me?" A look of anger flashes across his face.

"I'm not leaving you alone with Ra."

"I won't be with him. I'm going to bed."

"That's even worse!" I shout, surprised by the force of my own voice.

"Oh, I see what's going on here."

"What?" I say, blowing a stray hair out of my face.

He exhales through his nose, amused but wary. "Usually, a connection between craft and pilot is like one of lovers, or between teacher and student." Xion paces the concrete floor of the hangar. "But this... this is maternal."

"Maybe," I admit. "All I know is that the thought of leaving him here alone makes my stomach turn."

"Nevertheless, I can't have you sleeping in my hangar. You can come back and see him tomorrow."

"No. I'm staying here," I say firmly. "Even if these feelings are just the result of our connection, there's no way I'm leaving this little being alone in a cold, scary hangar overnight."

"Little being? He's three times your size," Xion deadpans.

"Whatever. I'm not going anywhere."

"Look, I can't have you staying alone with this thing..."

"Ra. His name is Ra."

"Okay, I can't have you staying alone with *Ra*. We don't know anything about him. He could be dangerous. For all we know, he could be the reason Bo is dead."

Anger flares up in me. "Don't you dare put that on him. For all I know, it was you."

A satisfied smirk turns the corners of Xion's lips as he steps slowly toward me. "Is that what you think of me, Synchronicity? That I'm a killer?"

My pulse quickens. "Maybe..."

"There's a lot you don't know about me, Synchronicity. And there's a lot you don't know about that craft over there. The last thing this school needs is another dead student."

"Ra's not going to kill me," I say, incredulous.

His gaze flicks to Ra. "Right now, you're seeing a lost

child. But what if it's not a child? What if it's a weapon? What if it's sleeping for a reason?"

"I'm not afraid of him."

"You should be. You don't even know what you are."

"I know enough to trust my intuition," I snap.

He looks at me for a long moment, then sighs, jaw tight. "Fine."

"Fine?"

"I'll go get some blankets."

"For me?"

"For *both* of us."

CHAPTER TWENTY

I wake up on the cement floor, curled into a fetal position beneath one of Xion's shabby blankets. My limbs ache, and my joints protest as I shift. Morning light streams through the high windows of the hangar, casting long beams that glint off Ra's surface. He's nestled back into his support arms, his symbols softly glowing with a quiet, dreamlike pulse.

Across the hangar, Xion sits in the same chair as last night, arms crossed, posture rigid as ever. His eyes are open. Watchful. Did he even sleep?

"Don't you have a class to be late for?" His voice breaks the stillness like gravel under a boot.

"Shit." I rub the sleep from my eyes. "What time is it?"

"Eight-thirty."

"Fuck." I groan, already picturing the scowl on Alien Sylestra's face. "I missed morning duties. Sylestra's going to be pissed."

I stand too quickly and nearly stumble. Then I look back at Ra. "Wait, what about him?"

Xion doesn't move. "Don't worry. He's been fine in here for weeks before you connected with him."

I hover, uncertain. "Are you sure?"

"Yes," he says, firm but not unkind. "Go. We'll figure this out later."

I hesitate again, fingers drifting along Ra's impossibly smooth hull.

"Can I come see him after craft today?"

"That'll be... complicated. No one's supposed to know we're keeping him here. If students see you coming and going from this hangar—"

"It'll look bad," I finish. "I get it. So make something up. Say I need remedial craft skills. Extra Earthseed credit. Whatever."

Xion exhales through his nose. "I'll talk to Isis."

I press my palm flat against Ra, reluctant to leave. "Can I at least come back tonight?"

He tilts his head toward me, eyes unreadable. "I'd tell you no... if I thought that would stop you."

I grin. "Smart man."

His smirk is barely perceptible, but it's there.

I sprint back to the Energy Work School, my feet barely touching the ground. I dart through hallways, flipping on the sauna and steam room, slapping towels onto racks like my life depends on it. By the time I reach the upstairs classroom, I'm breathless, hair frizzed from moisture, with just minutes to spare.

"Synchronicity," Alien Sylestra's voice slices through the room. Her antennae twitch, picking up on every frazzled inch of me. "The gua sha stones in the energy shop were not restocked."

"I... yes, I meant to. Sorry, I forgot."

Her black, bug-like eyes narrow. "You look terrible. Dignity and discipline are the foundation of an elevated auric field. If you can't tend to yourself, how do you expect to tend to others?"

"I understand, Alien Sylestra. It won't happen again." I bow, the act automatic by now.

"Somehow," she says, "I doubt that."

I ignore Vaylen's satisfied smirk and shuffle to my seat beside Cassandra.

"I made this for you." She hands me a small origami rose.

"It's beautiful, Cassy." I tuck it on the corner of my desk. "Thank you."

"I felt bad for what happened to you the other day," she says.

"It's fine." I force a smile. "We still have two exams left."

"Class," Sylestra begins, gliding to the center of the room. "Today we will be discussing the tidal pulse of the coccyx and its relationship to the sacral rhythm."

I try, truly try, to focus. But my mind slips again and

again to the hangar. To Ra. To his strange glowing symbols and the almost childlike way he engaged with me. The classroom fades, and when I blink back to the present, Sylestra is already dismissing us.

I throw on a fresh outfit in my room and hurry as fast as I can back to the craft site. Mae and Jasper are already sprawled in the grass, Mochi curled in Jasper's lap like a lazy sunbeam.

"Where were you last night?" Jasper fans himself with a notebook. "Mae made her famous mung bean crepes."

"Sorry," I say, trying to keep my voice light. "I had lab. It ran late." I settle down into the grass next to them, my eyes lingering on the hangar where I know Ra is hidden.

"Don't worry, we found a suitable replacement for you. Go on, tell her, Mae."

Mae blushes and turns her head away. "Stop. It was nothing."

"Kara joined us for dinner last night," Jasper picks a blade of grass and feeds it to Mochi.

"That's great, Mae," I say, but I'm worried for her. I remember the way Kara treated her the last time they hooked up. "I'm happy for you."

"It's nothing serious." Her cheeks flush as she shrugs. "She's not ready for a relationship, so we're just taking it slow and having fun."

I glance across the lawn. Kara, Vaylen, and June are deep in conversation, their heads bowed in a tight triangle. Kara doesn't even look in Mae's direction.

"If you call spending the night with her 'taking it slow,'" Jasper tosses out.

"Mae!" I exclaim, giving her a playful shove.

"Guys, she is *incredible* in bed. It's like our souls are melding. She's like a drug. The colors literally look brighter after being with her." Mae picks up her ukulele and strums a dreamy tune.

"Oh, you've got it bad," I say, although I have no room to talk, torn as I am between our alien flight instructor and a spiritual healer who's probably just playing games with me.

"Whatever." Mae gazes across the field at Kara. "I like her. Is that a crime?"

"Shh. Here comes Alien Death," Jasper drawls.

Xion steps out onto the field, and my heart flutters. This would all be a lot easier if my hormones didn't go into overdrive every time I laid eyes on him.

"Good morning, Starseeds." Xion's eyes sweep over the group, landing on me last. "And Earthseed." The ass has the nerve to smile.

I flip him the middle finger.

"Who wants to learn about particle condensers?"

Jasper groans dramatically.

"Since Mr. Collins has already taken this class, I'm sure he will get much more value out of deconstructing his craft's quantum drive."

"You got it." Jasper gives a thumbs-up without taking his attention away from Mochi.

"The rest of you will be using your craft manuals to locate the particle condensers and remove them. When everyone has their condensers out on the lawn, I'll teach you how to overhaul them. Now get to it."

I wander over to my Castor 5 and locate the release handle to open the hatch to the cockpit. I pull myself up into the run-down flying saucer and flip through the manual, looking for the part that Xion specified.

The cockpit is ringed with circular windows that let the daylight into the archaic interior. Cables and hatches to various compartments line the floor while the walls are covered with indecipherable control panels. After about twenty minutes, I've located the particle condenser and have it halfway removed when Xion pops his head up through the entry hatch.

"Permission to come aboard?" Xion asks, his voice a low rumble.

"If you must." I try to ignore the sight of his muscles as he pulls himself up with unsettling ease. The cockpit suddenly feels much smaller.

"I want to come over tonight," I say without looking up.

A pause.

"Wow. I've never been propositioned so bluntly by a student."

I lob a screwdriver at him. He catches it one-handed.

"Not for you," I say. "For Ra."

"Ah," he says. "Right. Your Eldercraft. How could I forget why I spent the night on concrete."

Fucking. Ass.

"You don't get it. It's like being away from a child. I can't stop thinking about him all alone in that hangar. Not that you would understand."

"You forget. I'm connected to an Eldercraft, too. And you're not a mother. You're a pilot. That is, unless you have some child that I don't know about."

"No. Just Ra."

"Interesting." The word rolls off his tongue like molasses as his piercing gaze passes over my body. The fact that I'm alone in a UFO with this massive, tattooed, alien of a man hits me like a freight train, sending a shiver of fear and excitement through me.

I push the feeling away and focus my attention back on the rusty craft part.

"Isis wants to see you."

I tense up. "When?"

"Tonight."

"So... does that mean I get to see Ra?"

"As long as you're good and continue to keep your promise." The smirk that follows is pure trouble.

"Who would I tell?" I purposely look away from him and focus on detaching the tubes from the condenser.

"You seem pretty tight with Collins and that Mae girl. One slip of the tongue, and the whole school would know we're hiding a rare Eldercraft. Next thing you know, Federation agents are swarming the campus, tearing Ra apart for ancient tech."

"You can't be serious," I say, but the look on his face is no longer joking.

"Why do you think Isis wanted it kept hidden? The Galactic Federation may seem like it's all love and light, but it has a dark political underbelly that you don't want to be on the receiving end of."

"I told you. I'm not telling anyone."

"That's a good Earthseed."

"Fuck you," I say, trying to pull the particle condenser out of my Castor 5 with brute force.

"Be at the hangar tonight by ten o'clock." He jumps back down through the hatch to the ground below, leaving behind the scent of smoke and steel in his wake.

"Oh, by the way," he calls up. "That's not the particle condenser. That's a plasma beam dump."

CHAPTER
TWENTY-ONE

I rush into the hangar and throw my arms around Ra. Not that it does much. Hugging him is like embracing a stone obelisk, smooth and massive and utterly unmoved. Still, I press my cheek against his shell. "I missed you, buddy. Were you okay in here?"

The ancient symbols on Ra's surface light up, and he lifts off from the support arms, hovering with a cheerful humming sound.

"Thank you for coming, Synchronicity," a serene voice says behind me.

I whirl around.

Alien Isis stands near the back wall, framed in an aura of lavender light. Her iridescent skin catches the glow of Ra's symbols and refracts it onto the surfaces around her. "I promise not to keep you long, but there are matters we must discuss."

"Alien Isis." I bow with as much grace as I can muster. "It's good to see you again."

She nods with quiet gravity. "You as well, Synchronicity. Alien Da'ath has informed me that you have connected with this Eldercraft."

I spot Xion leaning against the far wall, whittling some unidentifiable scrap of wood. He doesn't look up, but I can feel his attention narrowing like a blade.

"That's correct," I say.

"And what led you into this hangar in the first place?" Her crystalline gaze is both striking and inscrutable.

"Well, after I heard you and Xion talking in the pyramid, I got curious."

Isis tosses a glance at Xion. "I was unaware we had an audience that day."

Xion glowers at me from across the room, rage simmering in the depths of his amber eyes.

"I... uh... only heard a little bit," I say, struggling to

recover. "But then I saw you leaving the pyramid one night and followed you here."

Shit. I shouldn't have said that.

"I see." Alien Isis thinks for a moment. I can't tell if she's regretting allowing me into the school. "It seems," she says softly, "that I've been too careless with my nighttime wanderings. And that Alien Da'ath should double-check his locks."

I know I'm going to regret throwing him under the bus.

"But regardless," Alien Isis continues, "it appears that all of this happened for a reason. Against all odds, this remarkable Eldercraft has found its pilot. That is exceedingly rare in and of itself. But for that pilot to be an Earthseed? Unheard of."

"I don't know what to say," I murmur.

"You don't need to say anything," she replies. "Only listen."

Her tone shifts, sharpening slightly.

"As you said during our first meeting, your arrival here was fated. We are now seeing the proof and ramifications of that statement. I'm sure Alien Da'ath has informed you that the presence of this Eldercraft at Agartha is a matter of the utmost secrecy. If this information were to be leaked, everyone at the school, including you and me, would be put under investigation by the Galactic Federation. A previously unknown variety of Eldercraft like this would be seen as a technological goldmine. However, there are certain factions of the Federation with immense power whose goals are not necessarily aligned with the well-being of the galaxy. If they were to get their hands on this craft... the consequences could be disastrous. As such, I believe it is in all our best interests to continue keeping the existence of this craft a secret."

"Ra," I say.

"Excuse me?"

"The craft's name is Ra."

"I see. Ra. Yes, for the time being, no one else can know about Ra. Is that clear, Synchronicity?"

"Yes, Alien Isis." I shift my weight back and forth

between my feet.

"And yet..." She turns back to Ra, who hovers quietly, "Connection with an Eldercraft is a beautiful thing that does not happen very often in this universe, and I am of the mind that this connection should be fostered. As I'm sure you are already feeling, bonding with an Eldercraft can be quite intense. If it is not cultivated in a healthy manner, the connection with such an advanced form of consciousness can drive a pilot into spiritual psychosis. You've been granted access to a consciousness far older than anything we teach here. You'll need guidance."

She turns to Xion. "And you will give it to her."

Xion jerks upright. "Wait, you can't be serious. I don't have time to give her private lessons."

"And even if he did," I blurt out, "I wouldn't want lessons from *him*." I shoot Xion a glare.

"Enough," Isis says quietly, but it slices through the tension like a blade. "The three of us and a handful of other teachers, none of whom are craft instructors, are the only ones who know about this craft. Xion, you will instruct her privately. At night. No one must see."

Xion's jaw tightens, but he doesn't argue. Not with her.

"This connection," she adds, turning back to me, "isn't a mistake. It's part of something larger. But if you mishandle it, the consequences will ripple far beyond this school."

I nod, still catching my breath from everything I'm absorbing. "I understand."

Isis smiles faintly, just a small curve of her luminous lips. "Then I'll leave you two to work out the details. I trust you'll be discreet."

She glides toward the exit, her light fading with her, leaving only Ra's soft glow behind.

The hangar door closes, and Xion finally looks at me.

"Well," he says. "Looks like you're stuck with me."

I fold my arms. "Don't expect me to like it."

He smirks. "I wouldn't dream of it."

CHAPTER
TWENTY-TWO

A week later, I'm getting ready for my first private training lesson with Xion. But as soon as I open my door, a flyer flutters to the floor.

STARSEED SOVEREIGNTY SOCIETY

Maldekians have no place in Agartha! Terminate all Maldekian faculty now!

Harsh red letters scream across the page like a threat.

I look down the hallway. More flyers. On every door. A littering of hate disguised as pride. It takes me fifteen minutes to take them all down. I thought being an Earthseed was bad. At least I'm not the target of a propaganda campaign.

I crumple the stack into a ball and toss it in the trash on my way out. I head across campus to the craft site and knock on Xion's door.

"Good evening, Synchronicity." His voice rolls like thunder. "Are you ready for your first official Eldercraft lesson?"

I spot one of the flyers balled up on his floor.

"You got one too?"

His jaw tenses for a moment, but he shrugs it off. "Don't worry about it. Tonight is about you." With a single kick, he sends it rolling out of sight and steps past me. "I took the liberty of moving Ra to a new location."

I blink. "I'm sorry, you *what*?"

"Don't worry. I was careful," he says. "Just for tonight. I think this place will help you connect."

"If you damaged him in any way..."

"You mean besides the giant crack running up his hull?"

"You know what I mean."

"I promise, he'll be just like you remember him. Come on. I'll show you."

He leads me to Nyx Arcana, whose smooth black body glints like obsidian in the Agarthan night. Her entry hatch swings down into a staircase, and I follow Xion inside.

The air is dim and scarlet-tinged, like dusk frozen in time. The walls curve around us in fluid, seamless panels of dark crystal. Instead of metal bolts or rivets, everything feels grown rather than built, like the craft was coaxed into existence by will alone.

Amber light spills from hidden veins in the floor and ceiling, casting soft shadows that flicker and move like firelight. The cockpit is set into the forward chamber like a throne in a temple.

One wall holds an altar-like shelf of objects: a cracked metal ring, a scorched piece of stone with Maldekian runes, and a braided leather strap. Relics, maybe. Reminders.

The passenger area is sparse, utilitarian. Black benches are molded directly from the walls. But in one corner sits a meditation alcove with a single low mat and a crystal glowing a faint rose gold. A warship with a soul... or maybe just a ghost trying to remember what peace felt like.

"Nice digs," I say.

"Take a seat. This won't be long." He settles into the captain's chair.

Nyx Arcana lifts off, her movement so smooth it barely registers. The lights of the school recede beneath us, and soon we are flying over mountainous terrain.

As I admire the sleek interior, my eyes land on a neatly wrapped black package tucked under a seat.

Before I get a chance to ask him about it, the ship starts to descend.

"We're here," Xion announces. He brings the craft into a gentle hover, landing in a remote stretch of mountains. When I walk back down the entry hatch, I am greeted by the sight of a glimmering crystal cave.

"Is there a fire in there?" I ask.

"Nope. It's just the natural fluorescent minerals. I've found it enhances the craft connection experience."

He leads me inside, and the narrow entrance opens into a vast cavern lit on all sides by twinkling stalactites and stalagmites, like an infinity room of underground stars.

Right in the center, Ra hovers over a large crash pad.

"This place is... incredible," I whisper, gawking at the natural beauty.

"I discovered it once on a recon mission, for Isis."

I trail my fingers along one of the glowing mineral pillars. "Recon for what?"

He hesitates. "There are still a lot of mysteries in Agartha. One of my jobs is to protect the students from them."

"Is this where you found Ra?"

"A little bit further north, buried in the ice. Isis picked up his signal right after you arrived."

"You think that's a coincidence?"

"I don't believe in those," he says.

I cross the crystalline floor and wrap my arms around Ra's giant stone shell. He lights up and makes trilling sounds, bobbing up and down like an excited puppy.

"You two practice some remote piloting, just like you did with the Castor 5. Low hovers. Circles. I'll be right back. There's a spring around here with some of the best water in Agartha."

"Okay, but just promise not to get eaten by an alien bear and leave me stranded in the middle of nowhere."

"The bears out here are more afraid of me," he tosses over his shoulder as he disappears back out of the cave.

"Okay, Ra," I say, settling into the mat in front of him. "Ready to practice flying?"

The massive egg-shaped craft hums and hovers back and forth.

"Let me see if I remember how to do this."

I close my eyes and descend the spiral staircase into the deepest chamber of my mind, where my mental projection of Ra is waiting for me. I notice that the door, the one I'm not supposed to open, seems to be leaking water. Like it's holding back a deluge.

I do my best to ignore it and instead focus all my attention on Ra. I imagine floating over to Ra and having my consciousness move inside him.

But he won't let me in.

Can I come inside, buddy?

Ra... scared.

Hey, that's okay. Don't worry. We don't have to do that yet.

He hovers there, humming.

Maybe I can just instruct you on what to do. Would that be okay?

Ra.

How about this? Can you do a spin?

S—spin?

Like this.

I leave my meditative state and return to the cavern. Standing up on the crash pad, I reach out my arms and spin around once.

"Like that. Spin."

"Spin," Ra reverberates in his ancient, mechanical, stone voice and turns around in place a full three hundred and sixty degrees.

"Good job, Ra! Yes! Just like that!" A huge smile creeps across my face.

"SPINNN," Ra says, spinning faster like a top until his symbols blur into blue streaks.

"Okay, good job, buddy. Now slow down or you're gonna hurt yourself."

"SPINNNN," Ra says again as a wobble starts to propagate through his axis.

"Wait, Ra—slow down!" My voice cracks with panic.

The wobble takes over, and Ra goes flying into one of the cave walls with a sickening thud, sending a few small stalactites crashing to the floor.

"Ra!" I rush over to him as he hovers out of the debris, his crack now pulsing a dull red.

"Oh no. What did you do, buddy?" I say, running my hand over his shell.

He rotates, and I see a shard of crystal lodged in his

fracture.

"I think you hurt yourself, Ra."

"**H-hurt?**"

"Yes. Hurt. Like pain. But let me see if I can fix it." I grasp onto the crystal with both hands. "Okay, this might hurt a little."

With one swift motion, I pull out the shard and a ripple of red flares out across Ra's glyphs before returning to a gently pulsing blue.

"I'm sorry, Ra. But you have to be more careful with this wound of yours."

"**Wound?**" Ra tilts.

"Yes, a wound. It's a painful spot. A spot where you've been hurt." I run my fingers along the large rift in Ra's surface.

"**Wound... bad?**"

"Not necessarily bad," I say. "Wounds are how the light gets in."

"You two doing alright in here?" Xion's voice bounces off the walls.

"Ra had a little accident, but I think he's fine." I get up and walk over toward Xion, letting my fingers run along the twinkling stalagmites as I cross the floor.

"Do I need to go get an oversized doggy bag?"

"No, nothing like that. He just got a splinter."

"A splinter, huh? Did your healing hands take care of him?"

"So far these 'healing hands' haven't healed shit. But I pulled the splinter out if that's what you're getting at."

"Here. I brought you something." He hands me a steel bottle still dripping with cold spring water, and I unscrew the lid.

The water hits my mouth like sweet glacial snowmelt. I gulp it down in big appreciative swallows.

"Oh my God. That tastes amazing." I wipe the moisture from my lips on the back of my hand.

"Straight from the source. I grab some every time I come

up here." Xion sits down on the edge of the crash pad, and I join him.

We fall into silence, surrounded by a thousand glowing crystals.

Time suspends around us.

"So... if Eldercraft know the secrets of the galaxy, why don't they remember who built them?" I ask, gazing up at the shimmering stones above us.

"There's an abyss," he says, following my gaze. "A great forgetting before which no Eldercraft has memory. We think there must have been some kind of cosmic blast from an exploding star that wiped all their memories. Whatever it was, it probably ended the Elder civilization, too."

I turn to him. "Do you ever wonder if the same thing will happen to us?"

He drags his gaze away from the ripples of fluorescent light coursing through the minerals and turns toward me. "There's always the possibility of some catastrophic ending looming on the horizon."

His eyes flick to my lips and linger. The air between us tightens. Something in his gaze darkens, not with fear, but with gravity. Hunger.

"The trick," he murmurs, "is surrendering to the infinite mystery in spite of it all."

His breath brushes my cheek. I lean in, just barely, my lips parting, heart ricocheting off my ribs.

The space between us contracts.

Then...

"SPINNN!" Ra's voice booms through the cavern like a thunderclap in a cathedral, shattering the moment into a thousand electric pieces. He barrels between us, and we have to duck to miss hitting his spinning shell.

Xion lets out a laugh. A real laugh.

I burst out laughing, too.

"Sorry," I say. "It's his new trick."

"Impressive," Xion says. "Very useful in interstellar flight."

"Okay, Ra," I call. "That's enough spinning for now. You don't want to hurt yourself again."

The towering, egg-shaped craft slows its rotation to the speed of a record player, blue glyphs floating by like lines of code.

Xion stands and offers his hand.

"Come on, Jones. We've got a lot of work to do."

After nearly two hours of trying to get Ra to do anything more advanced than spinning, I collapse backward onto the crash pad, arms flung out in defeat.

"He's a very enthusiastic blender," I mutter.

Xion, leaning against an outcrop with his arms crossed, lets out a low grunt. "Takes time. A week ago, he could barely hover."

"And now I've taught my Eldercraft how to spin himself into a wall. At this rate, I'll be ready for intergalactic travel in... never."

I sit up and brush the glittering dust from my pants as Xion strides over. The crack in Ra's hull pulses faintly, a soft, cautious blue.

"All right," Xion says. "Let's pack it in."

I hesitate, looking back at Ra, who hovers there like a massive, docile egg lit from within. "We can't leave him here."

"Relax. It's late enough that no one will see us. I'll tow him back using Nyx's tractor beam."

Ra follows us out of the cave, where Nyx Arcana waits on the ridgeline like a sleeping dragon, her silhouette blending into the night. The hatch opens with a whisper, and we step inside.

I sink into one of the velvet-lined passenger seats while Xion takes the pilot's throne, his fingers dancing over floating control nodes. Nyx hums to life around us like a beast exhaling.

Through the window, I watch as a deep crimson beam lances out from Nyx's undercarriage and gently envelops Ra. He lifts off the mountainside like a sleeping child, cradled in red light.

Ra doesn't resist. He just floats there, trailing behind us, his glowing symbols flickering softly against the dark.

For a long time, I can't look away.

When I finally do, my eyes land on the empty space beneath the opposite seat.

The black package is gone.

CHAPTER
TWENTY-THREE

"The Galactic Federation is governed by what is known as the Council of Five," Alien Lumari drones from the front of the amphitheater. His voice echoes in harmonic layers, like five or six people are speaking through him at once, just a millisecond out of sync. "Their spiritual stewardship guides the Federation in all high-level decisions."

I try to listen, but my mind keeps drifting—away from the politics of alien empires and back toward a cracked, humming egg... and the brooding man training me to fly it.

I know I can't trust Xion yet, not after that mysterious package that disappeared during our flight lesson last week. But there's something more to him. Something that draws me in.

"The council includes one delegate from each major star system: Sirius, Lyra, Arcturus, and the Pleiades," Lumari continues, his glowing orbs rotating slowly above the podium like a hypnotist's pendulum. "The fifth seat belongs to Aldebaran—a symbolic position. They are the closest known descendants of the Elder civilization."

While Lumari goes on about the political structure of the Galactic Federation, I put the finishing touches on a sketch of Ra.

"What's that?" Mae whispers, leaning over to see my notebook. "Breakfast?"

"Nothing," I say, scrambling to hide the drawing under my hands. "Just a doodle."

Lumari's light dims slightly as he pivots to the next slide, which shows the sigils of the Council members. "The current leaders are as follows: Alien Kali from Sirius, Alien Hetros from the Pleiades, Alien Kitsune from Arcturus, Alien Calliope from Lyra, and the oldest of them all, Alien Mem of Aldebaran."

Jasper leans in from the row behind us. "Psst. Either of you up for another stakeout on Xion? If we catch one solid piece of evidence that he was involved with Bo, we could take it straight to Alien Isis."

We all glance to the end of the row where Bo's old seat still sits empty.

"I'm not so sure anymore," I say softly.

Jasper raises a skeptical brow. "You're kidding."

"I've just... seen another side of him," I admit, trying to keep my voice even.

Mae shifts beside me, watching me curiously.

Jasper looks back and forth between us, incredulous. "Wait. You mean besides the drill-sergeant-from-hell routine and the fact that he's the only Maldekian on campus?"

"He's more than that." The words come out before I can stop them. "I don't think he killed Bo."

Silence lingers between the three of us.

"You've been acting differently, Sync," Jasper says finally, his tone hardening just a fraction. "Is there something going on?"

"I've just been seeing things more clearly," I say. But I don't know if I'm trying to convince them or myself.

From the front of the room, Lumari's glowing orbs swirl in thoughtful patterns. "In the event of a tie," he says, "the deciding vote lies with Aldebaran. As you'll recall, theirs is not a political seat, but a spiritual one. A reminder of what came before."

My eyes fall again to the sketch of Ra, hidden beneath my hand. The fracture on his hull. The way Xion spoke of a great forgetting, a void in memory shared by every Eldercraft in existence.

Whatever came before... it didn't just vanish.

It broke.

CHAPTER
TWENTY-FOUR

"I want to try something new tonight." Xion closes the hangar door behind him, sealing us inside. The overhead floodlights click on with a rising hum, washing everything in white-blue light. His silhouette sharpens in the glow.

Tattoos coil up out of the collar of his aviator jacket, highlighting his taut, muscular neck.

My throat goes dry.

"It's a technique I picked up in the Prawn Nebula," he says, approaching slowly. "Their mystics believe Eldercraft aren't external. They're projections, born from the subconscious mind. Not machines. Not even beings. Interfaces. Between consciousness and the Divine." He stops in front of me, and that familiar smell of smoke and leather engulfs my senses. Ra hovers behind him, bobbing faintly like he knows we're talking about him.

"So... you're saying Ra is, like, my imaginary friend?"

"No," Xion says. "I'm saying Ra might be the part of you that still remembers God."

I swallow hard. "What do I do?"

"You sit. And you face him."

I lower myself to the cool concrete floor, crossing my legs and squaring my spine. Ra drifts slightly toward me in greeting, a low harmonic purring in his core.

"Should I close my eyes?" I ask, already halfway into a trance.

"No." Xion paces behind me, his heavy leather boots striking the floor with methodical regularity. "This exercise is about stripping away the preconceived categories that your conscious mind projects onto your surroundings. Try not to think of it as a meditation technique. It is simply a shifting of your awareness."

I settle in, grounding my weight on the floor.

"Now I want you to soften your focus." His voice rumbles deep in his throat, finding resonance in my chest. "The goal of this exercise is to see Ra as he truly is, without all the trappings of conscious perception. Your mind has all these categories like 'egg' and 'hieroglyphs' that it forces onto Ra, but the truth is far stranger and far more real."

His footfalls are like a metronome, lulling me into a relaxed state.

"Whatever you may think about Ra, be it alien, spaceship, artifact, whatever, I want you to momentarily put those qualities aside. Language is an amazing tool for communicating, but it can seriously impair true perception. I want you to imagine that you are not in Agartha. Not in the Hollow Earth. Imagine that you have never seen an egg or a spaceship before, and let the true essence of Ra reveal itself to you."

I blink slowly and relax my gaze, letting the edges blur, letting my breath slow until it feels like I'm exhaling through the soles of my feet. Ra begins to shimmer. Not literally, but in some subtle way that escapes the senses. Like the image of him is slipping off the hook of language.

And the crazy thing is that Ra has not changed at all. It is my perception that has changed. I realize that Ra is far more dense and intricate than I could ever have imagined. Our conscious minds strip out so much ineffable detail.

And then—

A sound. Or not a sound. A resonance.

Ra is humming. And somehow... so am I.

Our frequencies align, syncopating in a perfect chord that starts in my pelvis and rises like heat, unfurling up through my belly, my heart, my throat... until it bursts into a halo of sensation at the crown of my head.

And in that flash, Ra shifts.

Right in front of me, four curved panels on his surface retract in a slow, blooming motion, releasing soft jets of vapor and fine, ancient dust. The scent is earthy, electric— like ozone and petrichor, like the memory of rain on a planet I've never visited.

Where there was once only smooth surface, there is now an opening. A seat. Simple. Elegant. Waiting.

I hear Xion's boots approach again. He crouches beside me, silent and watching. When he speaks, his voice is lower than before, almost reverent.

"I'll never stop being amazed at how quickly you pick these things up." He holds out his hand, and I allow him to help me to my feet.

"What did I just do?"

"You," Xion says, stepping closer with a note of wonder in his voice, "just discovered Ra's cockpit."

I blink at the strange hollow in Ra's surface. It looks less like something designed to fly and more like something designed to envelop. The seat, if you can call it that, is molded from a smooth, pale material, somewhere between bone and muscle, shot through with pale veins and a lattice of glowing neural strands that vanish into the depths of Ra's interior.

"It looks... small," I murmur. "Claustrophobic."

"I have to admit, it's not what I expected either." Xion walks up to Ra's exposed interior and examines the jungle of white tendrils. "He's almost entirely biological. Even Nyx Arcana has metalwork, circuitry. But this? This is like stepping into a nervous system."

He turns, brushing dust from his palms. "Why don't you take him for a spin?"

I take a cautious step forward. "You mean... get in there?"

Ra's cockpit is nothing like the comparatively spacious interior of the Castor 5. Castor looked like a real spaceship. This looks like the inside of a brain.

"I bet these tendrils will connect you to Ra's consciousness." Xion seems fascinated by the craft's design. "Total synchronization. No need for buttons or levers. It will prevent you from losing focus during flight."

I reach out and poke the fleshy white armrest.

"What if I get trapped in there?"

"You know how to talk to Ra. I'm sure he'll spit you right back out whenever you want to leave."

I step up on the segment of Ra's shell that has descended like a step. "Okay. I'll try it."

"I'm opening the hangar doors," Xion says, striding off. "I'd prefer not to scrape you off the ceiling."

Ra lets out a little chuff of steam, like he's amused.

I step into the opening and lower myself into the seat. It's not cold like I expected. It's warm, pliant, almost... welcoming. The material gives just enough to cradle my spine and limbs, like it was made for me. It's less like sitting in something and more like being held.

I settle back against the headrest and with a hiss of warm vapor, Ra's petals fold inward, closing me inside.

The darkness is absolute. All sound has been cut off from the outside. It's like I'm in a sensory deprivation tank. I practice what Xion taught me and descend the imaginary steps to the deepest chamber of my mind. The door I'm not supposed to open is dripping water again.

Not tonight.

I turn, face my mental projection of Ra, and wait.

Tendrils slip forward and wrap around my temples, wrists, and spine, securing me to the seat.

Heat blooms through my skull where the tendrils attach, and bright lights appear in the peripheries of my vision.

Then, all of a sudden, my consciousness merges with Ra.

I see the hangar in flawless, surreal clarity. Every bolt, every cable, every mote of dust drifting in the filtered air. I see Xion by the doors, his form outlined by the glow of Ra's sensors. But it's more than sight. I know the pressure of his foot on the floor. The static electricity clinging to his jacket. The warmth of the hangar lamps. It's like the whole room is breathing. And I am breathing with it.

Fractals unfold inside everything I perceive. The grain of a screw expands into a constellation. The floor beneath me hums with molecular music. I have never felt so completely alive.

Is this how you always feel? I ask.

Yes. This is Ra's world.

It's... beautiful.

We hover in that shared awareness, awash in wonder.

Should we fly?

Ra... scared.

It will be just like hovering. Only faster.

We learn together, Synchronicity.

I smile.

Yeah. We do.

I don't so much command Ra forward as intend it, and the full mass of the Eldercraft lurches, my breath catching at the unexpected jolt.

Somewhere outside, I hear Xion shouting. It's muffled, garbled through the thick hull, just another piece of static in the symphony of my own disbelief.

Sorry, let me try that again.

Getting the neurological hang of it, I once again will Ra as an extension of myself toward the opening into the night beyond. This time the acceleration is slower, more gradual.

Nice! That was smooth. Let's keep going.

We glide out the bay doors into the craft field where multicolored indicator lights blink on the rows of RE craft.

Dark here.

It's nighttime. The sun won't be up for another eight hours.

Sun?

Not the real sun. The Agarthan sun. It's a big light that floats in the sky.

I sweep my gaze across the field, catching a flicker of movement. Xion bounds up the steps into Nyx Arcana. A second later, his voice crackles through the intercom.

"You hear me now?"

"Just fine," I say.

"I wasn't sure if this frequency would work with Ra.. Most crafts are embedded with specialized Logos Stones that allow for long-range communication." His voice is even more raw and gravelly over the intercom.

"So I pulled forward twenty feet." I speak it out loud instead of in my mind. "Do you want to call it a night?"

"Fuck no. I want to see what you can do. Follow my lead."

The sleek black frame of Nyx Arcana goes into a hover, then takes off toward the main pyramid, leaving me behind at the craft site.

"Hey, wait up!" I push Ra skyward. There's a moment, barely a breath, of stillness, then the world drops away.

The pyramid shrinks beneath us, its Logos capstone blazing like a cosmic lighthouse. The pull of gravity tugs my stomach into my tailbone as Ra pitches upward, rocketing toward the distant shimmer of fluorescent minerals embedded in the underside of Earth's surface.

Xion's voice crackles through the link. "Come on. I want to show you something."

"But I've never flown this high before," I say, and it's true. I only ever took the Castor 5 on low hovers and basic training maneuvers.

"Don't worry. If you lose control, I've got you."

He speeds ahead, tracing glowing arcs across the dark dome of the sky. I keep pace. We fly together across the Earth's inner expanse, racing over jagged mountains, then wide open deserts that glow faintly with moonstone reflections. Up ahead, a flare of brilliance... Sunlight breaking over the horizon from the curvature of the hollow world.

The Agarthan sun rises with the drama of a solar opera.

"Holy shit, that's beautiful," I whisper.

Holy Shit, Ra repeats.

"Not you, Ra. That's a bad word. Bad!"

Xion laughs over the channel. "You want to see more?"

"Is that even a question? Yes!"

Flying feels like molly, acid, and the thrill of riding a rollercoaster all rolled into one—an overwhelming cocktail that, under any other circumstance, would sound like a nightmare, but in this moment, it's the most exhilarating thing I've ever experienced.

Nyx Arcana shoots forward, carving a silver line across the false firmament, and I push Ra to follow. We arc toward Agartha's snow-covered pole, where the air grows sharper and rarefied.

Xion pulls into a steep ascent. I follow, zooming upward, up and up, until a giant hole resolves itself in the Earth's crust.

And beyond it: real sky.

We race through the rocky opening and flip inverted over the snow-laced surface of outer Earth.

"What the hell did I just see?"

"That's the North Pole," Xion says. "One of two openings to Agartha. The only natural entrances in or out."

"More like North *Hole*," I snort.

"Ha. Very funny."

"So... you're telling me every map I've ever seen was wrong?"

"Not wrong, just intentionally incomplete." Xion banks over a craggy peak and descends into a flightpath along a towering wall of blue ice.

"What is *that*?" It's like looking at an infinitely long glacier.

"The Ice Wall. What do you think holds back the oceans of Earth from flooding into Agartha?"

"I guess I never thought of that."

"Most people don't," Xion replies. "But I come here to think. There's something about the endless expanse of the sea lapping against immovable ice that really calms the mind."

"My mind is anything *but* calm right now."

"Focus, Synchronicity. This connection you have... It's powerful. But power without focus is a crash waiting to happen."

"Copy that, Captain."

"I'm not your fucking captain." Xion pulls up again, and I follow him over the rim of the Ice Wall. We shoot back across the Arctic landscape until I see the gaping hole on the horizon leading back into the hollow Earth.

I shoot ahead and take us into a gut-churning dive. We spiral through the breach in the crust, and the entire inner world of Agartha reappears like a pearl in a shell, radiant and waiting.

"You're picking this up quickly, Jones."

"It's easy," I say, high on adrenaline and awe. "I just go wherever my mind wants me to go."

And then that door at the back of my mind breaks open.

Thoughts of Aidan come flooding back. His face, his breath, his frozen body... Grief takes control before I know what's happening.

Red light flashes across Ra's interior.

We tilt.

We drop.

The world becomes a blur of descent and alarms.

Ra? I reach for him mentally, frantically.

Nothing.

Ra, are you there?

Still nothing.

Please, Ra, wake up!

But Ra is gone, vanished from our link. Like he's curled into himself, hiding from the storm inside me.

We spiral downward, falling fast through Agartha's inner sky, mountains rising up like teeth.

I brace for impact.

But at the last moment, the world holds its breath.

A deep, warm light envelops us, soft as a heartbeat.

We stop, floating inches above a jagged peak, cradled by the red shimmer of Nyx Arcana's tractor beam.

"What the hell happened back there?" Xion's voice is tense over the intercom.

"I don't know. I... lost control," I say. "There's something in my mind. Something I'm not supposed to see."

A long silence.

He lifts us gently, carrying Ra and me across the fractured peaks of the Agarthan range like some ancient guardian ferrying a wounded soul.

Then his voice again, low and steady this time. "Well, whatever it is, you're going to need to face it someday if you ever want to be a real pilot."

I close my eyes, still shaking, knowing he's right.

CHAPTER
TWENTY-FIVE

Xion says goodnight and shuts the door to his monastic, brutalist abode, leaving me alone in the silence of the craft site.

Or so I think.

"Sync?" a voice whispers from the dark.

I jump. Jasper steps out from behind an RE craft, followed closely by Mae, both of them wrapped in oversized cloaks.

"What was all that?" he asks. "We saw you come out of that hangar with Xion."

My heart kicks into overdrive. "I... It's not what it looked like."

Mae folds her arms, studying me with that intuitive gaze of hers. "Then what is it?"

I glance back towards Xion's ziggurat. All the lights are off. "Okay, I'll show you," I say, my voice barely a hush. "But you have to promise not to tell anyone."

We creep over to the hangar door, and I pull out the key Xion gave me to visit Ra.

"I'm serious, guys. You literally can't tell anyone about this. If Xion knew I showed you, he'd probably—"

"Were you going to say 'kill you?'" Jasper's eyes dart around the craft site. "Because he would, Sync. He's literally a killer. What are you doing with a key to his hangar anyway?"

"I'll show you, but you have to promise..."

"We get it. Top secret." Jasper makes an exaggerated sign of the cross. "Now show us already. It's freezing out here."

I look to Mae for a final check.

She nods. "We won't say a word. You have my oath."

"Okay." I take a deep breath and swing the door open.

"I can't see anything," Jasper says as the three of us walk inside.

"Just a second." I fumble for the switch in the dark and flip it on, flooding the massive interior space with light.

And there he is. Ra.

Hovering just above the platform, pale and otherworldly, his symbols flicker awake like fireflies sensing my presence.

"Oh my Source..." Mae holds her hand up to her mouth. "What is that thing?"

"Meet Ra," I say, a little breathless. "My Eldercraft."

"Your *what*?" Jasper says, blinking rapidly.

"I connected with him a few weeks ago. After Bo's death, I was suspicious about Xion and came snooping around, but instead of finding any evidence, I found Ra."

"You went spying on Xion... *without us*?" Jasper snaps.

"It was a spur-of-the-moment thing. Besides, Alien Isis wants this kept a complete secret. No one can know."

"Alien Isis is in on it, too?" Jasper says. "I can't believe you were keeping this all a secret from us. This is *huge*."

"He's beautiful." Mae walks up to Ra and runs her hand along his engraved surface. Ra makes the ancient stone equivalent of a purring sound and lights up even brighter on the areas that Mae touches. "He's cute, too."

"He's kind of like a baby. We're still figuring everything out. Xion's been giving me private lessons."

"So *that's* why you've been acting so strange," Jasper says.

"A baby Eldercraft," Mae muses. "I've never heard of such a thing."

"Neither has Xion. That's why we're keeping it secret. Alien Isis says if the Federation found out, they'd tear this place apart to get at him."

"That tracks," Jasper says, nervously rubbing his hands together. "Federation tech freaks would dissect him molecule by molecule. He'd never be safe."

"I don't even like leaving him alone in here," I say. "He should be flying, playing outside... But if anyone finds out—"

"They won't," Mae says, taking my hand. "We won't tell. Not a soul."

I nod, heart heavy with the weight of the risk. "Thanks. I'm sorry I didn't tell you earlier. Are you guys mad at me?"

Jasper's face twists in disbelief. "Mad? Sync, this is

amazing. Eldercraft pilots are rare enough, but an Earthseed connected to a never-before-seen egg craft? That's legendary."

Mae grins. "It's not just awesome, it's you. You're meant for this."

"Yeah?" I ask, throat tight.

Jasper places a hand on Ra's warm hull. "Hell yeah. And now you've got the perfect cover to keep an eye on Xion."

I stiffen. "You still think he—"

"I don't know *what* I think," Jasper interrupts. "But I know he's hiding something. And if we're gonna protect you and Ra... we need to find out what."

CHAPTER
TWENTY-SIX

A week later, Xion and I sit on top of the Castor 5 after another training session with Ra. The glowing underside of the Earth rotates overhead in its slow, celestial crawl, casting an ambient light on the field of dormant craft below.

"I had a bad day in Energy Work," I mutter, hugging my knees against my chest. "Sometimes I think I'm the least spiritual person in this entire school."

He rolls a cigarette with those deft, inked fingers, sealing it with a flick of his tongue. From his pocket, he draws a worn brass lighter, igniting the tip before taking a long drag. "You want some?"

"Fine."

He passes it to me. The first inhale hits like a punch, smoke curling hot down my throat, my head already floating. I haven't had one since... well, since the surface.

"You know," Xion says, his voice low and even, "being spiritual isn't always about prayer beads and meditation. Sometimes it's about sitting in the wreckage. Touching the darkest part of yourself without flinching."

"What if I don't want to touch those parts?" I say, passing the cigarette back to him. "What if they would quite literally kill me?"

"You remember that playwright I told you about?"

"Braggart Thickneck or whatever?"

"Braghzor Zhurn'ekk," he corrects with a ghost of a smile. "He said no warrior gets to heaven unless his soul has walked through hell."

Brooding, angry, deadly Xion is a sight that sends my heart racing, but Xion quoting spiritual truths with that deep yearning on his face has to be one of the most beautiful things I've ever seen. My stupid, broken soul feels like it might be ready to open again.

I shift closer. "Sounds kind of evil."

"It's not evil," he says. "It's honest. We all have darkness in us. Deny it, and it grows stronger. Acknowledge it, and maybe, just maybe, you can find a light worth keeping."

"I guess I'm still looking for the light," I say.

Silence settles between us, thick and alive.

"Is that why you sneak off to Moongate's house in the middle of the night?" he asks suddenly. "Trying to find the light?"

Is that a flash of jealousy in his eyes?

I freeze. "You're keeping tabs on me?"

He simply shrugs those massive shoulders. "Had to make sure you weren't giving away our little secret."

My pulse spikes. I have no right to be mad, considering Mae and Jasper talked me into spying on *him*. But part of me still bristles. "It's none of your business who I spend my nights with."

I don't tell him that he's right. Some part of me feels that if I could get someone like Kai to like me, maybe that would mean I wasn't such a bad person after all.

Xion's voice is a quiet growl. "Moongate's a good healer. That doesn't mean he's good for you."

I narrow my eyes. "And what, you are? At least he's trying to improve himself. What are you doing, Xion? Hiding in hangars and brooding about a dead planet?"

His jaw ticks, and I can tell I crossed a line.

"I'm sorry, I shouldn't have said that."

He doesn't answer immediately. Just takes another drag, the cigarette tip burning red in the dark.

"Fuck self-improvement," he spits. "It's masturbation for the ego. You want the truth? Real awakening comes from accepting the whole damn thing. Even the parts you're ashamed of. Hell, *especially* those."

He passes me the smoldering remains of the cigarette, fingers brushing mine.

"I wish I believed that," I say quietly. "But the truth is, I've been buried in the dark for so long... I don't know where the rest of me went. I'm not even sure who I am anymore."

I look over to him, and the tattooed lines that trace his

cheekbones seem to shimmer in the glow of the Earthlight. His eyes, those molten gold embers, don't burn. They ache.

A silence stretches between us, fragile as glass.

And suddenly I can't breathe. Because this—this is the moment before something irrevocable. This is standing at the edge of a cliff, and knowing if I take one more step, I won't be able to turn back.

This is so fucking dangerous.

He is so fucking dangerous.

And I want him anyway.

His voice breaks the silence, low and steady. "I want to teach you something. A way to talk to Ra even when you're not with him."

My eyes light up. "Really?"

"That way you don't spend the day worrying if he misses you." He turns to me, lifts a hand—and then both—cupping my face with such unexpected gentleness it stills my breath. His thumbs rest along my cheekbones, fingers threading beneath the base of my skull until my head is fully cradled between his hands. The warmth of him floods through me.

"Close your eyes." His voice rumbles like thunder across slickrock.

It occurs to me, briefly, that he could snap my neck with a flick of his wrists. But I trust him. And that's the scariest part.

I close my eyes.

"Start like you would when connecting with Ra, but this time don't envision any place in particular. Visualize nothing."

"And how am I supposed to do that?" I bite my upper lip but keep my eyes shut.

"Imagine you are in the vast expanse of space. Not the kind with stars. The kind before stars. Pure nothingness. An infinite void in every direction. Left, right, above, below. Just black silence. Endless and still. And you're floating at its center."

I settle into the strong embrace of his hands and try to visualize absolute nothing surrounding me. It gives me the uncanny sensation of floating.

"And now," he continues, "on your next inhale, I want you to pull up on your perineum."

My eyes pop open. "On my *what*?"

"You know, maybe this is too advanced a practice for you." He lets go and turns away with a smirk.

"No wait. I'm sorry. I want to learn."

"The perineum is located where the cerebral spinal fluid pools. By pulling up on it, you push that fluid up your spine, sending electromagnetic signals out into the cosmos. Believe me. Since we're from the same star system, we have a similar anatomy."

I groan under my breath. "Okay, fine. Let me try again.

He places his hands back on my face, and I close my eyes once more.

"When you pull up and inhale, focus on what you want to say. You and Ra are tuned to the same energetic frequency now. That bond will carry your message to him wherever he is."

I imagine myself floating in the center of it. An infinite void of nothing. I blow all the air out of my lungs and on my next inhale, I pull up on my pelvic floor, mentally vibrating the words: "Hello Ra."

"And now," Xion whispers, "on the exhale, listen."

I let my breath go, slow and steady, until my lungs are empty. For a moment, there's nothing but silence. Just when I'm about to give up and try again, Ra's voice comes echoing into my mind.

Synchronicity.

I smile but keep my eyes closed.

On my next inhale, I send out the words: "How are you?"

Ra.

That's it. Just his name. But I can feel his contentment in the tone, like a cat purring in a language beyond words.

I open my eyes to find Xion searching my face.

"It worked," I say softly.

His expression doesn't change, but I see it in his eyes. A

flash of impressed wonder. "That took me two weeks to figure out," he says. "You did it in one try."

Heat flushes across my cheeks. I try not to let the pride show too much. "Guess I just had a good teacher."

He brushes the tender skin above my cheekbones with those rough fingers, studying my face like it's some alien artifact he needs to decipher. His thumb traces an arc across my jaw. And then he stops.

His gaze drops to my mouth.

God.

The hunger in his eyes isn't subtle. It's a furnace. A starving animal on the edge of restraint. His jaw flexes, stone-carved and unreadable, before he suddenly yanks his hands away and turns his face to the dark.

"Shit," he growls under his breath. "That was a mistake."

My breath hitches. "What?"

"Touching you."

"A terrible mistake," I say, glancing over at him. "You should never have done it."

His voice is barely audible. "And kissing you would be..."

"Disastrous," I finish for him. The space between us feels like pure electricity, like trying to keep two magnets apart. If something doesn't relieve this tension, the whole universe might explode.

"We're going to regret this," he says, but his voice is unraveling. I can feel him fraying under the weight of his own willpower.

I look him in the eye and say, "I don't care."

Suddenly, the space between us collapses. His mouth crashes into mine like a comet against stone. All heat and gravity and ruin. My body goes molten.

Fuck. Yes.

Somehow, this is exactly what I need.

I don't even remember falling backward, but suddenly the cold metal of the Castor 5 is against my spine, and Xion is over me, devouring me like he's been waiting lifetimes to taste this.

I open for him—lips, heart, soul—and his tongue finds mine with slow devastation. His body is pure violence held barely in check, and I crave every deadly inch of him. Every fucked up, forbidden part.

He tastes like ash and leather and something ancient, like the ghost of a burned-down temple. And I want more. More of his mouth, his weight, his darkness.

He slides a hand beneath the hem of my shirt, palm scorching against my ribs. My hips respond before I even think, rising to meet him. We move together like we've always known how.

When he rolls onto me, pressing all that coiled muscle and Maldekian tension into my body, something inside me splits wide open. I wrap my legs around his waist. Arch into him. If I had any self-control left, it's all gone now.

He kisses my throat, my collarbone, every inch of me he can reach, and I swear to every star in the galaxy I've never wanted anything more.

No one has ever made me feel this way before. No first kiss has ever driven me so mad with desire. It's fucking terrifying because I know in this moment he has the power to utterly destroy me.

And that would be just fine.

Hell, I'd beg for more.

The last ounces of tension melt away from my body, and I give in completely, surrendering to the insatiable need in my core. I watch him lose all control, and for a moment, we are a coil of lips and hands and want, and it feels like I'm in the void of my mind again because nothing else exists.

But then, just as the last of my resistance burns away, a flicker of doubt flashes through the back of my mind...

That package.

That damn disappearing package.

I break the kiss. My voice comes out low, husky, trembling. "Can I ask you something?"

He goes still above me. I feel the tension in his spine even before I see it in his face.

"What?" he asks, already guarded.

"That package. The one in Nyx. We didn't go to that cavern just to train, did we?"

He gets up and sits on the edge of the craft. The silence stretches long and cold.

"No," he says finally.

"Who did you give it to?"

He looks away, jaw tightening, refusing to meet my eyes.

"You should go."

The words drop like a stone into my chest.

"Why?" I ask.

"Because this is stupid. I'm your teacher."

He pauses. Turns those amber eyes on me again. Eyes full of fire and pain and something impossibly tender.

"And because I'm Maldekian. You're an Earthseed. Interspecies relationships are forbidden."

"But we're from the same star system," I protest. "You said it yourself. We have the same anatomy."

He shakes his head like he's weighed down by something bigger than both of us. "It doesn't matter. We can't, Synchronicity. I won't."

"Why?" I whisper. "Because you're afraid you'll like it? Or because you already do?"

His silence is the loudest answer of all.

He looks back out at the night sky, Earthlight catching the edge of his tattoos like shattered obsidian.

I slide off the Castor and stand barefoot on the gravel. "You know," I say, keeping my voice soft, "this doesn't have to be so complicated. We could be good for each other."

But he doesn't even look at me.

He just lights another cigarette, exhaling smoke into the cold, uncaring night.

CHAPTER
TWENTY-SEVEN

To say the next six weeks are weird would be an understatement.

Xion doesn't so much as look at me unless it's to bark a flight instruction or correct my form. Our mandatory nighttime Eldercraft lessons have become tight-lipped drills in spatial awareness, entirely devoid of the intensity and fire that once crackled between us.

In daytime craft class, I might as well not exist.

Part of me wants to confront him about that night, but with my Energy Work midterm looming in just a few short weeks, I've got bigger problems to worry about.

Despite hours of study with Kai and relentless coaching from Mae and Jasper, I still haven't been able to manifest a single *wisp* of healing energy.

"Maybe you could borrow my ukulele," Mae suggests.

"Somehow, I don't think Alien Sylestra would allow that." I slump further into the barstool at the Larimar House kitchen island, cradling a mug of something warm I've already forgotten the name of.

"Speaking of your ukulele..." Jasper pops the last bite of a banana into his mouth and finishes chewing. "What time does your audition start?"

"Oh shit, we need to get going." Mae stands up from leaning on the counter and adjusts her colorful crocheted skirt.

"Let me grab my jacket, and we'll be off." Jasper bounds up the wooden stairs, Mochi scampering at his heels with a chirpy squeal.

I smile at Mae.

"I'm proud of you, you know. This is big."

"It's just an audition," she says, tucking a lock of hair behind her ear, "but maybe I'll be the next member of Supermoon." Her voice lilts with a quiet hope.

"They'd be idiots not to pick you."

Mae blushes, then calls out toward the common room. "Peter? Want to come with?"

Peter doesn't respond, at least not verbally. His curtain of black hair hangs low as he scribbles furiously into his ever-present notebook. Perched on the back of his chair, his raven spirit animal lets out a low, guttural sound that could mean *no*, or possibly *doom*.

"Are you sure?" Mae asks again, gentler this time. "It's gonna be fun."

He shakes his head, eyes never leaving the page.

"You're always welcome to join us if you want." Mae leans in closer to me and whispers, "I like to try and include him."

"That's good," I say.

A moment later, Jasper dashes down the stairs in a knee-length psychedelic pea coat. He strikes a pose. "Are you two witches ready to rock?"

A late November chill has descended over campus, and the few leaves that remain on the trees tremble in the brisk night air. We make our way past the main pyramid, lit from the inside by the crystal lamps of professors working late into the night.

We follow the lantern-lit path into the market district, where *Elixir,* the campus kava bar, is already pulsing with life. Trippy lights undulate from violet to blood orange, painting the crowd in liquid color. Ambient bass reverberates through the walls and floors, giving the space the feel of a waking dream.

Jasper forges ahead through the crowd, dragging us behind him like his personal entourage until we reach the bar. He elbows out a pocket of room so we can read the glowing menu.

"I'll take a Lotus Latte," I say.

"Just structured water for me," Mae says.

Jasper raises an eyebrow. "Really?"

"I gotta stay sharp." Mae shrugs.

He leans over the counter, flashing the bartender a

charismatic grin. "We'll take one Lotus Latte, one Celebration Jun, a glass of structured water, and three kava shots."

"Kava shots?" Mae arches a brow.

"Come on, you need a little something to loosen you up."

She rolls her eyes but concedes with a smirk. "Fine. But if I start dancing like June at last week's bonfire, this is on you."

I glance across the room. "Speaking of, Kara's here." Across the crowd, Kara, Vaylen, and June perch at a corner table, sipping martini mocktails, each wearing a matching wide-brimmed hat like some occult fashion coven.

"Oh Source," Mae mutters, half-hiding behind her hair. "That's just what I need. I'm gonna be so nervous."

"All the more reason for kava shots." Jasper picks up the three glasses of milky white liquid and hands them to us. "To Mae," he says, holding out his own glass. "The next member of Supermoon!"

"To Mae!" I clink glasses with my friends and shoot back the delightfully earthy and mouth-numbing substance.

The rest of our drinks arrive just as the house music fades and the bar dims, drawing attention to the small stage near the back.

A tall figure with waist-length dreadlocks steps into the spotlight. "Evening, everyone. First of all, shout out to Elixir for letting us throw this tonight. Big round of applause for the staff!"

The room whoops and whistles, hands raised in gratitude.

"I'm Jason Starsong," he continues, his voice honeyed and warm. "Tonight's audition will determine the next member of Supermoon. Traditionally, we're a seven-piece band, but one of our members graduated last year. So we're looking for someone new to join the journey. Doesn't matter what you play. We're looking for presence, resonance. Vibe."

He holds up a crumpled piece of paper. "I've got a list here, but if your name's not on it, just head over to my man Rojo by the side table. He'll sign you up."

"Shit, I forgot to sign up." Mae thrusts her water at me and disappears into the crowd.

Jason Starsong clears his throat. "One more thing. The winner of tonight's audition will not only be the newest member of Supermoon, but they will join us to play the Solstice Dance, which we just found out we are headlining this year!"

The crowd erupts into applause.

"So without further ado, I'd like to welcome..." He fumbles with the paper in his hands. "...Kara Volkova to the stage!"

Vaylen and June kiss their friend on the cheek before she takes her place in front of the crowd. Kara has her shamanic hand drum with her, and she coaxes the audience into silence with a steady beat. "This is an old Siberian journey song I was taught by my ancestors. May it take you where you need to go."

She sways to the rhythm with her eyes closed. As the beat grows stronger, the characteristic yellow glow of Lyran energy begins to radiate from her instrument. The steady thump of the drum has me halfway in a hypnotic state when Kara starts to sing.

"Damn, she's good." Mae is back by my side, her gold-tinted blush glinting in the light of Kara's music.

The song gets more intense, and the threads of glowing yellow energy spool out into the audience, wrapping around their crown chakras and gently piercing the spot on their foreheads known as the third eye.

Soon Mae, Jasper, and I all have our arms over each other's shoulders and are swaying right along with Kara, her enchanting song taking us all on an invisible journey.

When it ends, it's like waking from a trance. The applause is thunderous.

"That's going to be hard to follow," Jasper mutters, sipping his Jun.

"Not just hard. Impossible." A dejected look falls across Mae's face. "She's gonna get it for sure."

"Hey, we don't know that." I rub Mae on the back between

her shoulder blades. "You're gonna blow her out of the water."

The following act is a woman with a crystal flute. Then a man drags a massive gong on stage before inundating the crowd with a cacophony of reverberating metallic strikes.

Jasper orders another round of kava shots, and I chase mine with a second Lotus Latte. The drinks flow, as does the golden Lyran energy pouring out into the crowd. Not all the musicians are Lyran Starseeds, but most are. I am brought back to my festival-going days before all that shit happened a year ago, and for the first time since then, I'm feeling like myself.

Finally, Jason Starsong calls Mae's name. She's one of the last to perform, maybe the very last, and it's well past midnight. My nerves are tangled. Part of me wants to be fully present for her, but the other part is itching to check on Ra.

I take a deep breath and do the telepathic technique Xion taught me. I slip into the nothing. My lungs expand. The message goes out.

Ra? It's me. Just checking in. How are you feeling?

A pause. Then, faintly:

Ra... cold.

Shit. The hangar is drafty as hell, and I forgot to adjust the thermostat. I make a mental note to fix it before bed.

Don't worry. I'll be back soon to warm you up.

Mae takes the stage and swings her ukulele around to the front.

"Hi, everyone. My name is Mae Rivers, and I am truly honored to be up here." Her voice is bright but trembles slightly.

"Woo! Go Mae!" Jasper hollers beside me.

"You've all done so well tonight. I don't know how I'm going to follow some of your performances, but I'll give it a shot." Mae's crocheted skirt and crop-top show off her tattoos and beautifully tanned skin. Her golden dreadlocks crown her face like a halo, radiant even under the low lights. "This is a song I wrote called 'Feral Dreams.'"

The crowd murmurs its encouragement and quiets.

Mae strums her ukulele, sending out golden sparks of Lyran energy that twinkle in the air around her like tiny fireflies.

"Thorns in my hair and dirt on my skin,
I shed this world I've been living in.
Calling back to the beast I've become,
My voice is a flame, my heart is a drum..."

"She's so freaking beautiful," I whisper to Jasper.

"I *know*, right?" he whispers back. "If she doesn't win this, I'm setting Mochi loose on that Starsong guy."

Mae's voice grows stronger as golden rivers of energy pour out from her instrument, swirling through the crowd.

"Wolf-eyed visions in twilight's gleam,
Velvet shadows split at the seam.
I don't belong in glass and chrome,
My wild soul knows only..."

She falters. Her voice catches like a skipping record. A croak slips out instead of the next line. Her fingers stumble on the strings, producing a jarring chord that pierces the warm spell she had cast.

I wince. Her cheeks flush crimson as she tries again.

"My wild soul knows only..."

She tries to speak, but nothing comes out. For some reason, I am reminded of my first day in Energy Work class.

That's when I notice it. The blue flame under the teapot at the bar flaring far too high. And Vaylen, her hand subtly extended, lips moving in a whisper. It's hard to tell in this low light, but her eyes look almost... black.

I don't think. I move.

Shoving past a cluster of Lyran Starseeds in paisley shawls, I reach her and, without hesitation, throw the remains of my milky blue Lotus Latte straight in her smug, whispering face.

"Hey!" she sputters, drenched and furious.

"Knock it off," I snap. "I know what you're doing."

Vaylen blinks, stunned, then sneers. "Will someone get this fucking Earthseed out of here?"

The room tenses. A few heads turn. Jason Starsong, already moving toward the stage, grabs the mic.

"Thank you, Miss Rivers," he says gently. "And thank you all for coming out tonight. The vibes are getting a little... spicy, so let's go ahead and close our tabs. We'll announce the winner in the coming days. Be safe out there."

"You're fucking dead," Vaylen hisses before letting out a frustrated screech and stomping off toward the bathroom. June and Kara trail after her like rattled courtiers.

"I'm not going to say she didn't deserve it, but why exactly did you throw your drink in Vaylen's face?" Jasper has sidled up next to me at the bar, settling the tab with the bartender.

"She was making Mae choke. Just like she did to me on our first day in Energy Work. It's her fucked up Sirian healing powers. They hurt you before they heal you."

"That *bitch!*"

"God, I hope I didn't ruin Mae's chances of getting in."

"You did the right thing," Jasper says.

Mae finds us through the crowd, tears welling up in her eyes. When she reaches us, she breaks down and cries. "I choked, guys. I don't know if it was being nervous or what. That's never happened to me before."

"It wasn't you." I wrap my arm around Mae's shoulders. "It was Vaylen. She was trying to make you choke."

Mae starts crying harder. Her body trembles in my arms.

"You did amazing up there. I'm sure Jason heard your talent even from the small bit you played. It was beautiful, Mae."

I spot Jasper in the crowd, chatting with the lead singer and gesturing our way. "Look, Jasper's putting in a good word for you."

"I don't know if a good word is enough to fix what

happened." Mae wipes her nose on the back of her hand. "Let's just get out of here."

We jostle with the crowd out into the night. Jasper catches up with us just outside.

"Well," he says, flinging his arms around both of us, "I told him what really happened. If justice exists, you're still in the running."

"Thanks," Mae murmurs. "But I'm not holding my breath."

Just as we round the corner and the lights from Elixir fade behind us, a message trickles into my mind like frost on glass.

Ra... cold.

CHAPTER
TWENTY-EIGHT

"Do you mind if we swing by the craft site?" I ask. "I just need to check on Ra real quick. Maybe he'll cheer you up, Mae."

She sniffles. "I guess."

"As long as we don't run into Xion," Jasper mutters. "I'm not trying to get murdered tonight."

"He's probably asleep," I say. Truth is, I'm not ready to see him either.

When we reach the craft field, Nyx Arcana is gone, and the hangar looms quiet in the dark. I pull out the key Xion gave me and unlock the door.

As soon as we step inside, Ra pulses awake with a cheerful hum, lifting off the support arms and gliding across the hangar to greet me. He nudges my jacket with the smooth curve of his ancient shell.

"I know, buddy. I'm sorry I left it cold in here."

As I fumble along the wall for the thermostat, Mae plops down on Ra's crash pad with her head slumped. "Everything just... went so wrong."

Ra circles toward her, humming softly.

"Hey, Ra," she says, reaching out a hand to stroke the glowing glyphs on his side. "You ever bomb a performance before?"

Ra tilts his shell like a confused puppy and lets out a curious coo.

"Didn't think so," Mae mutters, lying back on the mat.

"Come on," Jasper says. "Let Ra be your emotional support egg."

That earns the tiniest laugh. Ra spins slowly around Mae and vibrates his favorite mantra: "SPINNN."

Mae giggles for real this time and pulls her ukulele into her lap. She strums a few soft chords. To our surprise, different glyphs on Ra's surface flicker to life with each note, glowing in sync with her melody.

"Oh wow..." I breathe, stepping closer.

Mae keeps playing, improvising now, weaving whimsy into every note. Ra glows brighter with each passing chord, his blue glyphs dancing like raindrops.

And then a symbol flares to life. Brighter than the rest.

A sudden burst of light projects from his hull, and a holographic vision blooms into the center of the hangar.

We go still.

A pristine civilization unfolds before us. Ivory towers rise toward turquoise skies, starships gliding gracefully between crystalline spires. Eldercraft drift like sentient stars above cities that pulse with peace and purpose.

"What is this...?" Mae whispers.

"It must be the Elder civilization," Jasper says, stunned.

But then, a dark shape cuts across the sky. A black comet, trailing smoke and rot in its wake.

It strikes.

There's a shockwave of blinding light.

Then, shadow erupts.

Clouds of writhing black energy spill forth, slithering like sentient ink across the glowing civilization, infecting everything. People collapse. Light dims. Buildings crumble. The Elders vanish.

Then: fast-forward.

Stars are born. Galaxies spiral.

A new planet emerges.

Maldek. Harsh, red, brutal. Obsidian temples rise. Red-skinned beings, Maldekians, build with tireless ambition. For a moment, it's almost beautiful.

Then the shadows return. More refined now. Hungrier.

The Maldekians fall to madness. A final flash, a supernova of destruction... And the world rips apart.

Asteroids drift. Silence reigns.

The hologram flickers and dies.

We're left in the quiet dark, the glyphs on Ra's hull still glowing faintly, as if catching their breath.

Mae's voice is barely a whisper. "Those shadows... they looked exactly like the things we saw over Bo's body."

It's like the veil thins for a moment, and I glimpse a pattern older than any of us.

"If those same entities destroyed both the Elders and Maldek," I murmur, the pieces snapping into place, "then whatever killed Bo... whatever might be connected to Xion... It's not just a threat to this school."

I meet their eyes.

"It's a threat to the whole damn galaxy."

CHAPTER
TWENTY-NINE

First thing in the morning, the three of us race across campus, our breath fogging against the paling dawn. We climb the stairs that lead up the center of the Great Pyramid and wait in silence outside the polished, crystal-laden doors to Alien Isis's office. Jasper paces. Mae wrings her hands. My heart hammers in my throat.

When the doors open, we step into that space that feels more celestial temple than administrative chamber. The high windows catch the golden glow of the Agarthan sun and scatter it across the walls in soft prisms. Tall plumes of white smoke drift up from censers hanging beside the angled windows.

Alien Isis looks up slowly. Her iridescent skin shimmers like moonstone, and her white robes fall around her in a perfect geometric drape. She clasps her long fingers before her and regards us with her usual serene intensity, equal parts benevolent goddess and executive high priestess.

"Alien Isis, I'm sorry to interrupt," Jasper blurts, "but we think Xion killed Bo."

Isis's face remains unreadable, but something flickers behind her eyes. "That's quite an accusation to hurl, Mr. Collins. I assume you have some evidence to support your claim?"

"Last night... we were in the hangar," he starts.

"Which hangar?" Her voice is calm, but the temperature in the room seems to drop several degrees.

"Ra's hangar," Mae blurts out, then winces.

Isis turns her gaze on me. "Am I to understand that you've exposed the Eldercraft to your friends here?"

"I'm sorry, Alien Isis. But I trust them. They're my family. They're not going to tell anyone."

"The more people who know about this, Synchronicity, the more fragile our safety becomes. You know what could happen if the Federation finds out about this."

"The Federation might need to find out," I say. "Ra showed us a vision last night—of the Elder civilization being completely wiped out. It was the same dark energy we saw hovering over Bo's body. It's coming back."

"Not only that," Jasper adds, stepping forward. "I've been researching this. I believe what we saw were Draconids. Fifth-dimensional parasitic entities that feed on negative emotion. I think they're responsible for the fall of Maldek. And if that's true... then Xion might be infected."

Mae looks up from the floor, her voice trembling. "I know it sounds crazy. But we saw it. We all saw it."

Alien Isis studies us in silence, her long fingers steepled under her chin. The ambient glow of the glyphs on her desk seems to dim.

"Energy vampires," she says at last, her tone slow and practiced, "are a myth. What you witnessed was likely a symbolic dramatization, a cautionary vision about the trappings of power recorded by the Elders and embedded in Ra's memory. Nothing more."

"Bo is dead," I say. "And I don't think it was an accident."

Her eyes flash. "That is not your conclusion to make."

"But what if it's real?" I press. "What if Ra's memory wasn't symbolic? What if that's what really destroyed the Elders, and Maldek, and now—"

Isis stands.

The radiant energy around her intensifies, and suddenly I feel like a child caught yelling in a cathedral.

"I suggest," she says, her voice now impossibly soft and terrifyingly final, "you focus on your studies. Midterms are approaching. If you allow yourselves to spiral into conspiracy and paranoia, you risk not only your grades but the security of this entire school."

"But Alien Isis—" Mae starts, tears brimming in her eyes.

Isis doesn't blink. "Put it out of your minds."

A long, uncomfortable silence.

And then she sits again. "That will be all."

We leave, walking out of her chamber with the heavy weight of silenced truth pressing down on all of us.

We descend the granite steps in silence, the sting of her dismissal still echoing in my ears. None of us speak. Outside, the Agarthan morning is still wrapped in shadow, and a frost has crept across the pathways.

Maybe she's right. Maybe we're just seeing patterns in the dark.

But the vision Ra showed us won't leave my mind—and the look on Isis's face, the flicker of something behind her carefully controlled expression, tells me she's hiding more than she's saying.

CHAPTER
THIRTY

Despite Mae's best efforts to recreate the melodic sequence that triggered Ra's vision, the mystery of the Draconids remains locked behind uncooperative glyphs. As November quietly dissolves into December, the school settles beneath the hush of approaching midterms, and I find myself caught between worlds. One ancient and celestial; the other bound by study guides and solstice exams.

Snow blankets the ground in Atum Crater, where we gather around the pristine blue pool for our herbalism midterm. Alien Thumgren waits in her usual leather sandals, her squat green toes poking defiantly from beneath a fur-trimmed parka.

"Glorious morning to all," she trills. "As you know, I don't believe in written exams. I prefer the wisdom of experience. And what better way to honor the solstice than with a living test beneath the open sky?"

My feet are already freezing inside my boots. I don't know how she does it.

"Midwinter is the time when almost all plant life has retreated into a state of dormancy. However, there is one plant that is begging our attention. The Siberian cedar, or *Pinus sibirica*, that grows in the upper reaches of the north-facing slope of the crater, has a very unique needle shape that gathers positive electromagnetic frequencies and concentrates them in the heartwood of the plant."

Myco, her mole-nosed squirrel companion, scampers up her parka and hands her a perfectly glossy acorn. "Thank you, sweetie." She kisses his tiny head and tucks the nut into her pocket like a treasure before brandishing a small ceremonial axe.

"When the Siberian cedar reaches the end of its life, its wood is so saturated with positive energy that the tree literally begins to ring. A tree like this is calling out to be harvested so that its energy can be shared with all beings.

Our job today is to find such a tree and cut it down for the Solstice Dance tonight."

Alien Thumgren trudges ahead through the snow-covered slopes of Atum Crater, a squat green Sherpa wrapped in furs, her ceremonial axe doubling as a walking stick. With each determined step, she carves a trail through the knee-deep powder, leading us toward a grove of solemn Siberian cedars. Ice crystals shimmer on their outstretched branches, catching the morning light like scattered diamonds. As we step beneath their canopy, the world falls hushed. The grove feels less like a forest and more like a sanctuary.

Alien Thumgren turns and addresses the class. "I want you to split up into pairs. Whoever finds the ringing cedar will win this persimmon as a prize." She holds out the immaculate orange fruit in her stubby fingers like some sort of rare gem. "Well, what are you waiting for? Get listening!"

I scan the crowd, hoping to spot Cassandra, but before I can move, Peter Quinn steps up beside me. Maybe it's the solstice season, but he looks a little cheerier than usual.

"Do you want to be my partner?" His black hair is slicked back, revealing a pale, acne-pocked forehead, and the raven on his shoulder scrutinizes me with its obsidian eyes.

"Sure." I'm surprised, but not unpleasantly so. He usually hovers like a shadow in the common area of Mae and Jasper's dorm, scribbling into his notebook like some arcane sorcerer. Today, he almost seems... open.

"I like the plot you picked for lab." He starts walking in a random direction, presumably in search of this ringing cedar. "You should be able to grow a wide variety of plants in the spring."

"Thanks. Yours is in the desert section, right?"

He nods, crunching ahead. "I've been studying the cryptobiotic soil there. I believe it has untapped potential for healing remedies."

"I've never heard of that," I admit.

"If you didn't know what it was, you would think it was just dirt. But actually, it's an advanced colony of lichen, mosses, and cyanobacteria that no one really knows about. Yet."

"That's actually pretty fascinating, Peter." We step further into the grove, and a branchful of snow comes tumbling down, catching the air and dancing in the sunlight like a vortex of stardust.

We both pause to admire the moment.

"I was wondering, well, if you weren't going with anyone else..." He turns to face me, and I can tell it's a struggle for him to make eye contact. "Would you go to the Solstice Dance with me tonight?"

I blink. I hadn't really thought about it. Mae's going with Jasper. Kara's out of the picture. Kai is chaperoning the damn thing, and I know Xion wouldn't be caught dead near a school dance.

"Sure," I say. "I'm all yours."

Peter's eyes go wide. "Really? That's... I mean, great. This is Persephone, by the way." He gestures to the raven on his shoulder. "Not sure if you two have been properly introduced."

Persephone lets out a low croak and takes flight, gliding through the grove before landing on the gnarled bough of a stately cedar. She taps her beak against the bark like she's trying to tell us something.

"Did you hear that?" I stop walking, my breath catching in the still air.

"Hear what?"

"Shhh." I hold up a hand.

And then there it is, faint and pure. A ringing. Like the sound of a glass harp echoing from deep within the tree.

We creep closer, and the sound becomes unmistakable. A resonant frequency, humming in the marrow of the wood.

"I think... this is it." Peter presses his ear to the trunk, and his expression shifts. Wonder. Awe. Maybe a little fear.

"Alien Thumgren!" I call out, turning toward the slope. "I think we found the tree."

CHAPTER
THIRTY-ONE

The same tree Peter and I found now stands proudly in the central plaza before the Great Pyramid of Agartha, strung with moonstone lights and garlands of orange peel and clove. Alien Thumgren reminded us that the Siberian cedar only sings when it's ready to give back the light it's stored across lifetimes. If we hadn't cut it down, it would've died in silence.

We'd all taken turns with the axe until the massive tree gave way with a groan and tumbled down the crater wall, its fall cushioned by the snow.

I did get to see Xion unexpectedly, or at least his ship, when he flew over to pick up the tree and transport it back to the main part of campus. I'm not going to lie, the sight of Nyx Arcana flying sleek and lethal over the horizon sent my heart thundering, not so much because of the ship, but because of the man I knew was piloting it.

"Damn, Synchronicity. You look hot," Mae says, adjusting the translucent scarf around her neck. She's gone full winter-rave fairy queen. White go-go boots, layers of shimmering mesh, and silver bangles stacked up both arms. She's traded her ukulele for a gleaming white hula hoop that catches the light like a prism.

I glance down at my black tights, hand-me-down Docs, and the thrifted sweater dress that hugs me in all the right places. "Shut up. You're the hot one. You look like a snow angel that dropped acid."

"Please, ladies, hold the compliments until after the celebration." Jasper swans in wearing a fur coat open to the navel, no shirt underneath, tight black trousers, and glitter in his hair. Even Mochi sports a festive red-and-green vest that jingles when he moves.

"I wasn't talking to you, Jasper." I roll my eyes in fake exasperation.

"Where's your hot date?" he asks with a mischievous arch of the brow.

"Don't remind me." Now that I'm actually here, having Peter Quinn as a dance partner feels like a tragic oversight. "I thought he was coming with you guys."

"Last I saw, he was combing his hair for about the hundredth time." Mae adjusts her flowing, iridescent skirt. "He must really like you, Sync."

"I don't know why," I casually toss out.

"What are you talking about, Synchronicity? You're a *babe*. No wonder Mr. Sexy Healer Man can't keep his eyes off you."

I glance toward the edge of the courtyard and, sure enough, Kai is standing there in a dashing, all-white linen suit. He sees me looking and turns away, flustered.

"What's up with you two anyway?" Mae presses.

"I don't know. Neither of us has made a move, and at this point, I doubt we will."

"Shame," Jasper says, scanning the crowd. "He's delicious."

"Probably doesn't want to get accused of abusing his authority," Mae suggests. "I heard the interim healers are under a lot of pressure if they want to be promoted to a permanent teaching position."

"So basically, it's up to me," I sigh, warming my hands on a mug of cider.

"I hate to break it to you, but yeah." Jasper shrugs. "Take the leap or die of regret."

"Uggh. I hate making the first move. Not that it will matter much if I fail the energy work midterm tomorrow."

"Stop saying that, Synchronicity. Worrying about something is just praying for it to happen." A look of genuine concern crosses Mae's face.

"I know, I know. Manifestation and all that. But seriously, guys. I have no healing powers. I'm fucked."

Before anyone can say more, the crowd shifts as Supermoon takes the stage behind the roaring bonfire, where students are roasting chestnuts. Jason Starsong taps the tourmaline-amplified mic. "Good evening, Agartha. Welcome to the twelve-thousand-and-twenty-fifth Annual Winter

Solstice Celebration. We're honored to bring some light to the longest night of the year. And now, please welcome our newest member... Kara Volkova!"

Applause thunders.

"I'm sorry, Mae," I say, squeezing her arm.

She shrugs it off and lifts her chin. "I'm over it. I just want to have a good time." She twirls off toward the stage, hips swaying, hoop glittering like a comet trail.

"Hey! There you are." Peter walks up to us from one of the many paths leading to the courtyard. He looks particularly dreary tonight in a funereal suit with a wilted boutonnière pinned to his lapel. Mochi reaches a curious paw out toward Persephone, but the raven squawks and flaps her big wings, sending Mochi scampering to Jasper's other shoulder.

"Well," Jasper says, "as much as I'd love to hang out, I really must go find my date. Toodleloo Peter. Take good care of Synchronicity for me."

I grasp onto Jasper's coat sleeve to convince him to stay, but he jerks it away and disappears into the crowd, leaving me alone with my gloomy date.

"You look nice, Peter," I say. "Did you see our tree? It looks pretty good."

"How could I miss it? The darn thing is like fifty feet tall."

"Maybe I'm crazy, but I feel like the ringing sound is even louder now. Listen, can you hear it?"

Peter squints an eye and tilts his head to the side. "Oh yeah, I think I can."

"Come on, let's go find Mae and Jasper." I take his hand and pull him into the crowd of students who have now mostly abandoned the bonfire and are packing in near the stage.

Supermoon has launched into an uptempo house beat, and from the reaction of the students, it seems like a favorite. It takes a second, but I find Mae and Jasper. Together, the four of us form a dance circle, alleviating the awkwardness of having to dance with Peter alone.

The music is really good. I can see why Mae wanted to be in this band so badly. We dance away the longest night of the year under the twinkling lights of the ringing cedar, losing ourselves to the oblivion of yuletide revelry. Even Peter lets loose a little, getting down with a halfway decent shuffle.

It must be getting late because Supermoon switches to a slow song. I can tell Peter is trying to work up the nerve to ask me to dance, but before he does, Kai appears. "Mind if I cut in?"

Peter looks taken aback, but doesn't protest.

"Thanks, buddy." Kai slaps his shoulder and offers me his hand. "May I have this dance, Miss Jones?"

"Absolutely." I slide into his arms as Peter sulks back toward the sidelines. "Thanks for saving me."

"You were looking pretty uncomfortable, but it wasn't just that." He looks at me with those big melt-your-heart eyes. "I know I'd regret it if I didn't get at least one dance with you."

Heat flushes my cheeks, and I look down, smiling despite myself. "I'm glad you did."

As he leads me out onto the floor, I catch a glimpse of Cassandra standing alone near the cedar tree. Her pale skin practically glows under the moonstone lights, and she's holding a cup of cider with both hands like she's trying to warm something deeper than her fingers. She watches us, unblinking. I offer her a small smile, but she doesn't return it.

I turn my attention back to Kai. He smells like an intoxicating mix of mint and eucalyptus. I glance back up at his freshly shaved jawline, and my pulse quickens.

"Has anyone told you you look beautiful tonight?" I try to look away again, but he pins me with his incorruptible gaze.

"Not in so many words." Why does being near this man make my stomach do flips?

"Well, you do. You look like a winter star."

I swallow. Hard. This is the closest we've ever been. Is this him finally making a move?

"Kai..." I start, but he speaks first.

"Listen, I know your midterm is tomorrow. I wanted to help."

"Oh yeah? Are you finally going to tell me the magic word that activates Earthseed healing powers?"

"I'm serious. I can help you, but the thing is..."

"What?"

He looks both ways. "I could get in a lot of trouble for telling you this, so you have to promise that no one will find out. Especially Alien Sylestra."

"I'll promise you anything if it helps me pass that exam tomorrow."

"There's a list," he says, glancing around like Sylestra might slither out from the crowd. "A master list in Sylestra's office. Every student is assigned to a volunteer with a different disease. I know it won't exactly help you with your healing powers, but if you know the disease ahead of time, you can tailor your study. Focus your practice."

He looks at me with a deep earnestness, and I can tell how much he's risking by telling me this.

"Kai, that's incredible! I don't know how to thank you."

"Thank me by not getting caught. The code to her office is 7-5-7-6."

"Kai, you're a lifesaver!" I push myself up on my toes and kiss him on the cheek.

Color flushes to his face. "Wait, you're going now?"

"I have less than ten hours between now and that midterm. If there's a chance I can pass it, I'm gonna use every minute I have left."

"Good luck." He smiles, but there's a bit of remorse behind his eyes, like he wishes our dance had turned into something more. "And remember, I didn't tell you anything."

"Your secret is safe with me. I'm pretty sure I'd get kicked out too, if Sylestra found out I was cheating. And Kai..." My gaze lingers on him a moment longer. "Thanks again."

I say goodnight to Mae and Jasper and weave my way through the crowd, but Peter intercepts me before I can leave the plaza.

"Hey, uh, I was wondering if you wanted to go back to the dorm with me." He runs his fingers through his greasy black hair. "I've got some pot we could smoke."

"I had fun, Peter," I say gently, "but I think we're better off as friends."

He shrinks back, clearly crushed.

"Besides, there's something I need to do tonight."

CHAPTER
THIRTY-TWO

The Energy Work School is quiet, the teachers having long since retired to the faculty housing. I'm no stranger to wandering its crystal-lit halls at night. It's the time when I do the majority of my work. But there are no linens to fold tonight.

I move up the spiral staircase to the third floor, my boots silent on the smooth stone. As I pass the corridor with the green light, the one with the locked door no one talks about, I hold my breath and keep moving. The air is colder up here. Thinner. Like the building itself knows I'm somewhere I shouldn't be.

Alien Sylestra's office sits at the end of the hall like a warning. The keypad glows dimly in the dark.

7-5-7-6.

I key in the numbers, my finger pausing for a half-second on each digit. The lock disengages with a muted click, and I slip inside, easing the door shut behind me.

Her office is as pristine as ever. The air smells faintly of sandalwood, like incense had burned hours ago. Everything is arranged with ritualistic precision: scrolls rolled tight and tied with silver cord, crystal vials labeled in alien script, and in the far corner, a rose-colored salt lamp glows faintly, casting shifting fractals across the walls.

She would notice if anything were out of place. I move slowly, carefully flipping through the documents on her desk. Workshop signups. Supply orders. A few glowing performance reviews—none for me, of course.

No disease list.

I check the drawers. Incense. Oils. A pouch of herbal smoking blend labeled *Sirian Dreamtime*. A tiny, smug smile threatens the corner of my mouth. It seems even Alien Sylestra is not without her vices.

But still no list.

I pause and scan the room. Kai said it was here. He

wouldn't lie about that. My gaze falls on a book resting on the end table, just slightly misaligned with the others.

Sacred Geometry of the Human Body.

It feels like a long shot, but I flip it open and out slips a folded piece of paper. I snatch it before it can flutter to the floor and unfold it on the velvet couch in the corner of the room.

Bingo.

Vaylen Blair: hip osteoarthritis.

Cassandra Holloway: gastroparesis.

Synchronicity Jones: heart palpitations.

Heart palpitations. Where had I heard that before? The glimmer of a memory from my first day of herbalism pops into my mind. Yes. Alien Thumgren had said something about heart palpitations. But what was it? A plant that healed them...

Hawthorne berries.

My pulse quickens. I just hope the tree still has some left.

Campus glistens like a gemstone half-buried in the snow, its spires and rooftops glazed in Earthlight and silence. The music from the courtyard has gone still, replaced by the hush of the solstice itself. As if the land is holding its breath, waiting for the sun to return.

As I pass the craft site, the RE ships sit like snow-draped relics from another world, their domed surfaces glinting like ornaments on some celestial tree. I mentally check in with Ra as I move past the hangar, but get no answer. Asleep, maybe. Or dreaming.

When I get to the forest that surrounds Atum Crater, I stop in my tracks.

There are voices. And firelight.

I creep toward the sound, silently cursing the crunch of the snow beneath my boots, when I see, gathered around a fire, three hooded figures.

Concealing myself behind a nearby tree, I peek my head out and watch. On the ground surrounding the fire, a pentagram has been drawn out of white and black stones. The same one I noticed on my first day of Herbalism. The cloaked figures occupy three points of the star, howling and beckoning the fire upward with their hands.

It might have taken me a second to recognize them if it weren't for the horse tied to a tree on the edge of the firelight, white as the snow that blankets the ground.

Edmund.

It's Vaylen, Kara, and June who are howling at the sky, performing this pagan rite. Using her elemental powers, Vaylen channels the fire to new heights, sending sparks racing up into the branches above.

"ARBATHIAO REIBET ATHELEBERSETH!" Her voice commands a dark power as she chants the strange words, raising her hands to the heavens. "Lady of the Crossroads, Queen of Night, Torchbearer, Mistress of Magic, and Guardian of the Underworld, I call upon you! Show us your magic on this, the longest night! When the veil is thinnest and your dominion complete!"

Kara and June cry like banshees, swaying wildly back and forth as the flames tower ever higher. Vaylen stands tall, her long hair billowing around her face with the force of the fire. "ARBATHIAO REIBET ATHELEBERSETH ARA BLATHA ALBEU EBENPHCHI!"

I duck farther behind the tree, heart hammering against my ribs.

What the fuck is this?

Vaylen's head turns in my direction, but her eyes don't register anything. Just glassy orbs sweeping across the trees, as if her consciousness is tuned to another station.

I don't wait to see what happens next.

Whatever they're up to, I want no part of it, and I certainly don't want them to find me out here when this weird ritual concludes. I tiptoe back through the snow, leaving them to contend with whatever dark forces they might be summoning.

I follow the well-trampled path to the edge of the crater and begin my long descent to the pool at the bottom. There is no moon in Agartha, but the fluorescent minerals etched into the undersurface of the Earth cast a silver-blue glow across the snow, almost like moonlight.

They say there are 525 steps to the bottom, though I've never managed to count them all.

Tonight, I lose count before ninety.

My mind's still tangled in what I saw in the woods—the pentagram of stones, the fire, the way Vaylen's eyes didn't seem... entirely hers. There was something else, too. A presence in the dark. Watching.

When I reach the final step, I pause, scanning the crater.

Nothing.

Only the pool, silent and crystalline, rimmed in snow like a mirror waiting to be shattered. And just beyond it, the hawthorn tree, its gnarled limbs sagging under the weight of vibrant red berries, as if they've been waiting for me.

I take a satchel out of my pack and start filling it with the ripe fruits, like miniature pomegranates, being careful to avoid the thorns that line the branches and trunk of the tree.

I've almost filled my satchel when out of the stillness of the night, a dark form comes flying at me. It is quick and ethereal and rabid, and it latches onto me like a jellyfish onto its prey. I stumble back, trying to fight the thing off, but it clings to my wrists and face, and I can't see for the swirling black clouds of energy whipping back and forth before my eyes.

I try to scream, but my voice is muffled by the wraith that seems to be trying to get inside of me at all costs. As I hopelessly flail, my heel catches on a rock and I fall backwards. My stomach drops just before I hit the surface of the pool.

The freezing water envelops my body, shocking me to the bone. Every nerve ending contracts in protest. But the creature falters too, its onslaught now more erratic as if it were fighting with both me and the frigid water that surrounds us.

I sink deeper into the bottomless pool, struggling to fend off the dark phantom as it continues to attack me. Precious oxygen escapes my lips and bubbles to the surface as I desperately fight with the incorporeal being that seems hellbent on consuming my very soul.

I'm losing air fast, and the water is getting darker and colder the further we descend. I can feel my muscles start to stiffen as the monster secures its deathly grip on my body.

The edges of my vision begin to go black, and I can feel the tendrils of the creature trying to force their way into my mouth. Down here in the depths of the pool, time seems to slow. I am surrounded by the crushing weight of the impossibly cold water, and just as my consciousness starts to slip away, I feel a white light filling my head. Then my whole body.

The power of the light courses through my bloodstream like electricity, and I push my hands forward, emitting a blast of blinding energy. The creature struggles to keep its grasp on me. I feel it letting go, then watch as it screams, disintegrating into ribbons of darkness that dissolve into nothing.

The light fades, but the strength of the energy lingers in my veins, and I use it to swim upwards, propelling myself to the surface with the last of my strength. The moment my head breaches, I gasp, lungs flooding with cold air like it's the first breath I've ever taken.

I claw my way to the shore and collapse in the snow, heart hammering, limbs trembling. My soaked clothes suck the warmth from my body like leeches. Even with that phantom gone, I realize I'm still in danger of freezing to death.

I force myself to stand.

The berries have spilled from my satchel like blood in the snow. I gather them up and, step by step, climb back up the crater, each stair an act of pure will. My body is shaking, my skin raw, but I make it to the top, across campus, and back into the Energy Work School, dripping water all over the neat stone floors.

I peel off my wet clothes, fingers numb, and stagger into the sauna. I crank the heat as high as it will go and collapse against the cedar wall, letting the warmth crawl slowly back into my body.

I close my eyes.

That thing... those dark clouds of energy... it looked exactly like the creatures in Ra's vision.

Like the thing that killed Bo.

And this time it was after me.

But why?

And then I remember the chanting, the flames, the eerie ritual in the forest.

Vaylen.

CHAPTER
THIRTY-THREE

I can't exactly prove it's her. Not without admitting why I was at the crater that late. After thawing my bones in the sauna, I spend the rest of the night brewing an extra-strength hawthorn berry decoction, then collapse into bed and catch a few final hours of sleep before class.

The alarm on my selenite tablet jolts me awake at 8:30, and I get ready for my most important midterm of the year. I'm putting all my faith in my last-minute elixir. If I don't find a way to get it into my patient without Sylestra noticing, my time at Agartha is through.

The desks have been moved out of the classroom and replaced with rows of massage tables—one for each student. On the tables lie third-year volunteers in various states of distress. I wonder what Sylestra bribes them with to convince them to be guinea pigs for first-year healers.

Each table has a name card. I find mine beside a kind-eyed barista I recognize from the cafe. I've helped her unpack bags of coffee a few times.

"Hi," I say.

"Please do not talk to your patients until I've started the timer," Alien Sylestra snaps from the front of the classroom, glaring at me in particular. "Once you have found your table, please wait quietly for further instruction."

The woman gives me a slight smile and closes her eyes. I thumb the vial of hawthorn berry elixir in my pocket. I'm pretty sure I can get her to drink it if I can just explain what's going on.

"You will have fifteen minutes to discuss symptoms with your patient, analyze their eating habits, and talk about any lifestyle stressors." Alien Sylestra paces back and forth at the front of the room, her immaculate white robes flowing behind her. "After that, you will have the remainder of the class to diagnose and cure your patient. Are there any questions?"

June raises her hand. She's in the front row with Kara and Vaylen. I try to catch her eye for some indication of what happened last night, but all three of them remain facing forward.

"Yes, Miss Molyneux?"

"Are spirit animals allowed, Professor?"

"I already went over that during our last session, June. Of course, spirit animals are allowed for Arcturian Starseeds."

"I was just making sure, Professor. Thank you!"

"If no one else has any questions, then we will get started. Oh, one last thing before we begin." Alien Sylestra's cold gaze narrows in on me. "Miss Jones, will you please trade patients with Miss Blair?"

I look back at her, dumbfounded. "But Alien Sylestra, my name card is here."

"I made some last-minute changes, Synchronicity. I think your unique abilities, or lack thereof, will be better suited for Vaylen's patient. Vaylen, on the other hand, is quite an accomplished healer and should be fine treating any malady."

Does she know I snuck into her office last night? Or is she just being unnecessarily cruel?

"But Professor..." I blurt out.

"No buts, Synchronicity. To the front of the class. Now."

I walk to the front of the room, passing Vaylen on the way. She gives me a smug, self-satisfied look, and I wonder if she's at all surprised to see me alive this morning after last night's attack.

I take Vaylen's place, front and center. My new patient is a middle-aged woman with steel-gray hair and tired eyes. Kara and June stand on either side of me, shooting me glares of disgust. I feel the noose tightening.

"Now then, if everyone's settled, we will begin." Alien Sylestra takes a seat at her table and starts a stopwatch. "You may now begin the pre-examination with your patient."

I take a shaky breath. "Hi. What seems to be the matter today?"

"I have pain in my hips, especially when getting up from

sitting or climbing stairs."

"I see." It sounds like a coached response. Like the volunteers memorized the symptoms of the disease they were given before the exam. "Are there times of the day that it feels more acute than others?"

"In the morning, right after I wake up."

I try to remember what the list said about Vaylen's patient. Hip dysplasia? Hip bursitis?

"And what are your eating habits like?" I ask, as if any of this will matter. My hawthorn berry elixir is completely useless.

"I usually eat oatmeal and fruit for breakfast, a light lunch, then generally a large dinner with grains and meat."

"And how's the range of motion in your hips?"

"Very poor."

"Okay, thank you. Let me see what I can feel." At this point, I'm just stalling. I have serious doubts whether my limited healing abilities can even make a slight impact on this patient, let alone cure her. I definitely don't want a repeat of last time.

I close my eyes and feel into her etheric body. There is a lot of turbulence surrounding her hips. Spikes of painful energy seem to be radiating out from the sockets...

Hip osteoarthritis! That's what it was.

I write the name of the condition down on the patient's intake form. Maybe I'll get a point for correctly identifying it.

But even if I do, that will be the *only* point I get. If I remember correctly, hip osteoarthritis is when the cartilage in the hip socket has completely worn away and the ball of the femur starts growing into the pelvis itself.

Like I'm supposed to regrow cartilage.

Shit.

I can barely stop a bloody nose.

Sylestra knew *exactly* what she was doing when she gave me Vaylen's patient. This has to be one of the hardest diseases to cure at our level.

I try to remember everything Kai taught me, feeling into

the rotation of her energy currents. They should be a clear, simple spiral flowing out from the body.

I do my best to align the currents surrounding the patient's hips. It should alleviate some of the symptoms, but won't do anything for the underlying cause.

Fuck. Sylestra is going to fail me, and I'll have to go back to living in my car, which is probably towed by now, and somehow figure out my shitty life back on the surface. I'll have to say goodbye to Mae, to Jasper, to Ra...

Just then, the same white light from last night floods into my mind.

Ra help Synchronicity.

Ra...

It was you last night, wasn't it? You channeled your powers to help me fight off that thing.

My power... is your power.

The light intensifies, saturating my head with a current so strong it makes my whole body hum.

This. Feels. Insane.

It's like liquid electricity is flooding my core, igniting every nerve ending. With each breath, I send it spiraling through my limbs.

Suddenly, the mental visualization of my patient becomes perfectly clear and detailed. I can see every energy current in her body, including the tangled mess surrounding her hips.

Even with my eyes closed, I can see the auric image of my hands, every vein and nerve radiating an electromagnetic field. I am seeing my own etheric body for the first time.

I raise one hand to my face and gaze in wonder at the intricate inner workings of a thing I took very much for granted. Every energy channel is visible, glowing and interacting with the network of other currents around it.

I hold both hands out above my patient, guiding the white current from the crown of my skull down through my arms and into my fingertips. Light pours from me in swirling vortexes, merging with the angry red pulse around her hips, realigning the disharmony.

I push harder. The white light streaming from my hands

engulfs the auric field of the woman lying before me, surrounding her in a cocoon of bright healing energy. I focus all my will on her hips, on restoring the blueprint of the cartilage. If I can repair the energetic pattern, the physical body will have no choice but to follow.

Just as the force flowing through me reaches its peak, I hear Alien Sylestra's voice, at first muffled and distant, then more immediate. "Synchronicity! Synchronicity, stop!"

I open my eyes and see arcs of white light shooting from my hands and creating a massive energy field surrounding not only my patient but most of the room. Papers are flying everywhere, and the crystal lights on the walls flicker and flare out. One by one, the windows shatter, sending shards of glass exploding into the classroom.

Then everything stops.

The arcs of energy streaming from my hands vanish, and a pregnant silence fills the room as sheets of paper float to the floor. Kara and June stare at me like I just brought someone back from the dead. Alien Sylestra's mouth hangs open in disbelief.

My patient sits up on the table and looks at me in awe.

"How did you do that?" she whispers.

"I... I don't know."

Sylestra shuffles out from behind her desk and hovers her hands over the woman's body, scanning her from head to toe. "Well, Source take me. I have no idea how you did it, Miss Jones... but your patient is completely cured."

CHAPTER
THIRTY-FOUR

I practically dance onto the craft field, waves of relief crashing over me as I scoop Mae into a hug and spin her around in the snow. "I passed! I passed!"

"I knew you would do it, Sync. I just knew it." Mae squeezes me tighter. Over her shoulder, I notice our crafts are conspicuously missing from the field.

"I wasn't so confident," Jasper chimes in. "I was afraid I'd have to draw up an application for a new friend."

"Oh, shut up," I say, punching him in the arm.

"Hey!" He rubs the spot with exaggerated tenderness. "I'm gonna make you heal that now, you know."

"How did you do it?" Mae asks. "Did Kai teach you some secret healing technique?"

"It's kind of a long story, but Ra helped me."

Mae's jaw drops. "*Ra?*"

"He channeled something through me, some kind of power. Or maybe it was already inside me. I'm not really sure yet."

"Wait, wait, wait." Jasper tosses a snowball, and Mochi goes bounding after it. "How the heck did you figure out how to do that?"

"Well, that's the crazy part." I look back and forth between them. "I got attacked last night."

"What?" Mae steps forward, all her warmth turning sharp with worry. "Sync, are you okay?"

"I'm fine. Maybe just some minor frostbite."

"Who attacked you?" Jasper's eyes narrow. "Was it Xion? Because I swear on Mochi's tiny life, I will *end* him."

"It wasn't Xion." I shake my head. "It was the same thing that attacked Bo. A cloud of dark energy, but it was sentient. It was like getting attacked by a rabid animal."

"How did you escape?" Mae brushes a dreadlock from her astonished face.

"I fell into the pool at the bottom of Atum Crater.

Thought I was gonna die. But Ra, he came through me. There was this white light, like pure Source, and it blew the thing apart."

"Synchronicity, that was still Xion," Jasper insists. "What you are describing sounds exactly like a Beta Draconid. Remember what I said about the fifth-dimensional energy vampires? They can remotely control the Beta Draconids to do their bidding."

"I don't think it's him." I lower my voice. "I think it's Vaylen."

Jasper scoffs. "Vaylen? *Miss Mindfulness Meditation?* You think she killed Bo?"

"She's not who she pretends to be. After the dance, I saw her in the woods with Kara and June. They were doing some kind of ritual with a pentagram. Chanting. Calling on a 'Queen of the Night.' That was right before I got attacked."

"Well, you did throw a blue drink all over that pristine linen jumpsuit she was wearing," Jasper concedes. "But that doesn't mean she's summoning dark forces to kill you."

"Like you said, if she's infected with one of those vampires, she may not even know she's doing it. Trust me. She's wanted me gone ever since she first laid eyes on me at the Entrance Obelisk."

Before he can answer, Mae whispers, "Shhh. Here she comes."

Vaylen, Kara, and June tromp over the hill in fur boots and leggings. Vaylen's white parka glitters like a threat.

They approach with slow, deliberate steps.

"That was some stunt you pulled in Energy Work today." Vaylen's eyes are locked on mine, the strands of her straight brown hair catching in the breeze. "You really had the whole room convinced."

"It wasn't a stunt," I say, taking a step forward. "I healed her."

"Everyone knows Earthseeds can't heal," Vaylen sneers.

"Well, apparently they can," Mae says, stepping up beside me.

"Stay out of this, second incarnation," Vaylen spits.

Jasper flanks my other side. "Alright, let's all take a deep breath. No need to brandish past-life karma before lunch."

Vaylen ignores him and keeps her gaze locked on mine. "I know you cheated, Earthseed. I just need to figure out how."

"She didn't cheat!" Mae blurts out. "She's connected to a..."

I stop her mid-sentence with a look.

"What my Lyran friend is trying to say," Jasper interjects, "is that Synchronicity here channeled the connection she has with her RE craft."

"That piece of junk?" Vaylen chuckles. "Yeah, right. That thing's barely capable of flight, let alone healing an advanced disease."

My nostrils flare, hot breath escaping in sharp bursts.

"I've got my eye on you, Earthseed. You're not gonna get away with this." She steps back, smoothing her expression into something falsely serene. "Come on, girls. Let's not let their low vibrations smudge our auric fields."

"The only thing giving off low vibrations is that fake Chanel coat!" Jasper shoots back at the women as they walk off toward the other end of the field. "Okay, I'm convinced. That girl is *definitely* harboring an Alpha Draconid. No one's naturally that awful."

"See? I told you. She has it out for me."

"Alright, aspiring pilots," Xion's voice resounds over the craft site as he steps onto the field. "Welcome to your midterm."

The breeze ruffles the fur-lined collar of his aviator jacket as he walks—cool, composed, devastatingly handsome. I hate how easily he sends heat pumping through my veins.

"I realize this is the final class of the semester for many of you, so we'll make this quick. This morning, I took the liberty of hiding your crafts in various places around the Academy. Your exam is simple: connect with your craft, ascertain its location, and remotely pilot it back to the craft site."

His gaze sweeps the group, and when it lands on me, it's like all the oxygen drains from the field.

Vaylen's hand shoots up in the air. "What if we don't have a strong connection with our craft, Alien Da'ath?" She's been angling to get a new UFO assigned to her all semester.

"At this point, that's on you, Miss Blair." He doesn't wait for another excuse. "Now, if we don't have any more transparent attempts to switch craft this late in the game, you may begin."

I know he must still think about that night we kissed, but if he does, he hasn't shown it in our late-night Eldercraft lessons. He's completely closed himself off from me.

"Let's get this over with so we can go have some mead." Jasper sits down full-lotus style in the snow, and Mochi curls into a ball in his lap. "The traveling honey man is going to be at Elixir tonight. I heard he brought back a batch from the Hadean Mountains."

Jasper closes his eyes, and his silence means he's begun the craft connection process.

Mae settles in beside him. "This should be a breeze. My craft and I are basically soulmates with GPS."

I join them, glad I picked up some snow pants from Deechin's earlier this semester. I close my eyes and try to get myself into a Theta brainwave state. It's not easy with everything that's happened in the past twenty-four hours bouncing around my head.

The ringing cedar. The dance. Vaylen's fucked up ritual. The attack. What does it all mean? Could a fifth-dimensional energy vampire really have it out for me?

I take all these thoughts and mentally lock them away in a big metal box, then I focus on relaxing the muscles in my face. From doing this practice, I've noticed my cheeks and jaw hold a lot of tension that I'm not usually aware of.

I let that tension melt away, and when I feel completely relaxed, I visualize myself walking down the stairs into the deepest chamber of my mind. Luckily, the door at the back of the room seems to be firmly shut.

I conjure up the image of my Castor 5 and port my consciousness into the cockpit.

Geminorum... geminorum...

I repeat the word that Xion says is used to boot the mainframe of all Castor models.

HeLlo. I aM zX240G, buT yOu CaN cAlL mE CaStOr. HoW cAn I bE oF sErViCe ToDaY?

Suddenly, I see the world as Castor sees it, a 360° panoramic view of a stone-laden field covered with snow. The only landmark I recognize is the gleaming Logos Stone on the top of the Great Pyramid that juts out just over the horizon.

Hey Castor. We're going to be doing a bit of flying today. Time to shine.

ExCeLlEnT. fLiGhT iS oNe Of My FiNeSt AbIlItIeS.

I know it is, buddy. Now, can you take off for me?

Castor's engines turn over with a metallic whirring sound but fail to start.

It SeEmS i'm HaViNg SoMe TrOuBlE wItH tHe IcE.

That's okay, Castor. Keep trying.

The engines turn over again, sputter out for a moment, then roar to life, sending a jolt through Castor's frame that I feel as if it were my own body.

Good job, buddy! Now let's see if we can gain some altitude.

Castor takes off with a jittery ascent, rewarding me with an uninterrupted view of the horizon and the Agarthan campus off to the west. From this height, I realize that the Academy is far bigger than I thought, with many more temples and buildings that I haven't explored yet.

Okay, Castor, all we have to do is get back to the craft site. You got this.

I mentally urge Castor forward, and his thrusters engage with a rickety jet propulsion sound. The ground gets sucked backward beneath us as we hurtle forward.

BeAm AcCeLeRaToRs HaVe FallEd To ReAcH oPeRaTiNg TeMpErAtUrE. mAiN eNgInEs ArE sHuTtInG dOwN.

The sound of the engines slows to a low hum, and we begin to lose altitude at a frightening rate.

Don't do this to me, buddy.

Not today.

MaIn ThRuStErS aRe OfFlInE. pRePaRiNg FoR eMeRgEnCy LaNdInG.

No!

I push with all my will, and Castor's engines roar back to life just before we hit the crest of a hill.

I've been working on those thrusters all semester. No way they are failing me now.

Just a little bit farther... We're almost there.

I can now make out the individual crafts on the field and see other students piloting their own saucers into place.

ThE pRoToN sYnChRoTrOn Is ExPeRiEnCiNg A cAtAsTrOpHiC fAiLuRe. AlL sYsTeMs ArE sHuTtInG dOwN.

No! I refuse to embarrass myself in front of Xion. Not after I've trained so hard. Lights flash on the edge of my vision, and multiple alarms all blare at once.

The ground is racing toward us far too quickly, and the craft site is still some distance off.

We're not going to make it.

I shut off my flight vision and go deep down into the recesses of my own mind. I block out all the alarm sounds. If we're getting out of this, it won't be through panic. It'll be through pure, focused Theta.

Just get to the craft site... Just get to the craft site.

I repeat it over and over in my head.

I visualize the spot right in front of my meditating body back on the field.

Here. I need you to land right here.

Outside of my control, the image of my mental cavern begins to fill with water.

I'm coming, Synchronicity.

Ra... *no!*

And then I hear another voice, deeper and far more urgent. "Synchronicity, stop!"

It's Xion.

My eyes snap open just in time to see Ra blast from the hangar like a cannonball, tearing through the corrugated roof and hurtling skyward at breakneck speed.

The massive stone egg reaches the apex of its trajectory and, for a moment, seems suspended high up in the atmosphere, hanging there like a big white balloon in the sky, before plummeting back down.

Right. Toward. Me.

I crab crawl backwards as fast as I can before Ra impacts the earth in front of me with a ground-shaking boom, sending clods of dirt and snow flying in all directions.

Before I can even process what's happened, Castor comes screaming overhead, trailing plumes of billowing black smoke. He has just enough altitude to make it over the craft field before crashing into the tree line, emitting a small, mushroom-shaped fireball.

Xion finishes his sprint towards me, slowing his steps with eyes glued on Ra.

The egg-shaped Eldercraft rises out of the impact crater unscathed, with bits of soil and grass falling from his hull, calm as a god surveying a battlefield.

"Source help us," Xion mutters under his breath.

Jasper and Mae's mouths are practically on the ground.

The symbols on Ra's surface light up like some ancient, unknowable algorithm. A monolithic hum reverberates from his shell.

Ra help.

Students pour across the field, faces slack with awe.

"What the hell is that thing?" I hear Kara say.

"That, class," Xion says, turning to address the students, "is an Eldercraft."

CHAPTER
THIRTY-FIVE

"No way Synchronicity gets to connect with an Eldercraft!" Vaylen's voice cuts through the stunned silence like a blade. She jabs her finger into Xion's chest, eyes blazing. "You said we couldn't switch crafts!"

Xion doesn't flinch. "Wrong. I said *you* couldn't switch."

"That's not fair!" she snaps. "Why should some Earthseed get an Eldercraft when there are way more spiritually advanced Starseeds available—"

"Synchronicity didn't choose the Eldercraft," Xion growls, barely containing his temper. "It chose her. And as far as I can tell, you still haven't returned your craft to the field. So unless you're hoping for a zero on your midterm, I suggest you focus your energy on *that*." He bites out the last few words through a clenched jaw.

"This is ridiculous. No wonder everyone thinks Craft is a joke." Vaylen storms off toward the far end of the field and drops into position, trying once again to connect with her craft.

"Everyone, listen up." Xion's voice commands an instant silence from the rest of us. "Yes, Synchronicity has bonded with an Eldercraft. Yes, it is rare, but it does happen. I'm bonded to one. Alien Isis is bonded to one. Does it change anything about our class? Not at all. For those of you who have already returned your craft to the field, good job, and have a nice break. The rest of you, get back to work."

Students scatter, glancing back at me and Ra with equal parts wonder and jealousy. Ra, for his part, hums softly at my side.

Xion strides toward me, his expression unreadable. "Well, I can't say you didn't understand the assignment. You certainly brought your craft to the flight field."

Ra lets out a cheerful thrumm, like he's proud of himself.

"I wish I could say the same for my other craft." I glance toward the tree line, where a thin column of black smoke coils into the sky.

"Luckily, you've got a more than suitable replacement to finish out the year." His eyes bore into mine like he's trying to figure out what the repercussions of all this will be.

"I really didn't mean to connect with him," I say. "He just... surged into my mind."

"It's okay. The bonds we have with our Eldercraft are incredibly strong. I knew at some point it would overpower your connection with the Castor 5."

"But what now?" I drop my voice. "The secret's out. People are going to talk. You said the Federation—"

"I'll handle it." Xion cuts in, voice low and firm. "I'll speak to Alien Isis. We'll come up with a plan."

"I don't want to lose him," I whisper, looking up at Ra. "I don't want them to take him away."

"I know, Synchronicity. I'll do everything I can to make sure that doesn't happen. But you're going to have to trust me."

I look up into those intense, unfathomable eyes, and to my own surprise, I realize I already do.

CHAPTER
THIRTY-SIX

"Are you sure you don't want to come back to the surface?" Mae and Jasper are bundled in their thickest winter layers at the Entrance Obelisk, where students vanish one by one through shimmering violet portals, homeward-bound for the holidays.

"I'm sure." I stare down at the snow gathering on my boots. "I'm not really on speaking terms with my family."

"You could stay with me," Mae offers. "Me and a few other people are throwing a Friendsmas party down in Big Sur. Ocean views, cacao, campfire ukulele sets. We would love to have you."

"Tempting," I say with a smile. "But I'd rather stay close to Ra. I don't think I could leave him just yet."

"That makes sense," Mae nods, readjusting her ukulele strap. "He's like your egg-baby."

"Exactly."

"Well, we'll miss you, Syncypoo." Jasper holds out his arms wide, and I give him a big hug, sending Mochi scurrying to his other shoulder.

"I hate that nickname," I mumble into his scarf.

"Too bad. I got you a present." Jasper holds out a wide, flat box wrapped in shiny red paper.

Mae lights up. "Oh shoot, I have one too!" She digs into her coat and retrieves a small, lumpy package bound with excessive tape.

"Guys... thank you so much." I take the gifts and stow them under my arm. "I feel bad. I didn't get you anything."

"Don't worry about it," Jasper says. "Just promise to sneak us in for one of those after-hours sauna sessions. It's always so packed during the day."

"Deal," I say, and pull Mae in for a hug. "I'm gonna miss you so much."

"We'll be back before you know it," she says, giving my hand a squeeze before she and Jasper disappear through shimmering portals just like the one I stepped through on my first day at Agartha.

I stand alone as the crowd thins out and the courtyard empties, the ancient obelisk casting its silent shadow across the stone. As the last students vanish, I make my way back to the Energy Work School. Alien Sylestra has given me an extensive list of tasks to accomplish while she is away, but I set it aside to make room for my gifts on my narrow bed. It's technically still Christmas Eve, but patience has never been one of my virtues.

I open Jasper's first. It's a gorgeous brown suede coat, vintage and soft, like something Rachel Green would wear in a snowy NYC montage. I slip it on and immediately feel ten percent cooler.

Mae's present looks like a feral animal wrapped— crumpled paper and a mess of tape. I tear off the adornments to find a little jewelry box with a sterling silver ring inside. The ring is inset with a polished piece of howlite cut in the shape of a teardrop, or more specifically, an egg.

"It looks just like Ra," I whisper, sliding it onto my finger. It fits perfectly.

I close my eyes and drop into the nothing, sending out a silent signal.

Ra, are you okay?

...Tired. But warm.

Xion must've patched the roof. I cranked the thermostat myself this morning.

Good. Get some rest. I'll come over to see you first thing tomorrow.

I pick up Alien Sylestra's to-do list.

- Restock linens

- Clean yoga mats

- Take out classroom trash

- Wipe dust off the indoor plants...

The list goes on.

I lay back on the bed, hands behind my head, staring up at the exposed pipes running along the ceiling, when I hear a low moaning sound.

It must just be the water moving through the old plumbing, I think.

But there it is again, this time more distinct.

I stand up on my bed and try to put my ear as close to the pipes as possible.

Ggggrrrrooooaaaan. GGGRRROOOAN.

Someone or some*thing* is definitely making that sound.

I walk out into the hall and follow it with my ear pressed to the wall.

It leads me down the corridor and to the stairwell where I trace it up to the third floor, following the guttural emanations around a corner to the mysterious green-lit hall.

I walk to the end and peer through the small glass window into the passage beyond.

It looks just like it did last time: sterile linoleum floors and glaring fluorescent lights. I press my ear up to the glass and hear the moaning even louder this time.

What could Alien Sylestra be keeping in this secret wing of the Energy Work School?

I look down and see a numerical keypad, lightly glowing near the handle.

I wonder...

I type in the code I used to get into Sylestra's office, 7-5-7-6, and to my surprise, I am greeted with a confirmation beep and the sound of a retracting dead bolt. I slip into the secret wing and quietly shut the door behind me.

The groaning is much louder now, and I easily trace the source of the sound to an unmarked door halfway down an adjacent hall. I look both ways, but the passage is eerily empty. Taking a deep breath, I turn the handle and enter.

Before me, hooked up to numerous tubes and wires, is a little grey alien sunken into a hospital bed. I jump in fright as he reaches out a trembling hand towards me, opening his mouth like he's trying to form a word.

The only sound that manages to escape is more of the groaning. Dried spittle cakes his tiny, wrinkled lips, and I realize he's not pointing at me, but at a container of water near the door.

"Are you... thirsty?" I say, taking a step closer.

He makes another, more urgent groan and slowly jabs with his long, bony finger toward the water.

I open the container and pour a glass. "Like this? You want some water?"

He reaches out further and groans in confirmation.

I walk over to the bedside and tilt the glass up to his lips. The little grey alien drains the glass in slow, grateful swigs before collapsing back onto his pillow. He turns his head toward me and tries to say something, but his lips just open and close without any sound.

"It's okay. You don't have to thank me," I say. "I'm glad I could help."

I almost reach out to touch his forehead when I hear footsteps echoing down the hall.

Shit.

I'm not supposed to be in here, and I'm definitely not supposed to know Alien Sylestra's code. If she ever found out I snuck into her office before the midterm, she'd fail me no matter how well I cured that patient.

I take the glass back to the shelf near the door and poke my head out into the hallway. Whoever's making those footsteps hasn't reached this corridor yet. I dart out into the hall and round the corner just as a healer I've never seen before turns the opposite corner, looking down at a clipboard of paperwork.

I tiptoe down the hall back to the door where I entered and slip back into the Energy Work School unnoticed.

CHAPTER
THIRTY-SEVEN

The rest of the break passes without incident, but the moment Mae and Jasper return, I jump at the first chance to show them what I saw.

"Synchronicity, what you're describing sounds like an *Elder*. No one's seen an Elder in, like, *eons,* and now you're telling us they're hiding one in a secret wing of the Energy Work School?" Jasper has returned from the surface with a fresh haircut that he refuses to show us.

"Kind of like the secret you're hiding under that hat!" Mae tries to swipe the oversized Russian hat off Jasper's head.

He jerks away with a dramatic gasp. "This cut is under magical protection... indefinitely."

"I'm serious, guys. It's just down this next hall." We step out onto the third floor, and I lead them down to the passage lit by the green crystal. It's the night before classes resume, and I had to wait till nearly midnight for Alien Sylestra to leave the building.

"Synchronicity, I love you, but you better make this quick. I'm only here under the condition that I get a full sweat in before bed. Come on, Mochi." Jasper rubs his fingers together in a beckoning motion, and the fluffy red panda bounds across the floor and climbs onto Jasper's shoulder.

"Pretty sure sauna protocol forbids fur hats," Mae chides.

"I could give a damn about the rules, although I wouldn't want to ruin this faux sable so you may actually have a point..."

"Look through the window," I insist, pulling them down the last few feet of the hall. "Doesn't that look weird?"

Mae and Jasper peer through the little rectangular window set into the door.

"It looks like a hospital from the surface." Mae tugs down her knitted skirt, and I notice a couple of new tattoos on her legs.

"Fluorescent light is literal violence to my skin tone," Jasper grumbles. "This entire hallway is a hate crime."

"Do you know the code, Synchronicity?" Mae turns toward me.

"Yeah. Just a second." I type Sylestra's code into the keypad and the door unlocks. I turn the handle but pause before I open it. "We have to be really quiet in there, guys. There could be nurses walking around."

"We understand, Synchronicity. Just show us the Elder." Jasper rolls his eyes.

I push the door open, and the three of us slip into the bright, sterile hallway. The smell of antiseptic clings to the air.

I lead them down the passage to a corner, check that the coast is clear, then wave them forward. Just a few more steps and we're at the door to the room where I saw the little grey alien.

"Okay, guys, just don't freak out. He's... not easy to look at."

I grip the handle, heart starting to race again, and push the door open...

"Wow, Synchronicity, you really stumbled upon a deep Academy conspiracy here." Jasper's tone is deadpan as he walks into the room. "Do you think this ficus is a dangerous fugitive from the Galactic Federation?"

"What?" I step into the room after them but find it made up like any other energy work studio in the school: a massage table, a few plants, and crystal lamps on the wall. "I swear he was right here. There were all these wires and machines hooked up to him."

"I believe you, Sync." Mae reaches out and rests her hand on my arm. "They probably just moved him somewhere else."

"Well," Jasper claps his hands together. "This has all been very stimulating. Now, if you'll excuse me, I have some toxins to sweat out."

Mae lingers a second longer, watching me. "You're not crazy, Synchronicity," she says softly. "Whatever you saw...

There's more going on here than they're telling us. We'll figure it out."

Then she turns and follows Jasper down the corridor, leaving me in the flickering quiet, staring at an empty room that should have held a secret.

But now, it's like he was never there at all.

"That's enough about my hair. Yes, I cried when I got home from the hairdresser. Yes, I buzzed it all off and dyed it blonde. End of story." Jasper leans back against the cedar wood wall, a white towel knotted tight around his waist.

"I actually like it," Mae says, stretching her legs across the wooden planks. Her bathing suit glistens with sweat, and a towel is tied like a queen's shawl over her dreads. "It's very Amber Rose."

"You look amazing, Jasper," I say. "You're the only person I know who could go full cyberpunk monk and pull it off."

"Flattery won't get you everywhere," he mutters, but I can see the corner of his mouth twitch into a smile. "Anyway. I'm over it. What I really want to know is, did our little Synchronicity get attacked by any more parasitic space ghouls while we were gone?"

"Nope," I say, grabbing the ladle and pouring water over the hot stones. A hiss of steam erupts between us, fragrant with eucalyptus. "Just the one Vaylen sent on the solstice."

"I've been thinking about that and I don't buy it," Jasper says. "Sure, that girl hates your guts, but why would she go after Bo? I'm pretty certain those two got along."

"I don't know." I lean back against the wall, watching the curls of steam rise toward the ceiling. "Maybe the thing missed. I was right behind him when we left class. It could've been meant for me and just... hit the wrong target."

"I suppose it's possible," Jasper says. "But my bet's still on Xion."

Mae perks up. "Speaking of, how are your Eldercraft lessons going?"

I hesitate. "The flying's fine. Ra and I are getting better at communicating. But Xion's been... off. Ever since we kissed, it's like he's slammed some internal door shut and swallowed the key."

Mae sighs, crosses her legs, and fixes me with a look. "Sync, you know I love you, right?"

"Oh god," I groan.

"Men like that?" she continues. "Dark, broody, emotionally unavailable? They're not projects. You can't alchemize a relationship out of a smolder and a death wish."

"She's not wrong," Jasper adds, resting his chin on his fists. "Even if he's not guilty of whatever conspiracy we're circling, he's still the kind of man who'd rather eat gravel than talk about his feelings."

"I guess we're kind of similar that way," I admit. "I just wish he could see it. There's something between us. A spark. But he won't admit it. Not to himself, not to me."

"Meanwhile, Kai Moongate is over here writing sonnets with his eyes and probably baking gluten-free scones in his spare time," Jasper says. "Emotionally intelligent, healing hands, cheekbones that could cut glass... what's not to love?"

"I *like* Kai," I admit. "I do. He's everything I'm supposed to want. But some deeply warped part of me is drawn to men like Xion. To chaos."

"Oh, Sync, you're hopeless." Jasper flops onto his side and starts rubbing Mochi's belly. The little red panda sprawls across the sauna bench, letting out a pleased yawn and a slow bicycle-kick with his back legs.

"Any word from the Galactic Federation?" Jasper asks, eyes half-lidded now but still tuned in.

"Not yet," I say, twisting the edge of my towel between my fingers. "Xion said he'd do everything in his power to protect Ra, but..." My voice falters. "I'm scared, you guys. What if it's not enough? What if they take him away?"

Mae reaches over, her palm warm against my wrist. "They won't."

"You don't know that."

"No," she says softly. "But I know you. And I know you won't let him go."

I nod, but a lump rises in my throat. Out on the craft site, Ra is asleep in his hangar. And I don't know how many days we have left.

CHAPTER THIRTY-EIGHT

Herbalism's been relocated to the main pyramid for the next two months—or at least until the weather decides to cooperate. I weave through the pyramid's labyrinthine corridors toward the room Alien Thumgren designated.

Compared to the stuffy cave that is the Galactic History classroom, this space is almost pleasant. The windows offer slivers of light and a view of the snow-laced outer courtyard. I slide into a seat next to Cassandra and try to toss Peter a friendly wave, but he acts like he doesn't see me.

Little shit.

He really thought I'd follow him back to his dorm after one awkward dance? Absolutely not.

Before I can ask Cassy how her break was, Alien Thumgren calls the class to order.

"Glorious morning, class," she says. Her green, elfin ears twitch beneath her halo of brown and silver hair. "As you know, being indoors is anathema to my soul, but I've found it's easiest on the students if we spend the colder months learning herb preparation in the classroom. I moved all the herbs you harvested from your plots to boxes at the back of the room with your names on them. We will be using these, as well as some extra herbs I gathered myself, to make balms, tonics, and tinctures."

She picks up a bundle of pale blue leaves and cradles them like a sacred text. "Now, the first category of herbs I want to discuss today is called nervines..."

But before she can launch into her usual impassioned tangent, the door swings open.

Alien Isis enters, flanked by two beings in black suits with translucent insectoid eyes and soft blue skin.

"I apologize for the interruption, Thalyssa," Isis says with an edge of formality. "But I need to borrow Synchronicity Jones."

Every head in the room turns toward me.

Alien Thumgren shuffles her sandaled feet. "Of course. Synchronicity, you can check in with me after class to find out what you missed."

I gather my things in awkward silence and follow Isis and her bug-eyed entourage into the hallway.

"Is this about Ra?" I ask once we've reached the privacy of the hall.

"No questions, please." Alien Isis leads us down a series of passages toward the interior of the Great Pyramid. I try to get a read on the aliens in black suits trailing just behind her. They look like Alien Sylestra, blue skin, little antennas, big insect eyes. I get the impression they're not here for a healing retreat.

We turn a corner, and Alien Isis takes us into a small, windowless study room, the kind students reserve for late-night cram sessions. She shuts the door behind us. "Take a seat, please, Synchronicity."

I sit across from the two agents, who lower themselves into chairs with the grace of spiders settling into their webs.

"This is Agent Kreth and Agent Marnox," Isis explains. "They're with the Galactic Federation's Vibrational Alignment Bureau. They'd like to ask you a few questions about the Eldercraft we recovered a few weeks ago."

Alien Isis levels me with a pointed look. I know for a fact they've been keeping Ra a secret for months, ever since school started, but it's clear she wants me to play along with the lie.

The taller of the two agents interlaces his long blue fingers and places them on the table. "Like Alien Isis said, I'm Agent Kreth, and this is Agent Marnox. Our job is to make sure that spiritual assets are being utilized in a way that best promotes the spiritual advancement of the galaxy."

"The Council of Five has requested a formal evaluation of your connection with the Eldercraft," Marnox adds. "Depending on our findings, the craft may be relocated for research purposes."

"Relocated?" I feel the sparks of anger begin to form in my chest. "You mean dissected in some Federation lab just so you can reverse-engineer some fancy new ship."

The agents exchange a look, and Kreth takes over the discussion. "We're going to do our best to keep you and your Eldercraft together, Miss Jones. If we don't find anything of sufficient value, the Eldercraft will be allowed to stay here at Agartha."

"He'll stay at Agartha no matter what you find," I say, my hackles rising.

"Unfortunately, that's not for you to decide, Miss Jones." The soft blue line of Agent Kreth's jaw flexes.

"Now, where were you when you first had contact with the Eldercraft?" Agent Marnox produces a selenite tablet and looks up at me expectantly.

"It was in a hangar at the school's craft site."

Agent Marnox types something into his tablet. "And why were you in this hangar, Miss Jones?"

"I was just sneaking around at night for fun. You know how students are." I shrug, innocently enough.

"And approximately when was this?"

I glance up at Alien Isis, searching her face for a signal. She gives nothing away, but her stillness is answer enough.

"It was two weeks ago," I say carefully. "Just before midterms." I drop my gaze to my hands, willing them to stay steady as the lie leaves my mouth.

"That would have been just a few days after the craft was recovered," Alien Kreth confirms.

"I wouldn't know about that," I say.

"Yes, that's correct," Alien Isis answers from the corner. If these agents find out we kept Ra a secret for the better part of a semester, who knows what the consequences would be.

"How would you characterize your initial interaction with the Eldercraft, Miss Jones?" Marnox's fingers are poised over the tablet, ready to type.

"I don't know. It was... beautiful and strange. Unlike anything I had ever experienced before."

"And have you flown this craft, Miss Jones?"

I answer honestly. "Yes."

"Have you had any experience piloting crafts before this?"

"Just an RE craft. In class."

"Who taught you to fly?"

"My instructor. Xion Da'ath."

"We'll have to talk with this Alien Da'ath next." Agent Marnox notes something down. "Miss Jones, just for our records, what is your Starseed classification and incarnation number?"

"I'm an Earthseed. First incarnation."

The agents exchange another look.

"That's... highly unusual," Kreth says slowly. He turns to Isis. "I wasn't aware the Academy was accepting Earthseeds."

"We made an exception for Miss Jones." Alien Isis's expression is cool and centered. "Since the portal allowed her in, we deemed her advanced enough for spiritual instruction."

"I see." Agent Marnox taps on his tablet. "One last question. Miss Jones, do you have any reason to believe that this craft could be used as a weapon?" Both agents look at me with renewed intensity.

"Ra? Are you kidding?" I scoff at the question. "He's like a toddler. The only way he could hurt anyone is if I crashed him into something."

Agent Marnox writes something down.

"Not that I would do that," I add quickly.

Kreth leans in closer. "Miss Jones, if Ra exhibits any signs of aggression or military design, you must report it to us immediately."

"Why?" I meet Kreth's stare. "Aren't you supposed to be some spiritually advanced, peaceful civilization? Are you fighting something we don't know about?"

Kreth flexes his jaw. "Our job is to ensure the vibrational alignment of the galaxy, Miss Jones. Any advanced military technology must be studied so that we can protect the collective consciousness of the Federation."

"Protect it from what?" I say, a little louder than I mean

to.

The agents look at each other, then back at me. "That's all we have for you today, Miss Jones," Marnox says. They both stand up, their chairs scraping sharply against the floor. "We'll be monitoring you throughout the semester to see if anything changes."

"I'm sorry. You'll be what?"

"We have been assigned to remain at the Agartha Starseed Academy for the remainder of the school year to monitor your connection with the Eldercraft in question. At the end of the semester, we will submit our report to the Council of Five."

"You mean you'll be following me around *for the rest of the year?*"

"You won't even know we're here, Miss Jones. Just go about your life as usual. We'll contact you if we need anything else. Now, Alien Isis, will you please show us to the craft site so we can see this Eldercraft for ourselves?"

"Wait," I say, standing up. "If you're going to see Ra, I should come too."

"That won't be necessary, Miss Jones. We want to get a baseline reading from the craft without the pilot's energetic interference."

I open my mouth to argue, but Isis steps in, placing a hand on my shoulder.

"It's alright, Synchronicity," she says softly. Her gaze meets mine. "I won't let anything happen to him."

CHAPTER
THIRTY-NINE

January turns to February, and despite the constant presence of Agents Kreth and Marnox in my classes, life goes on much as it had. Any flicker of heat I feel for Xion after our private flight sessions is swiftly extinguished by the agents' endless interrogations.

How would you characterize your connection with the craft during this flight?

Ecstatic.

Can you access any other abilities besides flight?

No.

Are you having any thoughts of violence toward yourself or others?

Does fantasizing about smashing that tablet over your blue alien head count?

I don't say that last part.

Even though I know the days are getting longer, it's hard to escape the weight of winter's lethargy. It's heavy, like a deep depression sinking into my bones.

On Valentine's Day, someone slides a little pink note under my door:

"I know this day is stupid, but I can't stop thinking about you."

Signed only with a heart.

Xion would never.

Kai, maybe?

On February 22nd, I wake up feeling like a sack of bricks. The body remembers, my ex once told me. Today is the one-year anniversary of his death.

I'd done my best to avoid thinking about what happened to Aidan and everything that unfolded afterwards, but now, exactly twelve months later, the memories come flooding back.

The creek. The ice. The axe.

I had been so sure of myself. So sure it would work.

Now I'm not sure of anything anymore.

I skip Energy Work. I skip Craft. I just lie curled in a tight ball as the winter wind howls outside. By six o'clock, I can't take the grief aching in my soul anymore. I get out of bed for the first time today, throw on some leggings and a hoodie, and walk out into the hall.

Before I reach the doors to the outside, Kreth and Marnox stop me. They're drinking tea in the lounge. "Where are you going, Synchronicity? We noticed you missed class today." Agent Marnox wears the same blank expression he always wears.

"Out." I walk past them without stopping.

The agents set down their tea and stand up. "Would you like accompaniment, Miss Jones? Agent Kreth and I would love to catch up with you and see how you're feeling."

"Fuck off," I snap. "Not today."

I push open the door and step out into the storm. Flurries of snow whip at my face, spiraling off into the darkening sky. I clutch my hood tightly around my face and trudge off into the cold, not knowing where I'm going.

Except... I do. Of course I do.

My boots crunch through the snow as the wind howls louder, stinging my cheeks and snatching my breath. I tell myself I'm just walking to clear my head, just moving to stay warm. But my feet betray me—carrying me down the winding path, past darkened buildings and frost-covered lights, until I'm standing in front of a familiar door.

Xion's.

I hesitate for a second, heart thudding in my chest, then raise my fist and pound against the metal, hard enough to be heard over the screaming wind. A moment later, he throws open the door, his tall, dark silhouette illuminated by the warm light inside.

"I... I need you," is all I can make out before I collapse into his arms.

"Come on," he murmurs, voice rough like it's scraped raw. "Let's get you out of here."

He lifts me without effort, cradling me against his chest

as he carries me down the steps and out into the wind-swept craft site.

"Should I connect with Ra?" I look up at him, and the hard line of his jaw flexes against the biting wind.

"You're in no state to fly right now." His tone tells me that there will be no arguing with him. His massive arms cradle me like some warlord carrying a fallen queen. He strides toward the deadly black shape of Nyx Arcana, hovering steadily two feet above the snow. Her hatch hisses open at our approach, and without breaking stride, Xion carries me inside his ship.

The interior swallows me like it always does—dark and timeless, all matte black and shadowed chrome. Ancient glyphs pulse faintly along the walls.

He lowers me gently onto the soft bench seat.

"I'm sorry I barged in on you tonight," I stammer. "I'm going through something and..."

"You don't need to apologize for anything, Synchronicity." His voice is low, steady, like it's trying to anchor something in me. Those haunting amber eyes hold mine, and for a moment, it's like he sees entirely too much. "And you certainly don't need to explain yourself. Not to me. Not to anyone."

The way he looks at me sends heat pooling low in my stomach. There's a quiet power in him, like he could break me open without even touching me. And tonight, I'm not sure I'd mind.

"Do you think everyone here is running from something?" I cross my legs and turn toward him on the seat. "Or is it just me?"

"I think to be a spiritual person at all, something in your life has to rip you open." He rakes his gaze over me, dropping his eyes from my lips, to my breasts, to my legs, and back up. "Something so crazy and unpredictable that it breaks you to your core."

"And what if I don't want to be broken anymore?" My voice comes out softer than I expect, nearly a whisper. I shift closer on the seat, drawn to him like gravity, my lips parting with a need I can't name—only feel.

His eyes darken. Not with anger. With heat. With something dangerous and reverent all at once.

"You don't have to be," he says, voice low and rough. "Not with me."

I let out a breath I didn't know I was holding. "You say that like you've seen it before. Like you know what it's like... to be wrecked and remade."

"I do," he murmurs. "And I know what it's like to want something so badly it terrifies you."

My heart stutters. He reaches up slowly, like he's giving me time to stop him. I don't.

His hand brushes my jaw, fingers trailing gently behind my ear. And then, finally, he closes the distance.

His mouth captures mine, and I melt—utterly, completely —into the kiss. His other hand tunnels into my hair, pulling me closer like he can't stand even an inch between us.

"Synchronicity..." he groans against my lips, and it's not just a name, it's a promise, a surrender, a prayer.

And I want him to say it again.

And again.

Until there's nothing left but the sound of it between us.

"I thought you didn't want this," I whisper, arching my back and pushing the tips of my breasts against his chest.

"You are exactly what I want." In one swift movement, he picks me up with his hands gripping the back of my thighs and pins me against the wall of his craft. The force of the motion sends Nyx Arcana swaying in the darkness.

My pulse hammers, a fierce thrill rising in my chest, knowing he feels it too.

"Good," I murmur, tilting my head to catch his lower lip between mine, teasing it with a playful nibble. "Because I've wanted you for a long time."

Our lips crash together in a kiss that's wild, ravenous, and all-consuming. I grind my hips into his, using the wall behind me for leverage and moaning into his mouth as need coils tight in my core. His hands find my ass, gripping hard, pulling me flush against him, so close I can feel every promise his body makes against mine.

His mouth trails down my neck, lips grazing my skin with maddening slowness until he reaches the hollow of my collarbone.

"Source help me..." he growls against my throat, and the next thing I know, he's hauling me into the cockpit. My ass hits the dashboard and I wrap my legs around his waist, locking my ankles to bring him closer. My body presses against a cluster of buttons, and Nyx Arcana roars to life, shooting upward with a lurch that steals the breath from my lungs.

I gasp. "Xion—"

"Don't worry. I've got it." He cradles my head in his hand, tilting it back for deeper access before plunging his tongue into my mouth. The ship levels out, and I realize he's flying her with nothing but his mind.

Every nerve in my body sparks to life. I'm molten, anchored only by his hands and the heat between us. I want him everywhere. Anywhere. Always.

"Tell me to stop and I will," he groans as his mouth explores the sensitive spots on my neck.

"If you stop now, I might just kill you," I say ragged and breathless, arching my neck back as his lips travel further down.

"I'd like to see you try that." He pushes a hand between us and the tip of his finger rubs against my clit through the fabric of my leggings, igniting a jolt of pleasure that radiates through my whole body.

I rock my hips against his fingers, desperate for more, but my leggings are in the way, tight, infuriating, a barrier I suddenly can't stand.

"Touch me," I breathe, voice edged with need.

He pulls back just enough to look at me. The hunger in his eyes is barely restrained. "If I take these off, I don't think I'll be able to stop."

I meet his gaze without flinching. "When did I ever give you the impression that I wanted you to stop?"

Something in his stony expression caves. He rips off my leggings and underwear, sending my shoes flying across the cabin in the process. I pull him back in, and he grazes my slick essence with his mechanic's fingers. His mouth is on mine again, and I tilt up, trying to taste all of him. The chaos, the ruin, the darkness.

He slides a finger into me, and I groan against him, clawing at his shirt. I manage to get it over his head, and my nails dig into his back as he curves his fingers inside me with expert strokes.

"Fuck, I want to be inside you, Synchronicity." His voice is a barely tamed growl.

"Then stop talking and take me." I rip off my sweater while he unbuckles his belt and drops his pants to the floor. I reach out and pull him into me, devouring his mouth in a shameless kiss.

He lifts me effortlessly, carrying me toward the center of the cabin. Every step he takes sends his shaft sliding against my swollen clit, a tease that has my breath hitching in his arms.

We sink to the floor in a tangle of limbs and heat, my legs wrapped tight around his waist, his breath warm against my cheek.

"Are you sure you want this?" he murmurs, voice thick with restraint, hovering just above me.

I meet his gaze, heart pounding, every nerve strung tight with anticipation.

All I can do is nod.

He kisses me again as he begins to ease inside, inch by aching inch. I shudder, nipples brushing his chest, and pull his lower lip between my teeth as he sinks deeper, filling me completely, stretching me to the edge of pleasure and pain.

I gasp. His fullness is almost too much. A sweet, burning ache that crashes through me like a solar flare, blinding and unstoppable.

"Source take me," he groans. "You feel... unreal." His hand finds the back of my neck, grounding me as his hips begin to move, each slow, deliberate thrust brushing against my clit and unraveling me further.

My fingers slide along the hard lines of his back, clutching at the muscle as he tilts my hips for a deeper angle, driving into me with growing intensity. I cry out, the sound half prayer, half demand.

I finally have him—Xion Da'ath—inside me. The thought alone sends a tremor through my body, stimulating every cell, every strand of my earthbound DNA.

He slams into me at a savage pace, driving the knot of pleasure inside of me ever tighter. "Xion..." I cry out his name as I writhe beneath him, arching my back for more.

"You're mine, Synchronicity. You're all mine." His hand grazes over my chest, calloused palm closing around my hypersensitive breasts, sending sparks straight to the tightening knot of pleasure deep in my core.

He claims my mouth with another kiss, and I lose all control. The pressure inside me snaps, and I shatter around him with a cry that tears from my throat, raw and feral. My body arches, trembling, as my inner muscles clench hard, trying to pull him deeper inside of me.

"Fuck," he groans, his breath hot against my skin. "I love feeling you come." His voice is black velvet, dark and addictive, and all I can do is whimper into the curve of his neck.

He picks me up and carries me to the bench seat, never breaking contact. As he settles between my legs and begins to move again, a new wave of pleasure grows inside of me, building on the crest of the last.

I brace my hand against the wall, pushing back to take him deeper. "Fuck—yes. Don't stop," I gasp between kisses.

"I've got you." His hand slips between us, fingers finding my clit and circling in perfect sync with the rhythm of his thrusts. The dual sensation wrecks me. My body tightens, spiraling, until another orgasm detonates inside me, blinding, infinite. It crashes through me like the echo of creation itself, rippling outward in uncontrollable waves.

"So. Fucking. Beautiful." He looks at me like I'm the only thing in the universe. Like he can't believe I'm real.

I ride the wave in complete surrender, every nerve lit up, every thought stripped away. Just as I start to descend from the high, he lifts one of my legs and thrusts deeper than he ever has before.

The first stroke sends a jolt down my spine; the next has me moaning in his ear, and on the third, he buries himself to the hilt, a shudder rolling through his body as he spills inside me.

He lingers there, braced above me, chest heaving, looking at me like he's not sure whether he just destroyed me... or brought me back to life.

"What the fuck did we just do?" I murmur, letting my fingertip glide along his jaw.

"Exactly what we needed to." He rolls off me and collapses onto the bench seat.

"I lean in, resting my cheek against his chest, syncing my breath to the quiet rhythm of his. "Thanks. I needed that." The memory of him inside my body still lingers as an aching warmth.

"It was one hundred percent my pleasure." He reaches out and cups my ass in his hand.

I trace my finger slowly along the dark tribal patterns etched into his crimson skin, following the bold lines that snake across his torso and upper thighs. The tattoos are black as void, stark against the living warmth of him.

"What do these mean?" I murmur, my voice barely a whisper against the quiet thrum of Nyx Arcana.

"They're Maldekian soulmarks," he says after a beat. His chest rises and falls beneath my hand. "Every one of us carries them. They're a link to what we were... to what we lost."

I pause, feeling the ripple of tension beneath his skin. My hand drifts lower, hovering over the sensitive place where his hip curves into his thigh.

"I read something once..." I hesitate, tracing a lazy circle with my fingertip. "That Maldek wasn't destroyed by war or power. That it was... something else. Fifth-dimensional energy parasites. Vampires."

I glance up at him through my lashes. "Have you ever heard of anything like that?"

For a moment, he's utterly still. Then I feel it—a subtle hardening of his muscles under my hand. His entire body tenses like a wire stretched too tight.

"Just stories," he says. But it's too fast. Too practiced. "We were a civilization drunk on our own power. Nothing more."

I study him in the warm glow of the glyphs.

"You don't believe that," I say, not as a question, but a truth hanging heavy between us.

He doesn't answer.

Instead, I tilt my face up toward his, catching the light in his amber eyes.

"And the package?" I ask, softer now. "The one you delivered. Who was it for?"

For a moment, he just breathes, slow and deep.

When he finally speaks, it's a threadbare whisper.

"For those still fighting in the dark."

His fingers graze my hairline, tucking a strand behind my ear with a gentleness that almost undoes me.

"Friends. Protectors. People you'll be safer not knowing."

"But I want to know," I whisper.

He leans in, resting his forehead against mine. His skin is warm, grounding me against the cold that's been eating at me all day.

"If I tell you," he says, "there's no going back. It's safer for both of us if you don't ask again."

His voice is so raw, so full of something unspoken, that I nod without thinking, pressing myself closer against him.

Whatever he's carrying... it's heavier than I could imagine.

I curl into the hollow of his chest, feeling the steady rhythm of his heart beneath my cheek. His arm wraps around me instinctively, pulling me closer.

The thrumming of Nyx Arcana fades into the background. The storm outside feels far away now.

Wrapped in his warmth, sheltered in the strange gravity between us, the exhaustion of the day finally catches up to me.

I let my eyes drift closed, the steady rise and fall of his breathing lulling me down into sleep.

The last thing I feel is the touch of his lips against the top of my head.

And the fierce, silent promise wrapped in his arms around me.

CHAPTER
FORTY

When I wake, I'm alone, wrapped only in a thin blanket. Pale winter light seeps through the windows, dusting the dark cabin in gold.

My clothes are strewn across the floor like the remnants of some wild dream. Piece by piece, I gather them up, my body still thrumming with the afterglow of the night before.

The exit hatch hisses open, and I step down into a dazzling bluebird morning. The storm is gone now, leaving behind only silence and untouched snow.

Xion is nowhere to be found.

I check his house. The door is unlocked, the hearth cold, the only sign of life a forgotten mug of coffee on the counter. The hangar's no different.

Only Ra hums faintly in the quiet, the hieroglyphs on his shell lighting up with a soft blue glow as I brush my fingertips across them.

He might be gone, but the fire he left in my veins still burns bright.

Last night I had him. Xion Da'ath. For a night at least, he was mine.

I linger after Herbalism, waiting until the other students shuffle out. "Alien Thumgren," I say, crossing to her desk. "May I talk with you for a moment?"

She peers up at me, her green skin crinkling into a patient smile. "What is it, my dear?"

"Well, it's a little embarrassing." I shuffle my feet.

"You can tell me. Anything said between us stays between us. You have my word." Her wizened eyes look like they've seen everything under the Agarthan sun.

"Well, I kind of need a contraceptive." My cheeks redden as I clarify: "an *after-the-fact* contraceptive."

Her expression doesn't change. She chuckles warmly.

"You'd be surprised how often I'm asked for that." She

turns around and retrieves a glass jar from the veritable apothecary that lines the wall behind her. She parcels out three spoonfuls of the herb into a cloth satchel and hands it to me. "Queen Anne's Lace seeds. Take a teaspoon, chewed well with water, this morning, tonight, and tomorrow morning. The Queen will take care of the rest."

"Thank you, Alien Thumgren," I say, genuinely relieved.

"Nothing to be ashamed of, dear," she says, pressing the satchel into my hands with a wink. "Life is meant to be lived."

The seeds have a mild, carroty taste and I wash them down with a swig of water in the bathroom before Galactic History. As I step out, I'm greeted by Agents Marnox and Kreth.

"Good morning, Synchronicity," Kreth says smoothly. "A quick word?"

I don't stop walking. "I'm late for class."

Undeterred, they follow. "We noticed you were heading toward the craft site yesterday evening. Did you happen to fly Ra?" Marnox has his selenite tablet at the ready.

I don't even turn around. "No."

"You realize that unauthorized flight of your Eldercraft is expressly prohibited. We must be made aware of any flight attempts to conduct a proper assessment of your performance." Agent Marnox trails behind me with Kreth in tow.

"I told you I didn't fly him." I push open the door to Alien Lumari's class, and the agents slink in after me, taking their usual post at the back.

"Do Tweedledum and Tweedledee ever take a day off?" Jasper slouches in his chair, rolling a coin on his knuckles.

"God, I wish. Those guys are creeps," I say, taking a seat between him and Mae.

"Sync, you're freaking glowing today. Did you finally try that beef tallow like I told you?" Mae leans forward, trying to get a better look at my face.

"Yeah, something like that." I tuck a loose strand of hair behind my ear and look down at my desk to hide the blush I feel rising to my cheeks.

"I know that look," Jasper says.

Please don't say it. Please don't say it.

"Synchronicity got laid last night, didn't you?"

I can feel my face go beet red. "Guys, stop. It wasn't anything."

"Oh my Source, who was it?" Mae puts her hand on my thigh. "Sync, you have to tell me. It was Kai, wasn't it?"

At the mention of his name, Vaylen turns around in her seat and gives me an absolute death glare. I've seen her talking with him around campus, twirling her perfect hair around her finger and laughing obnoxiously at his jokes.

"No. It wasn't *Kai*," I say firmly, staring right back at her until she turns back to face the front of the class, nose in the air.

Mae squeezes my thigh. "Then who?"

I drop my face into my hands and mumble, "Xion."

"What?"

She either didn't hear me or didn't believe me.

I hide my face with the palm of my hand and whisper, "It was *Xion*."

"Oh my Source, Sync!" Mae lets out a squeal and covers her mouth.

Now Kara, June, and Vaylen are looking back at us.

"Will you shut up?" I whisper emphatically, sinking further behind my hand. "Do you want the whole class to know?"

"Synchronicity, I am both horrified and obscenely proud that you would sleep with one of the prime suspects in our murder investigation." Jasper scratches Mochi behind the ears, who is sitting on his desk curled up in a ball.

"It wasn't like that," I mutter. "I *know* he didn't do it. He's... he's got a good heart." My chest warms at the memory of him against me last night. The intensity, the desire...

"Oh, Sync," Jasper says, dramatically fanning himself with a notebook. "I didn't think you could be swayed so easily. One night with Alien Death and now you're dicknotized."

"How was it, Sync? I have to know." Mae pats my leg

excitedly with both hands.

"It was good," I say, settling back into my seat as Alien Lumari floats to the front of the classroom. "*Really* good."

CHAPTER
FORTY-ONE

For the rest of the day, I'm floating on cloud nine. Even the sight of Agent Marnox and Kreth tailing me through the halls can't drag me down. When they finally retreat to their assigned housing for the night, I take my second dose of Queen Anne's Lace and slip away to the craft site.

I find Xion in the hangar, bent over a beam accelerator, the muscles in his back tense beneath a fitted black shirt. He looks up from his work as I approach, but the warmth I remember from last night is nowhere to be found.

"I wasn't expecting you tonight." His tone is as cold and as hard as the concrete floor.

"I thought we might have a private session." I step lightly towards him, hands held behind my back. "Without those pesky agents watching us."

"Synchronicity," he says, wiping his hand on a rag, "if this is about last night..."

Where is the man who was so full of passion? The one who told me I was his?

"It doesn't have to be about last night," I say, leaning casually against his workbench. "We could just hang out and talk."

"About what?" There is no joy in those eyes.

"I don't know. Tell me something about you. Something you've never told anyone else before." I crane my neck up at him, trying to evoke some sense of the emotions we felt last night.

"I don't have time for this right now," he says, turning his attention back to the machine in front of him.

Anger flares in my chest. "What the hell is wrong with you? Last night, you told me I was yours. You opened up to me."

"Last night, I gave you what you needed. That's all." His gaze remains fixed on his little project.

"Hey!" I slam my palm against his shoulder, feeling the

solid, immovable weight of him. "The least you could do is *look at me* while you rip my heart out."

Finally, he turns. "Synchronicity, I..."

"No, just shut up. This is so like you. One day we're connecting on a soul level, and the next you have your walls back up like it meant nothing."

"Synchronicity, you should..." he starts, but there's a flash of something behind his eyes. Fear? Regret?

"No, let me finish, because I know it meant something to you. I know it. Why can't you just fucking admit that there's something between us?"

"Please stop, Synchronicity. You don't know what you're..." He reaches out his hand toward me, but I smack it away.

"Don't fucking touch me, asshole. You should never have slept with me if you didn't have any intention of committing. God, I was so stupid to think you could change!" Spit flies from my mouth, and I notice a red glow has lit the room.

"Synchronicity, look behind you!" The urgency plastered across his face is real.

I whirl around.

Ra is hovering in the center of the hangar, his white shell blazing with red sigils.

And worse, he's armed. Two massive plasma cannons extend from either side of his hull, locked directly onto Xion.

"I don't fucking care!" I scream, wiping a tear away from my eye as I step toward Ra, furious and reckless, and his cockpit opens like a mouth inviting me inside.

"Do *not* get in that craft, Synchronicity. You're not thinking straight. He's connected to your emotions." Xion takes a step forward, but a blast of white energy shoots out of one of Ra's guns and obliterates the workbench.

Xion backs up slowly, hands raised. "Easy, Synchronicity. He's only reacting to you. You have to calm down."

But I'm past the point of calm. "Fuck you, asshole." I climb up into the cockpit, and Ra seals me inside. I feel his tendrils wrap around me, threading into my mind...

Then all I can see is red.

CHAPTER
FORTY-TWO

"Come on. Stay with me, Jones." Someone's slapping my cheek. I peel my eyes open, and the silhouette of Xion's head resolves against the night sky. "Oh, thank Source, you're alive.

The pain in my body screams with each step that he takes, nearly sending me into another blackout. "What... what happened?"

"Shh, just hold on. We're almost there." His voice is taut, unraveling at the edges.

He carries me in his arms for what feels like an eternity. Somewhere along the way, he adjusts my weight into one arm so he can knock on a door, sending a wave a nausea through me that almost has me retching.

"Come on. Come on, open up." His fist slams against the door again, harder.

A light comes on. The door opens. "Who is it?" I recognize Kai's voice, groggy, confused. "Xion? What the hell?"

"There's no time." Xion barrels through the doorway. "Where's your bed?"

"Just back there." I can hear Kai following close behind. "What the hell happened to her?"

"There was an accident." Xion lays me down on Kai's bed as carefully as he can, but the pain of shifting my body is so intense that all I can see is white light.

When my vision comes back, Kai has his hands over me. "Nearly every bone in her body is broken. What happened, Xion?"

"She flew. She flew when she was angry. I've never seen a craft move like that." All the color has drained from Xion's face.

"You let her fly in that state? God dammit Xion. What the hell were you thinking?"

"We can argue about this later. She needs medical attention. Now. Can you heal her?" I've never seen Xion like this before. He looks scared to death.

"Internal bleeding, severe head trauma... she needs a whole team of healers. Why did you bring her here?"

"If those fucking agents find out what happened, what Ra can do, they'll have that ship *and* Synchronicity locked up at a blacksite for the rest of her life. You know they would, Kai. Now, please, can you help her?"

Both men turn toward me, faces etched with worry.

"I can heal her," Kai says, turning his gaze on Xion. "But I need you out. Get the hell out of my house you irresponsible ass."

Xion's jaw ticks. "Just let me know when she's okay."

"I'll take it from here, flight instructor. Now get out." Kai is nearly a foot shorter than Xion, but he meets his gaze with a glowering intensity.

Xion looks like he might say something, but simply takes one last look at me before disappearing out of the house.

The second he's gone, Kai kneels beside me again, brushing a trembling strand of hair from my face. "Oh, Synchronicity. What has he done to you?"

I can barely breathe. My chest feels like it's filled with broken glass.

"Please," I whisper. "It hurts."

"I've got you. You're okay. You're going to be okay." His hands move over me, warm and glowing, drawing in breath after breath like a prayer. "Just stay with me, alright? Stay right here."

I manage the barest nod.

"Shit," he mutters. "This is going to be a long night."

Kai gently places his hands on either side of my neck and feels the individual vertebrae. "Compression fractures. I'm going to start with your neck." He holds out his palms above my throat and closes his eyes. A glowing aurora of rainbow light appears around his hands, swirling like a whirlpool and flowing down over my neck.

The intense pain there slowly melts into pleasure as the healing light caresses my throat like a lover. He moves like that, up to my head, down to my shoulders, and each injured spot becomes warm and soft and excitable. When Kai's hands are over me, it's like every nerve is standing on end, begging to be touched.

"You've got a lot of broken ribs. Just bear with me." His eyes are kind and compassionate, and I know that I am safe with him. He moves his hands over my chest and the tingling sensation floods over my skin. Heat races across my breasts as the iridescent light billows down, wrapping around and penetrating me. I can't help but arch my back as the healing light seeps into my bones, making them as sensitive as any erogenous zone. It's like torrents of down feathers are spiraling over my nipples and I feel them become erect, pleading for physical touch.

I want to tell him to grab them, to massage away the intensity that needs to be released, but I know it would be completely inappropriate. This man is trying to save my life, after all. Not get me off.

He moves down to my stomach, leaving my nipples desperate and unsatisfied. The erotic sensation follows, and as the healing light pours into my body, I can feel it rearranging my guts and filling every inch of flesh with hot, burning need.

I bite my lip and moan.

"I'm sorry. I know this is a lot." Kai slows the healing light to a trickle. "We can stop for a moment if you need a break."

"Fuck no. Keep going," I command, breathlessly.

He turns his healing power back on, igniting renewed lust in my veins as he transforms my broken bones and bruised insides into puddles of unquenchable desire.

Kai moves his hands over my hips. A jolt of pleasure shoots up my spine—then back down to my toes, reverberating through my body in waves. "Holy fuck, that feels amazing."

"One of the unfortunate side effects of my healing powers." The hint of a smirk curls his lips, and I realize he's enjoying this just as much as I am. "You're pretty messed up down here. This is going to be a lot."

"Don't hold back on my account." I try to tilt my hips upward to get a better angle but pain erupts deep inside of me.

"Just relax," he says, ever calm and present. "Let me do all the work." Kai closes his eyes and outstretches his hands. The healing light flows forth with renewed vigor, lighting my nerves aflame.

Normally I'd be worried that he could see how wet I'm getting through my leggings but right now I don't even care. His healing power is working a magic on me like nothing I've ever felt before.

I bite back another moan as the light spreads over my clit, massaging me with expert softness as it tunnels deeper inside of me. "Oh fuck, don't stop..." I blurt out as my core fills with a bright ball of pressure, begging for release.

Kai thrusts his hands forward and the light shoots into me, flowing past my clit like an endless stream, penetrating me in my deepest essence. He pulses his hands one more time and the ball of pleasure inside me explodes, sending a shockwave straight to my throat as I moan out his name. "Kai..."

The orgasm fades as Kai pulls his healing energy back, only to thrust it in again with another movement. It's like the ocean tide going in and out, making me come again and again with each onrush.

With one last earth-shattering orgasm he retracts the healing light completely and leaves me gasping for air on his bed.

"You did great, Synchronicity." Kai stands at the bed, next to me, stroking my hair.

"Are you done?" I ask, half-wishing it's not over.

"I still have to do your legs, but I figured this was a good time for a break."

"I'm sorry about all... that," I say, blushing. "Like you said, it was a lot."

"You have nothing to apologize for." Kai scratches his cheek. "As your medical professional, I shouldn't really say this, but seeing you like that kind of turned me on."

"Kai Moongate," I say slapping his thigh. "Are you flirting with a patient?"

"A very, very lovely patient." There's something more behind his eyes than kindness, but I'm afraid of what it might mean.

"Kai, I... don't know what to say." With everything that has been going on with Xion, Kai feels like a safe harbor in a storm.

"You don't have to say anything. Let me get you a glass of water. You're going to need a lot of it."

I drag myself up into a sitting position but the pain in my legs is still excruciating.

Kai returns with the water and I gulp it down.

"Are you ready for round two?" he asks, holding out those magic hands in front of him.

"Only if it ends with the same amount of fireworks," I say.

"We'll see about that." He moves down to the end of the bed and hovers his hands over my feet. "Let's begin."

With the same tantalizing energy he works his way up my legs, arousing every cell with exquisite pleasure. My pain melts away and is replaced by the overwhelming need to be touched. By the time he reaches my hips again I am completely insatiable. The current of healing light grazes my clit and I shudder as the sensation ripples through my body. "Kai, I want you..."

He brings his glowing hand up to my cheek. "Are you sure this is the right time?"

"I need you inside of me." It's not a request. It's an order.

I grab that beautiful face and pull his lips to mine. We meet in a gentle, chaotic embrace and his lips part for more. I run my fingers through his hair and pull his full weight on top of me. All the pain in my body has been replaced by a needy warmth that demands to be satisfied.

"Synchronicity, ever since that first day I saw you at the Entrance Obelisk, I've wanted this." He props himself up and looks down at me.

"Then you should have done something about it," I say,

guiding his lips to my neck. He kisses me down to my collarbone, releasing some of the want that has lingered there since his healing light first touched me. He unzips my jacket and makes his way to my breasts, pulling the fabric of my tank top aside with his unshaven chin.

"Oh fuck, I needed this." I arch my back and push the tip of my breast into his eager mouth. He circles his tongue around my nipple and nips it gently with his teeth, sending little jolts of electricity through me.

I claw at his flowy linen shirt and he pulls it off revealing a surprisingly athletic physique. I run my finger down his chest and over his abs to the spot where a hint of hair protrudes above his trousers. Shamelessly, I bite my lip and look longingly up at him.

"Not yet," he says, kissing me over my tank top and down to my belly button, running his fingers over my pantie line. He takes the band of my leggings between his teeth, and with his hands, pulls everything down to my ankles.

I rub my newly healed thighs against each other, and he pounces on them, looking up at me while his chin rests on my pelvic bone.

"Are you sure you're okay with this?" he asks.

"Mmm hmm," I say, nodding.

He buries his face between my thighs and takes all of me in his mouth, resting the full length of his tongue against my entrance before licking me from bottom to top. A shiver shoots through me and I whimper into his pillow. He swirls his tongue around my clit before settling into a steady rhythm, flicking it with expert strokes.

I arch my head back into his plush pillows and grab my breast, rubbing my sensitive nipple between my fingers.

He pauses for a second. "Do I have your permission to put my fingers inside of you?" I appreciate his concern for my autonomy. It's nothing like Xion's brute aggression that had me questioning the boundaries of my own desire.

"Yes, of course." I prop myself up on my elbows. "Thank you for asking."

He goes back to sucking my clit and eases two fingers

inside of me, holding them motionless while my muscles adjust to their presence. Slowly he starts stroking my g-spot with a practiced "come hither" motion as he increases the pressure with his tongue.

I feel the ball of pleasure building again, and with each stroke he concentrates it, like a star ready to go supernova. Just when I feel like I'm on the precipice of ecstasy, he turns something on and those healing powers flood my core, pushing me over the edge as that ball of pleasure explodes into a million leg-shaking pieces.

He holds his mouth and his fingers firm as I ride out the wave, grinding against him until the last echoes of the orgasm settle into my bones.

"Holy fuck, that should be illegal," I say, collapsing onto his bed. He crawls up beside me and pulls the covers up to our chins. I roll over and put my head on his chest. "How's a girl not supposed to get addicted to you?"

"I admit I cheated a bit at the end, you know, being a Pleiadian Starseed and all." He holds up his hands and the remnants of the healing energy dance on his fingertips like electricity.

"Are you sure you don't want to finish?" I ask tracing my finger down to his pants.

"I'm okay for tonight. I try not to spill my sexual energy too often." He runs his finger through my hair and places a comforting hand on my back.

"Suit yourself," I say, snuggling into him. I want to ask him about Xion, about what happened to me tonight, but the gentle rise and fall of his chest lulls me into an impossibly deep and peaceful sleep.

CHAPTER
FORTY-THREE

In the morning, Kai's still there. He didn't leave me.

The constancy of his presence is like a balm to my restless soul. I yawn and stretch, reaching my arms up into the golden sunlight illuminating his room. My body aches, but a good kind of ache, like I just hiked a wonderfully exhausting trail. Kai is still asleep, sprawled on his side with his face half-buried in the pillow.

I glance around. His room is neat, filled with subtle beauty: abstract paintings on the walls, a few thriving plants tucked into sunlit corners. Nothing like the stark brutalism of Xion's house.

I tiptoe around, pulling my clothes back on piece by piece, trying not to wake him. But as I slide on my second shoe, Kai stirs, blinking up at me with sleep-warm eyes.

"Good morning," I whisper.

He props himself up on one elbow, his bare chest and lean torso catching the light. He's almost heartbreakingly handsome like this. I resist the urge to crawl back into bed and press my mouth against the line of his collarbone.

"How are you feeling?" he asks, voice still rough with sleep.

"A little sore," I admit, flashing a smile, "but good. Really good."

I lace up my shoes and reach for my coat.

Kai pushes himself upright, raking a hand through his dark mahogany hair. "Do you want tea? I usually do a little morning tea ceremony. Helps clear the mind."

The offer is so him—gentle, grounding.

"Any other time I'd love to, but there's something I need to do." I make for the door, but his voice stops me.

"Synchronicity."

I glance back. The sunlight outlines him, half-bare and honest. There's no judgment in his gaze. Only concern.

"Please, try to stay away from Xion. What he let happen

last night... That was reckless. You could have died."

For a heartbeat, my chest tightens.

"I know," I say softly. "Trust me. I have no desire to be anywhere near that man."

Back in my own room, I find the Queen Anne's Lace seeds and chew up the remaining spoonful, washing the bitter mush down with a glass of water. It feels cleansing, like I'm washing away the last chance of Xion and me ever being together. The last thing I want right now is to get pregnant by that heartless ass.

I grab my towel and toiletries and make my way to the spa. After a long, scalding shower, I pull on a clean outfit and head back toward my room, only to find the ever-vigilant agents from the Vibrational Alignment Bureau blocking my door.

"Miss Jones, we have to talk." Agent Marnox has his tablet out, and he looks even more serious than usual.

"What else is new?" I say, adjusting the pile of stuff in my arms. "Do you mind if I put this back first?" I elbow my way through the agents and shut the door to my room behind me.

I wring my hair out in my towel and memories of last night come flooding back. The fight with Xion. Ra...

Ra had guns.

Oh shit.

Did I hurt someone? Did I destroy the craft site?

I was so pissed at Xion, I wouldn't be surprised if I blew a hole straight through the pyramid.

Relax, Synchronicity, just relax.

If I'd hurt someone, I'd already be in handcuffs.

I send out a signal to Ra.

Ra, is everything alright?

For a moment, there's no response, and panic starts to grip my chest.

Synchronicity...

What happened last night?

Ra scared. Synchronicity mad.

I'm so sorry. I didn't mean to scare you. You should never have seen me yell like that.

We flew. You were so... angry.

Ra, what happened?

I show you.

The world blinks out, replaced by Ra's memory. Vivid, visceral, total.

I see the hangar through his eyes: me, raging, screaming at Xion. He's waving for me to stop and looking at Ra in fear.

He steps toward me, and a targeting system locks on him. A white flash shoots from one of Ra's guns, instantly destroying the work table. Xion stumbles back. I charge toward Ra's cockpit as it opens to receive me. The moment I climb inside, we are *one*.

Without warning, Ra lurches to the side, knocking over a quantum drive, then jerks left, scattering sockets across the floor like marbles. I can feel it now: Ra mirroring my fury, both of us out of control.

Xion sprints to the bay door controls. He slams the switch just in time before Ra rockets through the opening into the night.

We shoot upward at breakneck speed, acceleration so brutal it would have turned anyone else into paste. Then we slam to a dead stop in an impossible, bone-snapping halt.

Ra thrashes, wild, lost in the storm of my anger, moving in ways that should not be allowed by physics and breaking nearly every bone in my body.

We plummet back toward the craft site.

Impact seems inevitable, until a shadow falls over us.

Nyx Arcana.

She locks onto us with her red tractor beam.

The sensation is instant, like being wrapped in a weighted blanket. Ra's guns recede into his shell. His whole being hums with relief.

Nyx Arcana lowers us safely onto the ground, where Ra spits me out, limp and broken.

The scene fades, and I am back in my room.

"Is everything alright in there, Miss Jones?" Agent Kreth is pounding on the door.

"Hold your horses. I'm coming." I pull on my jacket and yank my door open. "Well? What do you want?"

"Please follow us, Miss Jones." Agent Kreth and Agent Marnox turn toward the exit, and I reluctantly follow behind them. "What's this about? I have to get to class."

"Please save your questions until we arrive." They lead me outside into a blindingly blue Agarthan day, straight toward the one place I hoped they wouldn't: the craft site.

I scan the rows of RE craft but don't find any signs of damage. Agent Kreth holds open the door to the hangar, and the three of us file inside.

Ra floats quietly at the center of the space, innocent as a child who definitely didn't fire a weapon last night. And right next to him, arms crossed and brooding like a storm cloud, is Xion.

Fucking asshole.

"Alien Da'ath, thank you for meeting with us this morning." Agent Kreth adjusts his posture even though he barely reaches Xion's shoulder.

"What's this about, guys? I had a rough night. I'm not really in the mood for your bureaucratic bullshit." He doesn't even make eye contact with me. Not once.

"That's precisely why we're here. There were several reports of an explosion last night, accompanied by strange lights in the sky."

"And why should that concern you fine agents?" Xion picks his teeth with a toothpick.

"Because, Alien Da'ath," Kreth says, tugging his collar straight, "at least one student said the strange lights looked like Ra. We did not give either of you permission for a flight lesson, and if an explosion was involved, well, we certainly need to know about that."

"Why would I sneak off to get extra lessons with *him*?" I jab a thumb toward Xion. "He's intolerable enough as it is."

Now I have his attention. He shoots me a glare that says

I'm too old to be acting this way.

"Interesting," Marnox mutters, jotting something down on his tablet. "Is there something going on between you two?"

I look Xion right in his heartless alien eyes. "Nothing. At. All."

Marnox softens, just slightly. "The emotional strain of connecting with an Eldercraft can lead to... instability. Burnout. Irrational behavior. Would you like to take a break from your flight lessons, Miss Jones?"

"I think that would be best for everyone involved," I say through clenched teeth.

"That still doesn't answer the question of the explosion and the reported lights in the sky," Agent Kreth says, returning to the original line of questioning.

"The explosion was from a beam accelerator I was working on. You know how insufferable those things can be." The ass is looking straight at me when he says it, and we both know he's not talking about machinery.

"Insufferable?" Agent Marnox echoes. "Can you clarify?"

"You know, finicky. Unstable." He holds my stare. "I'm lucky I wasn't killed."

I step forward, fire simmering beneath my skin. "You'd think that such an experienced mechanic would be able to handle a sensitive part like that. After all, he was the one who ripped it out of the craft in the first place." I lace each word with a poison I hope sinks into his bloodstream.

Marnox looks up from his tablet. "Miss Jones raises a valid concern. Wouldn't beam accelerator maintenance be standard for someone of your expertise?"

"I don't know what to tell you, gentlemen. This piece was unusually... *volatile*." His eyes glow brighter on the last word.

I scoff. The audacity of this man.

"That still doesn't explain the lights that several students saw in the sky last night." It's clear that Agent Kreth won't stop until he gets answers.

Xion's jaw ticks, and he holds my stare a moment longer before turning to Kreth. "Beam accelerators hold a plethora of tightly packed particle-antiparticle pairs. What was seen was simply the escaped particles interacting with Agartha's magnetic field." He fixes Kreth with a look that dares contradiction. "You should have been here. It was quite the fireworks show."

"I see," Agent Kreth says, and Marnox taps something down on his tablet.

"Are we through here, gentlemen?" Xion's tone is final.

The agents exchange glances. "Yes, we're through," Kreth confirms.

"Good," Xion says. "Because I've got a replacement accelerator to find."

"Good luck with that," I toss over my shoulder as the agents lead me out of the hangar. "I heard the one you had was irreplaceable."

CHAPTER
FORTY-FOUR

I find myself waking up at Kai's more often now. It's nice. Simple. Uncomplicated. I didn't know being with a man could be so easy. He makes me tea in the mornings. He listens when I vent. He's vulnerable, patient, and lets the relationship move as fast or as slow as I want.

March flies by in a blur of studying and late-night hangouts at Larimar House, but no matter how late I'm out, Kai always lets me snuggle into bed with him.

Xion, for his part, barely acknowledges me during regular Craft class. I spend that time rebuilding the Castor 5, learning every part of an RE craft from the ground up.

Life starts to return to the soil after winter's ravages, and by April, the campus is in full bloom. Trees unfurl new leaves like pages in a book, and the air hums with birdsong and possibility. In the crater gardens, my hyacinths push up in tight purple coils, and the tulips I planted open slowly to the sun—hesitant at first, then bold, almost defiant in their color. They reflect something in me I can't quite name: a thawing, a cautious uncurling.

My feelings for Kai.

I don't know if it's love. Not yet. Love is such a loaded word, so full of expectation, of weight. This thing between us is softer. Quieter. We haven't even said boyfriend and girlfriend, but we talk all the time about what we are and what we want out of this fragile, tentative thing between us.

If anything, Kai is almost *too* emotionally intelligent.

Sometimes I feel like I'm pretending to be spiritual just to keep up with him, terrified he'll see right through me.

Kai wants intimacy, deep and whole, and I love that about him.

But there's one thing I cannot tell him.

One secret so ugly I fear it would tear everything apart.

Still, even with that shadow clinging to my heart, things between us are good.

So good that I find myself dreading the end of the school year, when I'll have to leave Agartha behind and return to my surface life. Despite my trepidation, finals loom with the approach of May.

"None of my plants have sprouted yet," Cassandra says one afternoon. Her plot, a barren patch of cracked earth, sits right next to mine.

"Don't worry," I say, brushing the dirt from my hands. "There are still a few days left. Alien Thumgren won't fail you just because your seeds are shy."

"I've always been a bit of a late bloomer," Cassandra mutters.

"If it'll help, you can have some of mine."

"Really?" Her pale face brightens, and she tucks a strand of platinum-blonde hair behind her ear.

"Here, you can help me transplant a few of these irises."

We kneel in the dirt together, our hands working side by side, mine tanned and calloused, hers so frail they could belong to a ghost. Her meteorite necklace dangles between us, swaying back and forth as we pat the soil into place around the relocated bulbs.

The Agarthan sun begins its slow descent behind the rim of Atum Crater, staining the sky in dusky gold.

Across the garden, I catch sight of Peter tending his own plot, dark and solitary, like the grim reaper cultivating a crop of chthonic saplings. In a barren tree above him, Persephone sits croaking omens into the listless breeze.

"Thanks for this," Cassandra says, looking down at the tender green shoots. "It really means a lot to me."

"Of course, Cassy. Anything for a friend."

She gives me a soft smile. "See you in class tomorrow?"

"Definitely."

"You'll have a slightly different schedule this week to accommodate testing," Alien Sylestra announces, pacing briskly at the front of the classroom. "Tomorrow, you'll attend each of your classes for a one-hour final exam. That will conclude your school year here at Agartha. The following day, we'll hold the Beltane Festival at the Great Pyramid, and on Saturday, the portals will reopen to return you home."

She stops and surveys the room, the usual sharpness in her gaze softened by something almost affectionate.

"Your final will be very much like your midterms. You'll be assigned a patient suffering from an unknown disease. Your grade will depend on how accurately you diagnose and heal them. Use of spirit animals and musical instruments for our Arcturian and Lyran Starseeds is encouraged."

She gives a rare, proud smile. "In lieu of regular class today, I'm dismissing you early to study. You've all made tremendous progress this year. I'm proud to call you my students."

After a year of sharp critiques and barely concealed judgment, the sentiment catches me off guard.

"Thank you, Alien Sylestra," Vaylen croons from the front row. "I think I can speak for all of us when I say that you were an amazing teacher."

"Thank you, Vaylen." Sylestra inclines her head, dignified as ever. "Now, you may use this classroom to study if you wish. Otherwise, you are free to go, and I'll see you tomorrow at 9:00 a.m. sharp."

I turn to Cassandra, who's seated quietly at the desk beside me. "Are you nervous about the final?"

"A little," she says. "I hope I don't get something hard... like endometriosis or something."

"You'll be fine," I say, smiling. "With your voice, I'm pretty sure you could sing someone right back from death's door."

Cassandra blushes and looks down. "Thanks. Um... would you want to stay and study with me?"

"Sure," I say, just as the classroom door opens.

Kai steps in, sunlight catching the soft waves of his hair.

My heart flutters at the sight of him. He gives a small wave, and I return it without thinking.

Vaylen twists in her seat to see who he's greeting, and the second she realizes it's me, her expression curdles into a grimace.

I shrug innocently.

"Hello, everyone," Kai says, addressing the class. "I'm running a study session tonight in the Talon Room of the main pyramid, six to nine. Snacks included. If you need some last-minute help or just want to hang out, feel free to come by. Thanks."

Students start gathering their things to leave. Kai weaves through the crowd, making a beeline for me. "I just wanted to say hi," he says, standing a little awkwardly with his hands behind his back.

"That's sweet," I say, smiling up at him. "This is my friend, Cassy."

"Nice to meet you, Cassy," he says warmly. "Anyway, I should get going. I'll leave you girls to your study time."

And then, before I can react, he leans down and kisses me.

Not just a quick peck. A real, passionate kiss.

Right there, in front of everyone. In front of Alien Sylestra. In front of Vaylen.

I lean into it, feeling the world spin slower for a few precious seconds, savoring every moment of his wonderful lips.

When he finally pulls away, I glimpse Vaylen over his shoulder.

She's staring right at me, nostrils flared, jaw clenched, like a thundercloud ready to burst.

CHAPTER
FORTY-FIVE

It's our last Craft class before finals, and when I arrive, a knot of students has gathered on the field, murmuring in hushed, uneasy tones.

Xion is nowhere in sight.

And Nyx Arcana, the gleaming shadow of her presence usually hovering at the edge of the field, is gone too.

I spot Mae and Jasper standing a little apart from the others and head toward them.

"What's going on?" I ask.

Jasper's face is unusually grim. He doesn't answer, just jerks his chin toward the far end of the field.

I follow his gaze and freeze.

"GO BACK TO MALDEK"

The words are painted in huge, red letters across the side of Xion's house.

Anger sparks in my chest, hot and immediate.

I turn back to the group, my voice low and trembling with restraint. "Who wrote this?"

No answer.

Just whispers and muffled laughter.

I step forward, my voice rising.

"Who wrote this?"

Silence.

Dozens of eyes, some ashamed, some indifferent, none brave enough to meet mine.

"This is ugly and hateful," I say finally, voice cutting through the quiet. "I hope whoever wrote it takes a long, hard look at themselves. Writing like that isn't spiritual. It's cruel."

I don't wait for a response.

I turn and start marching toward the hangar.

Footsteps patter after me as Mae and Jasper catch up.

"That was badass," Jasper says, a little out of breath.

"I thought you didn't like Maldekians," I shoot back.

He shrugs. "Don't get me wrong. Xion can be an ass. But all that Starseed Sovereignty crap? It's just propaganda to keep everyone divided. I draw the line at hate speech."

"It's just awful," Mae adds, shaking her head. "Xion doesn't deserve that."

She hesitates, watching me change direction toward the hangar.

"But Synchronicity... where are you going?"

I don't slow down.

"I think I know where to find him."

I don't want anything to do with this man.

But he was there for me the night I needed it most, and somehow, I owe it to him to return the favor.

I flip the switch that opens the hangar bay doors and stride towards Ra. "Ready for a flight, buddy?"

Ra doesn't answer with words. He just opens the four curved segments of his shell, revealing the cockpit like a blooming flower. I climb in and feel his nerve-like tendrils slip around me, connecting us.

The shell seals, and we shoot out over the craft site, whistling past Mae and Jasper and the rest of the students who have to whip their heads to follow our trajectory. I pull Ra into a sharp climb, slicing through Agartha's blue atmosphere until the curve of the Hollow Earth reveals itself in all its impossible beauty.

We bank just before the rocky crust, following the gentle curve of terrain falling away beneath us, weightless and free. Of all the things in Agartha, I'm going to miss flying the most.

We race through the vast, empty expanse until the ceiling of stone breaks into the northern hole, the pathway to the surface world. The opening is so massive I can barely make out the other side as we soar up and over the edge into the terrestrial sky beyond.

I slow my speed and descend into a low glide over the ice wall that holds the oceans of Earth at bay. It doesn't take long to spot Nyx Arcana and the dark figure of Xion brooding on the edge of the ice.

I pull Ra into a hover and land next to Nyx Arcana on the glacial expanse. Ra opens up, and I detach from the white, nerve-like tendrils. Xion doesn't even look over at me as I walk toward him on the blue, fissured ground. He just stares up at the moon, illuminated in the bright daylight of the Arctic like an ancient saucer in the sky.

"I thought I'd find you here." I sit beside him, clutching my knees to my chest and trying to avoid looking over the edge at what is surely a terrifying drop.

"The one bad thing about Agartha," he murmurs, "is that you can't see the moon." He sits right on the edge, feet perched on an outcropping slightly below the rim of the wall. "They say Maldek had three moons. The Three Sisters, we called them."

"I'm sorry about what those kids wrote back there," I say. "It was disgusting. No one deserves to be treated that way."

"It's fine. They're right. We were a doomed civilization from the start. We got what we deserved." He turns his head away in disgrace.

"Don't say that." I reach over and put my hand on his, rubbing the back of it with my thumb.

"When you're treated like the villain your whole life, you start to believe it's true." He turns back to me, and there's real pain in his eyes, something ancient and aching. For the first time, I wonder if there's a chance he might jump.

"You're not a villain," I say, reaching up to touch the sharp line of his cheek. "And just because you don't have a planet doesn't mean you don't have a home."

His breath catches, and a flicker of vulnerability breaks through. Tears gather in those beautiful eyes, and something in my chest shifts. Suddenly, I'm not afraid of falling off the ice wall anymore.

I'm afraid of falling for him.

"I'm Maldekian, Synchronicity. I carry death and destruction around wherever I go. It's so deep in my DNA I don't think I could ever be truly healed." A shard of ice crumbles beneath his foot and vanishes into the void below.

"Is that why you never committed to me?" I whisper. "Because you think you're carrying around this generational curse?"

His jaw flexes, but he doesn't say anything.

"Listen, Xion. You're frustrating and you're moody and you're closed off, but you're not cursed. We are not our fucked up pasts. And if I want to be with someone, it's not your responsibility to protect me from that choice. None of us knows what's going to happen. All you can do is follow your feelings, and if someone gets hurt, then that's just part of this crazy cosmic drama we're all playing out."

"Synchronicity..." His voice is ragged and velvety and smoky and, Source help me, but when he says my name, my heart simply implodes.

"I know you're scared that if we were together, you might hurt me, but you're hurting me more by trying to protect me from you. You want me, Xion. I see it every time you look at me in class, when you stop by my craft to give me extra tips. I saw it that first day when you whispered in my ear the secret to starting the Castor 5."

I'm putting it all on the line. If he rejects me now, *I* might be the one who jumps.

"You have a lot of loss in your past. So do I, but life is huge and messy and encompasses everything, from the destruction to the joy, and I know that if we run from whatever this is, then we're not worthy of the divine spark that chose to incarnate in us at this exact point in time."

I look at him and I see that same utter yearning I feel in my own soul and it floods me with something I haven't felt in a long, long time.

"What about Kai?" he asks, and I see jealousy flare up in his eyes. "I know you've been seeing him."

"It's complicated. Kai is great. Maybe he's what I needed for a while, but he's just so perfect. And it's not that I feel like I don't deserve someone like that, it's that he doesn't have the depth or the darkness that I see in myself. And also, what did you expect? That I wouldn't have sex with anyone else while you sulked around in that black cloud of depression that follows you wherever you go?"

"Fair point. Synchronicity, I..." he starts, but I don't want any more of his excuses.

"I know, I know. You're my teacher, *and* you're Maldekian, but school ends in two days, and you won't be my teacher anymore. And as for the Maldekian thing, maybe the Galactic Federation can make an exception for beings from the same star system."

"That's not what I was going to say." He puts his hand up to my cheek, and his touch ignites a fire under my skin. "I was going to say I've wanted you for longer than you know. Ever since that first day I saw you in the Entrance Courtyard, I knew. Something about you... it undid me. I've never wanted anyone like that. Not once. And it terrified me, because I knew that after seeing you, nothing would ever be the same."

He doesn't move. Doesn't breathe. Just stares at me with those ruinous eyes, burning like dying stars.

My pulse hammers in my throat.

I can't take another second of the space between us.

I press myself forward and lock my lips on his like I'm holding on for dear life. He leans back and pulls me on top of him, spearing his fingers through my hair and kissing me back with such fervor that I know he meant every word he said.

I fumble with the zipper of his jacket, breath shallow, fingers shaking—but I manage to get it undone without once breaking our kiss. He sits up, peels off his tight white shirt in a single motion, and I drink in the sight of his tattooed chest, all sharp lines and power beneath inked skin. I tug him back into me, kissing harder, rocking my hips against his with rising urgency. Why the hell did I have to wear jeans today?

He slides open my own jacket, and I twist free, clinging to his mouth like I might unravel without it. His hands skim down my back, slipping under the hem of my shirt. He pulls it over my head, leaving us both bare-chested in the brisk Arctic air. I arch into him, my breasts pressed against the heat of his skin, our hips moving in rhythm, the ice forgotten beneath us.

In one swift motion, he flips me around and lays me on his leather jacket. One by one, he lifts my feet with a tenderness that feels at odds with the brutal strength etched into his frame, slipping off my shoes like I'm made of something sacred.

"Are you sure you want this?" I ask, looking up at him, framed by the impossibly blue sky.

His voice comes out low but steady. "I'm tired of running. I need you, Synchronicity, and that scares the hell out of me. No one has seen me like you do. No one has ever looked into my soul and met the darkness, not with fear or even compassion, but with desire like you have."

That's all I need to hear. My heart thunders and I reach for the button of his pants.

"But are you sure *you* want this, Synchronicity?" He catches my wrist before I can get him fully unzipped. "I know I haven't been good to you. I know I've been an ass." He looks at me like whatever I could say might break him.

I nod, firm. "As long as you don't shut me out again. As long as you promise to be honest with me."

He pulls my wrist above my head and lays me back down until he has it pinned against the snow. "I promise," he breathes—and then he kisses me, raw and reckless.

With his free hand, he manages to get my pants undone. I wriggle out of them and kick them to the side. I don't care if they fall off the edge. As far as I'm concerned, this moment is going to last forever.

He pulls down his own pants, and I can feel his tip pressing against my entrance. "Synchronicity," he groans.

"Take me," I say. "I want all of you." My skin feels like a smoldering tinder pile ready to burst into flames at any moment.

He runs his hand over the lines of my hips, over my breasts, and brings it to rest around my throat. The weight of it—not rough, just firm—grounds me. Anchors me.

I tilt my hips into him, and with one deep thrust, he

enters me. I gasp, the pleasure sharp and overwhelming, every inch of him stretching me open, filling me completely.

"Fuck, you feel so good around me," he growls into my ear.

I writhe under his touch, rocking my hips to get him deeper. He drives into me with hungry purpose, gripping my throat and pulling me toward him at the peak of each thrust, like he needs every part of me, deeper, tighter, closer.

"Harder," I say, placing my hand over his and squeezing.

He increases the pressure on my throat and slams his hips into me at a savage pace.

Just then, a low, thunderous crack reverberates through the ice, like the spine of the world snapping in half. The sound echoes across the cliffs, sharp and primal. Tiny plumes of snow burst upward around us as the ice beneath our bodies begins to fracture, splitting away from the main wall with a groan that sends panic lancing through my chest.

"Xion—" I gasp, scrambling to grab hold of something, anything, but it's too late. The entire shelf lurches beneath us, shearing off in a deafening roar of rending ice.

The world tips sideways, the ocean rushing up to meet us, when Nyx Arcana appears—silent, sudden, a gleaming shadow overhead. Her crimson tractor beam locks onto us in the nick of time, halting our freefall in a weightless blur of motion. The iceberg plummets past, crashing into the sea with a force that sends a spray of glacial mist into the air, waves rolling outward like aftershocks.

I cling to Xion, my breath caught somewhere between fear and awe.

"Don't worry. I've got you." His voice is warm against my ear. He pulls me closer to him, hovering in mid-air in the light of the tractor beam as our clothes float around us like petals suspended in starlight.

But all I can feel is the knot of pleasure still coiled tight inside me, pulsing with need. The cold, the chaos, the cliff collapsing beneath us—none of it matters. Not with the way his body presses to mine, not with the way my nerves still hum, begging for release. I close my eyes, breath ragged, clinging to him like he's the only thing tethering me to this reality. Because right now, he is.

He moves his hand to the back of my neck and guides me up and down on his massive member as we float there over the abyss.

"Source dammit! You feel so fucking good!" His eyes nearly roll to the back of his head with the pleasure I know is coursing through his body.

"Don't come yet... I'm almost there," I gasp, digging my fingers into his back as he drives me to the edge of ecstasy.

"I wouldn't dare." With his other hand he grips my ass and I grind my clit on his pelvic bone as he times his thrusts with the undulations of my hips.

His eyes lock on mine, and I watch him lose all control, pounding into me with an intensity that pushes me past the breaking point.

I scream out as we ride the wave of absolute pleasure that shudders through us. My walls spasm, trying to pull him deeper as he empties his essence into me, throb after leg-shaking throb, until I collapse like dead weight in his arms.

Everything else seems to melt away as Nyx Arcana pulls us up into her hull and closes her sleek black doors beneath us. I don't know how long I lay there in the cold cargo bay, wrapped in his big warm arms, but at some point, when almost all the pleasure has drained from my veins and I am on the verge of sleep, he sits up.

"We should get back to school. Those VAB agents are probably shitting themselves right about now." He adjusts me so I'm looking up at him. "Was that alright?"

"That was more than alright." I run my fingers over his chest. "It was perfect."

"*You* are perfect," he says, threading his fingers through my hair. "You know, Maldekian women don't have hair. I didn't know what I was missing."

The thought of him with another woman, Maldekian or otherwise, sends a fire of jealousy shooting up my spine. "There better not be some Mrs. Da'ath waiting for you at the end of the galaxy after all that."

He lets out a booming laugh. "I haven't been with a woman in a very long time. That's partly why I finished so quickly. But don't worry, that will get better with practice." He smiles. Not one of those self-satisfied smirks, but a real, heartwarming smile.

"I like the sound of that," I say, pulling on my pants. "You know, we're going to have to work out how you'll come to see me during the summer break. People on Earth aren't used to seeing big, handsome, red aliens walking around."

"We'll figure something out. I promise." He stands up too and begins to get dressed. "Come on. I'll drop you back off at Ra. Then we'll have to come up with a really convincing reason why we disappeared for three hours in the middle of a school day."

"What if we told them the truth?" I say, walking seductively toward him till I'm right under his nose. "That we were having some of the best sex two beings have ever had in the history of the galaxy?" I run my finger under the band of his pants until I graze against his bulge.

"You forget," he says, pulling my hand out of his pants and pinning it to my side. "I'm still your teacher for two more days, and personally, I don't want to see my best student get expelled before she even has a chance to be my assistant next year."

I blink. "Are you serious? You want me as your assistant?" My whole being simply lights up at the thought.

"The rules about relationships among staff are less strict. If I had you on the payroll instead of those lousy work-study credits, we could be a little bit more open about, you know... us."

Us. Hearing the word come out of his mouth awakens a hunger deep in my bones, and I want him again. All of him.

CHAPTER
FORTY-SIX

Ra and Nyx Arcana spiral around each other like a double helix threading through the sky. Ra's tendrils have me strapped to the seat as we slice through the Arctic air, but it's not just the aerial stunts giving me butterflies. Xion confessed his love to me. Or at least everything short of actually saying the word.

There will be time for that. More than enough time. If I end up working for him next year, not only will I be free of Alien Sylestra, but I'll get to be around him every day.

Am I worried about his shit moods and his tendency to close himself off? Definitely. But we'll work on that. Together.

Nyx Arcana dives into the jagged hole that marks the entrance to Agartha, and I follow, leaving my stomach somewhere in Earth's atmosphere. We plunge headlong into the chasm below until the inner planet, blue and tranquil as the Earth itself, is revealed in the light of the ancient Agarthan sun.

As we descend, the rocks on the underside of Earth's crust fade into the pastel blue sky. Agartha has its own ice cap at the northern pole, and we arc into a wide curve to avoid crashing into the frozen expanse.

Below us, the snow gives way to vast forests, wild and untouched, rushing past in a blur of green and gold.

"I don't think I'll ever get tired of seeing that," I say over Ra's intercom.

"I hope you never do." Xion's voice is gruff and immediate, projected right into my ear as if the man himself were sitting right next to me.

I am becoming more familiar with the terrain of this dwarf planet hidden inside our own, and I can tell from the coastline that we are getting close to the Academy.

"Before we land, there's something I want to tell you." Xion pulls his ship level beside mine.

"Oh yeah? What's that?" I ask, wishing I could see his face.

"Well, if we're being honest, and if we're going to trust each other, then there's something you should know."

Heartbeats pass. If I could scoot to the edge of my seat, I would be on it. "What?" I call over the intercom.

"Synchronicity, there's..."

A black shape comes streaking across the sky and collides with Xion's craft, sending him into a tailspin.

"Xion! Are you alright?"

Static crackles over the comm. No response.

The black shape latches onto Nyx Arcana, clawing at the hull like a rabid animal, and I recognize it immediately.

The same thing that ambushed me on the solstice.

A Beta Draconid.

Ra reacts before I do, his outer shell unfolding, massive white guns assembling themselves like pieces of a living puzzle.

I yank Ra into a sharp turn, banking hard until Xion's spiraling craft is positioned right in front of us.

"Get this thing off me, Synchronicity!" Xion's voice finally punches through the static.

"I don't want to hit you!" I shout. "Remember what happened to your work table?"

Crosshairs appear in Ra's and my shared vision, and the Beta Draconid zooms in and out of them, scuttling around Nyx Arcana's hull like a deranged spider.

"Just shoot! Nyx can take it!"

Fire, Ra! Fire! I shout in my mind, but as I do, I realize the guns are under my control.

I suck in a breath.

The blaster tips charge, gathering energy into two glowing spheres of light.

The Beta jerks into the center of the crosshairs, and I fire.

With a jolt, twin beams of energy streak across the sky, missing the Beta Draconid by a hair.

"Shit!"

"Synchronicity, I need you! It's disabled all my controls!"

The ground rushes up towards us at a frightening rate.

I suck in another deep breath, focusing all my energy on the guns. The tips glow with a burning intensity, and I let loose another volley. One of the beams glances off Nyx Arcana's hull, ricocheting into the sky. The other misses entirely.

Fuck.

We're seconds from impact when a new craft blazes into view, rust red, angular, and veined with black lines like circuitry.

It opens fire, blasting beams at Nyx Arcana.

One beam nails the Beta Draconid dead-center, knocking it off the ship.

Xion wrestles his ship back under control, pulling up just in time to avoid smashing into a ridge.

The strange black-red craft barrels past us, and an unfamiliar voice crackles over the comms: "That's the second time I saved your ass this week, Xion. You owe me a new quantum drive."

Xion laughs, a rough, relieved sound. "Damn, it's good to hear your voice, Koop. Thanks for the save."

Koop's ship tears off after the Beta, red beams hammering after it.

Xion speeds up to follow.

I chase close behind, heart slamming in my ribs.

Nyx Arcana fires a volley of her own, three red beams slicing the sky, tearing the Beta apart into ribbons of oily darkness.

"I had him," Koop mutters over the comms.

"Not fast enough," Xion says. "What's that make us? Fifteen to eight?"

"If I had an Eldercraft, you know I'd be beating you," Koop responds.

I cut in, voice sharp: "Excuse me, but who *is* this?"

"That must be the girl you told us so much about," Koop says, teasing. "Was wondering when you'd introduce us."

A beat of static. Then Xion's voice, rougher than usual:

"Synchronicity, meet Kooprix."

Another pause.

"My brother."

CHAPTER
FORTY-SEVEN

I follow the two ships to a hidden landing field etched into the mountainside. A scar of flat stone surrounded by sharp cliffs and cloud-wreathed peaks.

The valley sprawls beneath us, rough and wind-scraped, a perfect place to disappear.

Along the valley floor, small houses crouch low to the ground, built from scavenged stone, rusted metal, and anything that wouldn't betray their existence from the sky.

We land on a narrow strip of cracked tarmac where a few battered red ships like Koop's sit in formation.

I step out of Ra and head straight for Xion, my boots crunching on the gravel.

"You have a lot of explaining to do," I say, anger and confusion twisting together in my chest.

"Synchronicity," he says, voice rough, "I should have told you a lot sooner. I wanted to. I just... didn't know how."

Before I can respond, Koop strides over.

He's smaller than Xion, with a restless energy in his stride that suggests a certain lightness to his being. His face is softer, more open, but there's something haunted in his eyes too, like someone who's spent a lifetime glancing over his shoulder.

"It's nice to finally meet you," he says, offering his hand.

I hesitate, then shake it, warily.

His grip is firm but careful, like he's afraid I might bolt.

"I would have told you if I could," Xion says again, rubbing the back of his neck like a guilty teenager. "But if the Federation found out... if they even suspected..."

"Suspected what?" I ask, glancing around.

As I say it, movement stirs at the edges of the valley.

Maldekian men and women, marked by the same sharp features and dark tattoos as Xion, begin emerging from the houses, wiping grease from their hands, and pausing mid-task.

Their expressions range from guarded to hopeful to simply curious, their eyes lingering on me like I'm some rare animal they never thought they'd see up close.

There are more of them than I expected. A whole village hidden away.

Xion lets out a sigh. "This will be easier if you're sitting down."

Xion, Koop, and a few other Maldekians gather around a battered metal table inside Koop's modest home.

The place is cluttered but alive: shelves packed with worn Maldekian artifacts, strange mechanical parts in various stages of repair, and the faint scent of oil and ozone hanging in the air.

Someone hands me a chipped mug filled with something steaming and strong.

"Aldebaran coffee," Koop says with a small smile.

"Seems to be a family favorite," I mutter, taking a seat in a plain metal chair, the legs scraping against the floor.

"Best in the galaxy," Koop replies.

Xion stands at the head of the table, shoulders squared, gaze steady.

"Synchronicity, I couldn't tell you about this because it wasn't just about me."

He pauses, eyes sweeping the room.

"There are dozens of us. Survivors. Refugees. Exiles. We're the ones who stayed behind, not because we were forgiven... but because we couldn't stand to see another world go down the way Maldek did."

I grip the warm mug, grounding myself. "So you've been protecting Earth from those... things?"

"The Draconids," Koop confirms, leaning back against the wall. "Though it's rare to see one breach the Hollow Earth. Most of the time, we catch them in the outer atmosphere."

My mind races back to the package, the secret delivery.

"The package—" I start.

"It was a craft part," Xion explains. "For them. We have almost no outside support. I bring them what they need to survive."

Across the table, a dark-haired woman with deep red markings on her skin speaks up.

"We'd be lost without Xion," she says warmly, and a flash of something sharp flickers in my chest.

Jealousy—quick, but undeniable.

"We couldn't ask for a better prince."

I blink. "I'm sorry, *prince*?"

Koop laughs and claps Xion hard on the back. "He didn't tell you our Dad was the Emperor of the Maldekians?"

"There's a lot he didn't tell me," I say, narrowing my eyes at him.

"Because it doesn't matter," Xion says grimly. "The throne's gone. Maldek is nothing now. Just a belt of broken stones and ghosts."

The table falls silent.

After a moment, Koop clears his throat. "That's one of our main jobs now," he says. "Tracking down fragments of Maldek that still carry Alphas, and sequestering them on Saturn."

My brow furrows. "Why not destroy them? Like you did that Beta?"

"Alphas are... different," Koop says. His voice drops. "We haven't found a way to kill them yet. Not permanently. For now, we've been trapping them in Saturn's magnetic field."

I glance at the grim faces around the table. "But why keep all this a secret?"

Koop spreads his hands in a helpless gesture. "We're not supposed to interfere with another planet's spiritual development. Not under Federation law. They call it interference. They want each species to ascend on its own."

"But these energy vampires," I say, "they're an external threat. Surely removing them wouldn't count as interference."

"They can only survive on planets with lower

vibrations," Koop says. "As far as the Federation is concerned, if you get infested, you weren't ready to ascend anyway."

Silence settles again, heavy, suffocating.

The Maldekians lower their eyes, the weight of old failures pressing down on them.

"If the Federation finds out what we're doing here," Xion says quietly, "they won't imprison us. They won't exile us again. They'll erase us. No questions. No trial. Just... gone."

I swallow hard.

The Galactic Federation, once a symbol of higher truth, suddenly feels more like a spiritual empire, quietly erasing anything that doesn't fit its pristine vision of the cosmos.

I lick my lips, forcing myself to ask:

"And Alien Isis..." I say. "She knows about this?"

"She's been in on it since the beginning," Xion says. "After Maldek fell, she gave us a home here. We owe her everything."

I nod slowly, my thoughts racing.

"And Bo..."

"She didn't want to cause panic at the school," Xion says. "Fear and chaos create the perfect breeding ground for the Draconids. We believe an Alpha has possessed one of the students. And the fact that more Betas are showing up in Agartha means it's getting stronger."

I grip the mug tighter, pulse hammering in my ears. "I think I might know who it is."

The words hang between us, electric and terrible.

Xion studies me, something hardening in his eyes.

"Then we'd better get back to the Academy. We don't have much time."

We step outside into the cold mountain air.

The sun is already sinking behind the jagged peaks, casting long violet shadows across the valley.

The Maldekians stand scattered near the houses, silent, watchful.

Their gazes aren't hostile, but they aren't casual either.

It feels like being weighed, measured... and, somehow, welcomed.

Koop jogs after us before we reach the ships.

In his hand, he holds something small, wrapped in a strip of cloth.

"Wait," he says, catching up to me.

He presses the bundle into my palm.

Inside is a thin, weathered ring, silver-black, carved with the faint sigils of Maldek.

"It's not much," Koop says, rubbing the back of his neck awkwardly. "But it's tradition. You saved a Maldekian's life..."

He nods toward Xion.

"You're family. Whether you like it or not."

I stare at the ring, the ancient marks catching the fading light.

It's heavier than it looks.

I slip it onto my thumb, where it fits snugly, like it was made for me.

"Thanks," I say, voice thick, "but I didn't save him."

Koop grins. "Oh yes, you did. Maybe not in the sky earlier today, but ever since he told us about you, he's been lighter. More like the brother I used to know. For a long time, we thought he was losing hope. But all that's changed now."

I look over at Xion, quiet and brooding next to his craft. I don't know if I can forgive him for lying to me. But I can understand why he did it.

Koop steps back, giving me a two-fingered salute.

"Just... be careful back there, Synchronicity," he says. "Not everyone at the Academy wants the truth to come out."

I nod, my throat too tight to answer.

Above us, the sky deepens into a bruised purple.

As I climb into Ra's cockpit, I glance back one last time.

The Maldekians stand there in the twilight, still and silent, like shadows of a broken world, and somehow, impossibly, the guardians of this one too.

CHAPTER FORTY-EIGHT

When we arrive back at the craft site, a crowd has gathered. Students are clustered together in a loose circle, each holding a candle against the falling night.

"That's not a good sign," Xion mutters under his breath.

Alien Isis rushes toward us, flanked by Kreth and Marnox, both agents taut and ready.

"Where have you two been?" Alien Isis demands, her voice razor-sharp.

"It's a long story," Xion says grimly.

"There's been another attack," she says, stone-faced.

The world seems to tilt sideways.

"What?" Xion says, incredulous.

"Who?" My voice cracks under the weight of dread.

"Kai Moongate," Alien Isis says.

My heart seizes. "Is he alright?"

"Sylestra and the other Energy Workers are working on him, but... it doesn't look good."

I scan the faces in the candlelight and spot Vaylen standing among them, a mask of concern poorly stitched over her face.

Fury rises in my chest like a tidal wave.

"What the hell is she doing here?" I demand, pointing straight at her.

"Vaylen was the first one to find Mr. Moongate collapsed in the courtyard," Alien Isis says evenly.

"Of course she was," I hiss, my whole body trembling. "She's the one who did it!"

My words hit the crowd like a dropped match. A circle begins to form around us. I catch glimpses of Mae and Jasper's wide, worried eyes.

Vaylen breaks from the crowd, stalking toward me.

"Excuse me?" she says, voice dripping venom.

I plant my feet and raise my voice so everyone can hear.

"They've all been lying to us," I announce. "Alien Isis. The Federation. All of them."

The murmuring rises, students shifting uneasily.

Xion steps forward, tension rolling off him.

"Synchronicity, wait..."

"No. They deserve to know." I turn back to the circle.

"The Earth is under attack by energy vampires. It's been happening for a long time, and they don't want us to know because it would 'interfere' with our spiritual development. Isn't that right, Agent Kreth?"

Kreth's jaw tightens. His hand strays too casually toward the blaster at his belt.

"We're all in grave danger. There's an energy vampire right here in this Academy, feeding off us. Growing stronger."

I glare at Vaylen.

"And it's inside her."

Gasps ripple through the crowd.

Vaylen blinks, stunned for a fraction of a second—then her lips curl into a smirk.

"You're insane," she sneers.

"I saw her," I say, stepping closer. "After the Solstice Dance. In the woods. Summoning something dark with Kara and June. That same night, something attacked me, something made of pure shadow. And now, Kai? It's jealousy, isn't it? You couldn't stand seeing him kiss me this morning."

The crowd ripples, hungry for a fight.

Vaylen throws her head back and laughs, a bright, terrible sound.

"Synchronicity... Synchronicity..." she gasps between giggles. "You're talking about my Hecate extra credit project?"

I blink. "What?"

Alien Sylestra steps into the fray. "Synchronicity," she says coolly, "Vaylen and her friends have been enrolled in an independent study, channeling the energy of the goddess Hecate. Is this what you are referring to?"

The ground seems to drop out from under me.

"I... I guess..." I mumble.

The righteous fire that fueled me fizzles out, leaving behind a hollow ache. My shoulders sag.

Vaylen's smile turns vicious. "It was probably *you* who attacked him," she spits. "I knew your low vibrations would ruin this school. And now that I think of it, didn't Bo trip you in class right before he got attacked? I think I'm starting to see a pattern here."

Her words slice into me, and suddenly the circle of students feels tighter, their candles flickering like torches at a witch trial.

"I am not a killer," I say through gritted teeth.

Vaylen tilts her head, studying me like a puzzle.

"What did you say?"

"I. Am. Not. A. Killer," I snap, every syllable a stone hurled from my throat.

Vaylen's eyes widen. Recognition flashes.

"That's it," she breathes. "I knew you looked familiar. You're that influencer, the cold plunge girl. The one who killed her boyfriend."

Ice floods my veins.

"Yeah, that's right," Vaylen says, loud enough for everyone to hear. "You were all over social media, sobbing into a camera. Saying those exact words: 'I am not a killer.'"

All the color drains from the faces around me.

A stunned, electric silence.

Alien Isis turns toward me slowly, her iridescent eyes hard as glass.

"Synchronicity," she says slowly. "Is this true?"

My head drops, shame crashing down like a black wave.

"It's true," I whisper.

A gasp shudders through the gathered students.

"Ha! I knew it!" Vaylen crows, her face twisting into something dark and triumphant. "You killed your boyfriend. You killed Bo. And now you've gone after Kai too."

"That's not true!" I scream, but my voice cracks, brittle as dry leaves.

Vaylen steps closer until our faces are almost touching, her breath hot with triumph.

"Which part isn't true, Earthseed?" she hisses. "The part about killing Bo because he bullied you? Or the part where you murdered your boyfriend?"

"I didn't murder him!" I roar, so much fire in my veins, I think I might explode. "It was an accident!"

And then the unthinkable happens.

Ra flashes to life, glyphs burning a sinister red. He shoots over behind me as his guns unfold, pointing right at Vaylen and gathering orbs of energy to fire...

"Ra, no!" I whip around and hold my hands up.

But before Ra can fire, Kreth drops to one knee and shoots. The blue electric energy spiderwebs across Ra's surface, disabling the guns, which fold down uselessly at his side.

A gasp ripples through the crowd.

"No! Don't hurt him!" I rush over to Ra and frantically run my hands over his glyphs, which flicker weakly in the dark. "Ra, are you okay? Ra answer me. What's wrong?"

"His systems are temporarily disabled," Kreth says.

"You can't do that! He's not a machine, he's alive!"

"And he was about to harm an innocent student," Kreth says with finality.

"See?" Vaylen shouts. "She was ready to kill me with that creepy egg of hers. If anyone's harboring an energy vampire, it's her."

"He was just trying to protect me..." I murmur.

But it doesn't matter.

The crowd has already decided.

I can feel it in the way they shift, the way the light of their candles flickers over faces twisted in fear, in anger, in doubt.

I turn to Xion, but he takes an unconscious step back, a look of confusion and fear on his face.

For the first time since coming to Agartha...

I realize I might truly be alone.

CHAPTER
FORTY-NINE

"You'll have to stay here until we can figure out what to do next." Alien Isis turns the key to a cell tucked deep within the lower levels of the main pyramid. "As the only Earthseed on campus, you are the most likely person to be infected with a Draconid, even without your... colored past."

"Alien Isis, I'm not infected with anything," I protest, rushing to the bars. "I can see why you might think I'd want to hurt Bo, but there's absolutely no reason for me to attack Kai. We were seeing each other. I cared for him. I still do."

Isis's expression doesn't soften. "You wouldn't know if you were possessed, Synchronicity. The Alpha Draconid amplifies negative emotions, twists them, uses them. It forces you to hyperfixate on someone until a Beta is drawn to feed on the unsuspecting victim. Unfortunately, lovers can often be the targets of such attacks."

Her words slice into me.

"It's not me," I say, hoarse.

"That remains to be seen." She steps back from the bars, the key cold and final in her hand. "For now, my hands are tied."

"What about Ra?" I ask, dread churning in my gut.

Alien Isis just shakes her head. "After that brazen display of military technology, I'm afraid the Agents have no choice but to bring him back to Federation headquarters. They're leaving first thing tomorrow."

"They can't do that!" I shout, pounding my fist on the bars.

"I did everything I could, Synchronicity." Her voice drops lower, almost sorrowful. "It's out of my hands now."

I stagger back from the bars, sinking to the cold stone floor.

"No," I whisper. "It's not possible."

"I'm sorry, Synchronicity. Truly, I am." Alien Isis turns to head back down the passage. "For the record, I don't think it's you, but until we find the Alpha, I'm afraid you're stuck here."

Her footsteps fade into silence, leaving me alone.

Alone with the darkness, the damp... and the gnawing fear that maybe, just maybe, they're right.

Kai, Bo, and before all this even started...

Aidan.

Kind, beautiful Aidan. The light in the world that, it seems, was my destiny to snuff out.

I lay in the cell for what feels like an eternity, letting the cold seep into my clothes, my skin, my bones.

Ra, I whisper silently, reaching out through the thread that once connected us.

Nothing answers. No pulse of warmth. No flicker of thought.

Just more silence, heavy and final.

I've lost everything.

My craft, my friends, the one man who I thought might actually accept me...

If I had just figured out a way to tell him.

Footsteps rouse me from my self-pity, echoing down the stone corridor. Two steady, human pairs... and one light, scampering set.

"Mochi!" I gasp.

The little red panda squeezes between the bars and barrels straight into my lap, curling up against me with a soft chuff. I wrap my arms around him, feeling the first real warmth I've felt in hours.

A second later, Mae and Jasper appear in the dim light, their faces full of fierce, stubborn loyalty.

"You guys came!" I say, my voice catching.

"Of course we did, Sync," Mae says. "We couldn't let them just leave you down here all night by yourself."

"I talked them into giving us visitor privileges," Jasper says, flashing a mischievous smile. "Reminded them that I was Arcturian royalty in a past life."

For the first time since being locked up, I almost laugh.

Then the fear creeps back.

"So... you guys don't think I'm the one who attacked Kai?"

Jasper's face twists like I've insulted him.

"Don't be ridiculous, Synchronicity," he says. "You practically lived at his place for the last two months. If anything, I was starting to get worried you'd forgotten the rest of us existed."

I smile weakly, but the knot in my chest refuses to untangle.

"What about..." I lower my voice. "The other thing?"

Mae and Jasper exchange a loaded glance.

Mae is the one who answers, her voice soft but sure.

"Bad things happen to good people," she says. "I just wish you'd known it would've been safe to tell us."

Guilt twists in my gut.

I stroke Mochi's fur, trying to steady myself.

"I'm sorry," I say. "You're my friends. I should've told you. I guess... I guess I was just scared. That if anyone at Agartha found out what I'd done, they'd kick me out and send me back to the surface."

I pick up a loose pebble and toss it across the floor, watching it skitter into the dark.

"Do you want to talk about it now?" Jasper asks gently.

I hesitate.

"I don't know. It's... kind of a long story."

Jasper lowers himself to the ground without hesitation, cross-legged just outside the cell.

"I'm not going anywhere," he says.

Mae sinks down beside him, her face open and patient.

"Whenever you're ready, Sync," she says. "We're here."

I sit there for a moment, Mochi warm against my chest, my friends a silent shield against the darkness.

And then I let out a breath.

A breath I feel like I've been holding for more than a year.

"Back on the surface, before Agartha," I begin, my voice low, "I was a coach. A spiritual influencer, technically."

I pick at a flake of lichen growing between the stones. "I

started with cold plunging videos—taking people into the mountains for 'therapeutic treatments.'"

"And by therapeutic treatments," Jasper says, unable to help himself, "you mean dunking them in freezing cold water."

Mae elbows him sharply.

"Okay, okay. Shutting up."

I manage a tiny smile before the weight of it pulls me back down.

"Anyway," I continue, "I wasn't really qualified to be doing these treatments. But the thing is, it let me quit my job in the service industry and a lot of my clients did experience improvements."

"You were helping people, Synchronicity," Mae says.

"That's what I told myself, but deep down, I knew I was doing it because it allowed me to live the lifestyle I wanted. More money. More free time. More followers. For the first time, I was actually succeeding at something."

"Sounds like you were surviving," Jasper says. "So you benefited from helping people. Not exactly a mortal sin."

"I wish it was that simple, but it wasn't. It was performative. I started wearing spiritual clothes, you know, the kind Vaylen wears, not because they were more comfortable or healthier, but because I knew I could charge more if I presented a certain image. And I never..."

I choke on the words.

"I never really cared about the safety of it. I figured no matter how cold the water was, people would survive."

Silence hums between us.

"But you're about to tell us someone didn't," Jasper says, softer now.

Mae hushes him with a glance.

"There was someone," I say. "Aidan. My boyfriend."

Their faces shift, somber, but they don't interrupt.

"We'd been together since high school. It wasn't a perfect match, but back then... it felt like love."

The walls of the cell press tighter around me.

"Aidan had health problems. Always getting hurt. Always sick. It prevented us from enjoying the things I loved, like mountain biking and skiing, together. There would always be some new symptom that would keep him bedridden for days. Near the end, I felt more like his nurse than his girlfriend."

"Go on," Jasper says.

"One day," I whisper, "I thought... what if I could heal him? Not for social media or anything, but because I thought I could really help him."

I pause, searching their faces. They don't look away.

"The day we chose to go to the mountains turned out to be one of the coldest that winter." A half-hearted chuckle escapes my lungs. "I actually thought that was a good thing."

I suck in a deep breath.

"I hacked a hole through the ice myself."

Mae's hand brushes the bars, reaching instinctively toward me.

"I made him a warming tea. Guided him in some breath work. Everything I thought would protect him. When we stepped into that water..."

I close my eyes. "Even I felt how fast it stripped the heat from my bones. But Aidan, sweet, trusting Aidan, he just did whatever I said. He trusted me. I could have told him to stay in the water for an hour, and he would have done it. He was so skinny, so pale in those days. I should have known better."

Nobody, not even my family, has listened to me as intently as my friends are now.

"I still remember that serene smile on his face as we held hands, sinking down till the water was up to our necks, like he was at peace with everything."

The air feels thinner now, harder to breathe.

"We closed our eyes and by the time the timer on my phone went off..."

I shudder.

"He was unconscious." As the memories flood back, tears stream down my face, and I feel myself begin to hyperventilate.

Mae reaches through the bars and puts her hand on my thigh. "I'm so sorry, Synchronicity."

"I pulled him out of the water, and I just remember thinking, 'His skin is so blue. He shouldn't be that blue.' I managed to get him into the car, wrapped in blankets, and we drove the forty-five minutes to the nearest hospital and... and..." I suck in ragged breaths between sobs.

"It's okay," Mae murmurs, reaching through the bars to pull me against her. "You're safe. You can say it."

I collapse into her arms, grief ripping out of me.

"He didn't make it."

We sit there, me sobbing, Mae holding me, Jasper silent and still.

"His family was friends with my family. He was practically like a son to my parents. They wanted us to get married. Our entire friend group was his friends. No one really ever understood my coaching practice, and after Aidan's death, well, everything fell apart."

I don't know how long we stay like that—me cradled against Mae's chest, Jasper quietly wiping his own eyes when he thinks I'm not looking.

Eventually, the storm inside me ebbs.

The cell feels a little less dark.

My breathing slows.

For a while, none of us say anything.

The only sound is the faint hum of the pyramid deep in its bones.

Mochi nuzzles against my side, trying to lift my broken heart back up from the floor.

"You know," Jasper says after a long moment, his voice softer than usual, "not to compare trauma... but when I was in high school, I sold some acid to this kid."

He looks away, staring into the flickering shadows.

"I knew he had mental problems. I told myself it might... I don't know, free his mind or something. Spiritual awakening bullshit."

His mouth twists bitterly.

"Turns out, he took it with a bunch of his friends. Ended up stabbing one because he thought he was a demon."

The words fall like stones into the silence.

I wipe my face with my sleeve, sniffling.

"Jasper... that's awful," I whisper. "I'm so sorry."

He shrugs, but the movement is stiff, hollow.

"It's fine," he says. "I've confronted it. Carried it around long enough that it doesn't crush me anymore. Figured since we're confessing our deepest, darkest failures..."

He tries for a smile, but it flickers out halfway. "You're definitely not the shittiest person here."

For a moment, we just sit there, heavy with the weight of what we can't undo.

Then Mae clears her throat.

"I got herpes in high school," she says plainly.

Jasper and I both turn to look at her.

Mae shrugs, a little embarrassed, but she meets our eyes without flinching.

"It was humiliating at the time. I didn't tell anyone I hooked up with."

She picks at a thread on her sleeve.

"I thought... if I ignored it hard enough, maybe it would go away. Maybe I could pretend I was still pure."

"Mae..." I reach out and rest my hand lightly on her thigh.

She covers my hand with hers, squeezing once.

"It's okay," she says. "I'm okay with it now. It's part of me. And thanks to the healing work we're learning here, it barely flares up anymore. Plus..."

She gives a small, wry smile.

"Now I tell any potential lovers *before* we hook up. No secrets."

A quiet, raw honesty hums between us, binding the three of us tighter than anything else could have.

Flawed. Bruised.

Still standing.

I let out a shaky breath, feeling something fragile and

essential start to mend inside me.

"Wait," I say, blinking through the emotion. "Alien Isis said something earlier... about how lovers are often the targets of Beta Draconid attacks."

Jasper shifts where he's sitting, rubbing the back of his neck thoughtfully.

"If that's true," he says slowly, "and if Vaylen isn't the host... then whoever it is would be someone who has strong feelings. Real, messy, pent-up feelings. Toward you, Synchronicity."

The words hang in the air like dust motes.

Jasper hesitates, glancing at me sideways. "Are you sure it's not Xion?"

I shake my head. "He and his friends basically run an anti-Draconid militia. If he wanted to hurt me, he's had about a thousand chances. I seriously doubt it."

Jasper raises an eyebrow.

"Friends?"

"Long story," I mutter. "I'll explain later."

But even as the words leave my mouth, something inside me twists.

A knot pulling tighter.

"Wait," I say, heartbeat spiking. "You said messy, pent-up feelings, right?"

A cold thread of realization slithers through me.

"I think I know who it is."

Mae and Jasper both look up sharply.

"Who?" Mae asks.

I barely whisper it: "Peter."

They blink at me, confused.

I nod, heart hammering.

"Everyone thought he was just shy," I say. "But what if it wasn't just shyness? What if it was... resentment? Obsession?"

Mae's face pales.

"It would fit," she says quietly. "It would fit perfectly."

The cell seems to shrink around us, the shadows pressing

closer.

Mochi lets out a low, uneasy growl, the fur along his back rising.

"In our first day of Galactic History," I say, "Bo called Peter a creep in front of the whole class."

"Yeah, so?" Jasper says.

"Right after that," Mae whispers, "Bo was attacked."

"Exactly," I say, voice tightening. "And then after the Solstice Dance, Peter asked me to go back to his room. I turned him down."

Jasper stiffens.

"That was right before you got attacked at the crater."

The pieces lock into place, ugly and undeniable.

"And on Valentine's Day," I add, "someone slipped a love note under my door. No name. Just: I can't stop thinking about you."

Mae shudders. "Creepy."

"Sounds exactly like Peter," Jasper says.

"He must have seen me and Kai getting close these past few months," I say, the horror settling in.

"That's why he attacked Kai," Mae says. "He was jealous."

For a moment, none of us breathe.

Then a spark ignites in my chest, small, wild, defiant. "Do you two think you can break me out of here?"

I flash them a reckless, conspiratorial smile.

"I have a plan."

CHAPTER
FIFTY

"Mae, can you distract the guard while Mochi grabs the key?" Jasper's eyes gleam with the excitement of imminent mischief.

"On it."

Mae flashes a grin and strides down the corridor. A few moments later, her flirtatious giggles float back to us, bouncing off the stone walls.

I press closer to the bars.

"You think Mochi even knows what a key is?" I whisper.

Jasper gives me a look like I sprouted a second head.

"Right," I mutter. "Stupid question."

"Mochi, come here, boy."

The little red panda scurries out of my cell, sitting on his haunches like a soldier awaiting orders.

"Can you go and get the key from the guard?"

Mochi cocks his head to the side.

"I'll give you this strawberry..." Jasper says, producing the bright red fruit from his pocket.

Mochi assesses the situation with a surprising air of gravity, then darts down the hall.

We wait in breathless silence.

Then Mochi reappears, a massive iron keyring clutched triumphantly in his tiny jaws.

"Good boy!" Jasper exclaims, tossing him the strawberry. Mochi devours it with a happy chirp.

"See? I told you he knew what a key was."

"Very impressive," I say. "Now get me out of here."

Jasper works quickly, trying key after key until one clicks with a heavy thunk. The old door groans open, and I step out into the corridor, heart pounding.

Mae jogs back toward us, casting glances over her shoulder. "I bought us some time, but I don't know how much."

"Okay," I whisper. "Now what?"

"Follow me," Jasper says, heading off at a brisk trot. "I may have, uh... spent a night in that exact cell last year for drunk and disorderly conduct."

I raise my eyebrows but say nothing.

Priorities.

Jasper leads us through a winding maze of corridors, the air growing cooler and mustier the deeper we go. Every twist and turn feels like a heartbeat ticking down against an invisible clock.

We arrive at what looks like a dead end: just a blank stone wall and a solitary statue of an alchemist in a cloak.

"This looks familiar," I say.

"You've probably seen his twin. Hermes Trismegistus. There are two statues of him in the school. If I can just..."

He presses one of the bricks.

A deep, ancient click echoes through the stones.

The wall shudders and slides sideways, revealing a hidden corridor and a matching statue beyond. We slip through, and the passage seals shut behind us with a grinding finality.

I know where we are now.

This is where I first overheard Xion and Alien Isis whispering about Ra.

We race through the corridors and up the stairs to the main level of the pyramid. Being careful not to be seen, we creep out into the night.

As we slip past the craft site, it looks like almost every student on campus is camped out in a silent vigil for Kai. Candles flicker in a sea of sleeping bags and blankets.

"I saw Peter at the vigil earlier," Mae says. "Hopefully, he's still there."

I glance toward the hangar where Ra sits, disabled, trapped between the twin tractor beams of the agents' ships.

"Hold on a little longer, buddy," I whisper. "I'm gonna get you out."

We slink through campus to Larimar House, its windows

darkened and vacant.

"Doesn't look like anyone's home," Jasper says, nudging open the front door.

Inside, everything is silent.

We tiptoe up the stairs, shoes barely whispering against the old wood.

Jasper leads us to Peter's room.

He tries the handle, and it swings open freely.

"I guess even Alpha Draconids don't lock their doors in Agartha," Jasper mutters.

We step into a room that looks like an arcane sorcerer's workshop. Strange sigils are scribbled on parchment and tacked to the walls. Animal bones lie splayed on the desk as if they had been used for scrying, and a crystal orb glows faintly in the gloom.

Mochi pokes at an animal skull, which wobbles, sending him scurrying behind Jasper's leg with a nervous chirp.

"Let's get to work," I say. "Anything that could show he has some sort of unnatural obsession with me. Or better yet, something that could tie him to Maldek, an artifact or something."

Jasper heads for the closet, grimacing as he rifles through Peter's wardrobe. Mae goes through the drawers and I search his desk. Other than some ancient-looking, but unfortunately Earth-derived tomes, I don't find anything.

"How will we know when we find it?" Mae whispers.

"I don't know," I admit. "I'm assuming it'll be obvious. Swarming with black energy, like Bo was."

I glance at the crystal orb, but even its gloom feels inert.

"Xion told me one of his jobs is tracking down fragments of Maldek still harboring energy vampires. Maybe Peter somehow found one before they did."

"I don't know," Jasper says, shaking his head. "All his stuff is creepy... but in a goth kid kind of way. Not a 'destroy the world' kind of way."

A hollow pit opens in my stomach.

"If Peter's not harboring the Alpha Draconid," I murmur,

"then who is?"

Before I can finish saying the words, a dark silhouette fills the doorway.

"I've been looking for you, Synchronicity." The voice is like two voices braided together—one horrifying and supernatural, the other small and meek.

"...Cassy?" I say, dread already pooling in my veins.

The wraith-like figure steps through the door, part Cassandra and part... something else. Her eyes have gone black, and distended veins spiderweb across her face. The meteorite necklace around her neck roils with oily clouds of dark energy.

"You shouldn't have ignored me, Synchronicity," she whispers, her voice cracking. "I... loved you."

Cassy shrieks, a sound like a thousand knives clashing, and lunges at me. I dodge out of the way just in time to see her body crumple on the bed. The thing shrieks again in frustration.

"Come on, Ra," I gasp, throwing out my hands, desperate to summon even a flicker of light.

Nothing.

Just dead air.

Cassy jumps at me again, bearing long, hideous fangs that protrude from her mouth like blades. I throw my hands up for protection, bracing for the strike.

But before it hits me, Mochi bounds into action, releasing a blast of green energy that sends Cassy crashing into the wall.

The green energy arcs around her, and the veins on her face fade as a hint of color returns. Her body slouches, unconscious.

"That's not gonna hold for long," Jasper pants. "We have to find Alien Isis. Come on. Mae, you and Synchronicity take her shoulders, I'll take her legs."

I stand up, stunned.

"It was Cassy this whole time?" I say.

"We'll figure it out later," Jasper says. "Right now, we

have to get her to Alien Isis. She's the only one powerful enough to deal with this."

We go over to Cassandra's body and lift her up. She feels impossibly light.

"Be careful that necklace doesn't touch you," Jasper says. "I think that's what we were looking for."

The cursed meteorite sits on her chest, pulsing with malevolent energy, like a black hurricane trapped in glass.

Of course. The necklace. I should have known.

The way none of her plants would grow. The way she looked at me at the Solstice Dance...

All the pieces crash together.

"That day in Galactic History," I say, breathless. "She was there when Bo tripped me. She was trying to protect me."

"Protecting you or displaying some really fucked up courtship ritual," Jasper says as we hurry down the Larimar stairs, Cassandra dangling between us.

"But why would she attack you on the Solstice?" Mae asks.

"Because," I say grimly, "I completely ignored her. She probably wanted to go with me."

"And Kai?" Jasper asks as we shove open the door to the night.

The cool air hits my face like a slap.

"This morning," I say, piecing it together, "She was right there when Kai kissed me in class. How could I be so stupid?"

"It doesn't matter now," Jasper says. "What matters is getting her to Alien Isis before that thing wakes back up."

"The Energy Work School," I say. "She'll be with Kai."

We sprint across the darkened campus, Cassandra's body swinging lightly between us.

We find Alien Isis along with a host of healers gathered around Kai's body in one of the larger classrooms.

"Alien Isis," I gasp as we practically stumble into the room, "we found the Alpha Draconid."

CHAPTER
FIFTY-ONE

Cassandra's body lies limp in the center of the classroom, pale and trembling, her breath shallow. The energy workers form a tight circle around her, candles at the edge of the room flaring slightly as they tune their focus.

"How did you know who it was?" Sylestra asks, her voice clipped and tight.

"We didn't," Jasper says grimly. "She attacked us."

Alien Isis stands near the head of the circle, arms crossed, robes brushing the ground.

"I'm not even going to ask," she says dryly, "how you managed to spring Synchronicity from her cell."

"How could this have happened?" one of the healers murmurs.

"It's the meteorite," I blurt out, pointing to the necklace throbbing against Cassandra's chest. "It must be a fragment of Maldek. That's how the Alpha's been anchoring itself to her."

Sylestra turns to Isis. "Should we remove it?"

She's already halfway toward Cassandra, hand extended.

"No!" Alien Isis snaps, making Sylestra freeze.

She steps forward slowly, eyes narrowing. "At this point, the fragment may be too deeply woven into her etheric body. Removing it might kill her."

"If you don't do something soon, *that thing* might kill her," I say. "It's sapping all her energy."

Alien Isis's jaw tightens.

I can see it, the gears turning, the grim calculations being made.

"We have to exorcise it," she says at last.

The word drops into the room like a hammer.

The energy workers glance uneasily at one another.

"Do we even know if that's possible?" one of them whispers.

"We have to try," Alien Isis says, her tone brooking no argument.

She turns her gaze to me, to Jasper, to Mae.

"You three, help stabilize her. If her spirit fractures during the separation, she won't survive."

"How?" Mae asks, voice small.

"Your connection to her. Your energy. Hold her in the memory of who she was before the infection spread."

Jasper rubs his hands together, blowing out a nervous breath. "No pressure," he mutters.

Alien Isis kneels beside Cassandra, hands hovering over her chest.

"This entity has bonded to her heart chakra," she says. "I'll work from the astral layers inward. You three, anchor her. Remind her she's more than the thing that's using her."

I swallow hard, glancing down at Cassy's frail, unconscious form.

The girl who sat beside me in class.

The girl who offered hesitant smiles.

The girl who, somewhere deep down, only ever wanted to be seen.

"I'm ready," I say, my voice steadying.

"Me too," Mae whispers.

Jasper cracks his knuckles and nods. "Let's bring her back."

Alien Isis glances around her circle of healers and gives a solemn nod. Each of them reaches out their hands over Cassandra's body.

The healers begin to chant, voices weaving together in ancient tones as light floods forth from their hands. A mixture of Pleiadian, Sirian, Lyran, and Arcturian energy swirls into a rainbow of light above Cassandra's body.

As the energy concentrates into a glowing ring, Cassandra's body starts to rise, being pulled up by the meteorite around her neck.

The chant grows louder, vibrating in my teeth, my bones, the floor itself.

Cassandra rises slowly through the floating halo of light, nightgown billowing, arms and legs dangling beneath her, limp as a puppet's. Her back arches and her eyes shoot open, black as night.

Alien Sylestra falters, and the stream of blue energy from her hands breaks.

"Focus!" Alien Isis commands, voice cracking like a whip.

Sylestra grits her teeth and renews her efforts. The ring of energy brightens just as Cassandra's jaw unhinges with an unnatural crack.

An otherworldly scream tears from her throat. The sound is not human. It claws its way into the air, rattling the windows and scraping down my spine.

Mae claps her hand over mine and squeezes. Hard.

Cassandra's body rises up above the heads of the energy workers, the meteorite taut, pulling at her neck. The clouds of dark energy swirling around it are more erratic now, and black plumes of smoke come billowing out of Cassandra's mouth.

Her body convulses as the black clouds twist around the meteorite, thickening, pulsing, forming the suggestion of a grotesque, demonic face.

Eyes. A snarling mouth.

The necklace snaps, and Cassandra's body drops like a stone, hitting the floor with a sickening thud. At the same instant, the Alpha Draconid tears free, howling with pure, feral rage.

The black meteorite, now fused to its center, smashes through the classroom window, and the phantom billows out into the approaching dawn.

Alien Isis drops to her knees beside Cassandra, gathering her broken form into her arms.

Cassandra blinks up, eyes a muted gray again, confusion dawning across her ravaged face.

"Where... am I?" she croaks.

"You're safe now, dear," Isis says gently.

She eases Cassandra onto a padded table, motioning for a healer to begin the slow work of mending the damage the parasite left behind.

I stagger to my feet, turning toward the front of the room.

My heart seizes.

Kai lies still, black clouds still hovering above him, sticky, malignant.

"Can you do for Kai what you did for Cassy?" I ask, hope burning in my throat.

Alien Isis meets my gaze and shakes her head. "Alphas part more easily from their hosts," she says, voice heavy. "Betas don't. They root too deep. Once a Beta takes hold, it never lets go."

A fresh wave of despair slams into me.

"Then what can we do?" I plead.

"Now that the Alpha's been freed, there's a chance. If we can trap it, contain it in a magnetic bottle, we might sever its link to the Betas. Including the one attached to Kai."

The fragile hope flickers.

But before I can cling to it, Alien Sylestra's voice cuts through the room. "Now that it's free," she says darkly, "it can activate a whole army of Betas. We're going to have a war on our hands."

A grim silence falls.

Even the air seems to hold its breath.

Alien Isis straightens her shoulders. "Sylestra, gather the students. Bring everyone to the Great Pyramid. They should be safe there. For now. I'll alert the Maldekians. We'll need every pilot we can find."

I step forward, fists clenched at my sides.

"Alien Isis," I force the words out. "I fought off a Beta before. With Ra. If you can convince the Agents to let him go..."

Alien Isis turns toward me with a heavy look. "I'm afraid the agents are leaving with Ra as we speak."

CHAPTER
FIFTY-TWO

I burst onto the craft site, lungs burning, feet slipping in the dew-slick grass.

And there, suspended in the pale light of dawn, is Ra, his hull shining like a pearl, caged between the twin tractor beams of the Federation's ships.

"**Synchronicity**," he intones, his voice strained and faint.

I try to throw myself against his side, but the tractor beams repel me like a force field.

"I'm gonna get you out of here," I breathe. "Just hold on."

"Please step away from the Eldercraft, Miss Jones." Agent Kreth's voice slices through the stillness, flat and deadly. "For your own safety."

I turn.

The same blaster that disabled Ra now points squarely at my chest.

"Stop," I plead. "You can't do this. He's not some machine to be taken apart. He's a living thing. He's *conscious*."

Across the craft site, Sylestra is beginning the process of moving the students to the main pyramid. Candles extinguished. Blankets abandoned. A silent vigil shattering into panic.

"That craft is a danger," Kreth drones. "To the Academy and every person in Agartha. We are bound by law to take it into custody."

Agent Marnox flanks Kreth, mirroring his aim. "Stand down, Synchronicity."

"There are Draconids," I shout, desperation cracking my voice, "heading for the school. We need every craft available to help fend them off."

"We're aware," Kreth says, "And we want no part of it. To defend Earth against such a low vibration attack would be a blatant violation of the Non-Interference Doctrine."

I stare at him, cold disbelief settling into my bones.

"So, you're just going to leave us here to die?"

A pause.

"To figure out your own spiritual path," he says, through clenched teeth.

"You can't do this!" I lunge toward Kreth, but before I can reach him, he fires.

The blue Sirian blast catches me in the chest, a paralytic web of light seizing every muscle, dropping me to my knees. I crumple into the grass as the stun blast completely incapacitates my body.

"**Synchronicity!**" Ra howls, his voice raw and furious.

The agents climb into their respective ships, cold, grey, soulless machines, and the engines roar to life. All I can do is watch as the Federation crafts lift off, hauling Ra between them, like a whale caught in a net.

Ra's glyphs flare as he strains against the twin tractor beams.

"Ra..." I croak, lifting a shaking hand.

"**Synchronicity... help!**" he cries, writhing in mid-air against his restraints like a caged beast.

But the beams hold.

As the Federation crafts engage their main thrusters, two dark shapes come screaming across the morning sky. Black, fast, terrible.

Beta Draconids.

They slam into the agents' ships like rabid spiders, scrawling and clawing over their hulls, fangs scraping metal with vicious precision.

The tractor beams flicker. Ra breaks through, in a sudden arc, spiraling down before catching himself and landing in the grass with a low, reverberating hum.

I shake off the stun blast and wrap my arms around him. "I couldn't bear to see them take you away."

"**No time,**" he groans in his ancient voice, like two stones grinding together. "**They're coming.**"

I look behind him to see the agents' ships plummet, their engines blown.

And from the sky, a darkness appears. A swarming, teeming madness.

More Betas.

Dozens of them.

"Everyone, *into the pyramid!*" Sylestra's voice slices through the chaos like a blade. "NOW!"

Screams erupt as students sprint for shelter, scrambling over blankets, colliding, dragging one another toward the Great Pyramid.

One of the Betas streaks ahead of the others, incorporeal and furious, black mist twisting around clawed appendages as it dives toward Kara, Vaylen, and June.

Ra's guns unfold like lightning, and a single white-hot blast obliterates the fiend into ribbons of darkness that scatter across the morning sky.

Kara peeks up from where she'd dropped to the ground. "Thanks," she says.

"Thank me later." I grab her arm and haul her to her feet. "Right now, we need to get everyone inside the pyramid."

Vaylen glares at me, but June just nods and swings herself onto Edmund's back, her spirit steed already bristling with readiness.

"June, do you think you can herd everyone away from the energy vampires?"

"I can try," she says with grim determination. She flicks the reins and goes galloping off toward the stampede of terrified students.

I turn to Kara and Vaylen.

"You two are powerful healers," I say. "You can fight. But I won't blame you if you take shelter instead."

Vaylen scoffs. "I don't take orders from an Earthseed," she snaps, already turning to follow the stream of fleeing students. "Come on, Kara."

But Kara doesn't move.

Vaylen halts, turning back. "What are you doing?" she demands, incredulous.

Kara bends to retrieve her shamanic drum, her voice

calm and certain. "I'm staying," she says. "To fight."

I give her a nod, then turn to Vaylen. "We could really use your firepower."

Vaylen snorts. "I'm not risking my life for you." With a sharp toss of her hair, she disappears into the crowd.

"I'm sorry about her," Kara murmurs.

"It's fine," I reply. "Just protect the others."

Kara starts a war beat with her drum, radiating pulses of golden energy just as Mae and Jasper run up to me on the field.

"Guys, what are you doing here?" I shout. "You should be in the—"

"Duck!" Jasper yells.

I drop instinctively as Mae strums a powerful chord on her ukulele. A blast of yellow Lyran energy shoots past me, vaporizing a Beta mid-charge. Its smoky remains scatter into the air.

"Thanks," I breathe.

Mae flashes a wild, determined grin. "There's no way we were going to leave you out here to fend for yourself."

"We'll follow you to hell and back," Jasper says. "Just say the word."

"Hopefully it won't come to that," I say. "Just make sure none of those Betas get too close to the other students."

"Any sign of the Alpha?" Jasper asks.

I shake my head. "Not yet." My eyes flick skyward. "I need to get back to Ra. I'll be more useful from the air."

"Go," Mae says. "We got it down here."

I race back to Ra, whose cockpit blooms open for me to step inside. I settle into his seat as the shell folds closed around me, locking into place with a low, harmonic hum. The neural tendrils slither around my arms, spine, and temples, and we are one again.

Ready to obliterate some negative energy, buddy?

Let's go.

We shoot off from the craft site, leaving behind a plume of dust. From this altitude, I can see the whole campus. More than half the students are already safe inside the pyramid, but on the outskirts of the group, chaos reigns.

I count at least five Betas engaged in battle with energy-wielding students and teachers.

I fly low and buzz by June just as Edmund rams into a Beta with an explosion of emerald light, sending it spinning across the grass. Kara and Mae are back-to-back, ukulele and drum echoing off each other in golden, rhythmic pulses that drive back two more. Meanwhile, Jasper and Mochi help stragglers on the edge of the fray.

For one heartbeat—

I think we might actually pull this off.

Then another wave of Betas appears in the sky, their bodies twisting like smoke and bone.

"Hang on, Ra."

I pull into a steep climb, positioning one of them in my crosshairs. Its form flickers in and out of visibility, like a nightmare refusing to solidify. I take a deep breath, charging up the blasters, and when I release, twin orbs of white light shoot across the sky.

They miss by a hair.

The swarm shrieks and dives, and I bank fast to avoid them. But not fast enough. One of them latches onto Ra's hull, claws sinking deep.

The lights inside start to flicker, and I feel myself lose control as the deranged entity crawls across Ra's surface. Our flight slows. For a moment, we are suspended in thin air.

Then Ra starts to drop.

I feel the Draconid gain purchase on the crack in Ra's hull. It's grasping, digging, trying to get in.

Fuck. Fuck. Fuck.

The ground approaches as the Beta rips off a fragment of Ra's shell. It feels like someone's peeling off my own skin. If that thing gets inside Ra's neural framework, we're doomed. I try to take control of the guns in a last-ditch effort, but it's no use. The Beta's attack has disabled all my controls.

We're hurtling straight for the Great Pyramid when a sleek black shape streaks across my periphery.

Nyx Arcana.

A volley of red beams erupts from her guns, knocking the Beta from my hull just in time to regain control. I yank us out of the dive, skimming so close to the Logos Stone that I feel the hum of its power radiate through Ra's shell.

"Thanks for the save," I gasp over the comms.

Xion's voice comes in low and rough. "Couldn't afford to lose one of our best pilots."

"I thought you hated me."

"You kept secrets. So did I. Call it even." He rockets past me, a blur of motion—then, behind him, a fleet of crimson Maldekian crafts bursts through the clouds like warbirds.

"Nice work, Synchronicity." Koop's voice cuts in. "We'll take it from here."

Xion leads the formation straight toward the onslaught of Draconids. The Maldekian ships peel off, each targeting a Beta with precision and fury.

Crimson beams tear through the sky.

One by one, the Betas disintegrate into spiraling black ash.

I swoop low over the school where Kara, Mae, and Jasper are ushering the last students into the pyramid. But then a stray Beta crashes against the glass exterior, claws raking wildly. It ricochets off and collides full-force with June, knocking her clean off Edmund.

I can't risk firing. The thing is already on her, clawing its way into her throat.

"No—!"

Kara sprints across the field, slamming her drum with frantic force. Golden waves pulse outward, but she's too late.

Clouds of dark energy surround June's body as she lies stiff and lifeless on the field.

"June!" I scream, my voice breaking. "No!"

Our only chance now is if we can capture...

A shriek, ancient and impossible, tears the sky apart.

The wind goes still. The field goes silent.

Every Beta lifts its head, sensing its master.

The Alpha Draconid.

It descends on the campus like a phantom. Two Maldekian ships fire at it, but it swats them from the air like insects, sending them both spiraling into the mountainside.

Shit.

I bank hard, diving to avoid its talons as they swipe inches away from Ra's hull. But it follows, close, relentless. Spectral claws outstretched, grasping.

Xion drops in behind it and fires a barrage of red beams. The creature snarls, more irritated than harmed.

I dodge between the dorms and the Entrance Obelisk, trying to lose it, but it stays close on my tail.

"I need you, Synchronicity..." The voice slithers over the comms, *wrong*, distorted, somehow inside the system. "You are more important than you know."

"Fuck you, creep!" I pull into a sharp ascent, and the Alpha Draconid crashes into a low wall.

Xion doesn't waste any time hammering the wraith with a hail of energy and pummeling it into the stone. He banks up, leaving behind a plume of dust and debris.

For a heartbeat, it looks like we've got it.

"Phew... that was close," I say, but as I do, the Alpha rises from the rubble, completely unscathed, and rockets past Xion straight toward me.

I try to lose it between the domes of the Energy Work School, but it's gaining on me, hollow eyes locked on Ra, mouth gaping wide like a portal to hell.

"Get this thing off me!" I shout.

"Trying," Xion growls back. "Nothing's phasing it!"

I loop back toward the craft site. Below me, I see Jasper and Mae running toward their crafts.

No. What are they thinking?

I pull Ra into a barrel roll and come down right behind the Alpha, letting loose a blast of white light from my guns that grazes the meteorite embedded in its chest. It recoils slightly, but the impact fades like smoke.

Moments later, I'm flanked by Jasper's cube-shaped craft

and Mae's copper saucer.

"What are you guys doing up here?!" I yell. "You should be in the pyramid with the others."

"We weren't about to let you have all the fun," Jasper responds over the intercom.

"If we're winning this, we're doing it together," Mae adds.

"Okay, we've got this thing on the run. Let's see if we can finish it off."

Green, yellow, and white light flares from our guns, pummeling the Alpha with a hail of blasts. But instead of diminishing the wraith, it somehow sucks in all of our light like a black hole, *feeding* off our energy.

"Guys, I don't think this is doing anything," Jasper says over the radio. Mochi chimes in with a concerned chirp.

Then, a blur of pink and cyan light streaks across the sky, unleashing a barrage of iridescent energy straight into the Alpha's core. The creature howls, veering violently off course.

A crystalline ship descends in its wake—like a fighter jet sculpted from pure opal. The morning sun refracts off its faceted hull, scattering into radiant halos.

"What the hell is that?" Jasper whispers.

"It's beautiful," Mae breathes.

Xion pulls Nyx Arcana in beside us. "That, students, is a Pleiadian Eldercraft."

Alien Isis's unmistakable voice comes in clear and resonant over the radio. "Everyone get into formation. Let's give it everything we've got. Once it's weakened, Xion and I will try to contain it in a magnetic field."

Isis rockets after the beast, releasing a continuous beam of iridescent light. The Alpha howls in agony and shoots skyward.

The rest of the Maldekians join us, adding their red beams to the mix as we chase the thing into the upper atmosphere of Agartha.

As the undersurface of the Earth comes into view, the Alpha begins to collapse inward, its black mass shrinking around the meteorite core, folding into itself like it's being devoured by its own hunger.

This is it.

We fire everything we have. A blinding supernova of healing light converging on one single point.

But just when it looks like it's going to shrink to nothing, the black hole implodes, sending out a shockwave of dark energy. It hits every craft like an atomic blast, and I feel Ra's systems go offline.

No.

This can't be happening.

Around me, every craft falters. Mae, Jasper, Xion, Isis, we all plummet toward the ground like stones as the Alpha reforms itself above us, larger, stronger, followed by a swarm of Betas that emerge from the Earth's crust.

"You thought you could stop me." Its hideous voice hijacks the intercoms. "I will not stop until the universe is MINE!"

It shrieks after us, followed by its demonic army. I try to take control of Ra, but we are in free fall. The ground spirals beneath us, and this time there's no one to save us.

I watch, powerless, as Jasper's craft slams into the edge of Atum Crater, tumbling end over end.

Then Mae's.

Then the Maldekians.

Then, Alien Isis.

Ra hits the bottom of the crater with a bone-snapping impact that tears his hull apart. Pieces of his shell go flying off as I'm ejected like a ragdoll, spilling onto the ground in a heap of pain and breathless terror.

I manage to roll over in time to witness Nyx Arcana careening out of the sky and, impossibly, break in two as she crashes into the rim. The cockpit tumbles off, spilling Xion's broken body onto the earth.

"Xion, NO!"

Around me, smoke and wreckage choke the air. The remains of my friends' crafts litter the crater floor like fallen stars. Mae stumbles from her ruined saucer, dazed and bleeding, just as a Beta Draconid slams into her, knocking her to the ground and clawing its way down her throat.

No, no, no. This can't be happening.

I crawl, half-paralyzed, useless, watching helplessly as she jerks once, then goes limp.

The horde of Betas descends on the survivors like locusts. Jasper falls. Then Koop. Alien Isis manages one last blast of diamond light that obliterates a group of Betas, but ten more take their place and swarm her until she, too, falls.

All that's left... is me.

The earth shudders.

The Alpha Draconid hits the crater with a force that splits the ground, sending cracks spiraling through the stone like lightning.

Its legs end in talons, shadow-velociraptor feet that churn the ash and debris with each thunderous step. Its body is draped in darkness, tendrils of void curling off its shoulders like smoke. Its face is a horror beyond comprehension.

It raises its head and locks its spectral gaze on me.

"The power in you is colossal, Synchronicity Jones. You were destined for more than this miserable little school." Its footfalls are like harbingers of doom as it plods slowly toward me. "Together, we will rule the cosmos. With you by my side... as my Dark Queen."

"No, please no," I pant, trying in vain to pull myself backward, away from the approaching beast.

"The galaxy will succumb to darkness..." It reaches out a clawed hand, pulling me so close to its sulfurous mouth that black vapors caress my lips. "And every. Last. Planet. Will. Fall."

Wait.

Geminorum, Geminorum, Geminorum...

"What are you saying?" it hisses.

Geminorum, Geminorum...

And then, a scream of engines.

Over the crater's rim, the Castor 5 comes streaking like a

comet through the smoky sky. It slams into the Alpha with explosive force, dragging it across the floor in a trail of fire and shattered stone, before embedding itself into the far wall in a flaming wreck.

Silence.

I push myself up onto a bleeding elbow.

Smoke coils through the air.

The Alpha rises from the wreckage, raining shards of metal from its jagged form. "You thought that pathetic little trick could stop me?" it snarls, voice wild now.

I close my eyes.

And go inward.

To the deepest chamber of my mind, in a desperate attempt to activate Ra's guns.

Ra... please.

If I ever needed you, *I need you now.*

I try to envision him just as I remember him, glowing blue glyphs, the crack in his shell pulsing like a wounded heart.

"Synchronicity..."

His voice is faint. Distant.

"Ra, I need your light. If we don't fight now, everything—*everyone*—will be lost."

But even as I visualize him, pieces of his shell crumble away, disintegrating into dust.

He's dying. Fading.

"Synchronicity... you must heal. You must face what is behind the door."

I turn around—

And there it is.

The door.

Cracked. Rotten. Weeping water from underneath like blood from an infected wound. The door I told myself I would never open.

From back in the crater, I hear the Alpha's voice. "You will not defeat me so easily."

I shudder.

Focus, Synchronicity... focus.

I step toward the door, feet splashing through the puddle pooling beneath it, and reach for the handle.

A wave of pain crashes through my heart.

"Ra," I whisper. "I don't think I can do this. That's a wound I cannot touch."

I turn back to him.

What's left of him.

He is barely holding together, his form collapsing, symbols dim.

"**Wounds...**" he says, his voice low and strained as more pieces of him break off and vanish.

"Ra, don't go. I need you!"

"**Wounds are how the light gets in.**"

The words strike me like a bell.

I whirl around and face the door.

You cannot rule me forever.

I reach out and turn the handle.

The door bursts open.

And I am annihilated in a flood of water.

CHAPTER
FIFTY-THREE

The cold is the kind where you welcome the numbness because it's better than feeling the white fire of your flesh freezing away. I clutch my coat tighter against the wind. The same one she was wearing.

Before she stripped down and eased herself into the axe-hewn hole.

With him.

So fragile against the brutality of nature. He was a light so pure and rare that it is seldom seen on this Earth.

And she.

She is a light so broken already and for so long that she thinks there is no other way to be. They hold hands in the bitter water, improbable as life itself.

I crouch down in the snow on the bank and watch as the color drains from his face. Hollowed cheeks taking on the hue of winter. He is serene. Quiet. Like a monk setting himself on fire.

And part of him knows that it's the end.

He's known all day.

Maybe he's known since he met her.

That it would end like this.

She sits across from him. Shivering yet confident. She does not know what finalities are to come.

To be a witness to their final moments together is a gift in itself. The world is all contrast: black tree trunks against the imperceptible latticework of frost. Time seems to slow. Stop. Indeed, has stopped for all these moons.

I alone can set it turning again.

The water flows on, bit by bit, carrying his soul into the world beneath the ice, until the timer on her phone goes off, and all that's left of him is a husk, as empty as the void that stretches between the stars.

My heart breaks now, not for him, but for the girl whose face turns to ash. She slaps his unresponsive cheeks and drags his lifeless body to shore.

No amount of her own breath forced into his lungs will revive him. The attempts to restart his heart are as futile as trying to win back a lover once love itself has fled. She punches his chest and cries out his name to the lonesome sky. Not even a bird deigns to answer her call.

And then I take her in my arms.

"It's not your fault," I whisper. "It's not your fault."

"Yes it fucking is!" she cries.

"You were trying to help him. It's not your fault."

She collapses in my arms and weeps.

"I forgive you," I whisper, running my fingers through her hair. She is the one I left behind. The one I will never leave again. "I forgive you. I forgive you."

CHAPTER
FIFTY-FOUR

"I forgive you... I forgive you," I whisper into the still-burning silence of the battlefield.

The ground shakes as the Alpha Draconid crunches its clawed foot into the rubble beside me, stone exploding outward like shrapnel.

"Is this another one of your tricks?" it growls, voice warping the air. "Another sad little craft come to die in a useless attempt at my destruction?"

It grips me by the throat and lifts me skyward, talons like rusted iron clamped around my neck.

Its face, a swirling mass of hunger and hate, leans close.

"You will know what it means to suffer," it hisses, "as my putrid. Groveling. Queen."

I choke against the weight of its grip.

"I forgive myself," I rasp, barely audible.

"What?"

"I forgive myself," I say one last time. A single tear rolls down my cheek, and the door in the back of my mind bursts open.

Glorious glowing rays stream through, flooding every corner of the place I'd kept locked for so long.

And I am filled with a warmth I thought I'd lost forever.

I stare into the void face of the monster and grit my teeth.

"Eat my light, motherfucker."

I thrust my hands forward.

Light erupts from me—pure, incandescent, unstoppable. It slams into the creature like a divine tidal wave. The beam widens, grows hotter, brighter, until the air crackles with it. The monster writhes in agony, ribbons of shadow flying from its body, disintegrating in the brilliance.

"You will not stop me, Synchronicity," it howls. "We... were... meant... to... rule... together..."

The light coursing from my hands rips at the Draconid,

stripping away its essence, hollowing out its soulless eyes until only the meteorite remains—blackened, empty, nothing more than a dead stone.

It drops to the ground with a hollow, final thud.

The light fades.

I struggle to my feet.

Above me, Ra descends, glowing like a risen god. His shell whole again, his glyphs radiant blue. The pieces I saw crumbling... made new by the light I finally allowed in.

Across the crater, the bodies of the fallen begin to stir.

One by one, the survivors awaken, the black clouds lifting from their bodies, their souls.

"Mae!" I run to her and pull her into my arms.

"You did it," she gasps, tears in her eyes. "You really did it."

"It's over," I whisper. "The Alpha's gone."

Jasper limps toward us, clutching his side.

"Synchronicity," he breathes, "that was insane. You *obliterated* that thing." Mochi comes bounding onto his shoulder with a triumphant chirp.

"You saw?"

"Every second. I couldn't move, the Beta had me frozen inside, but my eyes were open." He grins through the bruises. "It was like watching a supernova."

Alien Isis steps over, austere and regal despite the scorch marks on her crystalline skin. "Synchronicity, what you did was impossible. Unfathomable." Her halo flares a brilliant purple. "You have saved us all."

Jasper's smile fades as his gaze shifts across the crater. "Not all of us."

I follow his gaze to where Koop cradles Xion's body in his arms, kneeling in the rubble.

The weight of it hits me like a collapsing star.

"Xion?"

I close the distance between us, falling to my knees beside him.

Koop looks up, face streaked with ash and tears. "He... he

didn't make it."

"No. It's not possible." My voice breaks. "Xion, wake up. I did it. I killed the Alpha Draconid. You can't be dead... I did it."

"He's gone," Koop whispers.

I run my fingers over the fallen prince's head.

Those eyes that once burned with the fire of a thousand suns are now nothing more than a faint light, flickering in the dark.

"No," I whisper. "I won't accept that."

Koop looks at me in disbelief.

I stand, heart thundering in my chest. "Bring him to the water."

We carry him, his heavy, broken body, down to the center of the crater.

To the pool.

Ancient, still, and mirror-like, untouched by the surrounding carnage.

The waters eternally flowing from the depths of Agartha.

"Lay him in," I say.

Koop places him gently in the pristine blue.

I wade out, taking his weight in my arms, until my feet barely touch the bottom.

"Xion, you can't go," I whisper. "You can't leave me here."

Ra lifts off from the shore where the others have gathered, solemn witnesses to whatever is about to unfold. He comes into a hover directly above me, and every inch of his shell begins to glow with a holy light.

As I look up, a beam descends, piercing me in the forehead and flowing throughout my body like a river of light. It moves down through my fingers and into Xion, who begins to glow just like Ra, the three of us a luminous trinity of healing energy.

I close my eyes and focus on the pure sensation inside, washing away every last trace of fear, of guilt, of shame. I see myself on the edge of that creek that stole Aidan from me, screaming into a sky that never answered.

And I realize something.

I realize that I had to heal myself first.

I had to heal myself in order to save the man who now lies in my arms. The man who saw the darkness in my soul and wanted more. The man who awakened something in me, unlike anything I've ever felt before.

When the light reaches its peak, there's a pause.

A breath.

And when I open my eyes, Xion is staring back up at me.

Alive.

CHAPTER
FIFTY-FIVE

"In light of the horrifying events that occurred yesterday," Alien Isis announces from a stage erected in front of the Great Pyramid, "I have instructed your professors to give you all A's for your final exams."

The students, gathered on the curved stone steps of the amphitheater, erupt in wild applause.

In the field below, brightly dressed dancers twirl barefoot through the grass, flower crowns tangled in their hair. Ribbons stream from tall maypoles that sway in the breeze, and to the left of the stage, a massive bonfire blazes.

"Thanks to the valiant efforts of many brave students, Maldekians, and one Miss Synchronicity Jones," Isis continues, her robes catching the firelight, "not a single life was lost during the Draconid attack."

A roar of celebration rises from the students, some hoisting their spirit animals above their heads, others lighting sparklers.

Mae and Jasper beam at me as they clap, their faces flushed with joy and relief. Mochi is draped in tiny fairy lights and rides Jasper's shoulder like royalty.

"We have much to celebrate during this Beltane Festival," Alien Isis says, her gaze sweeping over the crowd like a benediction. "The renewal of the Earth. The return of spring. The triumph of light."

She pauses.

The drums still.

"But there is one final matter to address before the festivities can commence."

A hush descends on the crowd.

"Agents Marnox and Kreth of the Vibrational Alignment Bureau have submitted a formal report to the Council of Five, requesting not only the immediate seizure of the Eldercraft known as Ra... but also the disciplinary removal of the Maldekian protectors for violation of the Non-

Interference Doctrine."

The crowd gasps.

Jasper is the first to yell: "Boo!"

A tide of boos follows, swelling like a storm from the steps of the amphitheater.

Isis lets it wash over her, then continues.

"All that remains," Isis continues, "is for the Council to vote on the matter."

The faces of the council members shimmer to life, projected onto the side of the Pyramid, like an interstellar conference call. Alien Kali, majestic and severe, from Sirius. Alien Kitsune, with tufted ears and animal eyes, from Arcturus. Alien Calliope, with long neck, golden skin and ears that drape practically down to her shoulders, from Lyra. And Alien Hetros, austere and radiant, like a man carved out of crystal, from the Pleiades.

Their presence is enormous. Reverent silence sweeps the amphitheater.

"I'll begin," says Alien Kali, voice clipped and exacting. "I read the report submitted by Agents Marnox and Kreth, and I have concluded that, despite the brave efforts of its pilot in yesterday's... debacle, the craft must be studied for future attacks. I vote in *favor* of the proposal."

No one boos this time.

Everyone listens. Mae reaches over and squeezes my hand.

Next, Alien Kitsune leans forward. Her ears twitch gently as she speaks. Behind her, a forest city stretches down a lush, alien canyon. "I have read the report. I have also spoken with Alien Isis. And I've watched the recordings of what transpired." She pauses. "What I saw was a school worth saving. A valiant group of Maldekians worth believing in. And a young woman, Earthseed though she may be, who showed courage beyond her years."

She lifts her gaze, staring straight into the camera.

"I vote against the proposal."

A ripple of cautious applause.

"Eldercrafts are rare," begins Alien Hetros, his voice

musical but measured. "But Eldercraft pilots are rarer. Connections like the one Synchronicity has with her craft not only raise the consciousness of her home planet, but of the entire galaxy. We need more souls like Synchronicity and the brave Maldekians who helped save the school. I vote against the proposal."

The applause is louder this time, and I feel a swell of hope rising in my chest.

Then comes Alien Calliope, her long fingers steepled beneath her chin.

Her voice is like wind chimes across a glass lake.

"The events of yesterday have shown us much. The strength of your students. The dedication of your teachers. The promise of your Earthseed."

I inch closer to the edge of my seat. You could cut the silence with a ceremonial blade.

"But most importantly," she continues, "it has shown that the Draconid scourge is still very much a threat. We must study this strange new Eldercraft if we are to keep the Galaxy safe. Moreover, a failed race like the Maldekians has no business interfering in the affairs of a Federation school. I vote *in favor*."

A low groan echoes across the amphitheater.

I turn to my friends, worried. "What does that mean? It's a tie."

"Didn't you pay attention in Galactic History?" Jasper says. "In the event of a tie, the deciding vote goes to the Aldebaran Councilor. The fifth member of the Council of Five."

"But I only see four..." Mae murmurs.

Just then, a tiny grey alien hobbles onto the stage, stooped over a curved cane.

"Oh my God." A jolt of recognition hits me. "That's the Elder I saw in the forbidden wing of the Energy Work School."

"That's not an Elder," Jasper whispers in awe. "That's an *Aldebaran*. The closest living descendants of the Elders."

It takes him nearly a minute to walk to the center of the

stage. Alien Isis offers him a hand, but the little alien waves her off. He slowly and laboriously clears his throat.

"My name is Alien Mem. Though you may not have seen me, I've spent the better part of a year at your school. In my old age, it seems I'm in need of more advanced healing treatments, the kind that only the healers at Agartha can provide. I have learned many things during my stay here. First, I would like to commend the Maldekians, whose bravery in the face of darkness has protected Earth from suffering the same fate as their home planet. In the coming months, I will make an effort to grant them honorary membership in the Galactic Federation."

I look around for Xion, but his face is nowhere to be seen.

"Second, this attack has shown that our Non-Interference Doctrine may be woefully misguided with regards to the spiritual advancement of the galaxy. There is a wealth of resources within the Federation, and they should be shared freely to ensure the ascension of every planet, regardless of their spiritual status."

His gaze sweeps the crowd.

"Thirdly, I have seen that Earthseeds are far more powerful than we have given them credit for." He turns to me in the audience, and I swear there's a gleam in his alien eye. "Synchronicity Jones has proven herself to be not only an extremely talented Eldercraft pilot and healer, but also a genuinely good person."

He raises his cane.

"I vote against the proposal. Ra will stay in Agartha."

The student body erupts into applause. Everyone stands and claps, looking at me. I wipe away a tear.

Mae throws her arms around me. Jasper pounds me on the back.

"You did it, Sync," Mae says. "You get to keep Ra."

I laugh through my tears. "Everything's gonna be okay," I say.

And for the first time in a long time, I believe it.

The shimmering faces of the Council blink out one by one, fading into the stone and glass surface of the Great

Pyramid. In their place, Alien Isis steps once more into the golden wash of the Beltane stage lights while two healers help Alien Mem down the steps.

She turns back to us, thousands strong, gathered beneath the opal sky.

"Thank you, Alien Mem, for your wisdom and your courage," Isis says.

Then, after a beat, her voice lifts like a bell.

"Students, Starseed and Earthseed alike, the portals to the surface will open tomorrow. And for those of you who choose to come back..." Her eyes catch mine for a breathless second, "The portal to return to Agartha for the next year of classes will reopen October 10th. Don't miss it."

A ripple of cheers breaks through the crowd, but Isis raises her hand, and a hush falls again. Her face softens.

"This year has brought trials unlike any we've seen in centuries... and triumphs that shine just as brightly. You have proven that courage, compassion, and consciousness are the true tools of ascension. And I—" her voice catches, "— am honored to serve as your Spiritual Director."

Then, with a smile that catches the firelight, "Without further ado, please welcome Supermoon to the stage!"

A roar of applause. The audience rises as Jason Starsong and the six other members stride onto the stage in embroidered robes and boots that twinkle like stardust.

Jason steps up to the mic. "Thank you, Agartha. This... is a little unprecedented." He glances back at the band. "But our newest member, Kara Volkova, has requested that someone very special join us tonight."

He grins. "Mae Rivers, would you please join us to perform your song, *Feral Dreams*?"

Mae's jaw drops. She looks to me and Jasper like she's just been invited into heaven.

"Oh my God. Guys... I'm playing with Supermoon."

Kara beckons to her from the stage.

"You deserve it," I say. "More than anyone."

"Get up there and break some alien leg," Jasper says.

As Mae descends the amphitheater steps, the crowd parts for her like petals opening to the sun. Cheers rise in waves as Kara holds out her hand, beaming.

Just before she reaches the stage, I scan the crowd.

"I wish I could see the look on Vaylen's face right now."

Jasper snorts. "Didn't you hear?"

I blink. "Hear what?"

He leans in.

"When the teachers evacuated everyone during the battle, they found a stash of Starseed Sovereignty propaganda in Vaylen's room."

My jaw drops. "You're kidding."

"Nope. Hate speech doesn't fly at the Academy. Last I heard, she's either getting expelled or spending the next year scrubbing crystals with a toothbrush for work-study credits."

I shake my head. "Damn. That tracks."

On stage, Kara kisses Mae gently, and the two move to the front. Jason strums a low, ambient chord. The lights dim to a soft violet.

Mae steps to the mic.

She looks radiant, golden dreads haloed in fresh flowers, her aura humming with confidence and belonging.

"Thank you," she says. "This is a dream come true."

She swings her ukulele to her front and strikes the opening chord. The crowd hushes again.

Her voice is pure fire:

"Thorns in my hair and dirt on my skin,
I shed this world I've been living in.
Calling back to the beast I've become,
My voice is a flame, my heart is a drum..."

At the word *drum*, she winks at Kara. I can literally see the attraction between them as their Lyran energy entwines across the stage in golden threads, like a cord tying them.

The rest of the band kicks in for the second verse, as the crowd sways in waves of firelight and awe.

"I guess everything worked out," Jasper says, as the Lyran light flowing from the stage casts his grin in gold.

"Almost everything," I murmur, eyes settling on Kai, standing quietly at the edge of the stage beside Alien Sylestra, his hands clasped, his gaze distant.

Jasper raises a brow. "Good luck with that." He nudges me with his shoulder. "I'll be here. Holding down the vibes."

I smirk. "Thanks. I think I've got this."

I begin walking down the stone steps, but before I can reach Kai, a frail hand tugs at my wrist.

"Cassy," I say, heart catching in my throat.

For a moment, I barely recognize her. There's color in her cheeks now, a soft, human flush that wasn't there before, and her platinum hair is woven with tiny wildflowers like she's just stepped out of a meadow.

"I'm sorry," she says, barely louder than the music drifting from the stage. "For yesterday. For all of it."

She looks down, twisting her fingers.

"I don't know if I'll ever be able to explain what it felt like, with the Draconid inside me, but I know what I did. And I'm sorry I attacked you." Her voice cracks. "I'm sorry for the whole year."

"Don't say that, Cassy." I touch her hand gently. "It wasn't you who did those things. I know that. And I'm so grateful I got to know you this year."

Her eyes rise to meet mine, wet and gleaming. "Really?"

"Really." I squeeze her fingers. "Maybe next year we can just... try being friends."

"I would like that," she says.

I turn to leave, but before I do, I remember something. "Hey, Cassy?"

"Yeah?" she says, her pale grey eyes wide like the moon.

"If you see any falling stars this summer... promise me you won't go chasing after them?"

A crooked smile breaks across her face. "You have my word." She sticks out her pinky, and I link mine with hers.

I linger a second longer, watching the girl who nearly

unraveled our world. She glows now, not with power, but with possibility.

Then I disappear into the tide of bodies pulsing to Supermoon's rhythm.

Kai stands apart, still and centered like always, his silhouette painted in stage-light and shadow.

Sylestra sees me coming and steps aside. "Well, Synchronicity," she says, "I suppose I owe you an apology. I underestimated Earthseeds. Thank you for protecting this school."

"It was an honor, Sylestra," I say, nodding. "But... would you mind if I steal Kai for a moment?"

"By all means," she says and joins a group of other healers.

"Hey," I say.

"Hey," he echoes, the air between us heavy with things unspoken.

"A lot happened while you were out," I say.

"So I heard."

I hesitate. "About me and Xion..."

He raises a hand gently. "It's okay. I get it."

"You do?"

"I get why you're drawn to him. He's... complicated. So are you."

I laugh, but it's soft. Grateful.

"So you're not mad?"

"Not about him." He looks out toward the stage where Mae is glowing like a goddess. "I think I'm more hurt you didn't tell me the truth about your past. I would've understood."

"I know," I say. "And I'm sorry."

He nods, then smiles. A real one, touched with sadness but not bitterness. "You saved the whole damn school, Synchronicity. You saved me. That counts for something."

I nod, blinking fast. "You were good to me, Kai. And I needed that. Even if it wasn't forever."

He reaches out his hand. "Friends?"

I take it, holding on just a second longer than I need to. "Friends."

The word lands more softly than I expect. There's still an ache, but it's the kind that tells me I did the right thing.

Mae strums the final chords of *Feral Dreams*, and Kara's voice joins hers in harmony as I walk into the shadows beyond the firelight.

There's one last person I need to talk to tonight.

CHAPTER FIFTY-SIX

Inside the hangar, Ra floats in the stillness, the light beneath his glyphs shimmering like reflections on water. The crack that once split his hull is now a faint line, silvered over like a healed wound. Proof that even the most broken things can mend.

I step forward and rest my palm on his shell.

"Are you gonna be okay here this summer, buddy?"

"**I'll... miss... you.**" Each syllable echoes against the metal walls, heavy with feeling.

"I'll miss you too, Ra." I pause, letting the silence speak for us. "You helped me find myself again."

"**You healed yourself, Synchronicity.**" His light ripples outward from a central glyph. "**You healed us.**"

Before I can respond, a voice breaks across the hangar like low thunder. "Saying goodbye?"

I turn. Xion stands near a workbench, sleeves rolled, hands stained with the soot of rebuilt things. He looks at me the way only someone who's seen you shattered can—like every part of you matters, even the broken ones.

"Just making sure he'll be in safe hands."

"I promise I won't let anything happen to him," he says. "You have my word."

"Can I come visit him?" I ask, stepping towards him with my hands behind my back.

"The portal doesn't open again till 10/10." His eyes burn in the half-light like twin eclipses. "You'll need a ride."

I smirk. "Lucky for me, I know someone who knows their way around the Ice Wall."

"You sure you don't want to stay?" he asks, slowly closing the distance between us.

I want to say yes. I want to fold myself into the gravity of him and never leave. But something else is calling to me.

"There's some stuff I need to take care of," I say. "Back on the surface."

"I could really use the help," he says, pulling me into his arms. "I've got a new class of first-years coming in the fall. And someone needs to rebuild that Castor 5. Again."

"I think an older craft like the Castor 5 is well within your area of expertise, Alien Da'ath." I tilt my head to meet his gaze. "Besides, my old life was in shambles when I left. Right now, I need to focus on putting *that* back together."

He studies me, like he's committing every last facet of my face to memory.

"Fair enough, Jones." His lips curve in that rare smile. "But I can't promise I won't abduct you in the middle of some romantic..." He kisses my collarbone. "Starry..." then my neck. "Moonlit..." then my lips. "Night."

I laugh softly into his mouth, one hand rising to the back of his neck, our hearts beating as one in the mystical glow of the hangar.

"I'm counting on it," I say.

And in the sacred hush between us, illuminated by the stars etched across Ra's shell and the smell of mysteries older than the galaxy itself, I realize something.

I'm not leaving anything behind. I'm carrying it with me.

The craft.

The fight.

The love I didn't think I deserved.

And the light that found its way in, anyway.

EPILOGUE

As the last of the students disappear through the portals, Alien Isis moves alone through the quiet campus, past rows of gleaming RE craft. Her lavender halo pulses faintly as she knocks on the door of a low, bunker-like structure set apart from the rest of the craft site. A pair of dull, smoldering crystal sconces flicker like dying embers beside the heavy steel door.

Moments later, Xion ushers her inside.

The interior is sparse, almost monastic, with furniture made from polished stone. A place for a pilot. A warrior.

Not a high priestess.

He offers her a seat, but she does not take it.

She walks past the Maldekian, running her slender fingers along the relics and half-repaired machine parts that line the wall.

"We need to prepare for next year," she says, pausing in front of a dusty, ancient star chart. Her finger traces a thin elliptical orbit reaching far beyond the edge of the familiar planets. A path that doesn't circle back for millennia.

When she speaks again, her voice is low and final.

"Nibiru is coming."

Hello, and thank you for reading my book! Creating this story was a monumental journey, and I appreciate that you took the time to get lost in this magical little world.

If you want to be one of the first to find out what happens to Synchronicity, Xion, and all your other favorite characters when Nibiru arrives in the upcoming sequel, join my newsletter at nlmystic.substack.com.

However this story found its way to you, I hope it cracked something open—and let the light in.

- N.L. Mystic

P.S. If you enjoyed this book, please consider leaving it a review. As a self-published author, I can't tell you how much this helps.

Made in the USA
Las Vegas, NV
28 May 2025

22804623R00184